AGENT

Also by Tom Rob Smith

Child 44
The Secret Speech

AGENT 6

TOM ROB SMITH

SIMON &
SCHUSTER

London · New York · Sydney · Toronto

A CBS COMPANY

First published in Great Britain by Simon & Schuster UK Ltd, 2011
A CBS COMPANY

Copyright © Tom Rob Smith, 2011

Simon & Schuster UK Ltd
1st Floor
222 Gray's Inn Road
London
WC1X 8HB

www.simonandschuster.co.uk

Simon & Schuster Australia
Sydney

A CIP catalogue record for this book
is available from the British Library

Hardback ISBN 978-1-84737-567-4
Trade Paperback ISBN 978-1-84737-568-1

Typeset by M Rules
Printed in the UK by CPI Mackays, Chatham ME5 8TD

To Zoe Trodd

Moscow
Lubyanka Square
The Lubyanka, Headquarters
of the Secret Police
21 January 1950

The safest way to write a diary was to imagine Stalin reading every word. Even exercising this degree of caution there was the risk of a slipped phrase, accidental ambiguity – a misunderstood sentence. Praise might be mistaken for mockery, sincere adulation taken as parody. Since even the most vigilant author couldn't guard against every possible interpretation, an alternative was to hide the diary altogether, a method favoured in this instance by the suspect, a young artist called Polina Peshkova. Her notebook had been discovered inside a fireplace, in the chimney no less, wrapped in waxy cloth and squeezed between two loose bricks. To retrieve the diary the author was forced to wait until the fire died down before inserting her hand into the chimney and feeling for the book's spine. Ironically the elaborate nature of this hiding place had been Peshkova's undoing. A single sooty fingerprint on her writing desk had alerted the investigating agent's suspicions and re-directed the focus of his search – an exemplary piece of detective work.

From the perspective of the secret police, concealing a diary was a crime regardless of its content. It was an attempt to separate a citizen's public and private life, when no such gap existed. There was no thought or experience that fell outside the party's authority. For this reason a concealed diary was often the most incriminating evidence an agent could hope for. Since the journal wasn't intended for any reader the author wrote freely, lowering their guard, producing nothing less than an unsolicited confession. From-the-heart honesty made the document suitable for judging not only the author but also their friends and family. A diary could yield as many as fifteen additional suspects, fifteen new leads, often more than the most intense interrogation.

In charge of this investigation was Agent Leo Demidov, twenty-seven years old: a decorated soldier recruited to the ranks of the secret police after the Great Patriotic War. He'd flourished in the MGB through a combination of uncomplicated obedience, a belief in the State he was serving and rigorous attention to detail. His zeal was underpinned not by ambition but by earnest adoration of his homeland, the country that had defeated Fascism. As handsome as he was serious-minded, he had the face and the spirit of a propaganda poster, a square jaw with angular lips, ever ready with a slogan.

In Leo's brief career with the MGB, he'd overseen the examination of many hundreds of journals, pored over thousands of entries in the tireless pursuit of those accused of anti-Soviet agitation. Like a first love, he remembered the first journal he'd ever examined. Given to him by his mentor, Nikolai Borisov, it had been a difficult case. Leo had found nothing incriminating among the pages. His mentor had then read the same journal, highlighting an apparently innocent observation:

December 6th, 1936, Last night Stalin's new constitution
was adopted. I feel the same way as the rest of the country,
i.e., absolute, infinite delight.

Borisov had been unsatisfied that the sentence conveyed a credible sense of delight. The author was more interested in aligning his feelings with the rest of the country. It was strategic and cynical, an empty declaration intended to hide the author's own doubts. Does a person expressing genuine delight use an abbreviation – i.e. – before describing their emotions? That question was put to the suspect in his subsequent interrogation.

INTERROGATOR BORISOV: *How do you feel right now?*
SUSPECT: *I have done nothing wrong.*
INTERROGATOR BORISOV: *But my question was: how do you feel?*
SUSPECT: *I feel apprehensive.*
INTERROGATOR BORISOV: *Of course you do. That is perfectly natural.*

But note that you did not say: 'I feel the same as anyone would in my circumstances, i.e., apprehension.'

The man received fifteen years. And Leo learned a valuable lesson – a detective was not limited to searching for statements of sedition. Far more important was to be ever-vigilant for proclamations of love and loyalty that failed to convince.

Drawing from his experiences over the past three years, Leo flicked through Polina Peshkova's diary, observing that for an artist the suspect had inelegant handwriting. Throughout she'd pressed hard with a blunt pencil, never once sharpening the tip. He ran his finger over the back of each page, across sentences indented like Braille. He lifted the diary to his nose. It smelt of soot. Against the run of his thumb, the pages made a crackling noise, like dry autumn leaves. He sniffed and peered and weighed the book in his hands – examining it in every way except to actually read it. For a report on the content of the diary he turned to the trainee assigned to him. As part of a recent promotion Leo had been tasked with supervising new agents. He was no longer a pupil but a mentor. These new agents would accompany him on his working day and during his night-time arrests, gaining experience, learning from him until they were ready to run their own cases.

Grigori Semichastny was twenty-three years old and the fifth agent Leo had taught. He was perhaps the most intelligent and without a doubt the least promising. He asked too many questions, queried too many answers. He smiled when he found something amusing and frowned when something annoyed him. To know what he was thinking merely required a glance at his face. He'd been recruited from the University of Moscow, where he'd been an exceptional student, gifted with an academic pedigree in contrast to his mentor. Leo felt no jealousy, readily accepting that he would never have a mind for serious study. Able to dissect his own intellectual shortcomings, he was unable to understand why his trainee had sought a post in a profession for which he was entirely unsuited. So mismatched was Grigori for the job that Leo had even contemplated advising him to seek another career. Such an abrupt departure would place the man under scrutiny and would, in all likelihood, condemn him in the eyes of the State. Grigori's only viable option was to stumble along this path and Leo felt it his duty to help him as best he could.

Grigori leafed through the pages intently, turning backwards and forwards, apparently searching for something in particular. Finally, he looked up and declared:

— *The diary says nothing.*

Remembering his own experience as a novice, Leo was not entirely surprised by the answer, feeling disappointment at his protégé's failure. He replied:

— *Nothing?*

Grigori nodded.

— *Nothing of any importance.*

The notion was improbable. Even if it lacked direct examples of provocation, the things unmentioned in a diary were just as important as the things that were written down. Deciding to offer these wisdoms to his trainee, Leo stood up.

— *Let me tell you a story. A young man once remarked in his diary that on this day he felt inexplicably sad. The entry was dated 23 August. The year was 1949. What would you make of that?*

Grigori shrugged.

— *Not much.*

Leo pounced on the claim.

— *What was the date of the Non-Aggression Pact between Nazi Germany and Soviet Russia?*

— *August 1939.*

— *The 23rd of August 1939. Which means this man was feeling inexplicable sadness on the tenth anniversary of that treaty. Taken together with an absence of any praise for the soldiers who defeated Fascism, for Stalin's military prowess, this man's sadness was interpreted as an inappropriate critique of our foreign policy. Why dwell on mistakes and not express feelings of pride? Do you understand?*

— *Maybe it had nothing to do the treaty. We all have days where we feel sad or lonely or melancholy. We don't check the historical calendar every time we feel such things.*

Leo became annoyed.

— *Maybe it had nothing to do with the treaty? Maybe there are no enemies? Maybe everyone loves the State? Maybe there are no people who wish to undermine our work? Our job is to reveal guilt, not naively hope that it doesn't exist.*

Grigori considered, noting Leo's anger. With unusual diplomacy, he modulated his response, no longer as confrontational but sticking by his conclusion:

— In Polina's diary there are mundane observations about her daily routine. As far as my abilities allow I can see no case against her. Those are my findings.

The artist, whom Leo noted Grigori was informally referring to by her first name, had been commissioned to design and paint a series of public murals. Since there was a risk that she, or indeed any artist, might produce something subtly subversive, a piece of art with a hidden meaning, the MGB were running a routine check. The logic was simple. If her diary contained no secret subversive meaning, it was unlikely that her art would. The task was a minor one and suitable for a novice. The first day had gone well. Grigori had found the diary while Peshkova was at work in her studio. Completing his search, he'd returned the evidence to the hiding place in the chimney in order not to alert Peshkova that she was under investigation. He'd reported back and briefly Leo had wondered if there was hope for the young man: the use of the sooty fingerprint as a clue had been admirable. During the next four days Grigori maintained a high level of surveillance, putting in many more hours than necessary. Yet despite the extra work he made no more reports and offered no observations of any kind. Now he was claiming the diary was worthless.

Leo took the notebook from him, sensing Grigori's reluctance to let the pages out of his hands. For the first time, he began to read. At a glance he agreed that it was hardly the provocative content they might expect from a diary so elaborately hidden near a fire.

Unwilling to cede to the conclusion that the suspect was innocent, he skipped to the end, scouring the most recent entries, written during the past five days of Grigori's surveillance. The suspect described meeting a neighbour for the first time, a man who lived in an apartment block on the opposite side of the road. She'd never seen him before but he'd approached her and they'd spoken in the street. She remarked that the man was funny and she hoped to see him again sometime, coyly adding that he was handsome.

Did he tell me his name? I don't remember. He must have done. How can I be so forgetful? I was distracted. I wish I could remember his name. Now he'll be insulted when we meet again. If we meet again, which I hope we will.

Leo turned the page. The next day she got her wish, bumping into the man again. She apologized for being forgetful and asked him to remind her of his name. He told her it was Isaac, and they walked together, talking freely as if they'd been friends for many years. By happy coincidence Isaac was heading in the same direction. Arriving at her studio, she was sad to see him go. According to her entry, as soon as he was out of sight she began longing for their next encounter.

Is this love? No, of course not. But perhaps this is how love begins?

How love begins – it was sentimental, consistent with the fanciful temperament of someone who writes an inoffensive diary but hides it as carefully as if it contained treachery and intrigue. What a silly and dangerous thing to do. Leo didn't need a physical description of this friendly young man to know his identity. He looked up at his protégé and said:

— Isaac?

Grigori hesitated. Deciding against a lie, he admitted:

— I thought a conversation might be useful in evaluating her character.

— Your job was to search her apartment and observe her activities. No direct contact. She might have guessed you were MGB. She'd then alter her behaviour in order to fool you.

Grigori shook his head.

— She didn't suspect me.

Leo was frustrated by these elementary mistakes.

— You know that only because of what she wrote in the diary. Yet she could have destroyed the original diary, replacing it with this bland set of observations, aware that she was under surveillance.

Hearing this, his brief attempt at deference broke apart, like a ship smashed against rocks. Grigori scoffed, displaying remarkable insolence:

— The entire diary fabricated to fool us? She doesn't think like that. She doesn't think like us. It's impossible.

Contradicted by a young trainee, an agent deficient in his duties – Leo was a patient man, more tolerant than other officers, but Grigori was testing him.

— The people who seem innocent are often those we should watch the most carefully.

Grigori looked at Leo with something like pity. For once his expression did not match his reply.

— You're right: I shouldn't have spoken to her. But she is a good person. Of that I am certain. I found nothing in her apartment, nothing in her day-to-day activities that suggests she is anything other than a loyal citizen. The diary is inoffensive. Polina Peshkova does not need to be brought in for questioning. She should be allowed to continue her work as an artist, in which she excels. I

can still return the diary before she finishes work. She need know nothing of this investigation.

Leo glanced at her photo, clipped to the front of the file. She was beautiful. Grigori was smitten with her. Had she charmed him in order to escape suspicion? Had she written about love, knowing that he would read those lines and be moved to protect her? Leo needed to scrutinize this proclamation of love. There was no choice but to read the diary line by line. He could no longer trust the word of his protégé. Love had made him fallible.

There were over a hundred pages of entries. Polina Peshkova wrote about her work and life. Her character came through strongly: a whimsical style, punctuated by diversions, sudden thoughts and exclamations. The entries flitted from subject to subject, often abandoning one strand and leaving it unfinished. There were no political statements, concentrating entirely on the day-to-day motions of her life and drawings. Having read the entire diary, Leo couldn't deny that there was something appealing about the woman. She frequently laughed at her mistakes, documented with perceptive honesty. Her candour might explain why she hid the diary so carefully. It was highly improbable it had been forged as a deceit. With this thought in mind, Leo gestured for Grigori to sit down. He had remained standing, as if on guard duty, for the entire time Leo had been reading. He was nervous. Grigori perched on the edge of the chair. Leo asked:

— *Tell me, if she's innocent, why did she hide the diary?*

Seeming to sense that Leo's attitude towards her was thawing, Grigori became excited. He spoke quickly, rushing through a possible explanation.

— *She lives with her mother and two younger brothers. She doesn't want them snooping through it. Perhaps they'd make fun of her. I don't know. She talks of love, maybe such thoughts embarrass her. It's nothing more than that. We must be able to distinguish when something is not important.*

Leo's thoughts wandered. He could imagine Grigori approaching the young woman. Yet he struggled to imagine her responding fondly to a stranger's question. Why didn't she tell him to leave her alone? It seemed wildly imprudent of her to be so open. He leaned forward, lowering his voice, not because he feared being overheard but to signal that he was no longer talking to him formally, as a secret-police officer.

— *What happened between the two of you? You walked up to her and started talking? And she . . .*

Leo hesitated. He didn't know how to finish the sentence. Finally, stumbling, he asked:

— *And she responded . . .?*

Grigori seemed unsure whether the question was put to him by a friend or by a superior officer. When he understood that Leo was genuinely curious, he answered:

— *How else do you meet someone except to introduce yourself? I spoke about her art. I told her that I'd seen some of her work – which is true. The conversation continued from there. She was easy to talk to, friendly.*

Leo found this extraordinary.

— *She wasn't suspicious?*

— *No.*

— *She should have been.*

Briefly they'd been speaking as friends, about matters of the heart, now they were agents again. Grigori sank his head.

— *Yes, you're right, she should have been.*

He wasn't angry with Leo. He was angry with himself. His connection with the artist was built on a lie: his affection was founded on artifice and deception.

Surprising himself, Leo offered the diary to Grigori.

— *Take it.*

Grigori didn't move, trying to figure out what was happening. Leo smiled.

— *Take it. She is free to continue her work as an artist. There's no need to press the case further.*

— *You're sure?*

— *I found nothing in the diary.*

Understanding that she was safe, Grigori smiled. He reached out, pulling the diary from Leo's hands. As the pages slipped out of his grip, Leo felt an outline pressed into the paper — it wasn't a letter or a word but some kind of shape, something he hadn't seen.

— *Wait.*

Taking the diary back, Leo opened the page, examining the top right-hand corner. The space was blank. Yet when he touched the other side he could feel the indented lines. Something had been rubbed out.

He took a pencil, brushing the side of the lead against the paper, revealing the ghost of a small doodle, a sketch not much larger than his thumb. It was a woman standing on a plinth holding a torch, a statue. Leo stared blankly until realizing what it was. It was an American monument. It was the Statue of Liberty. Leo studied Grigori's face.

Grigori stumbled over his words:

— *She's an artist. She sketches all the time.*

— *Why has it been rubbed out?*

He had no answer.

— *You tampered with evidence?*

There was panic in Grigori's reply.

— *When I first joined the MGB, on my first day, I was told a story about Lenin's secretary, Fotievam. She claims that Lenin asked his chief of security, Felix Dzierzynski, how many counter-revolutionaries he had under arrest. Dzierzynski passed him a slip of paper with the number one thousand five hundred written on it. Lenin returned the paper, marking it with a cross. According to his secretary, a cross was used by Lenin to show he had read a document. Dzierzynski misunderstood and executed all of them. That is why I had to rub it out. This sketch could have been misunderstood.*

Leo thought it an inappropriate reference. He'd heard enough.

— *Dzierzynski was the father of this agency. To compare your predicament with his is ludicrous. We are not permitted the luxury of interpretation. We are not judges. We don't decide what evidence to present and destroy. If she is innocent, as you claim, that will be found out during further questioning. In your misguided attempt to protect her, you've incriminated yourself.*

— *Leo, she's a good person.*

— *You're infatuated with her. Your judgement is compromised.*

Leo's voice had become harsh and cruel. He heard himself and softened his tone.

— *Since the evidence is intact, I see no reason to draw attention to your mistake, a mistake that would certainly end your career. Write up your report, mark the sketch as evidence and let those more experienced than us decide.*

He added:

— *And Grigori, I cannot protect you again.*

Moscow
Moskvoretsky Bridge
KM Tramcar
Same Day

Leo exhaled on the window, causing it steam up. Childlike, he pressed his finger against the condensation and without thinking traced the outline of the Statue of Liberty – a crude version of the sketch he'd seen today. He hastily rubbed it away with the coarse cuff of his jacket and glanced around. The sketch would have been unrecognizable to anyone except himself and the tramcar was almost empty: there was only one other passenger, a man seated at the front, wrapped up against the cold in so many layers that the smallest patch of his face was visible. Having made sure no one had witnessed his sketch he concluded there was no reason to be alarmed. Usually so careful, he found it hard to believe he'd made such a dangerous slip. He was running too many late-night arrests and even when he wasn't working, he was finding it difficult to sleep.

Except for early in the morning and late at night, tramcars were crowded. Painted with a thick stripe in their centre, they rattled around the city like giant boiled sweets. Often Leo had no choice except to force his way on. With seating for fifty, there were typically twice that number, the aisles filled with commuters jostling for position. Tonight Leo would've preferred the discomfort of a busy carriage, elbows jutting into his side and people pushing past. Instead he had the luxury of an empty seat, heading home to the privilege of an empty apartment — accommodation he was not obliged to share, another perk of his profession. A man's status had become defined by how much empty space surrounded him. Soon he'd be designated his own car, a larger home, perhaps even a dacha, a country house. More and more space, less and less contact with the people he was charged with keeping watch over.

The words dropped into Leo's head:

How Love Begins.

He'd never been in love, not in the way described in the diary — excitement at the prospect of seeing someone again and sadness as soon as they went away. Grigori had risked his life for a woman he barely knew. Surely that was an act of love? Love did seem to be characterized by foolhardiness. Leo had risked his life for his country many times. He'd shown exceptional bravery and dedication. If love was sacrifice then his only true love had been for the State. And the State had loved him back, like a favourite son, rewarding and empowering him. It was ungrateful, disgraceful, that the thought should even cross his mind that this love was not enough.

He slid his hands under his legs, mining the space for any trace of warmth. Finding none, he shivered. The soles of his boots splashed in the shallow puddles of melted snow on the steel carriage floor. There was heaviness in his chest as if he were suffering from the flu with no symptoms except fatigue and dullness of thought. He wanted to lean against the window, close his eyes and sleep. The glass was too cold. He wiped a fresh patch of condensation clear and peered out. The tram crossed the bridge, passing through streets heaped with snow. More was falling, large flakes against the window.

The tramcar slowed to a stop. The front and back doors clattered open, snow swept in. The driver turned to the open door, calling out into the night:

— *Hurry up! What are you waiting for?*

A voice replied:

— *I'm kicking the snow off my boots!*

— *You're letting more snow in than you're kicking off. Get in now or I'll shut the doors!*

The passenger boarded, a woman carrying a heavy bag, her boots clad in clumps of snow. As the doors shut behind her she remarked to the driver:

— *It's not that warm in here anyway.*

The driver gestured outside.

— *You prefer to walk?*

She smiled, defusing the tension. Won over by her charm, the gruff driver smiled too.

The woman turned, surveying the carriage and catching Leo's eye. He recognized her. They lived near each other. Her name was Lena. He saw her often. In fact, she'd caught his eye precisely because she behaved as if she did not wish to be noticed. She would dress in plain clothes, as most women did, but she was far from plain herself. Her desire for anonymity struggled against the pull of her beauty and even if Leo's job hadn't been to observe people he would surely have noticed her.

A week ago he'd chanced across her on a metro. They'd been so close together that it had felt rude not to say hello. Since they'd seen each other several times, it was polite to at least acknowledge that fact. He'd been so nervous it had taken him several minutes to pluck up the courage to talk to her, delaying for so long that she'd stepped off the carriage and Leo, frustrated, followed her even though it wasn't his stop, an impulsive act quite out of character for him. As she walked towards the exit he'd reached out and touched her on the shoulder. She'd spun around, her large brown eyes alert, ready for danger. He'd asked her name. She'd assessed him in a glance, checking the passengers passing by, before telling him it was Lena and making an excuse about being in a rush. With that, she was gone. There was not the slightest trace of encouragement, nor the slightest trace of impoliteness. Leo hadn't dared follow her. He'd sheepishly backtracked to the platform, waiting for the next train. It had been a costly endeavour. He'd turned up to work late that morning, something he'd never done before. It was some consolation that he had finally found out her name.

Today was the first time he'd seen her since that awkward introduction. He was tense as she moved down the aisle, hoping she'd take the seat beside him. Rocking with the motion of the tramcar she passed him by without a word. Perhaps she hadn't recognized him? Leo glanced back. She took a seat near the rear of the carriage. Her bag was on her lap, her eyes fixed on the snowfall outside. There was no point in lying to himself: of course she remembered him, he could tell from the way she was studiously ignoring him. He was hurt at the distance she'd placed between them; each metre was a measure of her dislike for him. If she wanted to talk she would've sat closer. On consideration, that would have been too assertive. It was up to him to go to her. He knew her name. They were acquaintances. There was nothing improper with striking up a second conversation. The longer he waited the more difficult it would become. If the conversation fell flat, all he would lose was a little pride. He joked to himself that he could afford such a loss: perhaps he carried around too much pride in any case.

Standing up abruptly, committing himself to a course of action, he strode towards Lena with a false air of confidence. He took the seat in front of her, leaning over the back of the seat:

— *My name's Leo. We met the other day.*

She took so long to respond that Leo wondered if she was going to ignore him.

— *Yes. I remember.*

Only now did he realize that he had nothing to talk about. Embarrassed, hastily improvising, he remarked:

— *I heard you say just now that it's as cold on this tram as off it. I was thinking the same thing. It is very cold.*

He blushed at the inanity of his comments, bitterly regretting not having thought this conversation through. Looking at Leo's coat, she commented:

— *Cold? Even though you have such a nice coat?*

Leo's status as an agent provided him access to a range of fine jackets, hand-crafted boots, thick fur hats. The coat was tantamount to a declaration of his status. Not wishing to admit he worked for the secret police, he decided on a lie.

— *It was a gift from my father. I don't know where he bought it.*

Leo changed the topic of conversation.

— *I see you around a lot. I wonder if we live close to each other.*

— *That seems likely.*

Leo puzzled over the response. Evidently Lena was reluctant to tell him where she lived. Such caution was not uncommon. He shouldn't take it personally. He understood it better than anyone. In fact, it appealed to him. She was shrewd and that was part of her appeal.

His eyes came to rest on her bag, filled with books, notebooks — school exercise books. Trying to strike a pose of easy familiarity, he reached out, taking one of the books.

— *You're a teacher?*

Leo glanced at the information on the written on the front. Lena seemed to straighten slightly.

— *That's right.*

— *What do you teach?*

Lena's voice had become fragile.

— *I teach . . .*

She lost her train of thought, touching her forehead.

— *I teach politics. Sorry, I'm very tired.*

There was no ambiguity. She wanted him to leave her alone. She was straining against her desire to remain polite. He returned the book.

— *I apologize. I'm disturbing you.*

Leo stood up, feeling unsteady, as if the tramcar were travelling across a stormy ocean. He walked back to his seat grabbing the bar for support. Humiliation had replaced the blood in his veins, the sensation pumped around his body — every part of his skin burning. After several minutes of being seated, jaw locked, staring out the window, her soft rejection ringing through his head, he noticed that his hands were clenched so tight there was a series of curved fingernail impressions embedded in his palms.

Moscow
Lubyanka Square
The Lubyanka, Headquarters
of the Secret Police
Next Day

Leo hadn't slept last night, lying in bed, staring at the ceiling, waiting for the sting of the humiliation to fade. After several hours he'd got up and paced his empty apartment, moving from room to room like a caged animal, full of hate for the generous space appointed to him. Better to sleep in a barracks, the proper place for a soldier. His apartment was a family home, the envy of many, except it was empty – the kitchen unused, the living space untouched, impersonal, no more than a place to rest after a day's work.

Arriving early, he entered his office and sat at his desk. He was always early except for the day he'd stopped to ask Lena's name. There was no one else in the office, at least not on his floor. There might be people downstairs in the interrogation rooms, where sessions could run for days without interruption. He checked his watch. In an hour or so other staff would start to arrive.

Leo began to work, hoping the distraction would push the

incident with Lena from his mind. Yet he was unable to focus on the documents in front of him. With a sudden swipe of his arm, he knocked the papers to the ground. It was intolerable – how could a stranger have such an effect upon him? She didn't matter. He was an important man. There were other women, plenty of them, many would be thankful to be the subject of his attention. He stood up, pacing the office as he'd paced his apartment, feeling caged. He opened the door, walking down the deserted corridor, finding himself in a nearby office where the reports on suspects were held. He checked that Grigori had filed his report, expecting his trainee to have forgotten or to have neglected the duty for sentimental reasons. The file had been submitted, languishing near the bottom of a low-priority stack of case files, many of which would not be read for weeks, dealing with the most trivial of incidents.

Leo lifted Peshkova's file, feeling the weight of the diary inside. In a snap decision, he moved it to the highest-priority pile, placing it at the very top – the most serious suspects, ensuring the case would be reviewed today, as soon as the staff arrived.

Back at his desk, Leo's eyes began to close as if having completed that piece of bureaucracy he was finally able to sleep.

*

Leo opened his eyes. Grigori was nudging him awake. Leo stood up, embarrassed at being caught asleep at his desk, wondering what time it was.

— *Are you OK?*

Pulling his thoughts together, he remembered – the file.

Without saying a word, he hastened out of the office. The corridors were busy: everyone arriving for work. Quickening his pace, pushing past his colleagues, Leo reached the room where active cases were held for review. Ignoring the woman asking if he needed any help, he searched through the stack of files, looking for the documents on the artist Polina Peshkova. The file had been on the top. He'd put it there only sixty minutes ago. Once again the secretary asked if he needed any help.

— *There was a file here.*

— *They've been taken.*

Peshkova's case was being processed.

Same Day

Leo searched Grigori's expression for hatred or disgust. Evidently his trainee didn't know that the file on Polina Peshkova had been moved. He would find out soon enough. Leo should pre-empt the discovery with an explanation, an excuse — he'd been exhausted, he'd simply glanced at the documents then put it back in the wrong pile. On second thought there was no need to mention it. The evidence against the artist was thin. Her file would be reviewed and the case dismissed. It was going to be reviewed anyway: Leo had merely accelerated the process. At the very worst, she'd be called in for a short interview. She would be free to continue her work. Grigori could meet her again. Leo should put the matter out of his mind and concentrate on the task at hand — their next assignment. Grigori asked:

— *Are you OK?*

Leo put a hand on Grigori's arm.

— *It's nothing.*

*

The lights were turned off. The projector at the back of the room whirred. On screen there appeared footage of an idyllic rural village. The houses were made of timber and roofs were thatched. Small gardens were lush with summer herbs. Plump chickens picked at grain, overflowing from ceramic pots. Everything was in abundance, including sunshine and good humour. Farmers were dressed in traditional outfits, patterned shawls and white shirts. They strode through fields of corn, returning to their village. The sun was bright and the sky clear. The men were strong. The women were strong. Sleeves were rolled up. Soaring music gave way to a formal news commentary.

— *Today these farm workers have a surprise visitor.*

In the centre of the village were several men in suits, out of place and awkward. With smiles on their plump faces, the suited men guided their guest of honour through the picturesque surroundings. The visitor was a man in his late twenties, tall, well built and handsome. Either through some trick of editing, or through some trait of the individual, it seemed as if there was a permanent smile on his face. His hands were on his hips. He was not wearing a jacket and his sleeves were rolled up, just like the farmers. In contrast to the artifice of the rural pantomime playing around him, his excitement seemed genuine. The commentary continued:

— *World-famous Negro singer and dedicated Communist, Jesse Austin, has come to visit the countryside as part of his tour of this great land. Though a citizen of the United States, Mr Austin has proved himself to be a most loyal friend of the Soviet Union, singing about our way of life and this country's belief in freedom and fairness.*

The footage changed to a close-up of Mr Austin. His answers were dubbed in Russian, the English still audible in the gaps in the translation.

— *I have a message to tell the world! This nation loves its*

23

citizens! This nation feeds its citizens! There is food here! And plenty of it! The stories of starvation are lies. The stories of hardship and misery are the propaganda of capitalist big businesses that want you to believe that only they can provide the things you need. They want you to smile and say thank you when you pay a dollar for a cent's worth of food! They want the workers to feel gratitude when they're paid a couple of dollars for their labour while big business makes millions. Not here! Not in this nation! I say to the world – there is another way! I say again – there is another way! And I've seen it with my own eyes.

The men in suits surrounded Austin in a protective circle, laughing and applauding. Leo wondered how many of the farmers were agents of state security. All of them, he suspected. No real farmer would be trusted to pull off this performance.

The footage ended. From the back of the room, their superior officer, Major Kuzmin, stepped forward. Short and stout, with thick-lensed glasses, to an outsider he might appear comic. To officers in the MGB, he did not, for they understood the scope of his power and his readiness to use it. He declared:

— *That footage was filmed in 1934 when Mr Austin was twenty-seven years old. His enthusiasm for our regime has not diminished. How can we be sure he's not an American spy? How can we be certain his Communism isn't a trick?*

Leo knew a little of the singer. He'd heard his songs on the radio. He'd read some articles about him, none of which would have been published unless the authorities considered the American a valuable asset. Sensing Kuzmin's questions were rhetorical he said nothing, waiting for Kuzmin to continue, reading from a file:

— *Mr Jesse Austin was born in 1907, in Braxton, Mississippi, migrating with his family at the age of ten to New York. Many*

Negro families moved out of the South, where they experienced persecution. Mr Austin talks extensively about the experience in the transcripts I've given you. This hatred is a powerful source of discontent among black Americans and an effective tool in recruiting them to Communism, perhaps the most effective tool we have.

Leo glanced up at his superior officer. He spoke of hatred not as a crime, there were no acts of right or wrong, everything was weighed politically. It was not a question of outrage but calculation and analysis. Kuzmin caught Leo's glance.

— *You have something you wish to say?*

Leo shook his head. Kuzmin finished reading:

— *Mr Austin's family moved in 1917, along with many others, a period of mass migration from South to North. Of all the hatreds Jesse Austin experienced, we speculate that it was the hatred in New York that made him a Communist. Not only was he hated by white families, he also found himself hated by the Negro middle-class families who were already established in the area. They were terrified that the migrants were going to flood the northern cities. It was a pivotal moment in his life, watching people who should have stood in solidarity with the new arrivals turn on them. He witnessed the way class divides even the closest of communities.*

Leo flicked through his copy of the file. There was only one photograph of the young Mr Austin with his parents. Mother and father standing straight, as if nervous of the camera, the young Austin standing in between them. Kuzmin continued:

— *In New York his father was an elevator man in a run-down hotel called the Skyline, which has since gone bankrupt. The hotel specialized in all the corruptions typical of a capitalist city – especially drugs and prostitution. As far as we are aware, his father was involved in none of the illegal activity; although he was arrested on numerous occasions he was freed without charge. His mother was a*

domestic. Jesse Austin claims his childhood was untroubled by vio-
lence, or drink, instead his family was broken by squalor. Their
room was cold in the winter and hot in the summer. His father died
when Jesse Austin was twelve years old. He contracted pulmonary
tuberculosis. Though the United States has some admirable health
facilities they are not open to all. For example, the Metropolitan
Life Insurance Company of New York has built one of the most
advanced sanatoria for its employees. However, Mr Austin's father
was not an employee of the Metropolitan Life Insurance Company.
He could not afford a stay in a sanatorium. To this day Mr Austin
remains sure that had the facilities been available his father
would've survived. Perhaps this is another important event in
Mr Austin's political development. Watching his father die, in
a country where healthcare is contingent on your employment
circumstances, themselves dependent upon the colour of your skin,
the accident of your birth.

This time Leo raised his hand. Kuzmin nodded at him.

— *If this is the case why don't more Americans become*
Communists?

— *That is a very important question, and one we are puzzling*
over. If you come up with the answer, you can have my job.

Kuzmin laughed, a strange, strangled noise. Once he'd finished,
he carried on:

— *Though Mr Austin is full of praise for his mother, she was*
forced to work many shifts after his father's death. With so much
time on his own, he took up singing to keep occupied and a child-
hood fancy became a career. His singing and musical compositions
have never been separate from his politics. To his mind, they are one
and the same. Unlike many Negro singers, Jesse Austin's singing is
not rooted in the Church, but in Communism. Communism is his
church.

Major Kuzmin put on a record and they sat and listened to Mr Austin. Leo didn't understand the lyrics. But he understood why Kuzmin, the most suspicious of people, had no doubts about Mr Austin's sincerity. It was the most honest voice Leo had heard, words that seemed to come straight from his heart, not moderated by caution or calculation. Kuzmin turned the music off.

— *Mr Austin has become one of our most important propagandists. In addition to his polemical lyrics and commercial success, he is a brilliant speaker, and known around the world. His music has made him famous, giving his politics an international platform.*

Kuzmin gestured at the projectionist.

— *Here is footage taken from a speech he gave in Memphis in 1937. Watch carefully. There's no translation but keep your eyes on the audience's reaction.*

The reel was changed. The projector whirred. The new footage showed a concert hall filled with thousands of people.

— *Note that the entire audience is white. There were laws in the Southern states of America requiring audiences either to be all white or all black. There was no integration.*

Mr Austin was on stage, dressed in black tie, addressing the large crowd. Some of the audience members walked out, others heckled. Kuzmin pointed to some of the people leaving.

— *Interestingly, many of the people in this white audience will happily sit through his music. They will sit and clap, even give him a standing ovation. However, Mr Austin is unable to end a concert without also giving a political speech. As soon as he starts to speak about Communism, they stand up and leave, or shout abuse. Yet watch Mr Austin's expression as they do.*

Austin's face showed no dismay at their reaction. He seemed to relish the adversity, his gestures becoming more assertive, his speech continuing.

Kuzmin turned on the lights.

— *Your assignment is a crucial one. Mr Austin is under increasing pressure from the American authorities for his unwavering support of our country. Those files contain articles written by him and published in American Socialist newspapers. You can see for yourself how provocative they are to a conservative establishment, calls for change and a demand for a revolution. Our fear is that Austin might lose his passport. This could be his last visit.*

Leo asked:

— *When does he arrive?*

Kuzmin stood at the front, crossing his arms.

— *Tonight. He's in the city for two days. Tomorrow he'll be taken on a tour of the city. In the evening he's giving a concert. Your job is to make sure nothing goes wrong.*

Leo was shocked. They'd been given so little time to prepare. Cautiously, he channelled his concerns into the question:

— *He arrives tonight?*

— *You are not the only team to be given this assignment. It was a late whim of mine to ask you to be involved. I have a good feeling about you, Demidov. It would be understandable for our guest, finding himself under such scrutiny at home, to question his loyalty to our nation. I want my best people working on this.*

Kuzmin gave Leo's shoulder a small squeeze, intended to convey both confidence in his abilities and the gravity of his assignment.

— *His love for our country must be protected at any cost.*

Moscow
House on the Embankment
2 Serafimovich Street
Next Day

Leo's was one of three teams working independently to ensure Austin's itinerary went according to plan. The danger was not to his life, but to his high opinion of the State. To that end, the principle of three overlapping teams, each tasked with the same objective, was to inject a competitive element into the operation as well as factoring in redundancy – should one team fail another team would pick up the slack. The extraordinary precautions underscored the importance of his visit.

They'd been given the use of a car. It was only a short drive from the Lubyanka Square, the headquarters of the secret police, to Serafimovich Street and the exclusive residential complex where Austin was staying. It had been expected that he'd take a room in the Moskva Hotel, on the fifteenth floor with a view over Red Square, but he'd declined, stating his desire to stay in one of the communal housing projects, preferably with another family if there was a spare bedroom. He wanted to be:

Neck deep in reality.

The request had caused great anxiety since their role was to ensure that Austin was shown a projected vision of Communist society, a representation of its potential, rather than the reality of that society as it stood now. A principled idealist, Leo reconciled the dishonesty by rationalizing that the Revolution was still very much a work in progress. The time of plenty was only a few years away. Right now, a spare bedroom was unheard of in a city suffering from a chronic housing shortage. As for the idea of living with a Russian family: it was too much of a risk. Aside from the conditions, which were typically cramped, they might speak out of turn. Creating an idealized family for the benefit of Austin was too difficult to stage-manage at this short notice. Mr Austin had only requested the change on the way from the airport.

In panicked improvisation they'd put him here, at No. 2 Serafimovich Street. It was an outlandish notion, passing off a housing project designed for the political elite at the cost of over fourteen million roubles as typical of the many communal housing projects being built. In contrast to the layout of most apartment blocks, with small rooms side by side, shared cooking facilities and outside toilets, this had only two large apartments on each floor. The living room alone covered one hundred and fifty square metres – a space that would normally have been home to several families. In addition to the extra space, the apartments were furnished to the highest specification, equipped with gas cookers, running hot water, telephones, radios. There were antiques and silver candlesticks. For a guest sensitive to inequality, Leo was troubled by the proximity of an extensive network of servants who provided residents with everything from laundry to cooking and cleaning. He had managed to persuade the other residents to allow the servants time off during Austin's visit. They'd agreed, for no matter how powerful or wealthy a citizen, they feared the secret police as much as the poor, if not more. The previous occupants had hardly been ordinary citizens of the Soviet Union, including Communist theoretician Nikolay Bukharin and Stalin's own children, Vasily Stalin and Svetlana Alliluyeva. The life expectancy of the occupants was perhaps even less than those living in the worst kind of deprivation. Luxury was no protection from the MGB. Leo had himself arrested two men from this building.

Having parked the car, Leo and Grigori hurried through the snow towards the grand entrance. Stepping inside, Leo unbuttoned his jacket, showing his identity papers which were checked against a list of those granted access to the building. They headed downstairs, into the basement, where a cellar housed a team of agents maintaining twenty-four-hour surveillance, technology that had been in place long before Austin arrived. Since these apartments were home to some of the most important people in Soviet society it was essential the State knew how they behaved and what they spoke about. Austin was staying five floors above, in an apartment wired with listening devices in every room. Among the surveillance team was a translator — one of three, working eight-hour shifts. In addition, an attractive female agent had been posted to the apartment itself, in a separate bedroom, ostensibly as the occupant. She was pretending to be a widow, prepared with a story about how her husband had died during the Great Patriotic War. According to their profile of Austin such a story would be particularly endearing. He hated Fascism above all else and had many times stated that the defeat of Fascism was largely a Russian victory, bought with Communist blood.

Leo glanced through the transcripts of all Austin's conversations since he'd arrived – a chronology of his ten hours in the apartment. He'd spent twenty minutes in the bath, forty-five minutes for dinner. There were exchanges with the female agent about the Patriotic War. Austin spoke excellent Russian, a language he'd sought to learn after his visit in 1934. Leo considered this an additional complication. The agents would not be able to communicate openly. Austin would understand any slips. Flicking through the transcripts, it seemed their guest had already questioned the discrepancy between the enormous apartment and the single occupant. The agent had made a reply about it being a reward for her husband's valour in battle. After dinner, Austin had phoned his wife. He'd spoken to her for twenty minutes.

AUSTIN: *I really wish you could be here. I wish you could experience the things I'm experiencing and tell me if I'm being blind. I worry I'm seeing things the way I want them to be and not the way they are. Your instincts are what I need right now.*

In reply his wife had told him that his instincts had never let him down before and she loved him very much.

Leo handed the transcript to Grigori.

— *He's changed. He's not the same man we saw visiting the farm. He's having a crisis of confidence.*

Grigori read through the pages. He handed them back to Leo.

— *I agree. It doesn't look good.*

— *That's why he waited until the last minute to change his accommodation arrangements.*

The agent posing as the widow entered the surveillance centre. Leo turned to her, asking:

— *Was he interested in you?*

She shook her head.

— *I made several suggestive remarks. He either didn't notice or ignored them altogether. I pretended to become upset thinking about the death of my husband. He put an arm around me. But it was not sexual.*

— *You're sure?*

Grigori crossed his arms.

— *What is the point of trying to trap him?*

Leo replied:

— *We're not judging him. We must know our friends in order to protect them. We're not the only ones spying on him.*

In the corner an agent raised his hand:

— *He's awake.*

*

The party officials congregated in the marble hallway – a clump of middle-ranking, middle-aged men, suits and smiles, just like the group who'd shown Austin round the village. As important as Austin was, it was decided against arranging meetings with high-ranking Soviet personnel in case it played into the FBI's hands, enabling them to portray Austin as a Soviet crony, interested in the elite, rather than a man enamoured with the system itself.

Austin appeared at the foot of the stairs, dressed in a knee-length coat, snow boots and a scarf. Leo assessed his tailored clothes. They were not flamboyant yet were no doubt excellent quality. Jesse Austin was wealthy. Reports estimated his annual income to be in excess of seventy thousand dollars. Austin assessed his reception. Leo saw a hint of displeasure in his expression. Perhaps he felt he was being surrounded and crowded, overly managed. He addressed them in Russian:

— *Have you all been waiting long?*

His Russian was excellent, fluent, but it followed American patterns of speech and despite his good accent, his words sounded foreign. The foremost official stepped forward, replying in English. Austin cut him short:

— *Let's speak Russian. No one speaks it back home. When else am I going to practise?*

There was laughter. The official smiled and switched from English into Russian.

— *Did you sleep well?*

Austin replied that he had, unaware that everyone already knew the answer.

The group left the House on the Embankment, making their way through the snow, guiding their guest towards the limousine. Leo and Grigori broke off, heading towards their car. They would follow the party, rejoining them at their destination. As Leo opened the door, he looked back to see Austin eyeing the limousine with disdain. He began to petition the officials. Leo couldn't hear what they were saying. There was a disagreement. The officials seemed reluctant. Ignoring their protests, Austin hastened away from the limousine, arriving beside Leo and Grigori.

— *I don't want to be driven around behind tinted windows! How many people in Russia drive cars like that!*

One of the officials caught up.

— *Surely, Mr Austin, you'd be more comfortable in the diplomatic vehicle? This is just a standard working car, nothing more.*

— *Standard working car sounds great to me!*

The official was flummoxed by this alteration of their carefully laid plans. He hurried back to his group, discussing the matter, then returned and nodded.

— *Very well, you and I will travel with Officer Demidov. The others will go ahead in the limousine.*

Leo opened the door, offering the front passenger seat to Austin. But once again Austin shook his head.

— *I'll sit in the back. I don't want to take your colleague's seat.*

Putting the car in gear, Leo glanced in the rear-view mirror at Austin, his tall frame cramped into the ungenerous proportions of the car. The official peered at the rudimentary interior with dissatisfaction.

— *These cars are very basic. They were built for work not for leisure. I imagine they compare badly to many of your American cars. But we have no need for excess here.*

That sentiment may have carried more weight had the official not five minutes ago tried to impress his guest with the luxury of a limousine. Austin replied:

— *It gets you there, doesn't it?*

The official smiled, a smile designed to cover his confusion.

— *Gets us where?*

— *Wherever it is we're going.*

— *Yes, it will get us there. I hope!*

The official laughed. Austin did not. He disliked this man. Already the plans were unravelling.

Moscow
Grocery Store No. 1,
Yeliseyev's Grocery Store
Tverskaya 14
Same Day

Grocery Store No. 1 was the most exclusive shopping experience the city had to offer, open only to the elite. The walls were ornate, adorned with gold leaf. The pillars were marble, the tops decorative and intricate – flourishes that befitted a palace. Regal settings for tins of food, polished and stacked with labels facing forward, fresh fruit arranged in patterns, spirals of apples, hills of fat potatoes. Several days had been spent preparing the store. Each aisle overflowed with stock, the storerooms had been pillaged and everything had been brought forward, meticulously displayed. The end result was a venue that Leo immediately recognized as an entirely inappropriate choice for their guest, fundamentally misunderstanding the audience it was intended for. This store didn't represent a model for a new society – it embodied the past, a Tsarist-era snapshot of exuberant wealth. Yet the gaggle of party officials beamed at Austin, as if expecting him to applaud. They had let vanity get in the way of identifying what their guest truly

wanted, presenting him with ostentation, abiding by the calculation that the more they showed him, the more he'd be impressed.
Their profound fear of being seen as poor and shabby in relation to
their American foes had blinded them.

Leo paused beside tins of pea soup stacked in a pyramid formation. He'd never seen food arranged this way and wondered why a
person would be impressed by such a display. Austin passed the
pyramid, looking at it with disdain, while surrounded by a clump
of officials keenly pointing towards exotic fruits that Leo couldn't
name. In an attempt to integrate this excess with the ideology of
Communism, the shoppers, all MGB agents, had been selected
from across the age spectrum, dressed in plain clothes and scuffed
shoes, as though Grocery Store No. 1 were for everyone – the elderly grandmother and the young working woman alike. The staff
meanwhile – men for the meat counter, women for the fruit
aisle – had been instructed to smile as Austin passed them by, their
faces following him as if he were the sun and they were flowers
turning into his light. There were more shoppers outside, offstage,
shivering in the snow, entering at apparently random intervals in
order to maintain the impression of people coming and going.

Austin's expression grew increasingly sour. He was no longer
speaking. His hands were deep in his pockets, his shoulders
slumped, while all around him customers behaved like a flock of
magpies, swooping from aisle to aisle, picking up anything that
caught the light. Leo glanced in one shopping basket to see three
red apples, a single beetroot and a tin of processed ham, an
unlikely set of requirements for any shopping excursion.

Austin broke free from the clump of officials, once again
approaching Leo. He'd evidently decided Leo represented the ordinary man. Perhaps it was his coarse uniform and gruff reticence –
during the car ride here Leo had said almost nothing, in contrast

to the incessant pitter-patter flattery of the official. Austin put a hand on Leo's shoulder.

— *I feel I can talk with you, Comrade Demidov.*

— *Of course, Mr Austin.*

— *Everyone wants to show me the best. But I just want to see the ordinary stores, where ordinary folks shop. Is there something more ordinary around here? You can't seriously be telling me every store is like this one? Is that what you guys are telling me?*

Leo felt the pressure of his question like a hand tight around his heart. He answered:

— *Not all are the same. We are in the centre of town. This store might have a better range than a village store.*

— *I'm not talking about a village store. I'm talking about an everyday store. You know? This can't be the only place in town?*

— *There are other shops.*

— *Within walking distance?*

Before Leo could answer the officials hurried over, keen to divert their guest back towards their displays. They still had things to show him – fresh bread, the finest cuts of ham. Austin raised his hand, as if to keep them at bay. His mind was made up.

— *My friend is going to take me on a walk. He's going to take me to a smaller store, you know, one that's a little more . . . ordinary.*

The officials glared at Leo as if the suggestion had been his. Their survival instincts were acute. Suddenly the two other teams of agents pushed forward, addressing Leo.

— *That is out of the question. We must stick to our itinerary, for security reasons.*

Austin raised an eyebrow and shook his head.

— *Security? Are you serious? I'm not in any danger here, am I?*

They were trapped. They could hardly claim that they couldn't protect him on the streets of their capital. Austin smiled.

— I know you got rules and regulations. I know you got things you want to show me. But I want to be able to explore, OK? I insist. You hear that? I'm insisting.

He laughed to soften the order but it was an order nonetheless. They were under instructions to do as their guest requested. From the way the others were looking at Leo it was clear that he was going to be blamed.

Leo led the group out of the store, appointed head of this expedition in search of the ordinary. Austin was by his side, his mood already improving as they trampled through the thick snow. Leo glanced back to see the officials in animated conference by the store's grand doors as a new influx of carefully down-dressed, scraggy shoppers in cheap coats arrived to find the show was over. The party officials didn't understand what Austin wanted to see but they knew it wasn't long queues and poorly stocked stores. Since they were under strict orders to accommodate Austin's every whim they could hardly intervene.

Austin put a friendly hand on Leo's back.

— Tell me a little about yourself.

Leo had no desire to talk about himself.

— What would you like to know?

Appearing out of nowhere, one of the officials joined them, having evidently overheard their conversation.

— Leo Demidov is one of our bravest officers. He fought heroically during the war and was awarded numerous commendations. Please, Mr Austin, where is it you would like to be taken? Perhaps you could take some tea while we make preparations?

Austin was annoyed at the interruption, ignoring the notion of tea, a crude attempt to stall for time, and addressed Leo.

— What do you do now, Comrade Demidov?

Leo believed in his work as an agent. Communism faced

dangers from many sides. It needed to be protected. However, it was much too complex an issue to go into now. He simply said:

— *I'm a police officer.*

Leo hoped the questions were at an end. But Austin continued:

— *Is there a lot of crime in the city?*

— *Not crime as there is in America. There are no murders or theft. I deal with political criminals, conspiracies against the State.*

Austin was quiet for a moment.

— *Fairness has many enemies, am I right?*

— *Yes, you are.*

— *I'll wager your job can be difficult.*

— *Sometimes.*

— *It's worth it, my friend. It is worth it.*

They'd danced around the edge of this dark subject. Leo was thankful for Austin's discretion. The conclusion of the conversation seemed to require a long silence, a pause. Jesse Austin eventually broke the silence, opting for a lighter topic.

— *No more serious questions. What do you like to do for fun? A handsome man like you, you must be married?*

Embarrassed at being called handsome, and at being single, Leo blushed.

— *No.*

— *But why not?*

— *I don't know ...*

— *But there's someone you love, isn't there? Surely there's someone? There's always a love story, right?*

The question implied it was simply unthinkable that a person could be without love. Leo was desperate to move the conversation on. A lie was the easiest way to do it.

— *There is someone. We met recently.*

— *What does she do?*

Leo hesitated, thinking back on Lena's pile of schoolbooks:

— *She's a teacher.*

— *Bring her to the concert tonight!*

Leo gave a small nod of his head.

— *I will ask her. She is often very busy. But I will ask her.*

— *Please, bring her.*

— *I will try.*

They'd walked for ten minutes, down side streets, off the main road. An official tugged Leo's arm, smiling broadly to conceal his agitation.

— *Are we walking anywhere in particular?*

Before Leo could reply, Austin saw the queue. He raised his hand, pointing to a line of customers snaking outside a small grocery store. Grigori ran ahead, assessing the store. There were at least thirty men and women. Many of them were elderly, their ragged coats dusted with snow. Grigori looked at Leo with alarm. The crowd turned and stared at the unlikely visitors, an MGB agent and a well-dressed American celebrity — perhaps the most famous American singer in the USSR, one of the few that the media was allowed to promote.

Leo turned to Austin.

— *Wait here. Let me see what the problem is.*

Leo hurried to Grigori's side to hear him whisper:

— *They haven't opened yet!*

Leo banged on the store window. The manager scuttled out of the back room, unlocking the door. Before Leo could utter a warning, Austin was by his side.

— *They open a little later here?*

Despite the cold, Leo's shirt had become damp with perspiration.

— *It would seem so.*

41

As the door opened, Austin addressed the store manager:

— *Good morning. How you doing today? My name is Jesse Austin. Don't mind us, we're just here to look around. Please go about your business as usual and I promise we won't get in the way!*

The manager turned to Leo, eyes wide and mouth open.

— *Should I close the store for you?*

Austin replied, taking control of the situation:

— *Those people are waiting in the snow! Let everyone in. Don't do anything different!*

Cautiously, the shoppers trundled in, perplexed at the circumstances, forming a second line at the counter. Leo explained:

— *In the other store you saw customers browsing. Here things are more disciplined. The customers tell the staff what they want. They pay and then collect the items.*

Austin clapped his hands, pleased.

— *I get it. It's all about necessity! They shop for what they need, nothing more.*

Leo mumbled his agreement.

— *Exactly.*

Reading the transcripts of Jesse Austin's speeches and American interviews last night, Leo had encountered several heated exchanges where Austin had been accused of believing a falsified vision of Russia manufactured for gullible Westerners. The accusations had stung. He'd refuted the claims. But Leo was left with no doubt that Austin would be sensitive to his tour being overly managed. For this reason Leo and Grigori had spent the evening preparing several smaller stores close to the route of their itinerary. Leo had pre-empted the possibility of an impromptu visit. They'd alerted the managers and where possible they'd directed additional supplies to fill their shelves. He calculated that a polished version of reality might be more effective than an artificial model of perfection. Without the time to personally check every store their fate was in the hands of the store managers. Glancing from side to side, checking on the shelves, the state of the floors, he was relieved to see that the store was clean and reasonably well stocked. There was fresh bread and cartons of eggs. The customers were real, not hand-selected, and their good mood was entirely genuine as they marvelled at their luck, shopping on a day when there was so much choice.

The old woman at the front of the queue gleefully collected a carton of eggs. With the excitement of the purchase and the confusion of having MGB agents watch her, she lost concentration. The carton slipped from her grip, falling to the floor. Austin was the first to step up to help. Leo caught the store manager's glance – there was fear in his eyes. Something was wrong. Reacting quickly, Leo ran past Austin, picking up the carton and checking inside. Instead of eggs, there were six small rocks.

Leo shut the carton, handing it back to the manager.

— *They broke.*

The manager's hands were shaking as he took the carton. Austin called out:

— *Hold on!*

The manager stood, trembling. Leo imagined the six small rocks shaking inside the carton. Austin gestured at the elderly woman.

— *She's going to get another carton, isn't she? Without charge?*

Leo put his hand on the woman's shoulder, imagining her disappointment when she arrived home to find herself the proud owner of six small rocks.

— *Of course.*

Most of the officials were outside, pressed up against the window, too scared to move, trying to keep some distance between themselves and what they presumed was the ongoing debacle. Gradually they plucked up the courage to step into the store, wearing brittle smiles. Austin was pleased.

— *This is great, really great.*

The shop visit had been a success. The official who'd suggested tea before did so again.

Austin shook his head.

— *What is it with you and tea?*

The officials laughed. Austin declared:

— *I'm eager to see more. What's next?*

Next on the itinerary was a visit to Moscow University. Before an official could even begin to sell the idea, Austin had turned to Leo.

— *Your girl is a teacher, you said?*

Confused, Leo hesitantly replied:

— *My girl?*

— *Your girlfriend? The one we were talking about. The teacher. Wouldn't it be something to go see a school?*

Moscow
Secondary School 7
Avtozavodskaya
Same Day

Leo sat with his hands tight around the steering wheel, furious at Austin for not understanding the danger that he'd placed him in. The man's actions were naive – entirely foreign. Keen to prove his detractors at home wrong, he'd embarked on a programme of calculated sabotage, brushing aside their plans with the playfulness of a man who had no comprehension of the regime he flattered. It did not tolerate mistakes. Grave risks existed for the people organizing his trip, including Leo. Yet it hadn't occurred to Austin that there would be consequences if he saw anything that didn't chime with the idealized vision that the Kremlin wanted him to export to the United States. These attempts to duck the official preparations were little more than a game, evidenced by the way he'd whistled all the way to the Secondary School 7, where Lena worked.

Leo stared in dumb terror at Secondary School 7: a newly built box of classrooms supported on concrete legs. Fortunately there was no risk that the school building itself wouldn't pass inspection. The officials were greatly relieved that their guest had chosen an institution they would have gladly picked themselves. The risk was solely on Leo's shoulders. He'd lied. When he'd claimed Lena was the woman he loved, he'd presumed the lie would fold into the conversation, an irrelevance immediately forgotten. It had been intended to save him from the minor embarrassment of admitting that there was no one he loved and no one who loved him. Now he bitterly regretted his foolishness. Why couldn't he simply have admitted that he lived alone? There was no way to wriggle out from the trap. Austin was intent upon visiting a school and he wanted to see one that couldn't have been prepared in advance. Leo had set him up perfectly.

Stepping out of the car, he tried to think calmly, rationally, something he'd been unable to do for the past forty-five minutes. He knew that her name was Lena. He didn't know her full name. He knew that she taught politics. Most important of all, he knew that she didn't like him. His legs felt weak, like a condemned man walking to his execution. He weighed up the option of admitting the lie: he could stop the group and declare that he didn't know Lena. He'd invented a relationship because he didn't want to appear lonely. It would be a pitiful, humiliating confession. Austin would laugh it off, perhaps offering him some reassuring words about love. They could tour the school without visiting Lena. The officials would say nothing. Yet there was no question that Leo's career would come to an end. At best he'd be demoted. More likely he'd be accused of deliberately undermining the opinion of a key ally of the Soviet Union. Since there was nothing to gain by admitting the lie it was better to play along with it for as long as possible.

It was lunchtime. Children were outside playing in the snow.

Leo could use them to buy him some time, encouraging Austin to talk to the students while he slipped off and found Lena. He only needed a couple of seconds to prepare her. She didn't have to do anything other than smile, answer questions and play along with his lie. She was smart, he was sure of that. She would understand. She would improvise.

As they entered the gates, Grigori hurried to his side, their first opportunity to speak in private since Austin's request to visit the school.

— *Leo, what is going on? Who is this woman?*

Leo checked that no one else was in earshot.

— *Grigori, I lied.*

— *You lied?*

He sounded amazed, as if he considered Leo an automaton, incapable of anything as human as a lie.

— *About the woman – Lena, she doesn't love me. She barely even knows me.*

— *Does she work here?*

— *She works here. That much is true. I think, at least, I can't be sure.*

— *Why did you lie?*

— *I don't know. It just happened.*

— *What are we going to do?*

Grigori had not removed himself from Leo's predicament. He did not have the instincts of a typical MGB agent. They were a team. Leo felt a flush of gratitude.

— *I'm going to try and persuade Lena to play along with the lie. Stay with Austin, slow him down, try to buy me as much time as possible.*

The children ran forward, forming a circle as Austin entered the school. The playground had fallen silent. No doubt fearing that one of the children might say something out of turn, it was entirely possible that none of them had ever seen a black man before, an official spoke up, smiling broadly to cover the implicit threat.

— *Children, you have a very important guest today. This is Jesse Austin, the famous singer. You must show our guest how well you can behave.*

Even the youngest children understood the danger these men represented. Austin crouched down to ask a question. Leo couldn't hear what he was saying. He was already on his way to the entrance.

Once inside, out of sight, he broke into a run, his shoes heavy on the smooth stone floor. He stopped a teacher, grabbing her arms, startling her with his intensity.

— *Where's the director's office?*

The teacher remained dumbstruck, staring at Leo's uniform. Leo shook her.

— *Where?*

She pointed to the end of the corridor.

Leo burst into the room, causing the school director to stand up, paling with each second. Leo realized that the poor man believed he was being arrested. He was frail, in his late fifties. His lips were squeezed thin with anxiety. There wasn't much time.

— *I'm Officer Demidov. I need to know everything about a teacher working here. She's called Lena.*

The director sounded like a frightened child.

— *A teacher?*

— *She's called Lena. She's young, my age.*

— *You're not here for me?*

Leo snapped:

— *No, I'm not. I'm here for a woman called Lena. Hurry up!*

The old man seemed to come alive with these words – someone else was in trouble, not him. He stepped around the front of his desk, keen to be as helpful as possible. Leo glanced towards the door.

— Lena, you say?

— Her subject is politics.

— A teacher called Lena? I'm sorry: you have the wrong school. There are no teachers called Lena here.

— What?

— There are no teachers called Lena working here.

Leo was shocked.

— But I saw her books. They had the name of this school written across them.

Grigori opened the door, hissing a warning:

— They're coming!

Leo was sure of the school. Where was the mistake? She'd told him her name. Her name! That was the lie.

— How many teach politics?

— Three.

— A young woman among them?

— Yes.

— What is her name? Do you have a photograph of her?

— In the files.

— Hurry!

The director found the relevant file. He handed it to Leo. Before he could look through it, Grigori opened the door again. Austin and the officials entered the room. Leo turned to address them:

— Director, I'd like to introduce you to Jesse Austin, our guest. He wants to inspect a Soviet school before returning to America.

The director having barely recovered from the first shock was inflicted with a second – an internationally renowned guest and a group of top-ranking officials. The official who'd addressed the children outside now addressed the headmaster, using the same smile to mask his warning:

— *We want to show our visitor that the Soviet education system is one of the best in the world.*

The director's voice had become weak again.

— *I wish you'd given me some warning.*

Austin stepped forward.

— *No warning. No fuss. No ceremony. No preparations. I want to poke around, see what you get up to. And see how things work. Forget I'm even here.*

He turned to Leo.

— *How about we watch a lesson?*

Disingenuous, Leo answered:

— *A science lesson, perhaps?*

— *Is that what your girl teaches? Science?*

Upon hearing the claim that a teacher was Leo's girlfriend, the director stared at Leo. Ignoring him, Leo answered Austin's question:

— *No. She teaches politics.*

— *Well, we all like politics, don't we?*

Everyone laughed except Leo and the director. Austin added:

— *What was her name? Did you tell me before?*

Leo couldn't remember if he'd mentioned the name Lena or not.

— *Her name?*

Evidently he didn't know her name. The director was too scared or too slow-witted to step in and help him.

— *Her name . . .*

Leo deliberately dropped the file – let it slip from his hand, the papers falling out. He bent down, picking them, glancing through them.

— *Her name is Raisa.*

*

The director led the way to Classroom 23 on the second floor, Austin by his side, the officials behind him, stopping occasionally to examine a poster on the wall, or peer into another lesson. During these breaks, Leo was forced to wait, unable to stand still. He had no idea how the woman who'd lied to him about her name was going to react. Eventually reaching the classroom, Leo peered through the small window. The woman at the front was the woman he'd met on the metro, the woman he'd spoken to on the tramcar, the woman who'd told him her name was Lena. It occurred to him, belatedly, that she might be married. She might have children of her own. As long as she was smart, they were both safe.

Leo pushed forward and opened the door. The delegation followed, the entrance filling up with officials, the school's director with Jesse Austin at the front. The students stood up, amazed, their eyes flicking from Leo's uniform to their director's anxious face to Austin's wide smile.

Raisa turned to Leo, holding a stub of chalk, her fingers dusty white. She was the only person in the room, aside from Austin, who seemed calm. Her composure was remarkable and Leo was reminded why he found her so attractive. Using her real name, as if he'd known no other, Leo said:

— *Raisa, I'm sorry for arriving unexpectedly but our guest, Jesse Austin, wanted to visit a secondary school and I naturally thought of you.*

Austin stepped forward, offering his hand.

— Don't be mad at him. It's my fault. I wanted it to be a surprise.

Raisa nodded, assessing the situation with agility.

— It certainly is a surprise.

She noted Leo's uniform, before remarking to Austin:

— Mr Austin, I enjoy your music very much.

Austin smiled, asking coyly:

— You've heard it?

— You're one of the few Western . . .

Raisa's eyes darted towards the crowd of party officials. She checked herself:

— Western singers any Russian would want to listen to.

Austin was elated.

— That's kind of you.

Raisa glanced at Leo.

— I'm flattered my lessons were considered worthy for such important visitors.

— Would it be OK if I watched you teach?

— Take my seat.

— No, I'll stand. We'll be no trouble, I promise! You just go ahead. Do your normal thing.

It was a comical notion that this lesson would be normal. Leo felt faintly hysterical and light-headed. The sense of gratitude was so intense it was a struggle not to take hold of Raisa's hands and kiss them. She taught the lesson, managing to ignore the fact that none of the children were listening, all of them fascinated by the guests.

After twenty minutes a delighted Austin thanked Raisa.

— You have a real gift. The way you speak, the things you say about Communism, thank you for letting me listen in.

— It was my pleasure.

Jesse Austin was smitten with her too. It was hard not to be.

— *Are you busy tonight, Raisa? Because I'd like it very much if you'd come to my concert. I'm sure Leo has told you about it?*

She glanced at Leo.

— *He has.*

She lied with consummate skill.

— *Then you'll come? Please?*

She smiled, expressing a razor-sharp sense of self-preservation.

Moscow
Serp I Molot Factory
Magnitogorsk
Same Day

Planners for tonight's event had toyed with the idea of staging the concert within the factory itself, capturing footage of Jesse Austin singing, surrounded by machinery and workers, creating the impression of a concert that had sprung up spontaneously, as though Austin had burst into song while touring the premises. It had proved impractical. There was no clear stretch of floor space to act as an auditorium. The heavy machinery would block the view for many and there were questions about whether the machinery was suitable for international scrutiny. For these reasons the concert would take place in an adjacent warehouse emptied of stock and more traditionally arranged. A temporary stage had been set up at the north end, in front of which were a thousand wooden chairs. In order to preserve the notion that this was a concert in contrast to those performed in the West, the workers were being ushered directly from the factory floor, given no time to go home and change. The organizers not only wanted an audience of workers, they wanted an audience that looked like workers, with oil on their hands, sweat on their brows and lines of dirt under their nails. The event would offer a stark contrast to the elitism that typified concerts in capitalist countries with tiered ticket prices resulting in a stratification of the audience, where the poor were so far away they could hardly see the show while the truly impoverished lingered backstage, in the service corridors, waiting for the concert to finish so they could sweep the floor.

Leo supervised the movement of workers from the factory to the warehouse, his thoughts on Raisa. He'd cut a particularly unimpressive figure today at her school, desperate and dishonest. However, he was in a position of power and Raisa had proved herself to be astute: it was possible she would weigh up the offer to attend the concert purely in practical terms and those were favourable to him. He wondered what she thought of his occupation. Mulling over the possibilities, he urged the people around him to hurry up and fill whatever seats were available. There were no tickets. The concert was free. The men and women dutifully occupied any remaining places, some of them shivering as they sat down. The warehouse was little more than a steel shell. The roof was too high and the space too large for the gas heaters to warm the entire area. Workers seated at midway points between heaters were discreetly handed gloves and jackets. Leo rubbed his hands together, searching the crowd – there was not long to go and Raisa had still not arrived.

The programme had been arranged in advance although it was hard to know if Austin would change those plans too. The proposal was for him to take to the stage with a number of songs interspersed with short polemical speeches. His speeches would be in Russian; with a couple of exceptions, the songs would be in English. Leo glanced across the sweep of the audience, picturing how the scene would appear on the propaganda film intended for distribution across the Union and Eastern Europe. Leo snapped at a man seated a couple of rows back:

— *Take off your hat.*

Gloves wouldn't be seen in the film. Hats would be. They didn't want to give away that the auditorium was bitterly cold. As Leo was making the final checks for anything that might appear out of place he saw a worker rub some of the dirty grease from his boot across his face, blackening it. Leo didn't need to hear what was being said as several men seated nearby began to laugh. He pushed into the auditorium, reaching the man and whispering:

— *You want this to be the last joke you ever make?*

Leo stood over him as he wiped the grease from his face. He looked at the men who'd laughed. They hated him but not as much as they feared him. He sidestepped out of the row, returning to the front of the stage. After thirty minutes of shuffling, the seats were filled. There were workers standing, crowded at the back. The orchestra was onstage. The concert was ready to start.

It was then that Leo saw Raisa, being escorted into the auditorium by an officer. He'd only ever seen her dressed in her work clothes, practical and sturdy outfits, her features hidden beneath a warm hat, her hair tied back — her skin pale and without make-up. Misunderstanding the nature of the concert, she'd dressed smartly. She was wearing a dress. Though her clothes were hardly extravagant, they were dazzling when contrasted with the workers. Among the dirty shirts and ragged trousers worn by most of the audience, she walked nervously. She felt exposed, out of place and overdressed. The eyes of the workers followed her, and for good reason. Tonight she seemed more beautiful than ever before. Arriving in front of him, Leo dismissed the other officer.

— *I'll take our guest from here.*

Leo guided her to the front, his throat dry.

— *I've saved you a seat, the best in the house.*

Raisa replied, a hint of anger in her voice:

— *You didn't tell me the concert was so informal.*

— *I'm sorry. I was flustered earlier. But you look lovely.*

She registered the compliment and her anger seemed to dissolve.

— *I wanted to explain why I lied about my name.*

He noted the tension in her voice, politely cutting her explanation short.

— *There's no need to apologize. I'm sure men ask for your name regularly. It must be a nuisance.*

Raisa remained silent. Leo added, keen to stop the silence from becoming too long:

— *Anyway, it's I who owe you an apology. I surprised you today. Austin wanted to see a school. I put you on the spot. It was unfair. You could have embarrassed me.*

Raisa turned her head away.

— *It was an honour to have such important guests.*

A formality had crept into the way she spoke to Leo, no longer brusque or dismissive. She glanced about the auditorium.

— *I'm looking forward to hearing Mr Austin sing.*

— *So am I.*

They arrived at the front.

— *Here we are. Like I said, the best seats in the house.*

Leo stepped back, faintly amused at the incongruity of her radiance among the exhausted factory workers.

The warehouse lights were switched off and bright stage lights turned on, flooding the structure in a yellow glow. The cameras began to roll. Leo took position on the steps to the stage, looking out over the audience. Austin entered from the other side, striding up the stairs in huge bounds. His energy was remarkable. Onstage he seemed even taller and more impressive. With a small wave of his hand he modestly requested the applause to come to an end. Once there was silence he took the microphone, speaking in Russian.

— *It is an honour to be here, in Moscow, to be invited to sing in your place of work. The welcome you give me is always special. I don't feel like a guest. The truth is, I feel at home. At times, I feel more at home than I do in my own country. Because here, in the Soviet Union, I am loved not only while I sing, not only while I'm onstage and while I entertain you. Here, I'm loved offstage. Here, the fact that I'm a singer makes me no different from all of you even though our occupations could not be more different. Here, regardless of whether I am singing, regardless of my success, I am a Communist. I am a comrade, like all of you. The same as all of you! Listen to those sweet words. I am the same as all of you! And that is the greatest honour of all . . . to be different and yet treated the same.*

The orchestra began to play. Austin's first choice was the *Friends' Song*, written for the Communist Youth with lyrics that called for the building of new cities and the laying of new roads. It had been modified for orchestral backing, transforming it from little more than a propaganda hymn into a musical performance. To Leo's surprise, the performance overcame the rigid polemic of its lyrics. Austin's voice was powerful and intimate at the same time. It filled the cavernous space. Leo was sure that if he'd asked anyone in the audience they'd have stated that Austin appeared to be singing directly to them. Leo marvelled at what it must be like to have a voice that could move men to tears, a voice that could hush and soothe a room filled with a thousand tired workers. Among the front row, he sought out Raisa. She was concentrating on Austin, under the spell of his voice. He wondered if she would ever look upon him with the same admiration.

As the song finished, a disturbance broke out at the back of the warehouse. Members of the audience turned around, staring into the darkness. Leo stepped forward, straining his eyes, attempting to identify the source of the noise. A man appeared from the shadows, wearing an MGB uniform, his shirt pulled out, his trousers scuffed with dirt. He was a mess, staggering wildly from side to side. It took Leo a moment to realize this man was Grigori – his protégé.

Leo hurried forward, running past other agents in order to intercept him. He took his trainee by the arm. He stank of alcohol. Despite the danger of his predicament, Grigori seemed not to notice Leo. He was applauding Austin with loud, slow, erratic claps. When Leo tried to pull him away, out of the warehouse, Grigori growled like a feral dog:

— *Leave me alone.*

Leo clamped his hands on Grigori's face, staring him in the eye, speaking with genuine urgency.

— *Pull yourself together. What are you doing?*

Grigori replied:

— *Get out of my way!*

— *Listen to me—*

— *Listen to you? I wish I had never heard you speak.*

— *What has happened to you?*

— *To me! No, not to me, to someone else, Leo, the artist, Polina, you remember her? The woman I love? They arrested her. Even though I disobeyed you and ripped out the offending page …*

Grigori raised the page from the diary, complete with the doodle of the Statue of Liberty.

— *Even though there was nothing in that diary, they arrested her, even though I disobeyed you and ripped out the page, they still arrested her!*

He was repeating himself, slurring his words, running the sentences into each other as though they were a chant. Leo tried to cut him short:

— *Then they'll free her and the matter will be over.*

— *She's dead!*

He shouted out the words. A sizeable part of the audience had now turned from Austin to Grigori. He continued to speak, this time in a whisper:

— *They arrested her last night. She didn't survive the questioning. A weak heart, that's what they said to me. A weak heart . . . a weak heart! Was that her crime, Leo? If that is a crime you should arrest me too. Arrest me, Leo. Arrest me. Charge me with a weak heart. I would rather a weak heart than a strong one.*

Leo felt sick.

— *Grigori, you're upset, listen to me—*

— *You keep asking me to listen to you. But I won't, Leo Demidov, I won't listen to you! The sound of your voice is appalling to me.*

Other agents were moving closer, several rising out of the audience. Grigori bolted forward, running up the stairs, past the orchestra and towards Austin. Leo rushed after him, following up the stairs but pausing at the threshold of the stage. If he tried to make Grigori leave, they would end up in a fight. The cameras were rolling. Thousands were watching.

*

Grigori stood, blinking in the glare of the spotlights. He wanted to shout out the truth. He wanted to tell them an innocent woman had been murdered. As the faces of those seated in the front rows came into focus he understood that they already knew – not that Polina was dead, but they knew her story, they knew it many times over. They did not need to hear it from him. They did not want to hear it. No one wanted him to speak. They were afraid, not for him, but of him, as if he had some sickness that might infect their lives. He was a lunatic, a man who stood onstage and made himself a target – an act of suicide. There was nothing noble in his actions. What did it matter if he spoke the truth? It was a useless, dangerous truth. He turned to the man onstage with him, the famous Jesse Austin. What had Grigori hoped? Perhaps he'd hoped that a man full of dreams about this land would hear the truth and transform from an advocate to a critic – it would be a bitter blow to the regime, a suitable revenge for Polina's murder. But looking into Austin's kind eyes he realized that this man did not want to know the truth either.

Austin wrapped an arm around Grigori's shoulder, announcing to the audience:

— *I don't know if he's a fan, or someone telling me to shut up!*

There was laughter. Grigori slurred the words, drunk, but exhausted, defeated:

— *Comrade Austin.*

Grigori pulled out the diary page:

— *What does this mean to you?*

Austin took the page, examining the doodle. He turned to the audience.

— *Our friend has shown me a drawing of the most important symbol of our time. It is the Statue of Liberty, in New York. There in my country, that statue is a promise of things to come – a future of liberty for every man and woman, regardless of background, or race. Here your liberty is real.*

Grigori was crying, surrounded by people and yet alone. He

repeated Austin's words, speaking up, projecting to the back of the warehouse:

— *Here our liberty is real!*

*

On the steps to the stage an agent grabbed Leo's arm.

— *Do something! Fix this!*

— *What can I do? You want me to go up onstage?*

— *Yes!*

Leo edged closer but Austin shook his head, indicating that he'd deal with it. He began another song. It wasn't due to be performed until the very end, as the finale, but Austin had brought it forward, sensing that he needed something to finesse the interruption. It was *The Internationale* – the anthem of Communism.

> *Arise, you branded by a curse,*
> *You whole world of the starving and enslaved!*

Many in the audience stood up immediately. The rest quickly followed and Leo understood why Austin had chosen this song to mask the disturbance. The audience knew the lyrics. Though their singing was tentative at first, it was only because they were unsure whether they were supposed to join in. As Austin encouraged them, they became louder and louder, until each man and woman was singing as loud as they could, perhaps fearful that their loyalty to the State might be measured by their volume, perhaps fearful that if they didn't sing until they were hoarse they would become like the strange sad figure of Grigori. Leo was also singing, but half-heartedly, preoccupied with his doomed trainee. There were tears in the young man's eyes, glistening in the bright spotlights. He too was singing:

We will destroy this world of violence
Down to the foundations, and then
We will build our new world!

Austin ended the song after the first verse. As the calls for a new world died down, vigorous applause broke out across the auditorium. Agents stepped up onto the stage, clapping, false smiles on their faces, closing around Grigori, edging nearer, trying to disguise their murderous intent. Oblivious, Grigori stood, waving at some distant point, towards imaginary friends, biding the new world goodbye.

Leo felt another tug on his arm. It was Raisa. She'd left her seat, taking hold of him. It was the first time she'd ever touched him. She whispered:

— *Please, Leo, help that man.*

Leo saw fear in her eyes, for Grigori certainly, but also for herself. She was afraid. That fear had brought her to him. Finally Leo knew what he had to offer — safety and protection. It was hardly a great talent. But, perhaps, in these dangerous times it would be enough, enough to create a home, enough to satisfy a wife, enough to make a person love him. Putting his hand on top of hers he said:

— *I will try.*

FIFTEEN YEARS LATER

Moscow
Novye Cheremushki
Khrushchev's Slums
Apartment 1312
24 July 1965

Climbing the stairs, Leo Demidov's shirt became damp with sweat, clinging to his back and stomach in transparent patches. His socks seeped with each squeeze of his toes. On the ground floor the elevator was broken: the door jammed half open, the light inside flickering like the eyes of a dying animal. Despite having to climb thirteen flights of stairs he encountered no other people. It was eerie for an apartment block to be silent in the middle of the day. No children played in the corridors, no mothers with shopping, no doors slamming shut or neighbours arguing – the bustle of ordinary life muffled by the heatwave now in its sixth day. In housing projects constructed in this fashion the concrete hoarded heat with the greed of a miser collecting gold. At the top of the stairs Leo paused, catching his breath before entering apartment 1312, unseen by the other occupants of the floor.

Surveying the cramped surroundings, he pinched the shirt off his torso as though it were a series of leeches feasting on him. He crossed the living area into the kitchen and ran his face under the water. The pressure was weak, the water disappointingly tepid. Nonetheless the sensation was pleasant and he remained underneath the stuttering flow with his eyes closed allowing the water to run over his cheeks, lips and eyelids. He turned the tap off, water dripping from his face, snaking down his neck. Opening the small window, he found the hinge stiff even though the building was only a few years old. The air outside was still, not a trace of wind, a block of heat wedged around the building. Opposite him the identically designed residential tower shimmered like a mirage: the vertical lines of thousands of windows quivering in the sunlight.

The apartment was typical in almost every way. There was only one small separate bedroom and consequently the living room had been crudely partitioned to create an additional sleeping area. This makeshift division was common in many households, a line hung from wall to wall with a sheet draped for privacy shielding two narrow single beds from the kitchen area. Leo moved to the borderline between the communal space and the designated sleeping area. Bags had been packed, one beside each bed, ready to go. He tested their weight. They were heavy, one notably more than the other. Over many years, having searched hundreds of apartments, he'd developed an acute sense for anything out of place. A person's home revealed secrets in the same way that a suspect revealed their guilt, through the smallest details. In apartments, clues could be the amount of dust on a surface, tiny scratch marks on the floorboards or a single sooty fingerprint on a desk. Leo's eyes were drawn to one of the beds. With the intense summer heat there were no blankets, just a thin sheet, enabling an easy view of the mattress. It displayed a small bump, like a headless pimple, almost imperceptible, hardly worthy of attention except to some-one trained by the secret police.

Guided by these instincts, Leo crossed into the sleeping area and squeezed his hand under the mattress. His fingers touched the edge of a book. He pulled it free. It was a notebook with a hard cover. There was nothing written on it, no title or image. It was not one of the cheap flimsy books used by schoolchildren. The paper was expensive. The spine was stitched. He turned it over, checking to see how many of the pages were creased. Half the journal had been filled with writing, perhaps two hundred pages' worth. He tipped it upside down, shaking the contents. Nothing fell out. With the preliminary examination over, he flicked to the first page. The handwriting was neat, small, precise, written in pencil, the tip of which had been kept pinpoint sharp. There were several faint smudges where words had been rubbed out and written over. Time and care had been spent on it. He'd examined many diaries in his lifetime. Often entries were written in haste, scrawled, words flung down without much thought. Careful redrafting was a promising indication that the diary contained valuable admissions.

The first entry was dated a year ago and Leo wondered if that marked the beginning of this volume, or the beginning of the author's first diary. His question was answered by the opening sentence:

For the first time in my life I feel the need to keep a record of my thoughts.

Leo shut the book with a snap. He was no longer an agent: he no longer worked for the secret police. This was not the apart-ment of a suspect — it was his home. And this diary belonged to his daughter.

About to return the diary to its ill-considered hiding place, Leo heard the key in the front door. With a flush of panic, he calculated that he didn't have enough time to return the book – he'd be caught in the act. Instead, he placed his hands, and the diary, behind his back. He took a step towards the door, away from the bed, looking up, like a soldier coming to attention.

Raisa, his wife, regarded him from the doorway, a bag by her side. She was alone. She shut the door, stepping into the apartment and disappearing into shadow. Even in the dark, Leo could feel her eyes judging him. His cheeks turned hot with embarrassment, different from the heat of the day, a burning sensation under his skin. Raisa had become his conscience. He could not lie to her and rarely made a decision of any importance without imagining how she'd react. She exerted a moral force, a pull upon his emotions as powerful as the moon on tidal forces. As his relationship with Raisa had developed, his relationship with the State had weakened – he wondered if he'd always suspected that would be the case, that by falling in love with her he knew his marriage to the MGB would end. Leo now worked as manager of a small factory, overseeing shipments, processing receipts, with a reputation among his staff as being scrupulously fair.

She took a step closer, coming out of the shadow and into the sunlight. To Leo's mind she was more beautiful today than she had been as a young woman. There were faint lines about her eyes and her skin was no longer as taut and fragile as it had once been. Softness had crept into her features. Yet Leo loved these changes more than any ideal of youthful beauty or perfection. These were changes he'd witnessed: changes that had occurred while he'd been by her side, the marks of their relationship, the years they'd spent together, reminding him of the most important change of all. She loved him now. She had not loved him before.

Under her gaze Leo abandoned his intention to slip the diary back without her noticing and instead offered it to her. Raisa didn't take it, looking down at the cover. He remarked:

— *It's Elena's.*

Elena was their younger daughter, seventeen years old, adopted early in their marriage.

— *Why do you have it?*

— *I saw it under the mattress . . .*

— *She'd hidden it?*

— *Yes.*

Raisa thought about this for a moment before asking:

— *Did you read it?*

— *No.*

— *No?*

Like a novice in an interrogation, Leo capitulated under the slightest pressure:

— *I read the first line and then closed the book. I was about to return it.*

Raisa moved to the table, putting her shopping down. In the kitchen she filled a glass with water, turning her back on Leo for the first time since coming home. She finished the water in three long gulps and placed the glass in the sink, asking:

— *What if the girls had returned instead of me? They trust you, Leo. It's taken a long time but they do. You'd risk that?*

Trust was a euphemism for love. It was hard to be sure if Raisa was talking solely about their adopted daughters, or if she was indirectly referring to her own emotions. She continued:

— *Why remind them of the past? Of the person you used to be? And the career you used to have? You've spent so many years putting that history behind you. It's not part of this family any more. Finally the girls think of you as a father, not an agent.*

71

There was calculated cruelty in the detail of her response, laying out their history with unnecessary elaboration. She was angry with him. She was hurting him. For the first time in the conversation Leo became animated, wounded by the remarks.

— *I saw something hidden under the mattress. Wouldn't any man be curious? Wouldn't any father have acted as I had?*

— *But you're not just any father.*

She was right. He'd never be an ordinary husband. He'd never be an ordinary father. He would have to guard against the past as surely as he had once guarded against enemies of the State. There was regret in Raisa's eyes. She said:

— *I didn't mean that.*

— *Raisa, I swear to you, I opened this diary as a father worried about his family. Elena has been acting strangely. You must have noticed?*

— *She's nervous about the trip.*

— *It's more than that. Something is wrong.*

Raisa shook her head.

— *Not this again.*

— *I don't want you to go. I can't help feeling this way. This trip—*

Raisa interrupted him.

— *We made a decision. Everything is arranged. I know your feelings about the trip. You've opposed it from the beginning without giving any good reason. I'm sorry you're not coming. I would love you to be there. I would feel more at ease with you by my side. And I petitioned for you to come with us. But it was impossible. There's nothing more I can do. Except to pull out, without giving any reason, at the last minute, which would be far more dangerous than going, at least in my view.*

Raisa glanced at the diary. She was tempted by it too.

— *Now, please, put the diary back.*

Leo clutched it, reluctant to let it go.

— *The first entry troubles me—*

— *Leo.*

Raisa hadn't raised her voice. She didn't need to.

He put the book back, positioning it carefully under the mattress, spine facing him, roughly half an arm's depth away from the edge – the exact position he'd found it. He crouched down, examining to see if the mattress appeared disturbed in any way. Finished, he stepped back from the bed, conscious that Raisa had been watching him throughout.

Next Day

Leo couldn't sleep. In a few hours Raisa would be leaving the country. Only in exceptional circumstances had they been apart for longer than a day. He'd fought in the Great Patriotic War — was a war hero decorated for bravery — yet the prospect of being alone unsettled him. He turned on his side, listening to the sound of her breathing. He imagined that she was breathing for both of them, timing his own breath with hers. Slowly he reached out and gently laid his hand on her side. Remaining asleep, she reacted to his touch, taking hold of his hand and pressing it against her stomach as if it were a precious keepsake. After a gentle squeeze of his hand her breathing returned to its rhythm. His anxieties about the trip almost certainly sprang from the fact that he didn't want her to leave. It was possible he'd conjured worries about their plans, developed arguments about why they should stay at home — voiced opinions relating to safety and security merely for selfish reasons. He gave up on the idea that he might snatch even an hour of rest and slipped out of bed.

Navigating in the dark, his feet kicked her suitcase. It was packed and ready, at the foot of the bed as if eager to be on its way. He'd bought this case fifteen years ago, when he'd been an agent, when the exclusive shops were open to him. It was one of his first purchases, having been told that his duties would involve extensive travel. Excited by the prospect, puffed up by the importance bestowed upon him, he spent his entire weekly wage on this smart case, picturing himself criss-crossing the country, serving his nation wherever duty called. That proud, ambitious young man seemed a stranger now. The few luxury items he'd accumulated during his career had almost all been lost. This case, deposited at the back of a wardrobe, gathering dust, was all that remained from those days. He'd wanted to throw it out, and had expected his wife to welcome the decision. Despite having nothing but hatred for his former career, Raisa would not allow the luxury of such a symbolic gesture. With their current wages they'd never be able to replace it.

He checked his watch, holding it up to the window, catching the moonlight. Four in the morning – in just a few hours he would accompany his family to the airport, where he would say goodbye, remaining in Moscow. In the dark he dressed, stealthily leaving the bedroom. Opening the door he was surprised to see his younger daughter seated at the kitchen table in the dark. Her arms were in front of her, hands clasped, as if she were praying – deep in thought. Seventeen years old, Elena was a miracle to Leo: seemingly incapable of spite or malice, her character showing few scars, in contrast to Zoya, his elder daughter, who was often brusque, surly and aggressive, with a temper that could flare at the slightest provocation.

Elena looked up at him. He felt a shudder of guilt at the thought of discovering her diary, before reminding himself that he'd put it back without reading more than the opening sentence. He sat beside her and whispered:

— *Can't sleep?*

She glanced across the room in Zoya's direction. To avoid turning on a light and waking her, Leo lit a short stubby candle, tipping wax into the base of a tea glass and fixing the candle inside. Elena remained silent, hypnotized by the refracted light of the flame. His earlier observation that she was acting oddly was accurate. It was quite unlike her to be tense and reticent. If this had been an interview as part of an investigation Leo would have been sure that she was involved in something. But Leo was not an agent any more and he was annoyed that his thoughts were still organized according to the disciplines he'd been taught.

He took out a deck of cards. There was nothing else to do for the next couple of hours. Shuffling the deck, he whispered:

— *Are you nervous?*

Elena looked at him oddly.

— *I'm not a child any more.*

— *A child? I know that.*

She was angry with him. He pressed her:

— *Is anything wrong?*

She considered for some time, looking down at her hands, before answering with a shake of her head.

— *I've never flown before, that's all. It's silly, really.*

— *You would tell me? If there was something wrong?*

— *Yes, I'd tell you.*

He did not believe her.

Leo dealt the first hand of cards, trying and failing to reassure himself that he'd done the right thing in not refusing to allow the trip. He'd protested as far as he was able, capitulating only when it seemed as if he was opposing the plan merely because he'd not been allowed to go with them. His decision to leave the KGB was a permanent mark on his record. There was no prospect of his ever being granted papers for travel abroad. It did not seem fair that his circumstances should hold them back. Opportunities to visit foreign countries were exceptionally rare. It was possible they'd never get another chance.

They'd been playing cards for no more than thirty minutes when Raisa appeared at the door. She smiled, which evolved into a yawn, and sat down with them, indicating that she wanted to be dealt in, muttering under her breath:

— *I didn't think there was much hope of getting a full night's sleep.*

Across the room there was a loud and deliberate sigh. Zoya sat up in bed. She pulled back the cloth dividing screen and surveyed the game. Leo was quick to apologize.

— *Did we wake you?*

Zoya shook her head.

— *I couldn't sleep.*

Elena said:

— *Were you listening to our conversation?*

Walking towards them, Zoya smiled at her sister.

— *Only in an attempt to fall asleep.*

She took the remaining seat. The four of them, with hair dishevelled, lit only by the flicker of a candle, were a comical sight. Leo dealt to each player. He watched his family take up their cards. Had it been in his power he would've frozen time, halting the approaching dawn, stopping the sun from rising and delaying for eternity the moment when he'd have to say goodbye.

Manhattan
2nd Avenue Subway Station
Same Day

Leaving the subway station, Osip Feinstein walked slowly, ambling in a haphazard fashion, taking on the air of an eccentric gentleman down on his luck, an effective trick because it was not too far from the truth. His slow walk was a crude measure designed to expose anyone shadowing him, normally young FBI agents who were physiologically incapable of appearing casual, remaining stiff and upright as if their skin had been starched rigid along with their shirts. Normally Osip was followed once a month in what seemed to be routine FBI harassment rather than a concerted attempt to build a case against him. However, for the past month he'd been followed every day. The step-up in surveillance was dramatic. Members of the Communist Party of America were reporting a similar increase in FBI activity. Osip felt sorry for them. The vast majority weren't spies. They were believers, nurturing dreams of revolutions, equality and fairness – card-carrying supporters of a legitimate political party. It didn't matter that Communism was not a crime. Their political allegiance resulted in their lives being placed under intense scrutiny. They were plagued with accusations.

Their employers were presented with dossiers containing nothing more than speculation regarding their employees' out-of-hour activities, dossiers that concluded:

A company or firm is judged by the behavior of its employees.

Underneath there was a telephone number. Every employer was being asked to spy for the State. So far this year three men had lost their jobs. One had suffered a nervous breakdown as his family, friends and casual acquaintances were brought in for questioning. One woman no longer left the house, certain she was being watched.

Osip paused, glancing back, assessing the people behind him. None of them stopped or looked at him. He crossed the street abruptly then ambled at a slow pace for some hundred or so metres before breaking into a brisk walk. Turning down another street, then another, he'd almost looped back to where he'd started. He reassessed the people behind him before continuing on his way.

The location for the meeting was an ugly low-rise, cooked by the summer sun, filled with beaten-down immigrants, just like him. Maybe not just like him; he doubted many of them were working as spies, although you could never be sure. The entrance area was busy, people lingering outside, squatting on the steps in the balmy evening. Osip's clothes were appropriately threadbare, his face sallow. No one paid him any attention: maybe he fitted in or maybe they just didn't care about a down-and-out fifty-seven-year-old man. He entered the apartment building, his shirt becoming sticky with perspiration as he stepped into the corridors. The evening was humid and the putrid muggy air hung around him like a shroud. Climbing the stairs, he wheezed his way up to the seventh floor. Even with the lowest of expectations, he was surprised at how awful this place was. There were stains on the walls as if the whole building were sick, suffering rashlike symptoms. He knocked at apartment 63. The door gave a little.

— *Hello?*

There was no reply. He pushed the door wide open.

The dregs of sunset, filtered by filthy net curtains, threw skewed shadows about the room. A narrow corridor passed a narrow bathroom leading into a narrow bedroom. There was a single bed, a fold-down table and a chair. An exposed light bulb hung from the ceiling. The bed linen hadn't been changed in months, shimmering with grease. The smell was oppressive. Osip pulled out the chair and sat down. In the soupy warm air, he closed his eyes, drifting off to sleep.

Faintly aware of a figure in the room with him, Osip awoke from his sleep, straightening up and closing his mouth. There was a man at the door. The sun had set. The light from the overhead bulb was weak. Osip wasn't sure whether it had been turned on by the man or whether it had always been on. The man locked the front door. He was carrying a cracked leather sports bag. He surveyed the room, the greasy bed linen. From the disgust on his face it was obvious the apartment didn't belong to him. The man pulled the comforter across the bed before perching on the edge. He was in his late thirties, or early forties; everything about him seemed substantial, his arms, his legs and chest, his facial features. He rested the bag on his knees, unzipping it, taking out something small – tossing it towards Osip, who caught it. In his palm was a wrap of opium. In a movement perfected over many years, he secreted the wrap into an inside pocket of his jacket with a small hole that enabled it to drop into the lining. Many agents had addictions, some to gambling, some to alcohol. Osip smoked most nights until he passed out, lying on his back and feeling the most wonderful sensation in the world – nothing at all. Dependency on the drug served a secondary purpose. It made his superiors, and those in the Soviet Union reviewing his activities, less suspicious. His addiction allowed them to feel in control of him. They owned him. He depended on them. His code name was Brown Smoke. Though it conveyed a degree of contempt, Osip liked it. It made him sound like a Native American, which for an immigrant spy was an irony, he supposed.

It was doubtful that this man was an FBI undercover agent. He hadn't said a word. An undercover agent would have already told a hundred nervous lies. He reached into the bag for a second time. Osip leaned forward, anxious to see what he would pull out next. It was a camera, with a telescopic lens. Osip said:

— *This is for me?*

The man didn't reply, placing the camera on the table. Osip continued:

— *I think there's been some mistake. I'm not a field operative.*

The man's voice was coarse and low, more like a growl than speech.

— *If you're not an operative, what are you? You provide us with no useful information. You claim that you are developing spies. These spies give us nothing.*

Osip shook his head, pretending to be indignant.

— *I have risked my life—*

— *A calculated risk from a man with nothing to lose. You're an expert in doing as little as possible. Time has caught up with you. Many thousands of dollars have been paid to you, and for what?*

— *I am happy to discuss what more I can do for the Soviet Union.*

— *The discussions have already taken place. We've decided what you must do.*

— *Then I'd counsel that those demands be aligned with my skills.*

The man scratched his chest through his shirt then looked at his nails, surprisingly long, and spotlessly clean.

— *Something very important is about to happen. For it to succeed two things need to be done. You were given a camera. Let me show you what I was given.*

The man placed a gun on the table.

Airspace over New York City
Same Day

The cloud cover parted as neatly as if a hand had pulled back a theatrical curtain revealing New York City to the audience circling in the sky. The Hudson River split like a tuning fork around the narrow island of Manhattan, on which the fabled skyscrapers were so neat and numerous that the city appeared as a geometric creation composed entirely of straight lines. Raisa had expected New York to be vast, even from the sky, a colossus of steel, with eight-lane roads and cars in ant-like lines that stretched for miles. Regarding the United States for the first time, she found herself holding her breath, an adventurer who'd finally reached a place of lore and legend – comparing myth with reality. This was not only her first glimpse of America, it was her first time in an airliner, the first city she'd ever seen from the sky. The moment was dreamlike although Raisa had never actually dreamt of coming here. Her dreams, modest as they were in scope, had always been confined within the borders of the USSR. The prospect of visiting America had never crossed her mind. Of course, she'd speculated about the nation vilified by her government, posited as their greatest enemy, a society upheld as an example of corruption and moral degeneracy. She'd never believed these assertions outright. Occasionally it had been necessary as a teacher to repeat the statements, striking a tone of anger and outrage, fearful her students would denounce her if she moderated the descriptions of the United States. Yet whether she believed them or not, these lies must have influenced her. This city and this country were a concept, not a real place, an idea controlled by the Kremlin. The Soviet media was only allowed to publish photographs of soup kitchens, lines of the unemployed, juxtaposed beside images of the vast homes of the rich, men whose stomachs strained against the cut of their bespoke suits. After years of mystery, the city was sprawled beneath her, fully exposed, like a patient on a surgical table, ready for her without comment or qualifications, without the accompaniment of a polemical propaganda narration.

Suddenly fearful that she'd made a mistake in bringing her daughters to this strange new world, Raisa regarded Elena, beside her, peering through the small window as the airliner circled.

— *What do you think?*

Elena was so excited she didn't hear the question. Raisa tapped her shoulder, suggesting:

— *The city is smaller than I expected.*

Elena turned around, able only to say:

— *We're really here!*

She returned her attention to the window, staring down at the city. Raisa stood up, looking over the back of her seat at her elder daughter in the row behind. Zoya was also pressed up against the window, like a young child, her eyes hungry for every detail. Raisa sat back down, reassured that she'd done the right thing in bringing them to New York – it was a remarkable opportunity.

The pilot announced their approach, explaining that preparations were being made for their arrival at the airport, no doubt a ceremony of some kind. At an elaborate departure ceremony in Moscow they'd been told that the pilot was the same man who had flown Khrushchev to the United States on his countrywide visit in 1959 and that this was the exact same plane used by the Premier, one of the few planes that could travel such a distance without needing to refuel. Concerned about their international image, the Kremlin had insisted that the delegation land in New York in the most advanced airliner in the world.

As the Tupolev 114 circled out to sea, readying to land at John F. Kennedy airport, Raisa caught sight of a smaller island located off the lower tip of Manhattan. She pressed her finger up against the window, telling Elena:

— *You see that?*

Elena face was still close to the window, fearful that she might miss some wonder:

— *Yes, I see it. What is it?*

Raisa squeezed her daughter's arm.

— *It's the Statue of Liberty.*

Elena turned around for the first time since the cloud had parted.

— *What is that?*

At nearly seventeen years old Elena had no idea about the city she was about to arrive in. While Raisa had been prepared to risk her own life reading banned books and illegally imported magazines, she would never have allowed her daughters to read them. In the conflict between her instincts as a teacher and her instincts as a protective mother, the mother always won out. She'd deliberately sheltered her daughters, shielding them from any knowledge that might taint them. By way of explanation she merely said:

— A famous New York landmark.

Glancing at the excited faces of the Soviet students who filled the cabin, Raisa couldn't deny that she felt a sense of pride muddled with her anxiety. She'd been intimately involved in the planning and development of this trip. Her position on it hadn't been won through political connections. In fact, the opposite was true: she'd needed to overcome serious questions about her past. Leo was a pariah in the complex political landscape of Moscow: his reputation was ruined by his refusal to work for the State security forces. Over the last ten years he'd maintained a low profile while she'd become an increasingly prominent figure in the education system. Promoted to director at her secondary school she held regular meetings with the ministry on topics such as literacy levels. Her school had achieved improvements that she would've dismissed as propaganda had she not been involved. It was a peculiar reversal of fortunes. Leo, once powerful and well connected, was now isolated, cut off from advancement, while her career had grown, pushing her closer to the corridors of power. Yet there was never any suggestion of jealousy. He was far happier now than she'd ever known him. He loved his family. He lived for them. He would die for them: of that there was no doubt. She felt a pang of sadness that he was not here to share this experience with them. She wasn't sure whether he'd enjoy New York, he'd almost certainly be on edge, alert for plot and intrigue, but regardless, he would always enjoy being with them.

Considering the level of hostility between the two countries the trip had been labelled as naive by many commentators. A delegation of Soviet students was to perform concerts in New York and Washington DC in an effort to improve relations between the two nations. It seemed like a fanciful idea. Recent diplomatic incidents had been grave: the Cuban Missile Crisis had brought the countries to the brink of nuclear war. While other incidents were relatively trivial in comparison, such as the Soviet Union being excluded from New York's World Fair, they'd contributed to a worsening sentiment. Tensions were high. Against this backdrop the notion of a school visit had gained favour with governments on both sides. Since neither nation could be seen to capitulate on critical military issues, there were few avenues open diplomatically. Though seemingly slight, agreeing to these concerts was one of the few concessions either country was prepared to make.

Diplomats on both sides had thrashed out the official aim of the trip, entitled THE INTERNATIONAL STUDENTS' PEACE TOUR:

The hope is for the children of today to know only peace in their lifetime.

The Soviet students ranged in age from twelve to twenty-three and were drawn from every region. They were to be partnered with an exact match of American students drawn from across fifty states. On stage the two nations would be intermingled, standing side by side, hand in hand, performing before the world's media and diplomatic elite. It was a crude political exercise and on occasion the preparations had descended into farce: there had been discussions about whether the weight and height of each student needed to be balanced to avoid one set of students appearing more substantial on stage. Despite these absurdities, Raisa thought the premise admirable. She'd originally been asked to nominate a selection of students who'd best represent the country and had enthusiastically become involved with the planning. Unexpectedly she'd been asked to head up the tour. Her only stipulation had been that she'd didn't feel comfortable leaving her daughters behind. Elena and Zoya had therefore been included. While Zoya found representing her country problematic – she had no love for the State, with a rebellious spirit that she could barely manage to control – she was shrewd enough to appreciate that the opportunity to travel would almost certainly never arise again. Furthermore, it was unthinkable to decline such an offer. She wanted to become a surgeon at a prestigious hospital. She needed to appear a model citizen. They'd witnessed the repercussions to Leo when he'd declined to work as a secret-police officer. In contrast to her older sister, Elena had no qualms about the trip: she couldn't have been more thrilled and had begged Raisa to take the position.

The airliner made its descent, the gentle rocking briefly muting the excitement of the passengers. Several gasps could be heard among the group of students and some of the teachers. Considering their inexperience as travellers, they'd remained remarkably calm during the flight. As they passed through the patchy cloud, Elena took hold of Raisa's hand. Whichever way she looked at it, today was a remarkable moment. Not only had Raisa never dreamt that one day she would visit the United States, she'd never imagined she would have a family of her own. Her situation had been so desperate as a teenager – a refugee during the Great Patriotic War – that her ambition had been no grander than to survive. Even today she found it a miracle that she'd been fortunate enough to adopt two daughters that she both admired and loved.

Touching down, the cabin remained in a state of stunned silence, as if sceptical that they'd made the transition from the sky to the ground. They were now on American soil. The pilot announced:

— *Look out your window! On the right-hand side!*

At once everyone unbuckled their seatbelts, rushing to the windows and peering out. Raisa was ordered by the cabin attendant to hurry the students back into their seats, an instruction she ignored, unable to resist sneaking a look out of the window herself. There were thousands of people outside. There were balloons and banners, written in English and Russian.

WELCOME TO AMERICA!

Raisa said:

— *Who are those people for?*

The cabin attendant replied:

— *They're for you.*

The plane came to a standstill. The doors opened. As soon as they did, a school brass band began to play, the noise filling the cabin. In a state of dumb bewilderment the passengers lined up in the aisle. Raisa was at the front. The school band was at the foot of the stairway, playing with great gusto rather than great finesse. Raisa was nudged down the stairs, one of the first to step onto the tarmac. The press was to one side, perhaps as many as twenty photographers, flashbulbs popping. Raisa turned around, unsure what she was meant to do or where she was supposed to go. They'd been told to leave their bags onboard so they would be free to enjoy the reception. A welcome party greeted them, smiling and shaking their hands.

Raisa saw a small group of men, apart from the others. They were wearing suits, hands deep in their pockets. Their faces were hostile. She knew without seeing a badge, or a gun, that they were America's secret police.

*

FBI agent Jim Yates watched the Soviet delegation form three neat rows, the shortest at the front, tallest at the back. The band, the balloons, the audience, the photographers flashing their cameras like these kids were film stars, and not one of them smiled, their expressions rigid, their mouths narrow. Like machines, he thought, just like machines.

Manhattan
Hotel Grand Metropolitan
44th Street
Next Day

If asked whether she cared about the concerts Zoya would shrug and claim that she hoped they went well if only for the sake of her mother. She didn't feel personally invested and didn't have much belief in the value of the events – the notion of international goodwill being conjured by singing songs seemed comical in its naiveté. Her rule was to avoid getting involved in politics and ideologies. She was training to be a surgeon. She dealt with the body, flesh, bone and blood, not ideas or theories. She'd sought out a profession in which in her mind there was as little moral ambiguity as possible: she would do her best to help the sick. Her approach to these concerts was pragmatic. She wanted to travel: that was the reason she was here. She wanted to see New York. She was interested to meet Americans. She'd learnt a little English and was curious to put it to use. And there was no way she would have allowed her little sister Elena to travel without watching over her.

Sat on the edge of the bed, Zoya was less than a metre away

from the television, engrossed in the American programmes being shown seemingly at all hours. The screen was encased in a glossy walnut cabinet with the speaker on one side, a panel of small dials down the other. The instruction card on top had been translated into Russian. No matter what dials she turned, or buttons she pressed, the same set of programmes was on. There were cartoons. There was a programme with music called *The Ed Sullivan Show*, introduced by a man in a suit, Edward Sullivan, with live music from bands she'd never heard of. Afterwards there were more cartoons featuring talking dogs and racing cars that tumbled down cliffs, crashing in an explosion of gold and silver stars. Zoya's English was limited to a few phrases. It didn't matter since there was hardly any dialogue in the cartoons and *The Ed Sullivan Show* featured live music and even when it didn't, even when the presenter was talking, even when she didn't understand, she found it fascinating. Was this what America watched? Was that how America dressed? The shows were hypnotic. She'd woken up early to watch more. The fact of having a television in her bedroom, a bedroom with her own private bathroom, was so incredible it seemed a shame to spend too much time sleeping.

The cartoon was about to finish. Zoya strained forward, excited. Even better than the cartoons or the music were the programmes that ran in between shows. These shorts were no more than thirty seconds each. Sometimes they featured men and women speaking directly to the camera. They spoke about cars, silverware, tools and gadgets. This one featured a busy restaurant in which children laughed while being served wide glasses filled with ice cream, chocolate sauce and fruit. It was followed by a second short, this one featuring images of houses, impossibly large for a single family, more like a dacha than a house. Except unlike a dacha, situated in the countryside, there were many of these large houses side by side, with neat lawns and children playing. And every house had an automobile. There was a programme featuring devices to chop carrots and potatoes and leeks and turn them into soup. There were face creams for women. There were suits for men. There were objects for every chore, machines for every task, and they were all for sale, propaganda except not for a political regime but for a product. She'd never seen anything like them before.

There was a knock. Zoya turned the volume down, opening the door and finding Mikael Ivanov outside. He was the youngest of the staff accompanying them, some thirty or so years old and one of the propaganda experts assigned to the delegation. His purpose was to make sure none of the students embarrassed the State and to make sure the Americans were unable to unduly influence the students. Zoya didn't like him. He was good-looking, vain, arrogant and humourless — textbook party loyal. He'd joined the tour preparations three months before they were due to leave, spending several hours a week lecturing the students, highlighting the social problems in the United States and explaining why Communism was superior to capitalism. He'd provided them with lists of things they should be wary of. While abroad they were supposed to carry these laminated checklists around with them wherever they went. On the checklist were statements such as:

The ostentatious wealth of a Few
The deprivation of the Many

Zoya wanted to wince every time Mikael spoke. She understood the principle, that the poor would be on the fringes, hidden from view, and that it was easy to be impressed by symbols of wealth in the centre of Manhattan. All the same, his relentless emphasis on party dogma was tedious. Of the many people involved in the tour, he was the person she mistrusted the most.

Mikael strode past Zoya, across to the television, turning it off with an angry flick of his wrist.

— *I told you: no television. It's propaganda. And you're lapping it up. They're treating you like you're a fool and you're behaving like one.*

At first Zoya had tried to ignore him as much as possible. Since that ploy hadn't worked she'd decided it was more fun to irritate him.

— *I can watch something without being brainwashed.*

— *Have you ever watched television before? Do you think they haven't put a lot of thought into the programmes they're showing you? This isn't real television that the American citizen will watch – it has been created just for you, along with the contents of that bedroom bar.*

In their rooms they had found a small refrigerator stocked with Coca-Cola, strawberry- and cream-flavoured candy and chocolate bars. A note, kindly translated into Russian, explained that the contents were free and were to be enjoyed with the hotel's compliments. Zoya had moved with lightning speed, drinking the soda before squirrelling away the rest of the chocolate. By the time Mikael had arrived to confiscate the contents none remained. He'd been furious and conducted a thorough search of their room, failing to find anything, since Zoya had lined all the candy and chocolate along the window ledge. Leo would've been proud.

Mikael was now working himself into a fresh temper about the television, which he had unplugged as if Zoya would not be able to plug it back again.

— *Do not underestimate the power of their programmes. They*

serve to numb the minds of their citizens. It is not mere entertain-
ment: it is a key weapon in maintaining their authority. The
citizens of this country are given idiotic escapism in order to pre-
vent them asking deeper questions.

Though Zoya enjoyed upsetting him, finding him entertaining
when he was angry, the joke quickly grew tedious and she moved
to the door as a way of hastening his departure. He looked about
the room.

— *Where is Elena?*

— *In the bathroom. She is shitting. As an insult to the*
Americans, you should be pleased.

He was embarrassed.

— *You're only on this trip because of your mother. It was a mis-*
take to bring you. You are quite unlike your sister. Practise your
songs. Tonight's concert is important.

With that, he left.

Zoya slammed the door shut, angry at the comparison he'd
made between her and Elena. Like most party officials he ruled by
creating divides between people, families and friends. She was
closer to her sister than anyone alive and she would not allow any
agent of the State to imply otherwise. She pressed her ear to the
door to make sure he'd gone. He was the kind of man who'd linger
and eavesdrop to find out what people thought of him. Unable to
hear anything she crouched down, peering through the crack
under the door. There were no shadows, just a strip of light.

Passing the bathroom, she called out to her sister:

— *You OK in there?*

Elena's voice was faint.

— *I'll be out in a second.*

She'd been in there for a while. Zoya plugged the television
cable back into the socket and returned to the edge of the bed and

turned it back on, lowering the volume only slightly. Maybe the American programmes were supposed to brainwash the audience. But only someone brainwashed by the Kremlin wouldn't be curious.

*

Even though there was nothing left in her stomach, Elena felt as if she wanted to be sick again. She filled a glass with water and rinsed her mouth. Desperately thirsty, yet unsure whether she could manage even a sip, she spat out the water. She took one of the towels, drying her face, composing herself. She was shocked at how pale she looked. She breathed deeply. She couldn't delay any longer.

She opened the door, stepped out into the hallway, rooting through the cupboard, hoping that Zoya would remain preoccupied with the television. Zoya called out:

— *What are you looking for?*

— *My swimsuit.*

— *You're going to the pool?*

— *That is where people swim, isn't it?*

Elena was trying to be sassy in an effort to hide her nervousness but it wasn't her style and the words jarred. Zoya didn't seem to notice:

— *You want me to come?*

Elena snapped back:

— *No.*

Zoya stood up, looking at her sister directly.

— *What's wrong?*

Elena had made a mistake in being so abrupt.

— *Nothing. I'm going to have a swim. I'll see you in an hour or two.*

— *Mother's coming back for lunch.*

— *I'll be finished before then.*

Holding her gym bag, Elena left.

In the corridor she hastened away from her sister's room, checking up and down to make sure no one was watching. She didn't head to the elevator, instead stopping by room 844 and trying the handle. It was unlocked. She stepped inside, shutting the door behind. The room was dark. The curtains were drawn. Mikael Ivanov stepped out of the shadows, putting his arms around her. She rested her head against his chest, whispering:

— *I'm ready.*

He put his hand on her chin lifting her eyes up towards his. He kissed her.

— *I love you.*

Manhattan
United Nations Headquarters
1st Avenue & East 42nd Street
Next Day

Raisa's awe came not from the architecture – the United Nations headquarters were not particularly tall or beautiful – but simply from being here. It was her first full day in New York City and the experience of being abroad, in the nation described as their Main Adversary, was overwhelming. Waking up in her hotel room in the middle of last night she'd been disorientated, searching the bed for Leo. When she couldn't find him, she'd opened the curtains to reveal a view no more glamorous than a back alley and a fragment of city skyline, the edge of an office tower – a view of windows and air-conditioner units. Yet she'd stood in dumb wonder as if stretched out before her were snow-capped mountains.

She entered the lobby of the United Nations Headquarters, the only member of her delegation to attend these preliminary meetings, inspecting the General Assembly Hall where tonight's concert was to be staged. She was to discuss the event with key Soviet diplomats, the men involved with the complex and on-going negotiations with the American authorities. She expected the meeting to be tough. They would want to pick through every detail of her plans. Tonight's concert was to be a gathering of United Nations envoys, representatives from almost every country and the key diplomatic event of the tour. A second concert was planned for tomorrow, intended for a public audience. It was to be filmed then broadcast around the world. After that, the delegation would travel by train to Washington DC for a final set of concerts.

As part of the chess-game-like negotiations, the Soviet authorities had insisted that the group not be taken on a tourist trail of New York City or Washington DC. Officials in Moscow were keen to avoid photos of Soviet students staring in amazement at skyscrapers or the Statue of Liberty, or salivating over hot dogs and pretzels as if they were starved and deprived. Such photos would be exploited. Despite the stated peace agenda, both sides were hunting for an iconic image that would define the tour in one nation's favour – the image that would be remembered and disseminated around the world. These fears had resulted in two officials being appointed to stage-manage the group's public appearances, evaluating any situations set up by their American guides. Raisa had no interest in these games being played and was annoyed that despite being in New York, the only visit she would probably ever make to the city, many of the sights were off limits. She was giving serious consideration to the idea of sneaking Elena and Zoya out of the hotel at night and taking them on an unofficial tour. It would be difficult to slip past the security and perhaps her instincts as a teacher were asserting themselves too strongly. There would be a risk. She pushed the thought aside for now, concentrating on the upcoming meeting.

Although she lived in Moscow and held a prestigious job she was concerned that she'd seem provincial. Granted a generous allowance, she'd bought a new outfit. She was wearing it for the first time today, a steel-coloured suit. She felt uncomfortable in it, as if she were wearing someone else's clothes. In Moscow the exclusive stores had been temporarily opened to her and the other teachers on the trip, a strictly one-off event in order to ensure they were presentable. Even so, she had no sense of international fashions and while the staff working in the store had lectured her on what executives in New York would wear, she suspected they didn't know what they were talking about. The diplomats she was about to meet spent their lives immersed in a society of the most important people in the world. She imagined walking into the room, being assessed in an instant as a woman of limited means who rarely travelled outside of Moscow. They would smile, polite, condescending – certain that she'd been plucked from obscurity, from mediocrity, and pushed onto an international stage. And this would be gleaned from a quick glance at her plain shoes and the cut of her jacket. In ordinary circumstances she wouldn't have cared what a stranger made of her appearance. She was not vain. On the contrary, she preferred not to be noticed. But in a situation like this she needed to command respect. If they didn't trust her, they'd be tempted to interfere in her plans.

In the elevator, Raisa stole a final glance at herself. The guide caught sight of her nervous self-appraisal. The young man, educated, with hair slicked to the side, wearing a no doubt expensive suit and polished shoes, afforded her a patronizing smile as if to confirm that her anxieties were exactly correct: her shoes were plain, her clothes poor and her appearance not to the standards typical of those working in this building. Worse was the implication that he was being generous to her, understanding the limits of her situation and making necessary allowances. Raisa remained silent, feeling out of her depth. She composed herself, doing her best to dismiss the incident, before stepping into the offices of the Soviet representative to the United Nations.

Two men, in immaculate suits, stood up. She knew one of them already, Vladimir Trofimov, a handsome man in his forties. He worked for the Ministry of Education, where the plans for the trip had been formalized. She'd met him in Moscow. While she'd expected him to be a political creature, largely indifferent to the children, he'd proved to be gregarious and friendly. He'd spent time with the students, engaging them in conversation. Trofimov introduced Raisa to the other man:

— *Raisa Demidova.*

He switched into an imitation American accent:

— *This is Evan Vass.*

She hadn't expected any Americans in the meeting. The man was tall, in his late fifties. Vass stared at her with such intensity that she was momentarily taken aback. His eyes didn't casually wander over her clothes, or note her simple shoes. She reached out to shake his hand. He took hold of it, loosely, as if it were something awful. He didn't shake it: he merely held it. She found herself wanting to pull away. He seemed oblivious to the fact that he was making her feel uncomfortable. Though she'd been practising, Raisa's English was limited.

— *It is my pleasure to meet you.*

Trofimov laughed. Vass did not. He answered in perfect Russian, releasing her hand:

— *My name is Evgeniy Vasilev. They call me Evan Vass as a joke. It is a joke, I suppose? I have never found it funny.*

Trofimov explained his joke:

— *Evan has been in America so long and is so corrupted by American ways we have renamed him.*

Even this light exchange left Raisa confused – to claim someone was corrupted by American ways was hardly a laughing matter, yet it seemed the remark were no more than banter. These men existed in a rarefied atmosphere where even serious accusations carried no danger. As Trofimov poured her a glass of water she reminded herself that no matter what leniency they showed each other she was not of their level and rules that did not apply to them still applied to her.

Putting the disconcerting introduction behind her, Raisa reiterated the plans for the concert, pointing out the significance of the arrangements, from the choice of songs to the blocking. There had been one meeting in her hotel last night with her American counterpart: she was about to have a second meeting in the Grand Assembly Hall. There would be a dress rehearsal in the afternoon. Trofimov smoked throughout, smiling and nodding, occasionally watching his cigarette smoke swirl in the air-conditioned currents. Vass gave no reaction, regarding her with unmoving coal-black eyes. As she finished, Trofimov stubbed out his cigarette.

— *That sounds excellent. I have nothing to add. You seem to have everything under control. I'm sure the concerts will be a great success.*

The men stood up. It was her cue to leave. Raisa couldn't believe it, standing uncertainly.

— *You don't have any comments?*

Trofimov smiled.

— *Comments? Yes, good luck! I'm looking forward to the concert. It will be a great success. A triumph, of that I have no doubt. We will see you tonight.*

— *Won't you be attending the dress rehearsal this afternoon?*

— *No, that won't be necessary. And it might spoil the experience. We trust you. We trust you completely.*

Trofimov stepped forward, showing Raisa to the door. The

young guide was waiting outside, ready to escort her to the General Assembly Hall. Trofimov said goodbye. Evan Vass said goodbye. Raisa nodded, heading towards the elevator, perplexed by their response. They hadn't interrogated her. They hadn't imposed their authority. They'd behaved as if the concert that they'd spent so long seeking diplomatic permission for was of absolutely no concern.

She touched the arm of her guide, saying in English:

— *Where is the bathroom?*

He changed direction, taking her to the bathroom. She entered, checking that she was alone before leaning on the sink and looking at her reflection, regarding her ugly, unfashionable set of clothes, registering the tension in her shoulders. Leo's instincts about this trip had been correct.

New Jersey
Bergen County
The Town of Teaneck
Same Day

FBI agent Jim Yates stood beside his sleeping wife, looking down at her as if she was a corpse and he was the first officer on the scene. She was wrapped up in a thick comforter in the height of summer, in a bedroom that was as hot as a sauna. Hypersensitive to noise, twirls of cotton wool spiralled out of her ears like wisps of campfire smoke. A thick black eye mask protected her in perpetual darkness, closing out the world, for she despised even this brilliant sunny morning. He leaned down, his lips hovering above her forehead and whispered:

— *I love you.*

She rolled onto her side, turning away from him, creasing up her face in irritation, shooing him away with the furrows of her brow. She didn't lower her eye mask and didn't reply. As he straightened up, the image flashed through his mind of taking off that mask, placing his fingertips on her eyelids, forcing them open and making her look at him – repeating, calmly, in a measured voice, not shouting, or losing his temper:

I. Love. You.

He'd keep repeating it, louder and louder until she said it back to him.

I. Love. You. Too.

He would say thank you. She would smile sweetly. And that was how a normal day should begin. A husband tells his wife he loves her, she should tell him she loves him back. It didn't even have to be true but there was a formula to follow. That was how it worked in every other household, in every decent suburb, in every normal American family.

Walking to the window, Yates pulled back the curtain and looked out onto their garden – it was overrun, the flowerbeds choked with knee-high weeds knotted together like witch's hair. The lawn had died a long time ago, the earth split into rock-hard chunks: jagged fissures between clumps of lank yellow grass, like the surface of some inhospitable moon. Set among the perfectly tended gardens of their neighbours it was an abomination. Yates had proposed hiring a gardener but his wife had refused, unsettled by the idea of a stranger moving in and out of the house, making noise, talking to the neighbours. Yates had suggested asking the gardener not to speak, never to come inside and to make as little noise as possible, anything so that their house wasn't such a vision of shameful neglect. His wife had refused.

Ready to leave, he went through the exit routine, checking the windows, making sure they were shut. He stopped by the phone, making sure it was unplugged. With these checks complete, he descended the stairs. At great expense they'd been carpeted with the thickest and finest material, of exotic foreign origin, to muffle any noise. Yates left the house, pinning a note on the door:

PLEASE DO NOT RING THE BELL

PLEASE DO NOT KNOCK ON THE DOOR

Originally he'd concluded with the explanation that no one was at home. But that line had been cut since his wife was worried it might attract burglars. When he returned after work he'd take the note down. Whenever he went out, even if it was for an hour, even if it was for five minutes, he went through the checks and put up the note. His wife did not react well to disturbances of any kind.

Yates got into his car, grabbed hold of the steering wheel, but did not start the engine. He just sat there, surveying his home. He'd loved this house when he'd bought it. He'd loved the street with its beautiful front yard, located near parks and a range of stores. In the summer it smelt of freshly cut lawns and always seemed to be cooler than the city. People would wave and say hello. Nothing angered him more than people who didn't appreciate how lucky they were to live in a country like this. The race riots in Jersey City in August last year were a disgrace, men and women destroying the very place where they lived. Those riots proved he'd been right to oppose the desegregation of public schools in Teaneck. Many people had been proud of this development, which they called social progress. Yates hadn't said anything in public but he was sure it would lead to an influx of outsiders and that would lead to tensions. Paradise doesn't need progress. The photographs of Jersey City had shocked him – smashed shop windows, burning cars. Maybe there were some legitimate complaints in that part of town, problems with employment, there were always problems, but only a sick man, a blind man, would trash his own home rather than trying to fix it. Yates would fight to stop the same happening here.

He pulled out of the drive, heading towards Manhattan, thirty minutes away. He'd been in the city until late last night, wanting to be certain that every member of the Soviet delegation staying in the Grand Metropolitan was accounted for. Once the final checks had been completed and he was sure that they were in their rooms, he should have returned home, to his wife. Instead, he'd visited a basement bar called Flute, off Broadway, where a part-time waitress worked, a woman he'd been seeing for the past three months. Twenty years younger than him, this waitress was beautiful and interested in the mostly made-up stories he told about the FBI. She would lie on the bed, naked, holding her head in her hands while he sat, shirt unbuttoned, recounting his adventures. Almost as good as the sex was the way she hung off every anecdote, saying *Un Be Lieve Able* at the end of each story, pronouncing it as though it were four words, as though being unbelievable were the highest compliment a man could be paid.

A real wife would've been suspicious. He'd arrived home at four in the morning, silently ascended the carpeted stairs to see his wife, Diane, curled under the blankets like a sick animal. Days went by and he never saw her in any other position. It had been too hot to sleep and he'd lain on top of the comforter, naked, still smelling of Rebecca. He hadn't ever wanted to be a cheat. He didn't romanticize infidelity. He'd wanted to be a good husband: he'd wanted nothing more in the world. He'd tried not to blame Diane for the guilt he felt every day. There were times when he was so frustrated he wanted to rip their house apart with his hands, take it down plank by plank and brick by brick. He wished he could start his life over again – he'd do everything the same, everything single thing except for Diane.

Last year his parents had celebrated their fiftieth wedding

anniversary. They'd held a party in their garden. Over two hundred people turned up. People had travelled from other states. Several had caught a plane. Diane hadn't been able to make it. After two hours of pleading, after banging his hands on the tabletop, after smashing the bottle of twenty-year-old wine intended as a present, after punching his hand through a glass cabinet and cutting his knuckles, Yates had been forced to go without her, turning up late, knuckles bandaged and having already downed a quart of Scotch. He'd taken over the barbecue and stood there like a dumb mute servant, staring as the meat sizzled and spat globs of fat onto the fire. Yates had ended up in the most miserable, rotten relationship in the entire neighbourhood and everyone knew it. Some days the humiliation was enough to make him want to die, literally die, his heart to clog up, his lungs to turn as dry as dust.

Diane had seen doctors and therapists and they'd said more or the less the same thing. There was something wrong with her nerves. It sounded like the kind of diagnosis written a hundred years ago and Yates couldn't believe it was being handed out now. Was there a pill that could help? They gave him pills and she'd take them but none of them did any good. In an attempt to remedy the disintegration of their marriage they'd tried for a child. The baby had been lost in pregnancy. Even though Yates had prayed for the strength not to blame Diane, he did: he blamed her for his dead child. He blamed her for the waitress – he blamed her for everything that was rotten about his life because the rot spread from her. He'd wanted the dream, the perfect marriage, children, the perfect home, he'd been able to provide it materially and emotionally, he'd been ready, and she'd trashed it with her craziness. Maybe that was the definition of craziness – to trash a good thing for no reason at all.

He'd arrived at West 145th Street. Parking the car, Yates wound up the window. His was one of only four cars on the street – the kind of Harlem street where no one would notice if a home had been left to ruin and the occupant was a crazy woman who didn't get out of bed. This was the kind of neighbourhood where Diane belonged. She didn't deserve their home. There was no greenery here, no parks for the children to play in. The children ran about the streets, jumping in and out of hopscotch chalk outlines that covered the summer-hot tarmac as if the streets were built for them and not for cars. Yates took pause every time he saw these kids. No space to play, no future, no hope – what made him mad were the men sitting around in the doorways, doing nothing, when they should be working, they should be trying to get these children a yard, a front lawn. But they never did anything, huddled in conversations, as though they had important matters to discuss. It was a joke, the seriousness with which the dropouts would sit around and talk while old women, as old as seventy, carried heavy bags of shopping. Yates never saw them move to help, never saw them offer to carry the bags or open the door. He was convinced they looked down on work. Work was beneath them. It was the only explanation.

Stepping out of the car, the heat was oppressive. The redbrick houses soaked up every bit of the sun but the summer wasn't pleasant like it was in Teaneck, it was a sickly heat, like a tropical fever. If the main streets were dirty, the alleys were something else, piled up with trash like they were waiting for a flood to wash it all away. Not such a bad idea, Yates thought, a flood, an almighty deluge, maybe it could take some of these layabout losers at the same time. He crossed the street, feeling everyone's eyes on him, hundreds of eyes squinting at him in the sunlight. Kids stopped playing. Men stopped their conversations, following him with controlled dislike, not expressive enough to get themselves into trouble, just enough to make it clear they hated him. Let them hate him! Let them think his opinions had to do with the colour of their skin. But the truth was that he didn't care what colour their skin was: he cared what kind of men they were – the colour of their soul. And a man worked. He tried to make his country a better place. He wanted to tell them that a man without a job wasn't a man, and yet he was sure that they wouldn't get it. They were alien to him, as surely as those Soviet Communists were.

Yates had worked for COINTELPRO, the FBI Counter-Intelligence Program, since its inception in 1956. Over the past nine years he'd become one of the programme's leading agents, making his name hindering the efforts of the National Committee to Abolish HUAC – the House Committee on Un-American Activities. A committee to abolish a committee: but those activists hadn't the wit to even spot the ridiculousness of their name, let alone their entire enterprise. They were too busy arguing for the rights of traitors, engaged in an abstract academic debate about how the individual's rights were more important than the well-being of their society. He would've thought Communists would understand that the needs of the many outweighed the needs of the few. They had no interest in the fact that there were real plots intended to do real harm against his country. They dismissed those arguments as scaremongering. Their complacency disgusted him. He'd seen the plots, the plans – he understood their way of life was hated by a powerful enemy and needed protecting.

He'd been rapidly promoted to dealing with CPUSA, the Communist Party of America. The party's membership was in decline. He wasn't sure whether this was due to new members being ordered underground. They weren't taking any chances. COINTEL-PRO wanted the party dead. Nothing else would satisfy them. The new leader of CPUSA, Gus Hall, had been trained at the International Lenin School in Moscow and COINTELPRO had no intention of giving him the space to expand the organization's public profile, or create a secret network that could better evade the range of measures deployed against it. There were several methods open to them: infiltration, psychological warfare, legal harassment – such as tax, sending in the IRS to go over every scrap of paper, searching for the smallest of mistakes. They could deploy the local police force and finally but importantly use non-legal harassment. He didn't get involved in that: it was farmed out to retired officers or people with no connection to the FBI. He had no qualms with it, of course. According to Hoover:

The purpose of counterintelligence action is to disrupt and it is immaterial whether facts exist to substantiate the charge.

As COINTELPRO officers they were tasked with pinpointing and neutralizing troublemakers before they could exercise their potential for violence. And Yates was one of the best.

Entering the stairway of a redbrick five storey, the temperature seemed to jump. It was so hot Yates had to stop, taking out a handkerchief and mopping his brow. The smells were bad, mingled odours he didn't want to think about too much. Walking up the stairs, his pores seeping alcohol from last night, he surveyed the cracked plaster and broken floorboards, the shabby pipes and doors held together with mismatched planks of wood and cardboard, no doubt kicked apart in some argument or other. Yates could sense the hostility from the people in the walkways, people milling in the communal spaces, with no jobs to go to, no skills to offer, just an inbred sense of injustice. They'd talk for twenty-four hours a day about how they'd been wronged and how their country had failed them. At least twenty per cent of CPUSA membership was estimated to be Negro, far higher than the Negro proportion of the national population – that was their solution to not getting a job, ripping down the whole edifice of their nation. He smiled at them as he passed, knowing full well it would drive them crazy. Hatred radiated from their faces like heat off hot coals. If they thought it bothered him they were wrong. He wanted to ask the young man perched on the window:

You think your hatred matters?

Of all the hatred in the world, theirs mattered the least.

At the top of the stairs, Yates knocked on the door. He'd been on the threshold of this apartment before although he'd never been invited inside. He would have authorized a search of the premises but it was impossible to do anything without the neighbours knowing, they all lived on top of each other, in and out of each other's apartments. Personally, he didn't care if they knew. He didn't see any need to be subtle about it. He'd been tempted to authorize it anyway, not expecting to find anything, but as part of the psychological warfare. The issue of race had stopped him. He was told that an illegal search might inflame relations between the community and the police. They couldn't even make it look like a burglary since realistically no one would rob a shit-hole like this.

He knocked again, louder this time. He knew the apartment was small, no more than a single room. No matter what they were doing inside it should only take a second to reach the door. Perhaps they could recognize the sound of his knock – angry, impatient – perhaps no one else in this building knocked that way. Finally, the door opened. The man who stood before him had been codenamed by the FBI: Big Red Voice. Yates said:

— *Hello, Jesse.*

Bradhurst
Harlem
West 145th Street
Same Day

Agent Yates leaned against the frame of the door, as close to the inside of the apartment as he could physically manage. As though in response, Jesse Austin's wife stepped forward, joining her husband, shielding as much of their apartment from view as possible – a human barricade. The gesture amused Yates. He knew there was nothing illegal that they wanted to hide, no dope or stolen property like most of the other families around here. This was defiance for the sake of it; the pair were fighting for privacy – a splinter of dignity – pitifully trying to assert themselves against his authority.

Jesse was a big man, tall and broad. Once strong, not any more, his back was hunched, muscle had turned slack – tightness turned not to fat but baggy flesh. In contrast, his wife had lost weight. Fifteen years ago she'd been beautiful with a full figure and elegant curves. Now she was manual-labour thin, skin drooped under her eyes and deep lines ran across her forehead. As for the apartment, it wasn't much to be protective about: a bedroom that doubled as a living room, a living room that doubled as a kitchen, a kitchen that doubled as a dining room. There were only a couple of paces from the bed to the stove and a couple more to the bathroom. To be fair, it was a little neater and nicer painted than some of the other rat-infested slum apartments he'd seen in his time. The stand-out difference, the only sign that this apartment had a story to tell, was the occasional expensive items of furniture like museum pieces salvaged from the wreck of a sunken career. Out-of-place antique cabinets and decorative side-tables, fallen on hard times, wept for their former Park Avenue homes.

Yates directed his attention at Jesse's wife – Anna Austin. She was too composed and too savvy to lose control. He admired this lady, he really did. She had been beautiful once, photographed at prestigious events, dressed in furs and jewels like a princess, hanging off her traitor husband's arm. Looking at the photos Yates could've sworn her teeth were carved out of ivory, a perfect smile, unnaturally white. How the mighty had fallen, reduced to this – from diamonds to dust, splendour to squalor. Despite this hardship, this self-imposed poverty, this unnecessary misery of Jesse's creation, she was still hooked to her husband's arm. Except now she was more like a broken Christmas decoration, a cracked bauble that had lost its glitter and sparkle.

Yates watched as Jesse reached down and took hold of Anna's hand. Was that a way of reminding him that they were together despite everything he and his colleagues had thrown at them – including rumours about adultery and accusations that he'd molested white girls? Those allegations had been easy to manufacture. There were plenty of photos of Jesse after concerts, surrounded by admirers, most of them female, some of them young. He was a tactile man, always putting his hands on people's shoulders, wrapping arms around pretty young girls. The dirt had stuck. Enough newspapers had run with the story, enough girls had come forward claiming he had behaved inappropriately. Of course, they'd only done so after a little encouragement from Yates's men, a nudge, a threat, worried they'd be accused of being a Communist sympathizer. Anna had never wavered, calling them liars every chance she'd got, publicly pitying them for not having the moral courage to stand up to the FBI. If only she'd been a weaker person, if only she'd left Jesse then he would've been broken for sure. She'd stayed true, steadfast and constant – values a woman should show to her husband. Still in love, still by his side, still holding his big hand as if it could protect her. She needed to get real: those big gentle hands hadn't protected her, they'd done more damage to her than if they'd slapped her. Jesse and Anna were so proud of their love, so proud of their relationship, that it was as though someone had told them about Yates's useless, crazy wife. Speaking his thoughts aloud, Yates said:

— *Who fucking cares?*

They both looked at him like he was as strange as he was scary. Yates liked the idea that he was scary.

He felt his pocket for cigarettes. They were in the car. He realized he was still a little drunk from the night before.

— *Big Old Jesse, tell me, you got any plans to hook up with your Soviet friends while they're in town? They've been trying to make contact with you, over and over again. Letters, invites ... We intercepted them but there's always a chance one or two slipped past. Or maybe they sent someone in person?*

Jesse's face was blank. In the absence of a cigarette, Yates took out a match, picking his teeth.

— *Come now, no games, you and me go back too far. You trying to tell me you don't know about a bunch of Soviet Communist kiddies singing their hearts out at the UN tonight? They're singing about peace and world harmony and all the things we know*

Communists love. I thought I'd stop by, see if you were going to make an appearance.

Anna replied:

— *We don't know anything about that.*

Yates turned his face close to hers, forcing her to step back into the apartment.

— *You don't?*

Jess answered:

— *No, we don't. You have no right to interfere with our mail.*

Jesse had answered but Yates kept his eyes on Anna.

— *I normally find you attractive when you're being coy, Mrs Austin. Might even have worked twenty years back, when you strutted around town with your long fake eyelashes, attending galas and making the magazines. I might have fallen for it. I'm a sucker for a pretty lady. I would've struck a deal with the Devil and fucked you just to take the heat off your husband. I bet you would've enjoyed it but told yourself, as your nails scratched my back, that you were doing it for him.*

Yates noticed Jesse's fist was clenched. Anger was bringing the old man to life. He didn't move, didn't dare step closer. Yates said:

— *Go ahead, Jesse. Stand up for her. Be a man. Take a swing. Might even make up for this shit-hole apartment you've forced her to live in.*

Jesse's face quivered with hatred, like a cello string being plucked. He managed to keep his cool, just about, repeating what Anna had already said:

— *We no longer have any contact with the Soviet authorities. We know nothing about their arrival here, or their plans.*

Yates nodded condescendingly.

— *You don't even read the papers? You probably don't even know where Russia is, am I right? Soviets singing? What could be more your taste, Jesse, than a bunch of pretty young Communist girls singing songs? Am I right in thinking you used to sing? Didn't you used to do something along those lines?*

— I used to, Mr Yates, you put a stop to that.

— Nothing to do with me. It's no crime to sing a song. Just so happens that some songs are popular and some songs, your Communist-loving songs, don't seem to get any audience these days. Times change, tastes change: people are forgotten, don't you find, Jesse? It's sad. Don't you find it sad? I could cry a river, there's so many sad things going on in the world. Careers coming to nothing, talent going to waste, sad, sad, sad, so very fucking sad.

Anna flinched, her eyes on Jesse, sensing that her husband might say something imprudent. Yates certainly hoped so. She said:

— Why are you here, Mr Yates?

— I could almost be offended. I don't think you're listening to me very carefully. The Soviets have invited you to this concert. We might have intercepted a couple of their attempts to make contact but they don't give up easily. They want you there. I want to know why. It's my job to keep an eye on men like you—

Jesse interrupted:

— And what kind of man is that?

Yates grew tired of the playfulness.

— What kind of man am I talking about? A man who went on record saying that he'd refuse to fight for America if war broke out with the Soviets, a man who lives in this country and expresses his disloyalty to it every chance he gets. What kind of man am I talking about? A Communist, that's the kind of man I'm talking about.

Yates looked down at Jesse's shoes. They were old, worn, but excellent quality, maybe Italian, or something fancy, another relic from the days when he earned a lot of money, more money in a year than Yates would earn in his life. But who would know it now? Still looking at the shoes, he said:

— *Jesse, you know what really makes me angry?*

— *I'm sure a lot of things make you angry, Mr Yates.*

— *That is true. A lot of things get me hot under the collar. But more than anything else, it's people who have done well in this country, people like you, coming from nothing, making all this money, having all this success, people who turn around and get into bed with another regime. The Soviets have given you nothing. They can't even feed their own people. How can you love them and not us? How can you sing about them and not about us? You're the American dream, Jesse: don't you get it? You're the American fucking dream. And what a shame that is.*

Yates wiped his brow. His heart was thumping hard. This wasn't fun any more. He breathed deeply.

— *So hot in here, I don't know how you sleep. I don't know how you breathe. Must have different sort of lungs.*

Anna replied, her voice soft:

— *We breathe the same as you do, Agent Yates.*

Yates curled his lip, as though he wasn't convinced.

— *Your last place had air conditioning? You must miss that.*

Neither of them replied and Yates lost interest in goading them further.

— *Listen, I'm done here. I'm going to leave you two alone. Before I go, I have a final question, a philosophical question, for us all to think about. In the Soviet Union do you think there must be people who hate their country? Don't you think the world would be a whole lot simpler if those people lived here and you went and lived there?*

Jesse said immediately:

— *Mr Yates, insult me any way you want. But you can't tell me this country isn't my home as much as yours. It's—*

Yates interrupted, turning to leave.

— *Not only am I going to tell you that, Jesse, I'm going to make you understand it too. And take it from me: you'd be smart to keep far away from that concert. You'd be really smart.*

Manhattan
Same Day

To stop her hands from shaking, Elena clenched her fingers into a fist. Her heart was pounding in her chest, double beats to the second. She needed to calm down. The first part of their plan had worked. She'd slipped out from the hotel without being seen. Her lover, Mikael Ivanov, had studied the layout of the Grand Metropolitan, identifying a vulnerable area: the pool and outside sundeck on the fifth floor, monitored only from the main entrance. The American secret police had wrongly assumed there was no other way out.

The cab passed by the top of Central Park, heading into the north of the city. Part of her appreciated that she should take in the sights around, the park, the apartment towers, the people on the sidewalk, but she was too distracted, unable to concentrate, the city passing in a blur. She looked through the rear window to see if anyone was trailing the cab. She'd never experienced traffic like this, an incredible number of cars. Few were official: the majority seemed to be privately owned. She would've marvelled at the experience if she hadn't felt so sick and dizzy. Surely it was due to the motion of the vehicle. She hated the idea that it was her nerves.

Throughout her life she'd been the weaker, younger sister — quiet and well behaved, the sister who never caused any trouble. In contrast, her older sister Zoya was independent, strong-willed, impressive. She'd made decisions for both of them. Her authority was unquestionable. Elena had always been compliant, deferring to her sister's judgement. Their relationship had followed this pattern for as long as she could remember. But Elena was her own person. Now was the time for her to emerge from her sister's shadow and find her own identity. For the first time in her life she'd been entrusted with a matter of great importance. It had taken someone outside of her family to recognize her potential. Mikael had selected her. He considered her an adult and an equal. Even before they'd fallen in love, he'd never spoken down to her, choosing to confide in her the real reason that he'd been assigned to this trip.

Mikael worked for a secret department within the Propaganda Ministry called SERVICE.A. As he'd explained to Elena its purpose was to promote the positive differences between Communism and capitalism overseas, to point out the institutionalized inequities of capitalism, to make a case for Communism that didn't depend on military might or the use of fear — an attempt to rejuvenate an ideology that had been tainted by excessive measures against their own population. Hearing about the murder of Elena's biological parents by the Soviet secret police, Mikael accepted that the party had made mistakes. He believed those mistakes obscured their ideological superiority. Communism was about racial and gender equality, an end to economic hardship for the many and lavish luxury for the few. Persecution and prejudice were issues Elena cared passionately about. Presented with an opportunity to make a difference, she'd agreed to play her part. She had lost so much under Stalin's rule, including her parents, yet believed that the murderous excesses of one tyrant should not end the dream of a fair society. She would not allow it to make her cynical as it had Leo.

SERVICE.A operated only what Mikael referred to as passive protocols, such as funding publications and subsidies to sympathetic figures. They were a non-violent organization that stimulated dissent. They had recruited American academics and journalists to report honestly on the flaws within a capitalist society, founding a publishing house that accepted controversial manuscripts no other publisher would touch. Their backlist included a book about how Kennedy had been assassinated by extreme right-wing figures, a cabal of arms and oil magnates. The publishing house had found less commercial success, although a great deal of academic renown, with its feminist texts. But examining the response to these essays on gender inequality it proved impossible to imagine that there was any realistic chance of changing America through direct appeals to women. As a result of the relative failure of the feminist texts, selling only a hundred or so copies, it was accepted that a revolution was unlikely to be spearheaded by a gender-orientated manifesto and SERVICE.A changed direction, focusing its attention and resources on the issue of race. Pamphlets rather than books were given away for free on street corners in targeted cities such as Atlanta, Memphis, Oakland and Detroit. The pamphlets were intended to provoke, with a series of shock headlines:

AVERAGE BLACK MAN EARNS $4000!
AVERAGE WHITE MAN EARNS $7000!
BLACK CHILD THREE TIMES MORE LIKELY
TO DIE THAN A WHITE CHILD!
BLACK FAMILY THREE TIMES MORE LIKELY
TO LIVE IN SQUALOR!

Elena and Mikael would lie in bed, talking for hours about how Communism had neglected the heart of its appeal – its very reason for existing. She'd found his passion beguiling and was flattered to be involved. In contrast to Mikael's beliefs, none of her immediate family seemed to possess any ideology. Raisa never spoke about politics beyond issues that directly affected her school. Leo was silent on the topic, as if it were prohibited. Elena pitied him: he'd been forced to work for a tyrant and his idealism had been corrupted. For him, there was no going back. He had lost his sense of hope. Outside of his family, he didn't believe in anything any more. Just because he was disillusioned didn't mean that she had to be too. Mikael was a man she believed in. Her older sister had once confided in her about the experience of falling in love. Elena had never fully understood the feelings her sister had described until she'd met Mikael. Love was admiration and devotion; love was doing anything for him because she knew he would do anything for her.

The cab had just passed West 120th Street – approaching her destination, on West 145th Street.

Bradhurst
Harlem
West 145th Street
Same Day

As Yates walked down the stairs, he passed the same good-for-nothing young men slouching in the corridors. He nodded at them:

— *Busy day, gentlemen?*

They didn't reply. Yates laughed. He doubted whether any of them could name a single song that Austin used to sing. 'Big Red Voice' had once played to audiences in the millions and now he was forgotten by Negroes and white men alike, forgotten by the rich and poor. He doubted if these men in these hallways even realized who the old man on the top floor was. Certainly no one younger than thirty would have any recollection of his success. Jesse was no longer played on the radio. His records weren't in stores. His words were no longer printed in newspapers, nor was he interviewed in glossy magazines. So weakened was he that he didn't even have the strength of heart to stand up for his wife when she was insulted in front of his face. It was one thing to smash a man's career: that was relatively straightforward. It was quite another thing to break a man's spirit. Having watched Jesse move, seen how his body stooped, slumped in the doorway, barely able to argue back, Yates was sure he was close to that particular victory.

It puzzled Yates why the Soviets had made so many attempts to contact Austin, imploring him to attend the concert tonight. What did they expect him to do? They would never secure permission to have him enter the United Nations. He was certain Austin was lying when he said he knew nothing and Yates could sense something was wrong – something he'd missed, an agenda he couldn't see. He'd worked too hard, for too long, to allow Jesse to have any kind of final flourish in the limelight.

Feeling considerably less hung-over, he stepped out of the apartment building, checking his pockets for cigarettes, again forgetting that they were in the car. There was another group of young men to his side, perched on the steps, two sitting down and two standing up. For a group of nobodies they were comically overdressed, with neat shirts tucked in, waistcoats and jackets, and two even had ties, as if they worked in a bank. They were smoking roll-ups. Yates walked up to them:

— *Would any of you gentlemen be so kind as to roll one for me?*

It wouldn't have been difficult to fetch his own from the car but this was more fun. The men exchanged glances, silently weighing up his request. They knew he was law. They hated him. And yet they couldn't say no.

Repeat after me: Your hatred doesn't matter.

It was a thrill to watch, these tough young men totally powerless, full of swagger and attitude yet obedient and servile, suppliant before him, like the most limp-wristed of men.

The youngest man produced tobacco and rolled a perfect cigarette. He took care over it, making sure Yates had no reason to be
annoyed. He was smart: understanding that even the slightest sign
of defiance would inflame Yates. When it was finished, he offered
it. Yates accepted, but did not take out his matches, even though
he had them in his pocket.

— *I prefer my tobacco to burn a little before I smoke it.*

A different man lit a match, holding the flame steady in front of
Yates. Yates dipped the end of the cigarette into the flame, lighting
the cigarette and inhaling, smiling his gratitude.

— *Been a while since I've tasted tobacco this cheap. Reminds me*
of when I first started to smoke as a kid. You men have a produc-
tive day. Enjoy the sun.

The man extinguished the match with an angry flick of his
wrist — the closest he dared to a display of his emotions. Yates
sucked deeply on the cigarette, savouring this moment — a sub-
lime moment, on a beautiful sunny day.

*

The taxi came to a stop. Elena looked out the window. This must
be the place — West 145th Street. The street was busy in a very different way from 44th Street. Some people were busy: many were
hanging about. She was worried at how conspicuous she'd appear,
a seventeen-year-old Soviet girl dressed unfashionably, with no
sense of this city, this neighbourhood or its culture. She didn't
have much time, little more than an hour before she'd be missed
at the hotel. The group was due to meet at lunch, before the dress
rehearsal, when Raisa returned from her preliminary visit to the
UN Headquarters. She checked her watch. The cab ride had taken
over thirty minutes, longer than they'd calculated for. The delay
meant that she didn't have long to find and talk to Mr Austin.

She'd been told that he'd become a recluse, no longer performing, rarely leaving the apartment, unemployed, his spirit downtrodden by the oppressive measures used against him.

The driver — a white man — turned around, looking at her with concern.

— *You sure you want to be here?*

Elena's English was competent. But the phrase confused her. She repeated the address.

— *West 145th Street.*

The driver nodded:

— *This is the place for sure. Not the place for a girl like you.*

Elena didn't understand. She asked:

— *How much?*

The driver pointed to the meter. She took out the money given to her by Mikael.

— *Can you wait?*

— *How long?*

— *Twenty minutes.*

The driver looked uncertain. Elena paid him five dollars. She noted that the driver seemed pleased with the money. It must be a significant amount.

— *There is more if you wait.*

He nodded, his entire aspect changed by the money. Elena felt disgust for him, a man in love with money, whose character would change at the sight of a dollar bill.

— *I'll wait. But only twenty minutes, if you're late, I'm gone.*

Elena stepped out the cab, shutting the door.

In front of the taxicab was an old-fashioned wood wagon with a cloth-top screen for shade from the sun. The surface was loaded with heaps of ice, edges rendered smooth by the heat, melting fast. Among the ice, there were clams, some in their pale shells, many scooped out, cooked in spices, spitting in the heat, sold in cones of newspaper. Along the dusty street, instead of a mass of cars, there were children playing ball or jumping games or begging for shards of ice from the clam-selling man who struck out with his fist, shooing them away. At a glance the houses seemed nice to Elena, they weren't too tall and they weren't ugly concrete like the slums where she lived. They were handsome brick, framed by metal fire escapes. In one window there was a sign:

Absolutely no loitering
On the stairs

Elena didn't understand all the words. But she understood it was asking people not to sit on the front stairs, a comical request considering almost every set of steps hosted groups of men.

The apartment was a little further on. She walked past the vendor, past the children sucking on uneven chunks of ice, ice they must have stolen when the vendor wasn't looking. She had never felt so foreign in her entire life. Self-conscious, it took an effort to continue walking and not run back to the cab. She didn't have far to go. The building was directly ahead.

There was a man on the steps, a tall white man, dressed in a suit, smoking a cigarette. Elena had been warned that Mr Austin was under pressure from the American secret police. She didn't know if this man was an agent but he didn't belong here, that was obvious, almost as obvious as the fact that she didn't belong here either. Her eyes darted about, searching for somewhere to hide. But it was too late. He'd seen her. She had no choice. She increased her pace, pretending to be in a hurry. At the same time he descended the steps to intercept her. As he drew closer Elena kept her eyes down, towards the ground, holding her breath.

They passed each other on the sidewalk. She continued walking, missing Mr Austin's address as if there was somewhere else she was heading for. Once she'd turned the corner, she pressed her back against the wall. There was no way into Mr Austin's apartment. And no way back to the cab.

Same Day

For a man who considered himself an optimist, it was a strange sensation for Jesse Austin to feel despair stalking them, glimpsed from time to time out of the corner of his eye. Even as his wife walked across the apartment her body expressed profound weariness, a heavy sway instead of her once characteristic brisk pace, exhaustion that went deeper than working too hard or fretting about money, exhaustion sunk into her bones making them as heavy as lead. She'd been worn down. Constant worrying had matted her hair, dulled her eyes, squeezed the blood from her lips and even altered the way she spoke. Her words had lost their playfulness, no longer singing with mischievous intelligence. They dropped out of her mouth as if a burden sat on the shoulder of each syllable, revealing tiredness that couldn't be remedied by a good night's sleep, or even a couple of days off work. In recent years he'd wondered if Anna's strength and resilience had been a curse rather than a gift. Anyone else would've left him, broken by the strain. Colleagues and friends had cut him loose. A few had even testified against him, stood before a HUAC hearing, pointing at him with trembling outrage as though he'd been guilty of murder. Not Anna, not for a second, and not a day went by that Jesse didn't feel humbled by her love.

Anna had been right. She'd prophesied that the men he was making enemies of were vengeful and absolutely did not forget. Jesse had joked that the authorities could take anything but they could never take away his voice and as long as he had his voice he had a career. He'd been wrong. In the 1930s he performed to audiences of up to twenty thousand. On tour in 1937 the combined audiences around the world totalled over a million. Today no venue would book him, not the grand concert halls, not even the smallest, smokiest bars, places where the sound of bottles clanking was louder than the singing. It wasn't enough that Jesse signed a contract promising not to launch into one of his polemics, vowing merely to sing songs that had been vetted and cleared as inoffensive. The day after his performance the venue would inevitably receive an inspection from health and safety officials, or from the police regarding an alleged disorder, a fight on the street. In every case the venue would be shut down for several weeks. No matter how outraged they were by the principle, no one could afford to make the same mistake twice. If they did, their licence was revoked. The managers of venues, men who'd once shook Jesse's hand after one of his concerts with eyes filled with tears and a cash register brimming with dollars, didn't even have the decency to admit the truth. He couldn't blame them for looking after their interests but did they have to lie? They'd tell him he was too old, or that his kind of music was no longer fashionable. They'd rather insult him than admit that they were scared.

It was a cruel joke that Jesse's appearance at the House Committee on Un-American Activities in July 1956 would prove to be his last performance on a major stage. Questioning Jesse, the congressmen quoted words he'd spoken in favour of Communism and run them up against the words he'd spoken in criticism of America. Had he claimed that he felt more at home in the Soviet

131

Union than in the United States? Jesse tried to explain the meaning of his statements: that the notion of *home* referred to the way in which he was respected abroad and abused domestically, his people Jim-Crowed and kept down. Footage was shown of him speaking in Moscow in 1950, in the Serp i Molot factory, while in subtitles, incorrect translation ran along the bottom of the screen:

<u>JESSE AUSTIN</u>: *The Statue of Liberty belongs here, in Moscow, not in New York.*

He'd listened to the gasps of the congressional audience, the scratching of pens against notepads by the journalists. He'd spent vast sums on counsel only to realize that there was no defence against insinuation. Quotes, stripped of their context, were tossed about the room. The issue of his refusal to sign a non-Communist affidavit had been debated. Photographs of his visits to Moscow were passed from side to side with circles drawn around some of the men he'd stood beside. They were described as KGB agents, decried as monsters that had murdered and enslaved the civilian population. Jesse had protested: the committee had no evidence to support those accusations. They'd shouted back that the men circled were secret-police officers and the secret police was proven as an instrument of terror. Did he deny there were slave-labour camps in the USSR, labour camps that made a mockery of his talk of equality and fairness? He'd retorted that draconian measures, if they existed at all, were only ever used against a Fascist element, an element that when left unchecked in Germany had brought about many millions of deaths. He wasn't about to weep over a few dead Fascists.

Though no court had found him guilty of any crimes, his passport had been taken away. He was no longer able to visit the Soviet

Union or to accept invitations from non-Communist countries such as the United Kingdom, France and Canada. He was no longer booked for public performances. His recording career was starved of oxygen. No radio station would play his music. No record company would release his songs. No store would stock his albums, his back catalogue was removed from sale – his achievements made invisible. Royalties stopped. Although he was a taxpayer since the age of sixteen, a man who'd brought in thousands of dollars from other countries, the State had his livelihood, cutting off their own source of taxes. His income dropped to less than four hundred dollars a year. His savings had been drained by legal costs, including pursuing his record label for breach of contract. No court ever ruled in his favour. It had taken twelve years, but finally he was destitute. They had what they wanted. He was penniless, just as he had been when he'd started out. Forced to sell his apartment near Central Park, he'd been certain that the FBI informed all prospective buyers of his financial straits. The sale price was half its true market value and didn't cover the debts.

Anna opened the window, perching on the ledge, looking out at the street below. Strands of her hair hung around her face, waiting for a breeze that wasn't coming any time soon. Jesse joined her, putting his arm around her slim waist, resting his head on her shoulder, wanting to say sorry a thousand times over. The words dried up in his throat.

At the knock on the door they turned at the same time. Jesse could feel the tension in Anna's body. The difference between an agent's knock and the knock of someone who lived in the building was the silence that followed. A friend would call out. There'd be the normal bustle around the landing. An agent would silence the building – the stairwells fell quiet, everyone would stop and stare and wait. Jesse stepped towards the door, reminding himself that Yates was looking for the slightest provocation. Taking hold of the handle, bracing himself, he opened the door.

It wasn't Yates but Tom Fluker, a cantankerous man in his sixties who ran a small hardware store at the corner of the block. Beside him was a young white woman with long dark hair. He didn't recognize her. Before Jesse could speak Tom launched into a tirade:

— I found this girl trying to sneak around the back, skulking like a thief. She says she's looking for you. I ask why she can't use your front door like everyone else. She gets confused, like she doesn't understand. First I think she's playing dumb then I realize she doesn't understand English too good. Got an accent too. So I listen a little more. She's a Russian! What's a Russian girl doing round here, looking for you? We don't need any more problems than we've already got, and we've already got plenty.

Jesse looked at the young woman, and then at Tom, his face scrunched up in anger. The FBI had tried to isolate Jesse among the local community. Friends and strangers, ministers and businessmen, went on record repudiating his Communist views and claiming that he was a disgrace, entirely unrepresentative of their desire to work hard and build a more integrated America. There were some who wouldn't speak out against him on record but who thought the adverse attention Jesse generated was senseless. While they were trying to improve conditions for their communities and gain rights for their people, he was dragging them back. Tom was one such man. He'd worked hard. He owned a store. Jesse was an obstacle to his dream of success, of passing on money to his children, of getting them ahead in the world. He didn't have time for ideology. He counted the dollars in his cash register at the end of the week, and people like Jesse were bad for business. Jesse

had no time for this way of thinking. The fact that he'd been sub-
jected to injustice had never made him reconsider his beliefs. That
mindset was the worst kind of subjugation, to be fearful of doing
what is right in case you upset those who were in the wrong.

Tom turned to the young woman, saying:

— *You're a Russian. Tell him.*

She stepped forward.

— *My name is Elena. Mr Austin, please may I talk to you? I
don't have much time.*

She spoke English though it was obviously not her mother
tongue.

— *Thank you, Thomas. I'll deal with this.*

Tom was unsure whether to say something more. Though Jesse
knew that Tom was tempted to call the FBI and distance himself
from this event, he was sure that Tom — no matter how much he
disagreed with Jesse — would never rat him out. He wasn't that
kind of man.

Tom turned, hurrying down the stairs and not looking back,
shaking his head in disbelief, in disgust, and repeating aloud, as if
it were an ancient, wicked curse:

— *A Russian in Harlem!*

Same Day

Anna dropped her head, knowing that this would end badly. They had lied to Agent Yates — they were aware of the concert at the United Nations tonight. Four separate attempts to persuade Jesse to turn up had been made by members of the CPUSA. They'd wanted him to address the crowds that were expected to gather outside the gates, a pro-Communist demonstration. With each attempt they'd used a different technique: they'd sent a wise old man who could quote just about anything Marx had ever written, they'd sent a beautiful young woman to flatter Jesse with her attention, they'd sent a young militant Communist who'd aggressively demanded solidarity, they'd sent a middle-aged married couple who'd also suffered at the hands of the FBI, or so they'd claimed. But Jesse had rebuffed all of them, saying that he was retired, he was old and he'd given more than enough speeches for the cause. The fight needed to be made by someone else, someone new. When they'd accused him of being beaten he hadn't denied it, waving them out of the door and ordering them not to bother a beaten man any more.

Earnest and wide-eyed, sugar-dusted with innocence and idealism, this girl was surely their last attempt at persuasion. She was a much smarter choice. This girl wasn't stuffed full of theory and quotes. She was bright with hopes and dreams; she believed in something. Careful calculations had been made in choosing her and they had nothing to do with sex. Her husband had no sexual feelings towards the girl. It wasn't that Anna was blind, believing in her husband's fidelity while he cheated on her every chance he got. That was the lurid picture painted by the FBI. In nearly forty years of marriage Jesse had never cheated on her and there'd been countless opportunities. He was a handsome man with a voice that made women weep in admiration. In his early years, when he'd been touring, there were fans lining up outside his dressing room who would've stripped off every stitch if he'd so much as given them a suggestive look. Many called her a fool and him an expert liar, with a honey-sweet tongue and a siren's voice that could make her believe anything he wanted. Anna knew better. Fidelity was his problem, not promiscuity. He was loyal to a fault – loyal to his mistress Communism even when she'd cost him his livelihood.

Anna had never blamed Jesse for the hardship that his beliefs had brought them. Her friends had pleaded with her to make him shut up, to retract his statements and apologize even if he didn't mean it, just to alleviate the pressure. She'd refused to countenance the idea. He was outspoken and passionate – the characteristics of the man she'd fallen in love with. His music was an extension of his beliefs – they couldn't be pulled apart, his personality couldn't be unravelled or tampered with. He couldn't be made more palatable or less provocative. However much she held by this view, and held it today, in truth, there had been times when bitterness rose through her veins like a tidal surge. She'd been his manager. She'd developed his career: all that work, all those achievements washed away like marks on a sandy beach. When she thought about everything they'd gained and everything they'd lost, sometimes her strength left her, her spirit crumbled and she imagined their life without Communism. In those moments she hated the very sound of the word, despised each syllable, but she never loved Jesse less.

Anna noted her husband's quick step as he hurried their young visitor inside and shut the door. His despondency after speaking to Yates evaporated like morning mist burnt off by a new day's sun. The girl was nervous and trying hard to control it; far from making her less persuasive, her stuttering and awkward behaviour was beguiling. She spoke in English, stumbling over her words.

— *My name is Elena. I am a student from the Soviet Union, visiting the United States as part of a tour. We are performing a series of concerts in New York and Washington DC. Tonight we perform in the United Nations.*

Agent Yates, repulsive as he was, was no fool. He'd been correct – the Soviets hadn't given up. They'd made contact. Jesse had always been disillusioned with the CPUSA, but he'd never been able to say no to anything the Soviets had asked of him. The young Russian seemed uncertain whom she should address, perhaps not expecting Anna to be at home.

— *Mr Austin, and Mrs Austin, I volunteered to act as a messenger. My spoken English is not good. I was informed that you speak Russian, Mr Austin. May I speak in Russian? I am sorry, Mrs Austin. Please forgive me. There would be no mistakes if we could speak Russian.*

Jesse glanced at Anna. He said:

— *I will translate.*

Anna nodded her consent. The young woman switched to Russian. Her husband's face brightened with the sound of that language – a language Anna had never understood.

*

Jesse's Russian came back to him in a rush and he was amazed at his fluency after so many years. It didn't feel like a language he'd taught himself, it felt like a mother tongue.

— *I thought maybe I was no longer of any use to you.*

He'd not meant to sound self-pitying. The young Russian girl shook her head.

— *There was a school programme only two years ago to write to you when we heard of your difficulties with the authorities. Thousands of students composed letters of support. I myself wrote you a letter three pages long. They were posted to you. Surely some came through?*

— *No, nothing.*

— *We feared this would happen. They were intercepted. The American secret police open all your mail.*

Jesse had long suspected that his mail was being intercepted though had no idea it was to this extent. He pictured the young FBI agents given the job of reading them all, hundreds of letters by children, analysed and fed through the most sophisticated auto-mated code breakers. Elena continued:

— *We also asked members of the American Communist Party to talk to you but they failed to persuade you to attend the concert.*

Jesse became annoyed at the mention of the CPUSA.

— *American Communists spend all their time bickering among each other. They've never achieved a thing worth mentioning. Why would I do anything for them?*

— *We would have tried to call you . . .*

The Russian girl blushed, not meaning to draw attention to their depressed circumstances. They no longer owned a phone. She continued:

— *That's why I had to come in person. But that is not the only reason. I'm here to tell you that regardless of whether you come to the concert tonight, you have not been forgotten in Russia as you have been in the United States. I am seventeen years old and you are a hero of mine. You are a hero for many Russians regardless of their age. You are played on the radio. Your popularity today is greater than ever before. That is the reason I wanted to come here today, Mr Austin, because we have heard your enemies tell you so many lies. We want to tell you the truth. You are admired and you are loved! You will never be forgotten and your music will never stop being played.*

Jesse felt as if he'd been unfrozen from a block of ice, warm joy passing through his body. His music wasn't lost. His songs were being enjoyed in another country even though his library of work had been erased from America's consciousness. No longer listened to in his own country, his work could still be heard abroad. Overwhelmed, he moved to the table, forced to sit down. Anna moved towards him, taking his hands.

— *What is it? What did she say?*

— *My music is still being played.*

It was true that he'd felt abandoned by the nation and the party for which he'd sacrificed so much. To hear that this was not the case was a powerful salve to the many hurts inflicted over the years.

Turning back to the young girl, he asked:

— *Who sent you?*

Elena answered in Russian:

— *My instructions are from the highest levels of the Soviet government. If nothing else comes of this meeting than my message of appreciation then that is enough. However, we are keen for us to do more together. We understand that you can no longer speak onstage or in concert halls because those venues will no longer employ you. When that first happened we were told that you reacted by speaking on street corners, refusing to give in, improvising venues, turning a parking lot into an auditorium. Yet we have reports that you no longer speak in any capacity.*

Jesse dropped his head. He'd initially fought against the FBI's tactics by taking his words to the streets, standing atop a crate, a fruit box, the hood of a car, calling out to anyone who'd listen. That was the past. He hadn't given a speech like that for at least two years. It wasn't merely the frequent interruptions by patrol officers or being arrested for disturbing the peace. The passing audience was often indifferent and some were even abusive. He sighed a response in English.

— *That is a young man's game.*

Anna squeezed his hands. There was agitation in her voice:

— *Did Yates see her when she came in? Ask her, Jesse.*

He repeated Anna's question. Elena replied:

— *Yates is an American secret-police officer? I saw him. But I was very careful. That was why I approached the apartment from the back.*

Jesse translated. Far from appeasing his wife, it made her angry.

— *Do you understand what you've done by coming here? Do you understand the danger? What more can you ask from him? What more can he give you? Look around! What is there left to take?*

Anna rarely lost her temper. Jesse stood up, putting his hands on his wife's arms. But that only infuriated her further. She pushed him away, refusing to be silenced, pointing to the pile of albums stacked in the corner, addressing the Russian girl as though she represented the Soviet regime:

— *You see this? This is the only way he can sell his records now. He prints them privately because no record company will sign him. He sells them by subscription to the fans that still remember him. Once, he sold millions. Now how many do you sell, Jesse? How many subscribers do you have? Tell her!*

With Elena's limited English, she could piece together only a little of the meaning. She understood the conversation about the albums in the corner of the room. According to Mikael, the CPUSA had offered Mr Austin direct subsidies as soon as the FBI had started undermining his career. He had declined, repeating his stance that he'd never taken any money from the Soviet government – he'd never accepted a bribe or a payment or gift of any kind. Mr Austin crouched by the heap of records, his back to both Anna and Elena. He said in Russian:

— *Five hundred. That's all I have left. I have five hundred subscribers. Five hundred fans ...*

Elena knew that of the private subscribers who bought his self-produced albums, the CPUSA made up four hundred. It had been the only way to support Austin without him finding out. She ventured off her carefully prepared script:

— *May I ask you something? I was not told to ask this. It is a question I would like to put to you. It is a personal question.*

— *Please, ask me anything.*

Elena caught Anna's eye and switched into broken English.

— *Why do you support the Soviet Union? Why do you give so much?*

The question had a profound impact on both Mr Austin and his wife. They looked at each other and in that instant their conflict seemed to disappear. They did not answer. And for a moment they seemed to forget that Elena was in the room.

Elena checked her watch: she needed to return to the hotel. It was approaching midday.

— *Please, Mrs Austin, I do not have much time. I must speak in Russian again.*

She switched back to her native language.

— *As you know, tonight we're performing a concert at the*

United Nations Headquarters. The world's press will be there. The most important diplomats will be there. We want you to be there too. We tried to arrange for you and your wife to have official tickets but the organizers blocked us. So I am here to ask you to wait outside, on the street, to give one of your speeches, if you feel up to it, to show that you have not been silenced. When the concert is finished, a few of the Soviet students will exit through the main doors. We will surround you, cheering and clapping. This moment will be the photograph that defines the whole trip. Everyone in the United States will be reminded of the injustice done to you. Please, Mr Austin, tell me you'll be there. This is our way of doing something for you.

Carried away with the energy of her plea, Elena placed a hand on his arm.

Same Day

Osip Feinstein crouched on the rooftop of the block opposite Jesse Austin's apartment. If the Russian girl hadn't turned up, the job of persuading Jesse would have fallen to him and he doubted very much he would've succeeded. With his camera he'd followed the events in the apartment, taking photographs of the two of them together: the young girl and the singer, a man who could've been living in a penthouse apartment overlooking Central Park instead of this slum. He was doped up on a drug far more toxic and powerful than opium, addicted to righteous ideology. Osip clicked the camera, shooting the scene before him. The last photograph would be the most incriminating – her frail white hand on his big black arm, the rumpled bed sheets in the background.

Manhattan
Hotel Grand Metropolitan
44th Street
Same Day

As Raisa entered the lobby, twenty sets of eyes landed on her: American secret-police agents pretending to be guests, lounging on sofas and chairs, sipping coffee, following her – their eyeline skimming the rim of their cup and the tops of their newspapers. From the UN Headquarters she'd been driven back to the hotel and left unsupervised for no longer than it took her to step from the car to the revolving doors of the Grand Metropolitan. At the elevator she half expected one of the officers to step in with her. Contemplating the security around the hotel, she found it excessive, so many officers to guard over schoolchildren. The elevator doors closed. Raisa said:

— *Twentieth floor, please.*

Without turning around the man operating the elevator gave a small nod. She was certain he was an agent despite being dressed in hotel livery. She studied his peculiar uniform, red with white trim down the legs. He was an unlikely looking spy, and she wondered if her anxieties were running away with her. She was seeing spies everywhere.

Trying to focus on what was real, rather than dangers imagined, she told herself that preparations for the concert had gone well. The discussions with her American counterparts had been awkward but not unmanageably so. Raisa's opposite number was an American teacher with neat grey hair and thick oval glasses. Through an interpreter they'd found much to talk about, not out of polite obligation but genuine curiosity. Raisa sensed that he was forced to maintain an air of subdued hostility in order to prove that he was not a Communist sympathizer. During their discussions key Soviet officials were absent, having expressed no desire to watch the upcoming dress rehearsal, excluding themselves from the preparations despite the degree of worldwide exposure it was going to attract.

The elevator doors opened. The operator turned round.

— *Your floor, ma'am.*

She nodded, heading out, wishing Leo was by her side. His instincts for subterfuge were acute. Alone, she realized how dependent she'd grown on them.

In the corridor, before Raisa could reach her daughters' room, one of the propaganda officers stepped out in front of her, blocking her way. It was Mikael Ivanov. He was arrogant, handsome and an entirely unnecessary addition to their team. He asked:

— *How were the morning meetings?*

As tempting as it was to ignore him, Raisa said:

— *A success, the concert should go well.*

— *Were you photographed? I told them no photographs without me present.*

— *No, I wasn't photographed. There was no press.*

He raised a finger, keen to correct her.

— But you must be careful of what appear to be amateur photographs. Someone might pretend to be your friend, and claim the photograph is for a personal album, and that is merely a trick in order that you lower your guard.

— No one took my photograph.

Why was Mikael Ivanov delaying her with his unnecessary questions? Raisa moved off before he could say anything else, reaching her daughters' room and knocking. Zoya opened the door. The television was on in the background. Raisa glanced about the room.

— Where's Elena?

— She went swimming.

Instinctively Raisa looked over her shoulder only to discover Mikael watching her with inexplicable concentration.

Same Day

Jim Yates entered the lobby, giving a nod to his colleagues stationed around the room, ill disguised as hotel guests. He didn't care if the Soviets knew they were being watched, their sensitivities were not his concern. He approached the reception and was handed an up-to-date log of movements by the Soviet delegation. According to their records the only person who'd left the premises was a woman called Raisa Demidova, a teacher who'd been taken to the United Nations. She'd returned only a matter of minutes ago. Yates left the log on the receptionist's desk, heading to the elevator. The young FBI agent working as an operator gave him an embarrassed smile, acknowledging his ridiculous uniform. Yates asked:

— *Do you remember a young woman using the elevator?*

— *Sure, she was just in here.*

— *No, young as in eighteen years, something like that.*

— *I'm not sure. I don't think so. Maybe she used the other elevator.*

The doors opened. Yates stepped out, frustrated with the lack of urgency in his colleagues. Their minds were dulled by the fact that they were dealing with cute kids, too angelic to be up to anything.

148

Yates had been adamant from the moment the trip was announced that the Soviets were going to find a way to exploit the opportunity. He approached the ornate double doors to the ballroom. They were closed, a sign claiming the room was undergoing extensive renovation. He took out his key, unlocking the heavy doors, stepping inside the cavernous ballroom.

Over thirty desks were set up, stretching the length of the room, scores of officers seated with headphones scribbling notes. Every room occupied by the Soviet delegation had been bugged with multiple devices in the ceilings of the bedroom and bathroom, the walk-in cupboards – ensuring no area where conversations could take place in private. The televisions had proved divisive. Yates had thought them a risk since the occupants could use the sound to mask their conversations. He didn't see the value in exposing the students to cartoons, pop music and adverts. He'd been overruled. The televisions had been rigged, providing a bombardment of images projecting a lifestyle that Yates's superiors wanted to trickle back to the Soviet Union, a message of abundance and comfort. As a concession Yates had managed to ensure that the sets were fixed with a volume control so that they could never be loud enough to hide a conversation.

Each room had been designated two translators working twelve-hour shifts. Dialogue was recorded but to provide immediate feedback the team would translate in real time, jotting in shorthand. Anything of importance was immediately flagged up. Otherwise the translator would type up their notes during the downtime, when the students and teachers were outside, or sleeping. The operation was so large that the FBI had drawn together the highest concentration of Russian linguists in the country.

Yates picked up the folder containing photographs of the Soviet students. He'd already studied them many times. He'd seen them step off the plane, watched them enter the hotel. He wasn't entirely confident that the young woman he'd spotted on the streets in Harlem could be counted among their number. How did she manage to leave the hotel without being seen? In the bustle he'd only caught her face for a moment and then she'd passed him by before disappearing down another street, apparently not making contact with Jesse Austin, the best-known Communist sympathizer in the area. It had been such an unlikely appearance, and an improbable location for a young white girl. Yates had returned to his car, noting the waiting cab and deciding he was going to wait too. The young woman had not returned. In the end the taxi driver had left without a passenger. It was impossible to see into Jesse's apartment from the street. After forty minutes Yates had given up too, impatient to check his suspicions back at the hotel.

Flicking through the photographs, he stopped. The woman's photograph was in black and white. Her name was Elena. She was seventeen years old. She was sharing a room with her older sister. Yates walked to the table where the translator was stationed for that room.

— *What are they doing?*

The woman translating pulled down her headphones, speaking with a thick Russian accent. Yates hid his disapproval: he was dealing with an immigrant, the least reliable of the linguists.

— *The older sister has been watching the television.*

— *And the younger sister? Elena?*

— *She went swimming.*

— *When did she go?*

The translator checked the log.

— *She left the room at ten a.m.*

— *Did you report this?*

— *She was followed to the pool.*

— *Has she returned?*

— *No.*

— *All those hours at a swimming pool? You don't think it's strange she hasn't returned?*

Jim picked up the translator's empty coffee mug, banging it against the table – a startlingly loud noise in the otherwise hushed atmosphere of the room. Everyone looked at him.

— *I want to know the location of one of the girls, Elena, eighteen years old. She was reported to be in the swimming-pool area.*

An agent raised his hand, said nervously:

— *The girl was followed into the swimming-pool area. We have an agent outside.*

— *Is she still there?*

— *She hasn't left.*

— *The agent can see her? Right now – he can see what's she doing?*

There was silence, then a hesitant response.

— *The agent isn't in the pool area. He's stationed outside. But she hasn't passed him. She has to be in there.*

— *You're willing to bet your career on that, are you?*

The man's confidence fell away. He began to stammer:

— *That's the only way into the pool. If she hasn't passed him she's got to be in there.*

Yates didn't bother to reply, hastening towards the doors, running past the elevator, and taking the steps up to the pool two at a time.

Manhattan
5th Avenue
Same Day

Seated in a cab, Elena glanced at her watch. She was late. The students were due to meet up in minutes. Everything had taken longer than she'd expected – far longer to drive to Harlem, longer to get into Mr Austin's apartment and longer to get out again. Fearful that the American secret police were watching, she'd been guided out of Austin's building through the back. She'd waved goodbye to Austin unsure whether he would show up tonight. He had not made any promises. She'd done all she could.

The hotel was up ahead, only five hundred metres away, but the traffic wasn't moving. Not knowing the correct English phrase she said:

— *I pay now.*

She put some money down, far too much, not waiting for her change. She jumped out and ran down the street. Instead of heading to the main entrance she turned down the hotel service alley. A series of steel ladders were attached to the back wall, leading up to the sun terrace on the fifth floor – a fire escape for those caught outside if the main pool area and corridor were impassable. Before climbing the ladder, Elena took off her clothes. Underneath her blouse and skirt she was wearing a swimsuit. When she'd climbed down this morning a bundle of clothes and a pair of shoes had been left for her, disguised and hidden behind the huge trashcans. Elena had no idea who planted the clothes, a member of the CPUSA perhaps. She threw these temporary clothes into the garbage before climbing the ladder. Red-faced and out of breath, she reached the fifth-floor sun terrace, peering over the edge. It was a sunny day and the terrace was crowded. She climbed up, walking determinedly towards the pool, unsure whether anyone had caught sight of her unusual entrance.

The man she'd seen in Harlem, the American police agent, was by the edge of the pool. She couldn't enter without being seen. If he'd already checked the sun terrace he would be suspicious if she suddenly appeared. He might find the fire escape. He might find her clothes in the garbage. The only place he couldn't have checked was the women's changing rooms. It was accessible from both the pool and the outside deck. Elena switched direction, walking away from the agent. She pushed on the door and stepped inside.

Heading towards her locker, a hand came down on her shoulder. Startled, she turned. It was Raisa.

— *Where have you been?*

— *I was in the sauna.*

The lie was a flash of improvised genius. Elena's face was red and sweaty. Raisa seemed to mull over this explanation and Elena realized had Zoya been in this position Raisa would've questioned her further. Instead, Raisa nodded, accepting it as the truth. Elena picked up a towel, wrapping it around her. Raisa asked:

— *Did you come down from the room in your swimsuit?*

Elena shook her head, retrieving her clothes from the locker. She was about to change when Raisa stopped her.

— *You can shower and change in your room. Hurry, we're late.*

Elena was annoyed at being spoken to as if she were a child and any guilt she might have felt about her secret enterprise quickly faded.

Stepping into the corridor they came to face to face with the American secret-police officer — the man from Harlem. His eyes were bloodshot, red capillaries like the roots of a tree branching out from his black pupils, patches of perspiration on his shirt. Elena tried to remain calm. Raisa asked, speaking in English:

— *Can I help you?*

Yates looked down at Elena, ignoring Raisa. He reached out, placing a finger on the side of Elena's face, catching a drop of sweat. He held the drop of sweat up to his eye, as though it were evidence.

— *I'm FBI officer Yates. I'm going to be watching the both of you very closely from now on.*

Raisa glanced down at Elena, then back at Yates. Yates stepped out of their way.

*

Raisa remained silent in the elevator. When Elena tried to speak she angrily gestured for her to say nothing. On the twentieth floor they walked at a brisk pace to the girls' room. Not until Raisa was inside and had locked the door did she speak.

— *I need you to tell me if something is going on. Don't lie to me.*

Raisa grabbed Elena's arm tight. Elena was shocked.

— *You're hurting me!*

— *What is going on?*

Zoya joined them.

— *What's happened?*

Raisa was looking at Elena.

— *Elena, tell me, right now, what are you involved in?*

Uncomfortable under her stare, Elena turned to the television. On the screen a brightly coloured cartoon car drove off a cliff, exploding in a shower of blue and green and pink stars. Her reply was a whisper.

— *Nothing.*

Raisa let go of her daughter's arm, in quiet disbelief at what she was about to say.

— *I don't believe you.*

Moscow
Novye Cheremushki
Khrushchev's Slums
Apartment 1312
Same Day

Leo was not expecting to have any word from or contact with his family for the duration of their trip. The same was true for every family who'd said goodbye to a son or daughter. They'd been told it was too complicated to arrange a phone call unless there was an emergency. Two days had passed since Leo had watched their plane take off for New York while he remained at the airport, among the remnants of the farewell ceremony. When everyone made their way from the viewing platform as the airliner disappeared into the distance, Leo remained standing long after it could no longer be seen. His family would be gone for eight days. To Leo it felt an impossibly long time.

The heatwave showed no sign of abating. It was approaching midnight and Leo sat at his kitchen table, wearing a vest and a pair of shorts, a glass of lukewarm water on the table, cards spread before him, his life on hold until his family returned. The cards were a distraction, an anaesthetic that gently numbed his impatience. He concentrated on the game at hand, achieving a meditative state of thoughtlessness. The nights were more difficult than the days. At work he was able to keep busy, resorting to cleaning the factory floor, perhaps the only manager ever to do so, in an attempt to push towards a state of physical exhaustion so that he might be able to sleep. At home, his strategy revolved around playing cards until he was on the brink of sleep, until he could hold his eyes open no longer. Last night he'd slept at the table, concerned that if he made the move to the bedroom he'd wake up and his chance of catching even an hour's sleep would slip away. Tonight he was waiting for that same moment, the point at which his eyes became heavy and he could lower his head onto the table, face pressed against the upturned cards, relieved that another day had passed.

About to place down a card, his arm froze, the two of spades pinched between his fingers. He could hear footsteps in the corridor. It was almost midnight, an unlikely time for someone to return home. He waited, tracking the footsteps. They stopped outside his apartment. He dropped the card, hurrying to the door, opening it even before the person had even knocked. It was an agent wearing KGB uniform, a young man – his brow was dripping with sweat having climbed the thirteen flights of stairs. Leo spoke first.

— *What's happened?*

— *Leo Demidov?*

— *That's right. What's happened?*

— *Come with me.*

— *What is this about?*

— *You need to come with me.*

— *Does it concern my family?*

— *My instructions are to collect you. I'm sorry. That's all I know.*

It took a concerted act of discipline not to grip the agent by his shoulders and shake an answer from him. However, it was probably true that he knew nothing. Controlling himself, Leo returned to the apartment, hurrying towards Elena's bed, sliding his hand under the mattress. The diary was gone.

*

In the car Leo placed his hands on his knees, remaining silent as he was driven into the centre of the city. His thoughts were ablaze with possibilities of what might have happened. He paid no attention to the journey, breaking from his anxious theorizing only when the car finally stopped. They were outside his former place of work, the Lubyanka – the headquarters of the KGB.

Manhattan
Hotel Grand Metropolitan
44th Street
Same Day

While the students ate lunch at the hotel, Raisa requested a phone call to her husband in Moscow, arguing that this was the only opportunity before the dress rehearsal that she would have to speak to him. The ability to lie convincingly was a talent that she had been forced to acquire as a young woman trying to survive during Stalin's years of terror, fearful that every rejection from every man who made a pass at her would bring an allegation of anti-Soviet behaviour. In this instance she claimed that Leo's elderly father was sickly and she wanted to make sure his condition had not worsened. She faced no resistance from the American authorities, who were more than happy to make arrangements, instead facing pressure from her colleagues, particularly Mikael Ivanov, who did not want members of the group phoning home. Raisa dismissed his objections: she was leading the delegation, not a homesick student, and a phone call to her husband was hardly an issue that need concern him, particularly if the Americans did not object. Of course, Raisa never believed the phone call would be private. The Americans and the Soviets would listen to every word. In view of such constraints, her dialogue needed to be coded. In her favour, Leo would understand from the mere fact of the phone call that something was wrong and she hoped, with careful phrasing, to communicate enough of events that he could offer an opinion. He would know very quickly whether there was something genuinely wrong or whether her anxiety was unwarranted.

Sitting in her hotel room, perched on the edge of the bed, she waited, staring at the phone on the side cabinet. If authorities in Moscow agreed to the request, Leo was going to be brought from their apartment to a phone. Once he was ready, the international call would be put through. Rationalizing both the Soviet and American position, she guessed that they were keen to hear what she had to say. If she made any remark the Soviets didn't approve of the call would be cut short.

Almost an hour had passed, the students would be finishing lunch soon – the dress rehearsal was due to begin. Time was running out. Raisa stood up, pacing the room, uncertain if the call was going to happen. Belatedly it occurred to her that she'd never spoken to Leo on a telephone before.

The phone rang. She jumped for it. A voice in Russian said:

— *We have your husband. Are you ready to take the call?*

— *Yes.*

There was a pause, a click – a sound like the rustling of papers.

— *Leo?*

There was no reply. She waited. Her impatience got the better of her.

— *Leo?*

— *Raisa.*

His voice was distorted, almost unrecognizable. She pressed the phone close to her ear, fearful of losing a sound. It took restraint not to simply spill her emotions: she needed to tread carefully and remember the lies she'd told to set up the call.

— *How is your father? Is he feeling better?*

There was a long delay and it was difficult to interpret it as either Leo's confusion or the connection. Finally he replied:

— *My father is still unwell. But his condition is not any worse.*

She smiled: Leo had not only realized that the lie was a pretext for calling, he'd left the excuse open in case she needed to call again. He asked, failing to conceal his anxiety:

— *How is the trip?*

Raisa was forced to respond indirectly, stating the points of concern without elaboration.

— *Today I met officials at the United Nations, where the first concert is to be held, and they had no questions regarding the plans. Previously they'd been involved very closely. Today they accepted the plans without comment.*

Once again there was a delay. Raisa waited, wondering what interpretation he'd offer. Finally he said:

— *No comments?*

His response was the same as hers. It was unusual for Soviet officials not to stamp their authority on plans, not to interfere.

— *None.*

— *You must be . . . pleased?*

— *Surprised.*

Raisa didn't know how much time she had. It was essential she bring up the second point troubling her.

— *Leo, the girls are nervous. Elena particularly.*

— *Elena?*

— *She doesn't seem herself. She spends a lot of time on her own.*

— *Have you spoken to her?*

— She says nothing's wrong.

The phone crackled against Raisa's ear, reminding her of the fragility of the connection, it could be cut at any point. Suddenly frantic, she blurted out:

— Leo, I don't believe her. What should I do?

The delay was so long that she was sure the call had been terminated. She asked:

— Leo? Leo!

Leo's voice was firm.

— Don't allow her to attend the concert. Raisa, you hear me? Don't allow—

There was a click. The phone crackled. The connection was lost.

Moscow
Lubyanka Square
The Lubyanka, Headquarters
of the Secret Police
Same Day

Leo repeated Raisa's name, raising his voice each time. The phone was silent. The connection was dead.

The door to the office opened. He'd been left alone during the conversation, an absurd illusion of privacy and a deeply cynical ploy, no doubt in the hope that he would lower his guard. It was simply ridiculous to imagine that his conversation hadn't been recorded and scrutinized. A woman entered the office, saying:

— *I'm sorry, Leo Demidov: the connection was broken.*

The woman appeared to be a secretary. She was not in uniform. He asked:

— *Can we reach my wife again?*

The woman squeezed her lips, compressing them into a feeble imitation of a sympathetic smile.

— *Perhaps you can talk tomorrow.*

— *Why can't you put me through now?*

— *Tomorrow.*

Her condescending tone, heavy with the implication that she was reasonable and he was not, infuriated Leo.

— *Why not now?*

— *I'm sorry, that's not possible.*

The woman's apologies were flat and insincere. Leo was still clutching the phone, holding it out towards the woman as if he expected her to bring it back to life.

— *I need to speak to my wife.*

— *She's on her way to the dress rehearsal. You can talk tomorrow.*

The lie increased Leo's unease. For her to have the authority to lie meant that she was an agent. He shook his head.

— *She's not on her way anywhere. She'll be doing exactly the same as I'm doing right now, holding the phone, asking to speak to me.*

— *If you want to leave a message I can try to arrange that she will receive it tonight.*

— *Connect us, please, now.*

The agent shook her head:

— *I'm sorry.*

Leo refused to let go of the telephone.

— *Let me speak to someone here.*

— *Who do you wish to speak to?*

— *The person in charge.*

— *In charge of what?*

— *In charge of whatever is going on in New York!*

— *Your wife is in charge of the New York trip. And she's now on her way to the dress rehearsal. You can speak to her tomorrow to find out how it went.*

Leo imagined the agents in nearby offices; agents who'd listened to his telephone call and who were now listening to this exchange. He imagined the discussion they were having. They'd established one vital point: he didn't know what was happening in New York and neither did his wife. There was no chance he'd be allowed to speak to Raisa until she was home, no matter what scene he made, no matter how hard he pressed his demands. She was on her own.

Manhattan
Hotel Grand Metropolitan
44th Street
Same Day

Raisa was still holding the receiver, demanding Mikael Ivanov re-connect her with Leo. Mikael shook his head, as though he personally controlled the telephone exchange. His smug sense of authority was utterly infuriating. Sounding reasonable and meas-ured, he said:

— *The dress rehearsal starts in less than an hour. The students have finished lunch. We need to leave. You're behaving irrationally. You're here to ensure the smooth running of this concert. That is your priority.*

Raisa was taken aback by the intensity of her hatred for this man.

— *One minute more isn't going to make a difference.*

— *If you didn't think you could manage your duties without your husband perhaps he should have led this trip rather than you. It's disappointing to see you so incapable.*

It was a shrewd attack; any further request to speak to Leo was a humiliating confirmation of the allegation that she was weak.

She would not be allowed a second conversation. She would not beg.

Raisa hung up the phone, remaining by the cabinet, running Leo's advice through her mind.

— *Where's my daughter?*

— *As I said, the students finished lunch. They're in their rooms. They're waiting to assemble on the coach. We're all waiting for you.*

Raisa noted that he didn't ask which daughter: he knew she was referring to Elena. How did he know? He'd listened to the call, or perhaps he was also involved, but involved with what?

Without another word, she strode out of the room, past Ivanov, fully aware that he was going to follow her.

— *Raisa Demidova!*

She reached the end of the corridor, knocking on the door to Elena's room. Ivanov was running to catch up:

— *What are you going to do?*

Elena opened the door. As Raisa entered, she turned to Ivanov.

— *Get the other students in the coach. I'll be down in a few minutes. My family is none of your concern.*

She didn't wait for a reply, shutting the door in his face.

Zoya and Elena stood side by side, in the clothes they would be wearing tonight – ready to leave for the dress rehearsal. Raisa said:

— *Elena, I want you to stay here. If tonight goes well, you can attend tomorrow's concert.*

After a fractional pause, stunned by the news, Elena sprang forward, flush with indignation.

— *What are you talking about? How can I not attend the performance?*

— *I've made a decision. There's nothing more to be said.*

Elena's face reddened. Her eyes glistened with tears.

— *I've flown from Moscow only to be told I must stay in my room!*

— *Something is wrong!*

— *What is wrong?*

— *I don't know. But I've spoken to Leo and he agrees—*

As soon as she mentioned Leo's name Raisa regretted it. Elena jumped on the idea that Leo was behind this.

— *Leo! He's been against this trip from the beginning. What has he been saying? He's paranoid. He sees intrigue and deceit and treachery everywhere. He's sick. Truly, he's sick to his soul. Nothing bad is going on. I promise you. There is no reason to keep me in my room just because a bitter former agent has forgotten that not everything in the world is twisted and sinister.*

Elena referred to Leo as a former secret agent, rather than her father. Raisa had undermined Leo's relationship with the girls.

Elena began to cry.

— *Am I the only student to be locked in their room? For no reason? While all the other students perform? I'm going to sit here? My real mother would never have behaved like this. A real mother would understand the humiliation . . .*

Zoya reached out and touched her sister's arm, in a reversal of their usual roles, trying to rein her anger back.

— *Elena . . .*

Elena pulled her arm free, staring at Raisa.

— *No, I will not be told how I should feel. I will not be told how to behave. I'm not a child any more! You can stop me from going to the concert. You have that power. If you do, I will never forgive Leo.*

Same Day

Yates struggled to understand the translator's thick Russian accent. She'd lived in this country for over forty years, was employed in an Ivy League university as a professor of linguistics, yet she couldn't even speak English properly. He asked:

— *The mother gave in?*

— *The daughter is coming to the concert. She's been allowed to attend.*

— *Did the girl mention any plans? Say anything else?*

— *She denied there was anything sinister about to happen.*

— *You're sure?*

— *I am sure.*

— *No mention of any plot?*

— *I've been speaking Russian all my life.*

This translator didn't like him and wasn't afraid to show it, peering over her thick-framed glasses as if Yates were beneath contempt. She'd been the only linguist who'd objected to helping with this operation, stating that she was an academic not a spy.

— *Speaking Russian all your life? That is a long time: maybe you still have feelings for the country? Sentimental feelings that might make you omit an important detail or two?*

The woman's face tightened with anger.

— *Have someone check the transcript, someone you trust, if there is such a person.*

Yates sunk his hands into his pockets.

— *How about you just answer my questions? Right now I'm not interested in you. I'm interested in what that family was talking about. Was there any mention of Jesse Austin?*

— *No.*

Yates addressed the entire room, clutching the rushed, hand-written transcript of Raisa's phone conversation with Leo.

— *The Russian woman is a better detective than all of you. She knows something is going on. She can feel it in her gut. I agree with her. I need you to do your jobs!*

He picked up the file they had on Raisa Demidova and her daughters. It contained nothing more than the official information provided by the Soviet authorities, statistics such weight and academic grades. He threw it down again.

An officer called out:

— *The students are boarding the coach. Do you want to go with them?*

Yates considered.

— *Have our agents keep contact with that family. I want them watched every step of the way from the coach to the United Nations building. Don't let them out of your sight, even for a moment.*

As the agents busied themselves with the movement of the students to the coach, Yates paced the line of translators' tables, frustrated that he couldn't even approximate an answer to the question of why the Soviets were so keen to arrange for Jesse Austin to attend the concert. They'd sent this girl: they'd risked her slipping out of the hotel. Jesse Austin's presence wouldn't even make the news. He called out:

— *I want to know if we've had any activity in Harlem recently.*

A field agent approached.

— *The team watching a suspected Soviet operative reported that he was in Harlem this morning. Normally he's pretty good at giving us the slip on the subway. Not today, they followed him.*

— *Where did he go?*

— *West 145th Street.*

— *Who was he?*

— *His name is Osip Feinstein.*

Manhattan
Global Travel Company
926 Broadway
Same Day

In the storeroom behind his office, Osip Feinstein developed the photographs he'd taken of Jesse Austin towering over the Russian girl, the rumpled bed sheets in the background appearing to carry the fossilized impression of their sexual encounter. It would've been preferable for Jesse's hand to be clasping her arm rather than the other way round. No matter, the sordid implications were striking. What couldn't be seen in the photograph was Austin's wife. She was out of shot. Nor would anyone know that the bed had been unmade before the girl had arrived. Those passing judgement were unlikely to spend time analysing it: the snap response would be outrage. The roles of the villain and victim were clear. Though the meeting had been entirely innocent, the photograph produced showed striking guilt and moral compromise – an exploited, fragile white girl pathetically bidding farewell after a squalid escapade with a lecherous old Negro.

Osip dropped his head in shame, staring at his wrinkled hands clasped around the photographs. He noted with interest that he still had the capacity to feel shame. He wasn't entirely dead inside, numbed with opium but not yet oblivious to his failings. This was not the life he'd sought when he'd come to America, to frame a man he admired, a man of great integrity.

A long time ago Osip had been a man of integrity too. Though he was now a spy, the truth was that he had no love for the Soviet Union and plenty of affection for the country he was betraying. He reconciled the contradiction, to some degree, by smoking opium – which helped a lot – and rationalizing – which helped a little. When he'd arrived in New York as a young man, he'd felt certain that success of some kind was inside him. He'd achieved success but not the kind he'd expected. At the age of fifty-nine, Osip had become one of the longest-serving Soviet spies to work in 'the main adversary', spy slang for the United States of America.

As a young man, forty years ago, Osip had been an ambitious nineteen-year-old living in the Ukraine, attending Kyiv University, with aspirations to spend his life in academia. Feeling the grip of prejudice around the neck of his fledgling career – the door to his room defaced, the Star of David scratched into it, the contempt of his tutors – it was evident that he would never achieve a professorship. Sitting in his cold room, looking over a snow-covered street, he could no longer imagine a future in Kyiv. Without close family to root him in the city, he made the decision to leave, motivated less by a sense of fear than a determination to fulfil his potential. He'd originally intended to travel to France. However, leaving Kyiv was akin to stepping off a cliff and falling into the ocean, buffeted by the waves, with no control over his direction. He eventually washed up on the shores of the American consulate at Riga, Latvia, where he'd remained in the State Emigrant House for two days, suffering the indignity of being examined and disinfected. He'd paid his entire worldly fortune to the Sovtorgflor

Company, which specialized in arranging travel for emigrants. Clutching his transit papers and doctor's certificate, six months after he'd made the decision to leave, he'd boarded a boat. For the first time he could imagine a future again: his future was New York.

He arrived in 1934 – the worst period in living memory to look for work. To make matters worse, his gifts were intellectual. Even so, he'd failed to complete his degree, meaning that the only work open to him was as an unskilled labourer, yet he lacked the physical strength to compete within the vast and desperate labour pool. From the window of his run-down room, shared with five other men, he'd watch the Unemployed Union marching through the streets, slow-moving lines of jobless workers that filed south on Broadway. He'd scratched together a meagre, desperate existence for a couple of years, living hand to mouth, before chancing across Communist activists trying to tap into the disenchantment of the unemployed. His survival instincts had taken over and sensing an opportunity he approached them, explaining his history. Since he was Jewish and fluent in Russian, they presumed he had an predisposition to Communism. He'd lied about the reasons he'd left the Soviet Union, explaining that he'd come to the USA in the depths of the Great Depression certain that the capitalist society was in crisis and wishing to ferment a revolution. Familiar with the jargon, the slogans, aphorisms and theory, he'd dazzled his audience. Though the Communist Party of the USA didn't know it, they were at the apogee of their success. The Communist presidential candidate William Foster and his Negro running mate James Ford had received over a hundred thousand votes in the 1932 election – claiming to be at the forefront of change: progressive socially and offering a radical alternative to the broken capitalist system that had driven workers to jump from office windows and families to live in shanty towns in Central Park. Almost everyone involved with the CPUSA hoped the Depression was the beginning of the end for capitalism, every-one, that is, except for their newest recruit, Osip.

Osip was starving, sick and unemployed. He didn't care about the party. He cared that they had money. They could pay him – the CPUSA received substantial illegal subsidies from the Soviet Union, transferred via a system of mail drops. They could feed and clothe him. For the first time since arriving in New York he ate well, without counting the cost of each mouthful. His strength returned. After several months of leafleting and performing rudi-mentary services for the party, it was decided he would set up a legitimate business called the Global Travel Company, selling tourist packages for Eastern Europe and the Soviet Union. Under this cover, Osip was tasked with importing potential spies from the Soviet Union, academics and scientists who could infiltrate key military and scientific operations in the United States. The American authorities would accept the applicants because they would be too brilliant to pass over. He'd run this tourist agency, which lost thousands of dollars, ever since.

The store bell was ringing. He had a customer. There were very few legitimate customers: rarely more than four or five a week. Osip wiped his hands and stepped into the store regarding the customer, a man in his forties. He was wearing a crumpled suit. The cut was poor and his shoes were cheap and scuffed but he wore his clothes with a swagger and bravado that concealed many of their faults. He was an FBI agent and Osip was sure it was the man he'd seen outside Jesse Austin's apartment. The agent had yet to look at him, flicking through one of the brochures. Osip said:

— *Can I help you?*

The agent turned, answering with mock formality:

— *I was wondering how much it would cost for a one-way ticket to the Soviet Union? First class, of course, I only want to see Communism if I can travel in luxury.*

He switched into his regular way of speaking.

— *Isn't that how it works in rackets like this, people with lots of money paying to see how people live with none?*

— *The point is for the traveller to experience a different way of life. What they make of that society is entirely up to them. We merely make the arrangements.*

Osip offered his hand to shake.

— *My name is Osip Feinstein. I'm the owner of this agency.*

— *Agent Yates.*

Yates produced his credentials but didn't shake Osip's hand. Instead, he sat on a chair, slumped, as though he were at home in front of his television. He lit a cigarette, inhaled, exhaled and said nothing more. Osip stood, waiting.

— *I take it you're not here for the travel.*

— *Correct.*

— *How can I help you?*

— *You tell me.*

— *Tell you what?*

— *Listen, Mr Feinstein, we can bounce this back and forth all day long. Why don't I lay my cards on the table? You've been under surveillance for many years. We know you're a Communist. You're described as a cautious man and a canny operator. Yet today my men are able to follow you to Harlem. You go into an apartment building not too far from a man called Jesse Austin. After several hours you left, returning to the store with a camera slung over your arm. We saw it all. That's what troubles me. It's not your style to be this careless. It feels like you're flirting with us,*

Mr Feinstein. If I'm wrong, if I have insulted you in some way, that's fine: I'll walk out of here right now and say sorry for taking up so much of your time, I'm sure you're busy selling these tours.

Yates stood up, walked towards the door. Osip called out:

— *Wait!*

He had not intended to sound so pitiful. Yates turned around, slowly, a toxic smile on his face.

Osip tried to ascertain quickly what kind of man he was dealing with. He'd hoped for someone businesslike. This agent seemed emotional and angry.

— *You queer, Mr Feinstein? In my experience most Communists are either queer, Negro or Jew. I know you're a Jew. I can see you're no Negro. I'm not all that expert at guessing queers, though. Sure, there might be other kinds of Communists, but the ones who aren't ashamed to stand up and say 'I'm proud to be a Communist' are always queer, Negro or Jew.*

Yates sucked on his cigarette and exhaled, jabbing it at Osip's chest.

— *I've been following your career with interest, Mr Feinstein. We've known for some time that this tourist agency is a cover. Did you think we were stupid? Those spies you sent us? We let them in. Why? Because we were confident as soon as they arrive in this country and start living in a nice house, and driving a nice car and eating nice food, they're going to forget about that god-awful Communist hole they left behind. They're going to be loyal to us because our lives are better than yours. And you know what? We were right. You've arranged for what, maybe three hundred people and their families to come over?*

The exact number was three hundred and twenty-five. Yates sneered:

— How many have given you anything confidential? How many have given you even a scrap of information or a single blueprint?

Despite his doubts about Yates, there was no way back. Osip had to proceed with his plan.

— Agent Yates, I left the Soviet Union fearing for my life. I have no love for that regime. I began working as a spy for the Soviet Union only because I couldn't get any other work in New York. I was hungry. It was during the Great Depression. The CPUSA had money. I had none. That is the truth. After I joined them, there was no going back. My card was marked as a Communist. I had to behave as one. The men and women whose visas I arranged were never likely spies. They were people in danger, scientists and engineers. They feared for their lives and the lives of their children. I never expected them to become spies. I never expected them to provide a scrap of information, as you say. I used Soviet resources to get them to safety under the guise of infiltrating American universities or factories or even the military. That is the truth. The measure of my success was not how many spies I created, but how many lives I saved.

Yates stubbed out his cigarette in the ashtray.

— Mr Feinstein, that's an interesting story. Makes you sound like an American hero, is that what you're saying? I should be patting you on the back?

— Agent Yates, I no longer wish to work as a Soviet agent. I wish to work for the United States government. In saying this, my life is now in terrible danger, so you should have no reason to doubt my word.

Yates moved close to Feinstein.

— You wish to work for the United States government?

— Please, Agent Yates, follow me. I can prove my sincerity.

Osip escorted him through to the temporary darkroom,

showing him the photographs of Jesse Austin. Only now did Osip notice that Yates had drawn his gun, fearing a trap. Keeping the gun by his side, Yates asked:

— *Why did you take the photographs?*

— *They're part of a plan drawn up by a Soviet department called SERVICE.A. The Soviet authorities intend to exploit these concerts for their own benefit. They have asked Jesse Austin to speak outside the UN tonight.*

— *They've been trying to get him to attend for months now. So what?*

— *He turned down every request, so they sent this girl, a Russian girl, an admirer of Jesse Austin. They want him to address the crowd. The world's media will be present.*

— *The world's media will be inside the hall, not on the sidewalk. You're telling me their plan is to persuade a washed-up singer to shout about his Communist brothers to a rabble on the sidewalk? Let him speak! I don't give a shit.*

Yates began to laugh, shaking his head.

— *Feinstein, is this really what you brought me over for?*

— *Agent Yates, after tonight, Jesse Austin will be more famous than ever, more famous than you can possibly imagine.*

Yates stopped laughing.

— *Tell me everything.*

Bradhurst
Harlem
West 145th Street
Same Day

The night was as hot as the day. Red-brick walls baked in the full glare of the sun leached the heat back out, slow-cooking the residents. For about an hour either side of sunrise there was some respite, when the bricks were cool and the sun wasn't yet beating down, the only time of day that was fresh and human. Jesse sat on the window ledge with no expectations of a breeze. Outside the sound of children playing ball or skipping ropes no longer cut the air. Having sold its day's stock the clam wagon was pushed off, arthritic, rusty wheels creaking into the distance. Beggars, who'd set up position next to it in the hope of catching loose change, were moving off, breaking into different directions, looking for somewhere to sleep or for new places to beg. The card players took their games from the shade onto the sidewalk, on fold-out flimsy tables. Those who'd slept during the day came alive with the night. There was drink and dope and laughter – the light side of the night, the first drink, the first smoke and it was always a good time. Later the fights would start, the arguments and shouting, the women crying and the men crying too.

Jesse watched the street evolve into darkness as the last of the sunlight seeped away. This was his entertainment now, for they no longer owned a television set, sold it years ago. They didn't miss it. They didn't want to watch the programmes it showed, the music that was aired, suspicious of the powers that controlled it, powers that would block him being on television in a heart-beat. Jesse wondered about the other men and women he might have known and loved if their careers hadn't been swallowed up by a disapproving state. How many artists, musicians, writers, painters, had been lost to fear? He wished he could bring them together, these lost souls, sit them round his table, pour them a drink, hear their stories, listen to their troubles and delight in their talents.

Anna was dressed for work. She was on a late shift, working for a restaurant that stayed open twenty-four hours a day. Nine at night to nine in the morning was a shift that not even the younger waitresses volunteered for. Anna claimed to prefer it, saying the heavy night-time drinkers always tipped better than the daytime diners and they never sent any of the food back. She stood by the door, ready to go. Jesse got down from the window ledge, taking her hands. She asked:

— *Have you decided?*

— *I don't know. I just don't know. Standing on the sidewalk outside the United Nations, giving a speech? I'm not proud, Anna, but it's not like an invitation to perform at Madison Square Garden. It's not what I had in mind for us. I don't know how I feel about it all.*

— *Jesse, I can't take tonight off, not at this late notice, I've got to work.*

— *I don't even know if I'm going, so there's no point you wait-ing around.*

She was uneasy.

— *I don't want you to think that I'm against it, should you choose to go.*

— *I know that.*

— *I'd never ask you not to do something when you believed in it, when you thought it was the right thing to do.*

— *Anna, what's wrong?*

She looked like she was about to cry. It was only for a moment, a ripple of emotion across her face, and then she recovered her composure. Anna never cried.

— *I'm late, that's all.*

— *Then don't waste any more time worrying about me.*

Anna kissed him on the check, but instead of pulling away, she remained close by his face, whispering:

— *I love you.*

Those three words were too much for him to bear right now. Jesse looked down at the floorboards, his voice faltering.

— *I'm sorry, Anna. For all this trouble, for all this . . .*

She smiled.

— *Jesse Austin, don't you ever apologize to me, not for what they've done, not for something that was never your fault.*

She kissed him again.

— *Just tell me you love me.*

— *Sometimes 'I love you' doesn't sound like it's enough.*

— *It's all I've ever wanted.*

She let go of him, straightened her clothes, opened the door and hurried down the stairs, without looking back and without shutting the door behind her.

Jesse waited by the window. Anna appeared on the street,

snaking her way through the card games on her way to the restaurant. Almost out of sight she stopped, turning back and waving at him. He waved back and by the time he'd lowered his hand she was gone.

It was time to decide. He checked his watch. There was only an hour until he was meant to address a group of unknown demonstrators. He didn't even know what they would be demonstrating about. In all likelihood they would not recognize him and he'd struggle to be heard. The concert started at nine. According to the Russian girl it only lasted seventy minutes. Jesse tapped the face of his handsome watch bought in better times. As he pondered on whether to accept the invitation, the memory of another watch crept into his thoughts, a watch he'd never worn. It had been given to him at the very start of his career while he'd been on his first national tour. The manager of the concert hall had been so pleased with the unexpected success of the performances, three sold-out events in the town of Monroe, Louisiana, that he'd presented Jesse with a handsome box, containing a nicely made watch with a leather strap with MADE IN MONROE embossed on the back. Jesse didn't remember too much about the watch itself but he remembered the manager very well. The man had knocked on his dressing-room door after the final performance, snuck in with the stealth of a mistress. Anna had been in the room and witnessed the manager nervously offering Jesse the watch as a token of his gratitude before hurrying out again. Jesse had laughed out loud at the odd manners of this pleasant man until he'd noticed that Anna wasn't laughing. She'd explained that man wanted show his gratitude, he just wasn't able to show it in public. He couldn't come onto the stage at the end of the show and give Jesse the watch. He couldn't invite them to dinner since he didn't want to be seen with Jesse and

Anna in a restaurant. He could employ Jesse to sing, he could be seen applauding, but as soon as Jesse stepped off that stage he couldn't be seen near him. It was a fine watch, a handsome watch, particularly for a young man who'd yet to make much money, but Jesse hadn't kept it, leaving it behind in the dressing room with a note:

Dinner would've been plenty.

He'd never been booked there to play again.

Anyone could love a person while they were singing and danc-ing on a stage. Jesse had learnt this lesson when he was seven years old. He and his family had been living in Braxton, Mississippi, before they'd made the decision to move north. Autumn 1914, a night so hot that after walking no more than a hundred paces Jesse's shirt was as wet as if a cloud had followed his every step. His mother and father had made him promise that he would stay inside tonight, they both had to work and they were leaving him alone. But just last week, they'd run out of wood and his father had scolded him for not pulling his weight around the house and Jesse didn't want to be told off again, deciding it would be better to find some more wood. So he'd been collecting timber without too much trouble since everything on the forest floor was a dry as thatch, bark coarse in his hands. Twigs crunched underfoot, the snap of dry wood, noises that echoed through the trees. Though he'd never admitted as much to his family, he'd always been afraid of the woods – his imagination ran free, his mind played tricks on him. He'd call himself silly. Sometimes he'd even call himself silly out loud.

— *Jesse, don't be scared. There's bugs and mosquitoes in these woods, that's all there is.*

But when he stopped talking the sound of voices continued. He shook his head as though there were water in his ears. The voices continued, not one, but two or three.

— *You've done it wrong!*

— *Like this!*

— *Stand there.*

— *Help me over here!*

— *That's it.*

— *Get the camera ready!*

He moved in one direction, deeper into the woods and the voices became softer. He changed direction, heading out of the woods, towards town. The voices became louder. He should've run home. He should've dropped his bundle of wood and run but he carried on, following the sounds.

Coming to the edge of the forest, not far from town, Jesse was surprised to see a large crowd, surprised since his parents had been so vocal in ordering him to remain inside that night when it seems so many other people were doing just the opposite. The crowd had their backs turned to him, in a semicircle, maybe one hundred in total; less like a crowd, he realized, and more like an audience. Those at the back and on the edges were holding burning branches, flickering lanterns, stage lights spitting red sparks into the night sky. They needed the lanterns since there wasn't much moonlight, only a glimmer every now and then when the heavy clouds lumbered out of the moon's way. Jesse thought that this was a well-dressed group of people, considering they were in forest. There were women in crisp dresses. There were girls wearing matching outfits. The men wore shirts, tucked into their pants. It was like they were dressed for church, or the theatre. Some people were fanning themselves with straw hats, ladies were shooing away mosquitoes and flies with dainty swipes of their dainty fingers, but Jesse could see the sweat stains on their backs; they weren't so different from him after all.

They hadn't noticed little Jesse, standing silently behind a tree – his arms full of wood, his hair knotted with leaves, his clothes as scruffy as if they'd been knitted from the foliage on the forest floor. The audience were captivated by what was happening in front of them but Jesse couldn't figure out what could be so entertaining this far into the woods. He was too short to see what was happening and he didn't dare move from behind the tree for the audience was all white and it wasn't wise to interfere.

As though a spell had been cast, every single man and woman and child in the clearing looked up into the trees at exactly the same time. Jesse looked up too, hoping to see a firework, a burst of brilliant stars. Instead, he saw what they had gathered to watch – it was a dance, two legs dancing in the sky; a jerky dance, not like one he'd ever seen before, a dance where the two black, shoeless feet didn't touch the ground, a dance without rhythm and without music, a silent dance that lasted no more than a minute or two.

By the time those legs were done with their dance, Jesse had crushed all the twigs in his arms and his shoes were covered in ground-up bark. A man in the audience lifted up a bulky box camera and a bulb flashed, burning bright for an instant and exposing everything hidden by the night. To this day Jesse wondered why the man waited till the end to take his photograph. Maybe he didn't want to miss a moment of that entertaining dance.

When the young Russian girl had asked him earlier why he'd sacrificed so much for Communism, when strangers and friends and families had asked him why he couldn't shut his mouth about politics and enjoy the money, he'd never told them the truth.

What had turned him into a Communist? It wasn't the hatred his family encountered when they'd moved to New York, or the insulting things that anyone had ever said to him. It wasn't the poverty, or the struggle his parents had faced just to make ends meet. On the opening night of his first major concert, onstage in a crowded auditorium, looking out at the well-heeled white people clapping as he danced and sang, he knew that they loved him only while his legs moved to a rhythm and only while his lips made song and not speech. Once the show was over, once his legs no longer danced, they wanted nothing to do with him.

Being loved onstage wasn't enough. Singing wasn't nearly enough.

Manhattan
United Nations Headquarters
The General Assembly Hall
1st Avenue & East 44th Street
Same Day

It was an audience of the most important diplomats in the world –
every United Nations envoy had been invited. The assembly hall
was full. The concert was due to start. Like a child before a school
play, Raisa stole a glance from backstage, wondering if her nervousness about tonight's performance had manifested itself as
paranoia. Her imagination had run away with her, drawing inspiration from her past when every word was loaded with danger and
intrigue. It was not her clothes that had revealed her as provincial
but the way in which she'd panicked, unsettled at being given such
a grand platform. She was embarrassed at the way she'd behaved.
The successful dress rehearsal had steadied her, calmed her down,
given her a sense of proportion and made her earlier outburst feel
ridiculous.

She regarded the Soviet students: they'd lined up and were
ready to walk out onto the stage. Her job was to reassure them,
not to be flustered. Passing each one with a smile and words of

encouragement, she approached Elena. Raisa had reluctantly relented, allowing Elena to sing, fearing that if she did not, Elena would blame Leo and hate him. However, they'd barely spoken since the argument and a sense of awkwardness remained. Raisa crouched down, whispering:

— *This is new for me too. The pressure became a little too much. I'm sorry. I know you're going to be amazing. I hope you can enjoy the evening. I hope I haven't spoiled this for you – that was never my intention.*

Elena was crying. Raisa hastily wiped away her daughter's tears.

— *Don't cry. Please, or I'll start.*

Raisa smiled, to cover the fact that she was close to tears, adding:

— *It's my fault. Not Leo's, don't be angry with him. Just concentrate on the performance. Have fun. Enjoy tonight.*

Raisa was about to return to the front of the students when Elena took her hand, saying:

— *Mother, I would never be involved in anything that wouldn't make you proud of me.*

The use of the word mother had been deliberate. Fearful that she would not be able to control her emotions, Raisa uttered a quick response:

— *I know.*

Raisa hurried back into position, composing herself, ready to lead her students onto the stage. She breathed deeply, determined to succeed. This was a remarkable event. Many years ago, in the Great Patriotic War, a refugee, her only thought had been to survive. As a teacher in Moscow during Stalin's reign, her only ambition had been to avoid arrest. Were she to go back in time and show that fearful young woman a glimpse of her future – a prestigious international audience in this remarkable hall with two beautiful daughters by her side – it would be impossible to believe. Her only wish was that Leo could be here with her, not because of any plot or treachery – she bitterly regretted putting the idea into his head – but because no other person understood the journey she'd made.

The musical cue was given. The orchestra was ready. The audience fell silent. Side by side with the American head teacher, Raisa led her students out. The applause was polite and she sensed not without an undercurrent of uncertainty. No one was quite sure how this unprecedented performance was going to turn out.

*

Walking onto the stage, Elena reassured herself that she hadn't lied: her mother was certain to be proud when she understood what she was trying to achieve – a much-needed show of love and admiration for Jesse Austin, a man wrongly persecuted for his convictions, a brilliant man beaten down by state oppression because of his belief in fairness and love. Of course, Raisa would be angry at first, furious by the fact that it had remained a secret. She would be angry that she'd not been told. Once that anger faded, then surely she would understand, perhaps she would even admire Elena's courage.

Regarding the hall, the decorations, the flags and the elitist audience, the political aristocracy dressed in fine clothes, Elena considered the spectacle artificial, disconnected from any real problems or issues. The concert carried no promise of social change or progress, sterilized, stripped of any anger or outrage to avoid offending their hosts. The protests on the street were not against one government or another, they would be universal, against intolerance and hatred, against inequity and an approach to human life that was inhumane. The world needed a second Revolution, a revolution of civil rights. Communism was the best vehicle for that Revolution. How could Raisa not be proud of what she and Jesse Austin were about to achieve? The applause came to a stop.

Harlem
Bradhurst
8th Avenue & West 139th Street
Nelson's Restaurant
Same Day

Reasonably priced and always busy, the restaurant was named after its owner, Nelson, a man much loved by those who lived in the area. He was fair to his staff and always knew whether to trade jokes with the customers or listen to their problems. Anna had never met a man with a more highly developed sense of what people were looking for. When she'd been desperate for money, searching for work, he'd helped her out. He didn't need to hire a woman her age with no experience when there were younger, prettier girls who could flirt with the customers and bring in extra business. Anna paid back the favour by never letting him down, never being late or slipping off early. She told everyone that he'd taken a chance on her, fearless of the repercussions. Customers liked the fact Nelson had given her a job, maybe he'd known that too. In the end, the FBI never kicked up a fuss, not like they did with Jesse. Anna suspected that they liked the idea of her washing dishes and scraping trays clean. If they thought hard work was a humiliation, then they were wrong.

As she stepped inside the restaurant, getting ready for her shift, she understood with sudden clarity that Jesse was going to accept the young girl's invitation to speak tonight. No matter how many shrewd reasons there were for not talking outside the United Nations, standing on the street in a hubbub of protestors sounded more like a Jesse Austin gig than any she could think of. She couldn't allow him to be there alone.

Anna hurried over to Nelson, taking him by the arm.

— *You know I've never done this before and I'll never do it again. But I have to go back home. I can't work tonight. I have to be with my husband.*

Nelson looked her in the eyes, saw her expression, registered her tone and nodded.

— *Is there something wrong?*

— *No, nothing's wrong. There's something my husband has to do and I have to be there with him.*

— *All right, Anna: do whatever you have to do. Don't worry about this place, I'll serve the food myself if I have to.*

At his kindness, Anna kissed him on the cheek.

— *Thank you.*

She turned around, taking off her apron, leaving the restaurant and heading back as fast as she could. She ran all the way home, across the street, through the men playing cards, through the haze of cigarette smoke, reaching the stairs up to her apartment building. On her way up, striding up two steps at a time, she felt the eyes of her neighbours. They pitied her, imagining that she'd suffered because of Jesse. They were wrong. She was the luckiest woman alive to have shared her life with him.

She threw open the apartment door. Jesse was standing on the bed, addressing the open window as though it were an audience of ten thousand. Around his feet were the handwritten pages of all the speeches he'd ever performed.

Manhattan
United Nations Headquarters
The General Assembly Hall
1st Avenue & East 44th Street
Same Day

Jim Yates slipped into the back of the hall and watched the performance. Communists mingled with American students, dressed
identically: boys in white shirts and black pants, girls in white
shirts and black skirts, nothing distinguishing one nationality
from the other. According to the programme, framed with a mul-
titude of international flags, the songs had been composed by
musicians from around the world. Not even the liberal organizers
of this event could allow Communist propaganda songs, Soviet
hymns about being the strongest nation ready to crush all enemies including the United States. The Communists would save
them for when they got home, as soon as they stepped off the
plane in Moscow. As the Russians weren't able to sing their songs,
neither were the Americans for fear of offending their guests. Not
allowed to sing their own songs in their own country! Of course,
this wasn't his country – the United Nations Headquarters did not
fall under the authority of the United States, even though it was

in New York. Without a shot being fired the land had been handed over to an international organization. Yates wasn't even an FBI agent here. He was a guest.

As the song came to an end and the audience applauded, Yates regarded the diplomats. White people seemed to be a minority. Several envoys stood up to applaud. Yates couldn't make them out clearly from where he was standing – probably Cubans or South Americans. The truth was that while the students sang on stage, arm in arm, their nations planned the other's annihilation. The charade was grotesque. He was appalled that there were American parents who'd agreed to put their children into this concert. Those mothers and fathers warranted further investigation.

Yates checked his watch, fingernail tapping the dial face. The real performance was about to take place outside.

Manhattan
Outside the United Nations Headquarters
1st Avenue & East 44th Street
Same Day

Jesse Austin was carrying an apple crate that he'd taken from Nelson's restaurant kitchen. He'd spoken on street corners before and without elevation of some kind he didn't stand a chance of being heard, even as a tall man and a practised orator. Every performer needed a stage and though an apple crate wasn't much of one, it was better than a sidewalk. Arriving from the subway, he saw that part of 1st Avenue was closed to traffic. Instead of subduing the atmosphere, the absence of cars heightened the sense that the demonstration was out of the ordinary. Surveying the scene before him, set against the backdrop of the United Nations building, he saw hundreds of people gathered, far more than he'd expected. Anna took hold of his free hand. She was nervous.

The police were positioned in a perimeter formation: some were wearing full riot gear, several were on horseback, patrolling the front line of the protest, their horses snorting as if disgusted by the rabble. The protestors were barricaded in, like cattle, garish homemade banners rising up among the crowd: bed sheets stretched tight over wooden posts, brilliant colours – a tapestry of different material. Letters had been cut out individually, unevenly, giving them a childlike naivety. Reading the slogans, Jesse deduced the protestors were a muddle of different groups. There was something he'd never seen before in New York, anti-Vietnam-War demonstrators with guitars and drums side by side with clean-cut men and women in starched shirts attacking the Communist Party, some with placards demanding that Hungary be liberated from Soviet rule, others using the tired phrase:

THE ONLY GOOD RED

IS A DEAD RED

It was reproduced so many times that Jesse wondered why they couldn't think of something else to say – it made him want to speak even more. The more they threatened him, the stronger he became: that's what he'd always believed.

He was too late for the most prominent locations in the demonstration, and he wouldn't be able to plant himself near the gate as Elena had requested. He and Anna would have to make do with the far side, down towards the scraggly end of the crowd. It was less than ideal and he was annoyed with himself for not getting there earlier. As they began to walk down the length of the demonstration, a voice called out:

— *Jesse Austin!*

Turning around, he saw a man near the gate gesturing for him to come over. They obeyed, despite having no idea who the man was. He was young, with a pleasant smile.

— *This spot is for you! I saved it!*

The space was beside the main entrance, as Elena had requested.

He took hold of Jesse's crate, lifting it over the barricade. He tested it to see that it was stable, before looking up at Jesse.

— *Climb over!*

Jesse laughed.

— *Thirty years ago maybe!*

Holding Anna's hand, he moved into the crowd, slowly working his way through the people until he reached the crate. The man was protecting the makeshift stage from other protestors, several of whom were trying to push their way onto it. Seeing Jesse, he put a hand on his shoulder.

— *This is your time. Give them everything! Don't hold back!*

Jesse shook his hand.

— *Who are you?*

— *A friend. You have a lot more of them than you know.*

Same Day

Yates left the United Nation's premises before the concert finished. Normally a demonstration wouldn't have been allowed so close to the headquarters, but redirected to Ralph Bunche Park or Dag Hammarskjöld Plaza at 47th Street and 1st Avenue, one block away from the visitors' entrance, four blocks away from the entrance used by top-level diplomats. The decision to allow the demonstration unprecedented proximity to the United Nations was symbolic, the idea being that unlike the Soviet Union, America had nothing to fear in the face of open criticism. And there he was – Jesse Austin, making full use of the liberties granted by this nation, freedom of speech, a freedom that didn't exist in the nation he so extolled.

Exiting onto the street, Yates saw a uniformed cop approaching Jesse, interrupting his speech and pointing at the crate he was standing on. Yates hurried forward, grabbing the supervising officer by the arm and shouting over the din:

— *Tell your officer to pull back! No one moves Jesse Austin!*

— *Who is Jesse Austin?*

The name meant nothing to this police officer. Yates was pleased.

— *The tall man, the Negro standing on the box! He stays where he is!*

— *He's not allowed to be so high, not so close to the main entrance.*

Yates lost his temper.

— *I don't care about your rules. You listen to me! That man is not to be moved. The Soviets have invited him here hoping that we'll force him to leave. If we do, he'll resist and we'll end up on the front page of every newspaper dragging him away. That's what he wants! That's why he's here! He's a famous Communist sympathizer, a popular Negro figurehead. Five white police officers manhandling an old Negro singer is not the kind of image we want. We're in the middle of a propaganda war. I don't want any displays of force tonight. I don't care what the provocation is. Do you understand? No one moves that man!*

Same Day

Jesse couldn't believe that the police officer was backing down, walking away, allowing him to remain on the crate. He glanced at Anna. She seemed equally puzzled, but with the press here, their orders must be to show restraint, not to interfere, to allow the demonstration free rein, a tactical decision to show off the notion of American free speech, a cynical decision: but if free speech was being granted, even if it was a one-night-only show, he intended to exploit it.

From the apple crate he could see over the entire demonstration, hundreds of faces, some painted like flowers, others contorted with anger and outrage. Jesse began to speak. Timid at first, no one apart from his wife was listening to him, not even those closest to his crate. It was less like a speech and more like a crazy old man talking to himself.

— *I'm here tonight . . .*

A faltering start, unsure whether to read his material or to improvise. Deciding to use the material he'd written in his apartment, he tried to ignore the fact that no one seemed to care and concentrated on a fixed point in the crowd, pretending that he was back on the big stage with an audience of thousands of paying guests. However, his rhythm was thrown out of kilter by the incessant banging of the war protestors' drums. His words were jumbled: he stopped midway through one point and began making another. He stopped again, returning to his first point only to wonder whether it mattered if he spoke Russian or English since no one was listening anyway. Despondent, he felt Anna take his hand. He looked down at her. She squeezed his palm and advised him:

— *Just say what you feel. Talk to them like you talk to me, from the heart, that's why people have always listened to you. Because you never lie, you never pretend, you only ever say something if you believe in it.*

Jesse blocked out the sound of the drums, preparing to speak, raising his hand. Before he said a word a man called out, one of the elderly war protestors with sinewy arms, a scruffy beard and a guitar hanging around his neck. His chest was bare, painted with a red peace symbol.

— *Jesse Austin!*

Being recognized took him by surprise and Jesse lost his train of thought. Before he could recover, the protestor had pushed through to him, shaking his hand and saying:

— *Always loved your music. Tell me, Jesse, did they kill Malcolm X because he opposed the Vietnam War? I'm sure of it. They'll kill anyone who speaks out against this war. Malcolm X said every black man and woman should support the Vietnamese, not the US soldiers, that's got to be why they shot him, don't you think? Who do you support? The Vietnamese or the Americans?*

Malcolm X had been shot at the beginning of the year. It had crossed Jesse's mind that his murder might be more than it seemed. To blame the Nation of Islam was a convenient explanation, and normally when there was a convenient explanation the truth was somewhere else. As he began to answer, the man called out to his friends:

— *Hey! It's Jesse Austin!*

Though people hadn't reacted to the sight of him on a crate, at the sound of his name people turned around and paid attention. Voices shouted out from the anti-Communist crowd, coarse with disgust:

— *How come you said America wasn't your home!*

— *You said you'd be glad to fight American troops!*

The old protestor winked at Jesse.

— *Better be careful what you say.*

Jesse called back:

— *I never said anything of the sort! I believe in peace, not war.*

The first accusation had burst a dam, more insidious lies poured out, increasingly extreme, from the group of anti-Communist protestors who knew Jesse better than anyone, as a figure of hate and ridicule.

— *Isn't it true you seduced a bunch of white girls?*

— *Why don't you pay taxes?*

— *Haven't you been in prison?*

— *Don't you cheat on your wife?*

— *I heard you hit her when you're drunk!*

Jesse couldn't always see the faces of his accusers, voices disconnected. He struggled to control his anger, in contrast to his accusers, and answered the allegations:

— *I pay my taxes! I've never spent a day in prison, except to visit those people in need of help. And I never touched any white girl, not like that, just like I never hit a person, let alone my wife, the woman I love more than anyone else. What you're repeating is nothing more than slander! A campaign of hate and lies!*

His voice was trembling. The pain of these lies welled up inside him, the memory of being helpless, watching his reputation being destroyed.

Sensing he was in trouble, Anna stepped up onto the crate with him, putting an arm around his waist to steady herself.

— *Would I be standing beside my husband if it were true? Would I have stuck with him when the government took our home? When they took our jobs? When they took our money and the food from our table? We lost everything. Now, you've gladly listened to the lies. Let me tell you the facts. Jesse's never hurt another person in his life. He's never been in a bar fight, or street altercation. He's never raised his voice against me! As for war, he couldn't dream of taking up arms against another soul. He doesn't believe in violence. He believes in love! He believes in love deeper than anything! He believes in fairness for all men and women, no matter where they're born or the colour of their skin. You can disagree with what we believe in if you want. You can tell us we're fools for our ideas. But don't tell us that we don't love each other.*

As she stepped down from the crate, Jesse saw how her words had turned the crowd in his favour, pulling more attention his way. He regretted his retreat from public speaking. He'd allowed insinuation to fill the silence. It was his duty to put the truth out there even if the mainstream channels were closed to him. It was his duty to stand up to his enemies no matter how heavily the odds were stacked against him. He'd been beaten down into believing that the truth had no valuc. It did: it was stronger than their lies and the audience heard it in their voices when they spoke. Encouraged, he tried to move from a conversation to a polemic. It was time to say what he'd come here to say.

— *Now that we're done rebutting the false allegations, can we speak about what really matters? What matters to millions of Americans up and down this great country? The unfairness, the bias, the intolerance and the institutionalized discrimination not only of black Americans but of all poor Americans!*

He put aside his prepared material, speaking off the cuff. Just as his Russian had come back to him in satisfying, rolling waves of words and phrases, so did the words of outrage perfected over hundreds of speeches, years of protests. His audience swelled, unified in his direction, men and women of different ages and races. Some of the anti-war protestors joined him, putting down their drums, allowing his words to be heard. It was the biggest audience he'd addressed in nearly ten years and they weren't there for his songs, or to be entertained, they were there to change the world. And the crowd continued to grow, more and more people arriving, pressing into the area behind the steel barricades.

An angry woman called out:

— *If you love the Soviet Union do much why don't you go back with them to Russia!*

His confidence growing, Jesse relished the adversary.

— *Why would I go anywhere when this is my home! I've lived here all my life. My parents are buried here! Their parents are buried here! I'm as American as you are, perhaps more so, surely more so, because I truly believe in freedom of speech, in equality, concepts I doubt you even think about. You're too busy waving the American flag to think about what that flag symbolizes!*

The woman was joined by a breakaway group of anti-Communist protestors, taking turns to heckle Jesse, shouting above the noise, some of their comments disappearing, some breaking through.

— *You live in America and you insult our country!*

— *The only people I've ever insulted were people like you, people who don't understand that every man and woman on this earth shares a common humanity. While you may not understand it, the hope for a better life is understood all over the world. The desire to be treated fairly does not change depending on where you live, or what language you speak.*

Jesse gestured at the United Nations Headquarters.

— *That building represents the world under one roof. That is the reality of our existence. We live under one sky. We breathe the same air. We get warmth from the same sun. Government policy does not create human rights. Those rights came first! Governments exist to serve and protect those basic human rights. Those rights have nothing to do with how you vote in an election, where you live, the colour of your skin or the money in your wallet. Those rights are inalienable. I'll fight for those rights as long as I have air in my lungs and blood in my heart!*

Jesse knew the concert would finish soon. The Soviet delegation would exit onto the street, the young students spilling into the crowd, surrounding him. He could only smile at the thought.

Global Travel Company
926 Broadway
Same Day

Cuffed to the radiator in the back office, locked in the dark, Osip Feinstein had lost track of the time. He was now sweating from withdrawal sickness. Normally by this time he'd be smoking opium and his body's desire for the drug overpowered all other sensations, including the emotion any normal person would be feeling in these circumstances – fear. His trousers were soaked where he'd wet himself. His wrist was hurting as the metal dug into his skin. He could no longer move his fingers. The photographs of Jesse Austin and the Russian girl had been taken and Osip's initial impression of Agent Yates had proved to be correct: the man was extremely dangerous.

In his dazed state he became aware of someone outside the office. Slowly the door opened. He blinked at the light. Standing over him was the Soviet operative who'd given him the camera. As Osip's eyes adjusted to the light he saw that the man was holding a gun.

— *Trusting the FBI was a poor decision, an unexpected misjudgement considering how shrewd you have been in the past.*

Osip did not have the energy to resist — he did not even have the energy to fight for his life.

— *I've been running from you for thirty years.*

— *No more running, Osip.*

The man picked up a bottle of hydroquinone, one of the chemicals used to develop film, highly flammable, and poured it over Osip's clothes and face, splashing it down his throat and into his eyes. It was a powerful bleach and Osip's skin stung as painfully as though it were burning, even before the man had set him alight.

Manhattan
United Nations Headquarters
The General Assembly Hall
1st Avenue & East 44th Street
Same Day

The concert was over. The audience was applauding. The young American student beside Zoya was so excited by the standing ovation he squeezed her hand. Only twelve or thirteen years old, the boy was smiling. Right now he didn't care that she was Russian — they were friends, part of a winning team. The success was theirs equally. Belatedly she appreciated that her mother's plans were much more than about the quality of the performance. It had been Raisa's idea for everyone to wear the same clothes, American and Soviet students alike, and it had been her idea that they commission new music from international composers. The world's diplomatic elite was applauding the way in which the concert had navigated the many potential traps, offending no one and including everyone. Raisa had tiptoed between different sensitivities with the aplomb of a diplomat, and the diplomatic audience was showing their appreciation.

Zoya followed the young American boy offstage, applause still ringing in the Assembly Hall. Once in the corridor the students broke formation, hugging each other, thrilled with their success. Raisa was talking to the American school principal, both of them laughing in contrast to their cagey conversations during the dress rehearsal. Zoya was pleased for her mother. She deserved to be proud of her achievements and Zoya regretted being so cynical about the entire event, wishing that she'd been more supportive, just as Elena had been.

Glancing around the students, Zoya couldn't see her sister. She'd only been positioned a few students away in the line-up yet was nowhere to be seen. She began looking for her, nudging through the crowd now mixed with members of the audience streaming out from the main auditorium. More and more people were pushing into the corridor, keen to congratulate them, men she didn't recognize shaking her hand. She caught sight of Mikael Ivanov, the propaganda officer, cutting a path through the students, with apparently no interest in them despite the fact that they were being photographed.

Zoya followed him.

*

Flushed with success, Raisa eagerly tried to find her daughters. It was difficult to locate them since the corridors were so full. She stood on the spot, slowly turning around, searching the crowd. They were nowhere to be seen. A tingling anxiety rose up through her legs into her stomach; she paid no attention to the congratulations offered to her, ignored the very men and women she'd been sent here to impress. Pushing through the group she saw Zoya and felt relief. She hurried towards her.

— *Where's Elena?*

Zoya looked at her, pale with worry.

— *I don't know.*

Zoya raised her hand, pointing in front of her.

Raisa saw Mikael Ivanov with his back to her and the children, staring out of the large lobby windows at the street and the demonstration. Behind him photographers flashed their cameras at the children and yet he didn't turn around, his attention concentrated on the events outside. She walked up to him, grabbing his arm and turning him around, staring into his handsome face with such determined ferocity that he recoiled but she did not let go of his arm:

— *Where is Elena?*

He was about to lie: she could see the process as clearly as if she were regarding the mechanics of a watch.

— *Don't lie to me or I swear I'll start screaming in front of all these very important guests.*

He said nothing. She glanced at the demonstration and whispered:

— *If anything happens to her, I'll kill you.*

Manhattan
Outside the United Nations Headquarters
1st Avenue & East 44th Street
Same Day

Elena left the United Nations Headquarters without being stopped. Preparations had been made, the route arranged, passage through security, a blind spot in the building leading to an exit where she escaped without being questioned. As she stepped out she'd been handed a dark red coat with a hood to conceal her face. Nothing had been left to chance. She'd been siphoned off from the main group as soon as the concert was finished. Mikael was not going with her. It was important he was not involved in the photograph since the presence of a propaganda officer would undermine its authenticity. During the dress rehearsal the plans had changed. Mikael had explained it was impossible for a small group of students to join the demonstration: they could only manage to sneak Elena out. The American authorities had arranged for a coach to take the students doorstep to doorstep: straight from the United Nations to the hotel. FBI agents were going to drive it. Elena would have to go alone. The operation rested on her shoulders: a chance to redefine Communism in the eyes of the world, to create a modern progressive image that would be embodied in the photograph of a young Russian hand in hand with an older American, two nations, two generations bridged. The photograph would carry a powerful message of an inclusive ideology, reminding the world of the Soviet Union's ability to embrace different races and cultures across a vast geographical space. Finally Elena would step out from the shadow of her sister, proving to Mikael that she was worthy of his trust and love.

The exit from the United Nations was located up the street, away from the main body of the demonstration. To reach Jesse she would have to walk past the police line. Hood up over her head, she hurried towards the protests, terrified of being intercepted. She kept her face down, her heart beating fast, glancing up to see Jesse on the crate. He was oblivious of her approach, engrossed in his speech. The easiest way to reach him would be to climb over the barricade but, fearful the police officers would swoop and arrest her, she joined the main body of the crowd. Surrounded by people, she breathed deeply, dropping her hood, feeling far safer than she did exposed on the street. Pushing forward, making slow progress, bustled by the protestors, she observed that this wasn't a chaotic crowd but an attentive audience – they were facing the same way, listening to Jesse Austin, the tallest of the speakers and by far the most prominent, throwing his voice over the crowd. He had no microphone, no prepared notes in his hand. He was altogether a different person from the quiet, polite gentleman she'd met in his apartment. Addressing the crowd he was angry, powerful. Elena was captivated by his performance: the protest was elemental to him, as natural to him as taking a breath.

Compared to the stultified concert inside, the carefully

selected and inoffensive songs washed clean of any provocation or genuine desire for change, this was noisy and raucous and the better for it. Elena had never been part of a demonstration before. She'd never seen one in Moscow and couldn't imagine such a protest being allowed with the militia standing by idle. The New York police officers were concentrated in the street, not the sidewalk, seemingly having surrendered to the crowd, patrolling it, holding their distance, curiously disengaged. The substantial police presence didn't seem to worry Austin. On tiptoes, Elena watched as his arms moved with the rhythm of each sentence, his hand punctuating each phrase. He was wearing a white shirt, his sleeves rolled up as if speaking was an act of intense physical labour. His communication transcended words – there was magic to it. Compared with the moody introspection of Leo, his cynicism, Jesse Austin was most intensely alive individual she'd ever seen.

Moving forward was like swimming against the current, her small frame shunted from side to side, jostled by an audience that didn't want to part. No one wanted to lose position near Jesse. Elena didn't have much time. The authorities would soon realize that she was missing and when they caught up with her she would be punished. It didn't matter as long as she managed to pose with Jesse. From her pocket she pulled the Soviet flag. This was her opportunity to make a difference: her way of proving to Jesse how much his efforts were appreciated and how he would never be forgotten. She would embrace him, flag flapping behind them, achieving the photograph they desired – the two of them side by side. Abandoning good manners, Elena forced her way through, clawing the audience aside. Jesse saw her as she breached the front rank. He reached down and took her hand, pulling her up onto the crate. For a man his age he was remarkably strong.

Elena saw his wife for the first time. Mrs Austin did something she hadn't done earlier: she smiled.

At the sight of Elena on the crate, the crowd broke into a chorus of comments. Elena didn't understand what they were saying but she knew exactly what she had to do. She released the flag, its full length spreading behind her. Jesse caught it. For a second there was fear in his eyes; he understood its provocation. Elena wondered if he might even fold it away. But he let go of the flag, allowing it hang behind them. The audience surged forward, like the crash of a wave against the crate. There were multiple flashes of cameras across the crowd, journalists asking questions, furious protestors and delighted supporters. Jesse cut his hand through the air, as if his arm were a scythe:

— *I want to introduce you all to a friend of mine. She's a young student from the Soviet Union!*

He was forced to raise his voice as the audience roared, some in approval, some in disgust. The audience were scandalized, unable to believe the scene before them. Elena couldn't help but laugh. Austin lifted her hand, still gripping the flag, into the air.

— *We could not be from more different backgrounds. Yet we are united in our desire for equality. We were born on different continents yet we believe in the same things! Fairness! Justice!*

Cameras continued to flash. Elena was euphoric with her success. The moment was everything she'd hoped for.

The deafening noise brought Jesse Austin and the entire crowd to silence, a noise like a clap of thunder, so loud and sudden it was as if the entire island of Manhattan had split in two. The crate shook. Vibrations travelled through her leg. Stunned silence remained after the sound stopped and this was as shocking and strange as sunlight breaking through the night sky. The silence lasted no longer than a second, replaced by a painful ringing that seemed to grow louder and louder until her ears hurt. She smelt smoke. She smelt metal. Some of the demonstrators were standing dumbstruck, motionless and frozen. Others had their mouths wide open. Elena slowly lowered her arms – the Soviet flag was gone, it lay on the sidewalk, spread out like a picnic blanket. Austin was standing beside her with one hand on his chest as though the national anthem were playing. He moved nearer to Elena, closer, leaning into her, about to whisper some secret. But he didn't say a word, falling, knocking into her, toppling like a tree, a giant ancient oak. They both fell to the sidewalk, pushed in different directions. Austin clattered into the steel barriers, while Elena fell into the protestors, her head against someone's chest, grabbing on to clothes to slow her descent, before hitting the sidewalk.

Elena lay among the demonstrators' feet, kicked as panic took hold and the crowd stampeded. She wrapped her arms around her head and watched through the feet and legs as Mrs Austin dropped to her husband. The crowd broke free of the confines, pouring onto the street, smashing down more of the barricades. A handmade banner landed on the ground near her. She stood up, only to be kicked down to her knees. She tried again, her ears still ringing, managed to get to her feet. From the opposite direction the police marched forward, batons raised, protestors smashing into them.

Elena limped forward before falling beside Jesse. His white shirt had turned red, the colour spreading at speed, conquering every visible patch of white. Through the ringing in her ears, she heard Mrs Austin cry out:

— *Help us!*

The police were forming a circle around the scene of the crime. Only a few demonstrators remained.

Someone took hold of Elena's face, looking into her eyes.

— *Elena! Are you hurt?*

The woman was speaking Russian.

*

Checking her daughter, Raisa couldn't see blood on Elena's shirt or see any sign of injury. She pulled off the red coat she was wearing, a coat Raisa had never seen before. There was something heavy in the pocket. She reached in, taking hold of a cold metal handle. It was a gun.

She knew immediately, and without any doubt, that this was the gun that had shot Jesse Austin.

Manhattan
Bellevue Hospital Center
462 1st Avenue
Same Day

Clutching the sides of the sink, Anna was certain that if she let go she'd fall to the floor. Each breath was snatched, not a natural rhythm, but ripped from the air, as she repeated the six words, unable to reconcile that they were true.

Jesse is dead.
I am alive.

Tentatively lifting her right hand from the sink, she reached out and turned the tap, running cold water. She cupped her palm under the water – filling it and raising it to her face, water leaking through her fingers. By the time it reached her face her palm was empty save for a few cold drops that she pressed against her forehead. They ran down her face, collecting in her eyes, like tears, had she been able to cry.

She tried speaking the words aloud, wondering if that would make them real to her.

— Jesse is dead. I am alive.

It was impossible to imagine her life without him, impossible to imagine waking up tomorrow without him beside her, going to work and coming home to their empty apartment. They had survived adversities together and enjoyed success together. They'd travelled the entire country together and shared a cramped space in Harlem. No matter what they'd done, they'd done it together.

It had taken the authorities nearly fifty years but finally they'd got him. There might not have been a length of rope tied around his neck, they might not have killed in him on the edge of a forest, and though the killers couldn't show their faces and proudly pat each other on the back, make no mistake, it was a lynching just the same, complete with photographs and audience. She would not cry, not yet. She would not mourn his death as a widow weeping by his graveside. Jesse had taught her better than that. Jesse deserved better than that.

Feeling her body come under some semblance of control, she straightened up, shutting off the cold water. She walked to the door of the restroom, opened it. In the corridor, in the distance, she saw the police officers waiting to interview her. She turned in the opposite direction, knowing exactly what she had to do.

Manhattan
17th Police Precinct
167 East 51st Street
Same Day

Raisa had foreseen the danger, spoken to Leo, heard his confirmation that the danger was real and then wished the threat away.
For many years she'd trusted in nothing, doubted every promise,
and presumed that all interactions were based around self-interest
and deceit. It had proved an exhausting, corrosive existence but it
had worked – she'd survived while the regime had murdered
many thousands. However, it was not a state of mind, nor a way of
life, that she'd wanted for her daughters. She'd not taught them to
lie when asked their name by a stranger. She'd not drilled into
them the need for caution and suspicion as a matter of routine.
She'd not wanted them to second-guess every display of affection
and interrogate every friendship. In so doing she'd failed as a
mother and she'd failed as a teacher. Just because Leo had left his
past behind did not mean those dark forces no longer existed. He'd
changed. But she'd been wrong to believe that the world had
changed too.

Watched over by a female police officer, Raisa refused to sit down, standing in the corner of the cell, her back against the wall, her arms crossed. She'd been given no news of Elena. They'd been taken into custody in separate cars, pulled apart in the chaotic aftermath of the murder. In the few seconds that Raisa had been able to hold her daughter, Elena had been a little girl again, the girl she'd adopted twelve years ago – lost and confused and seeking protection from a world she didn't understand. She'd buried her face in Raisa's shoulder, hands wet with Jesse Austin's blood, and wept like a child. Raisa had wanted to say everything was going to be OK but it wasn't, not this time, and she couldn't manage even a comforting lie, too stunned at events to tell Elena that she loved her. It would be the first thing she said the moment they next met, even if it was for a second. Raisa didn't know the details of the plot Elena had become embroiled in. Whatever it was, she could only have been seduced by the promise of a better world. With her quiet optimism, she was like Leo, a dreamer who'd ended up with blood on his hands. Raisa's heart broke to think that her idealistic young girl would never be the same, no matter what she was told, or how she was reassured. Leo would help her. He had gone through the same process – he would know what to say. They just needed to get home.

The door opened and the agent from the hotel, Yates, stepped into the room. For a man who'd presided over a security disaster, he seemed peculiarly satisfied. There could only be one interpretation: he was involved somehow. An older woman stood beside him – she was not in uniform. She spoke first, in perfect Russian.

— *You're to come with us.*

— *Where is my daughter?*

The woman translated to Yates. He said:

— *She's being questioned.*

Raisa followed them out, saying in Russian:

— My daughter did not kill anyone.

The woman translated and Yates listened but offered no response, leading them into the main office – an open space with desks and chairs, and many people, mostly police officers, phones ringing, people shouting over each other, pushing past each other.

— Where am I being taken?

After hearing the translation, Yates said:

— You're being moved.

— Is my daughter also being moved?

To this question she received no reply. Yates was busy talking to another man.

Waiting, disorientated and afraid, Raisa peered about the room, feeling dizzy. She was about to ask for a glass of water when, among the crowd, she glimpsed a woman – the only black woman in the room. She was wearing civilian clothes. There was a uniformed officer by her side. He was talking to her but she wasn't paying him any attention. She was concentrated on them, staring towards them with startling intensity. Belatedly, Yates also saw the woman and reacted strongly, shouting orders. The uniformed officer grabbed the woman's arm, trying to pull her away. She shook him free, raising her other arm. She was holding a gun.

Raisa had seen the woman before, by the body of Jesse Austin, screaming out to the sky for help when no help would come. She recognized love and pain in the woman's expression, love turned to anger. As the gun flashed explosions of white light, she wished that the last thing she'd told Elena was that she didn't blame her for anything and that she loved her very much.

Harlem
Bradhurst
8th Avenue & West 139th Street
Nelson's Restaurant
Next Day

None of the staff were working, none of the customers were eating, all were turned towards the radio, listening to the news broadcast. Nelson was standing, hand on the volume dial, turned up as loud as it could go. Several of the women were crying. Several of the men were crying. In contrast, the voice on the radio was clipped and without emotion.

— *Last night the once-popular singer Jesse Austin was murdered, shot dead in public. The suspect is a Russian woman, a Communist, suspected of being his lover. A source inside the NYPD reports that the Russian woman told police officers after the murder that she shot Mr Austin because he failed to live up to his promise to marry her and rescue her from Soviet Russia. Mr Austin is already married. The tragic affair did not end there. Last night his wife, in revenge for the murder, took a gun and entered the police precinct, where she shot the Russian woman. After killing the suspect Mrs Austin turned the gun on herself ...*

Nelson picked the radio off the counter, pulling it from the power socket, raising it above his head. The customers watched. He reconsidered, put it down. After a moment, he addressed the room.

— *Anyone want to listen to those lies, they can do it someplace else.*

He walked into his office, returning with a large glass jar that he placed on the counter by the cash register.

— *I'm setting up a collection. Not for the funeral, this isn't a time for flowers and Jesse wouldn't want them anyway. I'm going to hire someone to figure out who really murdered Jesse and Anna. We need lawyers. Private detectives. I can't speak for you. But I need to know. I have to know.*

He took out his wallet and emptied it into the jar.

By the end of the morning the jar was full, waitresses contributing their tips, customers donating too. As Nelson counted out the collection, noting it down in a ledger, he heard one of Jesse's songs. He left his office to find his customers and waitresses standing by the window, looking out onto the street where the music was coming from. He crossed the restaurant, opened the door and stepped outside. A young man called William whose parents Nelson knew well was standing on top of a crate, singing one of Jesse's songs. He didn't have any music in his hands. He knew the words by heart.

People stopped in the street, gathering around the crate, forming an audience. Men held their hats in their hands. Children paused from their games and stood, listening, staring up at the young man.

I'm only a folk singer
And that's enough for me
I'm only a folk singer
Dreaming one day we'll all be free.

225

Regarding the audience, Nelson knew that with a little effort he could pull together a crowd of thousands – he could address the crowd himself, he had plenty to say, maybe not with Jesse's voice but he'd find his own. Remembering what Jesse used to answer when asked why he'd risked so much, Nelson finally understood. Running a restaurant, even a successful restaurant, just wasn't enough.

ONE WEEK LATER

USSR
29 Kilometres North-West of Moscow
Sheremetyevo Airport
4 August 1965

Frol Panin watched the heavy rain across the empty runway. The weather had broken and brooding, angry clouds had replaced blue sky and a blazing sun. At the side of the runway the soil had cracked in the weeks of heat, grass turned yellow, so dry that the rain ran off the surface. As the weather deteriorated air-traffic control considered diverting the incoming flight. They were being overly cautious and Panin had pushed back against the idea. Extensive preparations for the passengers had been made. Unless there was an emergency, they would land here.

The returning students couldn't know the extent to which the murder of Jesse Austin had become news in the Soviet Union and abroad. Internationally the story was a sensation. At home, a less hysterical and more measured approach had been taken, with *Pravda* casting doubt over the official version of events without actually stating them to be false. All the same, these young men and women needed careful briefing and help adjusting after the shock of the past few days. The airport was busy with

KGB agents, psychologists and propaganda officers. Unlike the joyous departure ceremony, there were to be no celebrations for their return, no band, no colourful ribbons, no alcohol and only a very limited number of journalists. Family and friends had not been allowed to come despite their requests. The airport was sealed off.

At sixty-one years old Frol Panin's hair had turned imperial silver-white, like a well-barbered wizard. His frame was trim. The lines in his face were less like wrinkles and more like victory notches, each carved after one of his many grand career triumphs. His most recent had been acquired after working closely with Chairman Brezhnev to oust the ageing and increasingly erratic Khrushchev. In the end it had proved a quiet accomplishment since Khrushchev had gone without a fight, depressed at his demotion. The former farmer had not lost his life but wisely retired into rural obscurity, an appropriate end since that had been his beginning. Panin was a political kingmaker, one of the most important men in the Kremlin. Even so, he was here, on a seemingly trivial errand, prepared to sit and wait for the return of a airliner and its passengers, becoming personally involved in an operation that he'd had no hand in, or awareness of. As he waited, he made a note to review all the protocols of SERVICE.A, an intelligence department he'd overlooked. Clearly their ability to provoke had been underestimated.

Agents and officials gravitated around him, providing information, answering requests and queries. Even air-traffic-control officers came to him, as though he had some sway with the clouds. His bodyguard and driver stood behind him occasionally asking if there was anything he needed and bringing fresh cups of tea as the plane became increasingly delayed. He was here for the sake of one man – Leo Demidov. They had worked together in the past and, feeling a curious sense of loyalty, perhaps it might even be termed affection – emotions he felt rarely – Panin had decided this particular task should fall upon him.

The sky was so dark and the rain so heavy Panin couldn't see the airliner until it was a few hundred metres above the ground. The wings wobbled as it adjusted position. The landing was uneventful. He stood up as it taxied to a standstill. His driver, a conscientious young man, was already holding an umbrella.

Standing under the umbrella, Panin surveyed the delegation as they disembarked. One of the first to step down was Mikael Ivanov, the propaganda officer assigned to this ill-thought-out operation. A handsome young man, he seemed nervous as he slowly descended the stairs, perhaps expecting to be arrested as soon as he touched the tarmac. He noticed Panin and though he did not recognize him, he feared the worst. Panin stepped forward.

— *Mikael Ivanov?*

Rain streaming off his face, he nodded.

— *Yes?*

— *My name is Frol Panin. You've been reassigned. You're to leave the city immediately. I have a car waiting to take you to the train station where there is a departure this evening. I don't know where you'll be taken, you'll find out on the train. A new post has been arranged for you. There is no time to return home, no time to pack. You can buy whatever you need once you arrive.*

Mikael Ivanov was afraid and exhausted, unsure whether this was an arrest in other guise, or merely a demotion. Panin explained:

— *Ivanov, you do not know me. But I know what you have done and I know Leo Demidov, Elena's father. When he is told what happened, he will seek you out, and he will kill you. I am quite sure of this. You must leave the city immediately. It is important I do not know where you end up because Demidov will ask me and he will know if I'm lying. For the same reason if you tell anyone, any of your family, he'll find you. Your only chance is to do as I say and to disappear, without a word. Of course, it is your decision. Good luck.*

Panin patted him on the arm, leaving him standing dumbfounded in the rain.

Staring up at the disembarking students, he compared their reactions to the news footage of them as they boarded the outbound flight, bathed in sunlight, smiling, waving to the cameras, excited with the prospect of flying transatlantic in an airliner. They were tired and scared. He waited for the girls he was supposed to meet, girls he hadn't seen since they were very young – Zoya and Elena.

Seeing them step down, Panin moved forward, his driver following so that the umbrella remained in position over his head as he intercepted the two girls.

— *My name is Frol Panin. You don't know me. I'm here to take you home. I am a friend of your father. I knew your mother only a little. I'm very sorry for your loss. She was a remarkable woman. This is a terrible tragedy. But come, hurry, let us get out of the rain. My car is nearby.*

The two girls looked at him blankly. They were sick with grief. The younger girl, Elena, peered out across the runway, blinking away the rain, as Mikael Ivanov was led away to his car. He did not look back. Elena was pained. Panin was amazed that even now, after everything that had happened, she still loved him and still believed he must have loved her.

In the car Panin briefed the girls, outlining the reaction to events in New York and the way in which those events had been portrayed, accurately or not. The American version, printed in newspapers from New York to San Francisco, London to Tokyo, was easy to sell to the public, containing drama and sensation. The story depicted the beautiful Raisa Demidova having an affair with the womanizer Jesse Austin. The relationship dated from 1950. They'd met during one of Jesse's tours. He'd visited her school and invited her to a concert performed in a factory warehouse. There was even film footage of the two together, Soviet propaganda film, with Raisa congratulating him at the end of the concert. She'd fallen in love and begged him to rescue her from the Soviet Union. They'd had a sexual encounter, incidental to him but life-changing for her. She was obsessed with him and had corresponded regularly, going so far as to organize a mass letter-writing session by the students in her school when she'd heard of his troubles with the American authorities. Elena interrupted at this point, exclaiming:

— *It's not true!*

Panin gestured for her to remain silent. He had only claimed this was the truth as the world knew it. In this truth, Raisa was a romantic figure besotted with Jesse Austin, convinced they were in the midst of a perfect love affair separated by nations. For Jesse it was no more than a forgotten night of sexual gratification. When she'd heard of the Soviet delegation going to New York, she'd forced her way onto the tour to reunite with him. Her dream was to claim asylum, live with him, abandoning her hated husband, Leo, who happened to be a secret-police officer. When she'd visited Jesse in Harlem they'd enjoyed a second sexual encounter. There was a photograph of Raisa Demidova, standing beside an unmade bed, crumpled sheets, dwarfed by the figure of Jesse Austin. Elena exclaimed again:

— *I was there, not Raisa!*

Impatient, Panin suggested that Elena appreciate that this version was the one created by the American authorities to defuse the situation. Continuing with the events, he explained that during this meeting between Jesse and Raisa, he'd told her that he would never leave his wife and she would have to return to Russia, to her husband. Consumed by jealousy and despair, Raisa had purchased a gun. Outside the United Nations, she'd shot Jesse Austin dead. She'd been caught holding the gun.

Elena could control herself no longer.

— *It's a lie! It's all a lie!*

Panin nodded, it was a lie. But it was the version of events that the United States had released to the press: it was the version of events they were demanding the Soviet Union support. The Soviet Union had agreed without condition. A lone shooter, no conspiracy and no greater powers at work — a story of unrequited love and a woman's fury at being spurned. The remaining peace concerts had been cancelled. Frol Panin and many others in the Kremlin had worked hard in order that the delegation might return without too much of a delay. Finally, the students had been released and returned home. There was no news on when the body of Raisa Demidova might be returned.

In the back of limousine, observing the two girls absorb the narrative crafted around them, Panin addressed them on a separate matter.

— *You must understand that Leo is a changed man. The news of his wife's death has . . .*

Panin searched for the correct word.

— *Disturbed him. I'm not referring to the normal expression of grief. His reaction has gone far beyond that. He is not the man you remember. To be honest, I'm hoping that your return might help ground him.*

The older girl, Zoya, spoke for the first time.

— *What can we tell him?*

— *He will want to know everything that happened. He is trained to detect when he is being lied to. He is certain that the official version of events is a lie. Which of course it is. There is no question in his mind that there has been a conspiracy. You must decide for yourselves what you tell him. I place no limits on what you may talk to him about. Maybe you, Elena, are afraid of telling him the truth. But in his current state of mind, I would be more afraid of telling him a lie.*

Moscow
Novye Cheremushki
Khrushchev's Slums
Apartment 1312
Same Day

The elevator was still broken, and forced to walk up thirteen flights of stairs, Elena began to feel weak, her legs trembling. Coming up the final flight she could see their door. She stopped, unable to go any further, panicking at the thought of the man inside the apartment. How had Leo changed? She sat on the step.

— *I can't do it.*

Leo had never hurt them, never raised his hand in anger or even shouted at them. Yet she was scared. There had always been something about him that had unsettled her. From time to time she would catch him sitting on his own, looking down at his hands as if wondering if they belonged to him. She would catch him staring out of the window, his mind elsewhere, and even though everyone drifted into daydreams with him it wasn't idle thoughts. Darkness collected around him like clumps of static dust. If he realized he was being watched he would force a smile but it would be brittle, on the surface only, and the darkness remained. The thought of Leo without Raisa frightened Elena.

Zoya whispered:

— *He loves you. Remember that.*

— *Maybe he only loved us because of Raisa?*

— *That's not true.*

— *Maybe he only wanted children because of her? What if everything we love about him was because of her?*

— *You know that's not true.*

Zoya did not sound entirely convinced. Frol Panin crouched down.

— *I'm going to be with you. There's nothing to worry about.*

They reached the landing. Frol Panin knocked on the door. Despite neither trusting Panin nor knowing anything about him, Elena was glad he was here. He was calm and measured. Physically he was no match for Leo; however, she couldn't imagine it would be easy for anyone to ignore his instructions – they were spoken with such authority. The three of them waited. Footsteps could be heard. The door opened.

The man standing before them was unrecognizable as their father. His eyes were swollen with grief and appeared to be inhumanly large. His cheeks were sallow, sucked inwards. There was insanity in his movements. His hands would clench together for no reason, as though he were about to pray, then separate and return to his side. When he looked in a particular direction, rather than turn his head he'd turn his entire body. He glanced over their shoulders into the corridor and the stairway, perhaps in the hope that somehow Raisa would be there, his enormous eyes expectant despite everything he'd been told. This pitiful hope was so painful to Elena that she began to cry, having not yet said a word. They might have stood there for some time, for Leo seemed incapable of speaking. Panin took charge, leading them inside.

Disorientated by the long flight, the time difference, the emotions of the past week and this reunion, Elena briefly wondered if she'd walked into a different apartment. The furniture had been moved, their beds stacked up, chairs pushed aside as if to make space for a dance. The kitchen table had been positioned in the centre of the room directly under the light. The tabletop was covered with clippings from Soviet papers about the murder of Jesse Austin. There were sheets of intricate handwritten notes, photographs of Jesse. There were photographs of Raisa. A chair had been placed opposite the table. The set-up was unmistakable. It was ready for an interrogation. Leo's voice was scratched and hoarse:

— *Tell me everything.*

Fingers knotted tightly together again, Leo listened with ferocious concentration as Elena recounted events in New York. She became emotional, muddling some of the points, confusing names and offering rambling justifications. At such points Leo interrupted, asking for nothing more than the facts, requesting clarification and demonstrating a pedantic desire for exact details. He didn't lose his temper, he didn't shout, and this absence of emotion was perturbing. Something has died inside of him, Elena thought, as she reached the end of her account. Leo said:

— *Please give me your diary.*

Elena looked up, confused. Leo repeated the request:

— *Your diary, give it to me.*

Elena looked up at her sister, then back at Leo.

— *My diary?*

— *Your diary, yes, where is it?*

— *Everything was confiscated by the Americans, they took our clothes, our suitcases, everything. My diary was in it.*

Leo stood up, pacing the room.

— *I should have read it.*

He shook his head angry with himself. Elena didn't understand.

— *My diary?*

— *I found it before you left, under your mattress. I put it back. It would have contained information about this man Mikael Ivanov. Am I right? You would've speculated on his feelings for you. You would have detailed what he'd asked you to do. You were in love. You were blind. I would have seen the relationship was a fraud.*

Leo suddenly stopped walking, raising his hands to his face.

— *If I'd read the diary I could've figured it all out. I could've stopped the whole thing. I could've stopped you from going. Raisa would be alive now. If I'd just behaved as an agent. I thought it would be wrong to go through your things. But that is who I am. That is what I do. Those are my only skills. I could have saved Raisa's life.*

He was speaking so fast his words were running into each other.

— *You love him, this man, Mikael Ivanov, who worked for this secret department? He told you his motivation was equality and justice. Elena, he didn't love you. Love was how you were manipulated. Some people want money. Some people want power. You wanted love. That was your price. You were bought. It was planned. The love was a lie, the most obvious and simple of tricks.*

Elena wiped away her tears, feeling a wave of anger for the first time.

— *You can't be sure of that. You don't know what happened.*

— *I am sure. I've planned operations like this myself. What's worse, they knew that only a person who wasn't aware of the plot could have persuaded Jesse Austin to attend the concert. They needed someone in love. They needed someone full of love and optimism. Otherwise, Jesse Austin would have sensed a trick. He would have sensed if you were lying to him, or if you didn't really believe the things you were saying. He would never have attended that concert if you hadn't asked him to.*

Elena stood up.

— *I know it's my fault! I know!*

Leo shook his head, lowering his voice.

— *No, I blame myself. I taught you nothing. I let you into this world naked and naive and this is what happened. Raisa and I wanted to shelter you from those things – lies, deceit, trickery – but they are the truths of our existence. I failed you. I failed Raisa. I had only one thing to offer her, protection, and I couldn't even provide that.*

Leo addressed Frol Panin.

— *Where is Ivanov now?*

— *I know that right now he is on a train. I don't know where that train is heading.*

Leo paused, sensing this was the truth but suspicious of it all the same.

— *Who killed my wife?*

— *To the world, the answer is Anna Austin.*

— *That is a lie.*

— *We don't know what happened.*

Leo became angry.

— *We know that the official version of the events is a lie! We know that much.*

Frol Panin nodded.

— *Yes, that version seems unlikely. However, to avoid a diplomatic crisis we have agreed not to contradict the American version of events.*

— *Who killed Jesse Austin? Was it us? Was it the Americans? It was us, wasn't it?*

— As far as I know, the plan was merely to have Jesse Austin turn up outside the United Nations. The hope was that he would be arrested, dragged off by the police, and if one of the students could become embroiled in the ruckus that would be useful from a propaganda point of view. It was a plot conjured up by a department that is desperate to make some inroads into the anti-Communist sentiment that prevails in the United States. They wanted to repair Jesse Austin's career. They wanted him to be famous again.

Leo began pacing the room again.

— I knew all along it would be impossible for you not to try something. You couldn't merely stage a concert. You had to go further. You had to do more.

— It was an ill-conceived plan that has gone badly wrong.

— Let me go to New York. Let me investigate.

— Leo, my friend, listen to me: what you ask is impossible.

— I must find out who murdered my wife. I must find them and kill them.

— Leo, you will never be allowed to go. It will not happen. There is nothing you can do.

Leo shook his head.

— There's nothing else! This is all that's left for me to do! I promise, I will find her killer. I will find the person responsible. I will find them.

Same Day

Leo had no clear sense of how long he'd been sitting on the roof of the apartment block – several hours at least. After Panin had left, he and the girls had put the room back as it should be, resembling a home, the two beds side by side. Leo had begun to make dinner but abruptly abandoned his efforts, leaving the food uncooked. The only place he could think to go was the roof.

Teenagers sometimes came here to kiss and fool around if they couldn't find anywhere else. Tonight, in the pouring rain, it was empty. Leo did not feel cold, even with his clothes soaked through. He could see out across the city, the night lights of Moscow smudged by rainfall. He stood up, walking to the edge of the building and looked down at the drop. He remained there for many minutes, trying to reason why he should step back. He remembered his promise. Stepping away from the edge, he turned his back on the city, heading downstairs to an apartment he'd once thought of as home.

EIGHT YEARS LATER

Soviet–Finnish Border
Soviet Checkpoint
760 Kilometres North-West of Moscow
240 Kilometres North-East of Helsinki
New Year's Day 1973

The rucksack belonged to a man shot trying to cross the border into Finland. Despite it being a savage winter with the snow in the forests lying waist deep, the man had attempted the perilous crossing perhaps hoping that the weather and near-permanent darkness would make it easier to pass undetected. To trespass into this heavily controlled area by accident or design was considered an attempt to defect to the West, an act of treason. The soldiers patrolling, many on skis through the forest, were instructed to shoot to kill. There would be wide-reaching repercussions if a traitor managed to slip through and seek asylum abroad, revealing classified information about the Soviet Union to its enemies. On a personal level, Eli Romm, in charge of this zone, would be called before a tribunal and would almost certainly lose his job and possibly his freedom, accused of neglect or, worse, of wilfully allowing an act of sabotage.

Eli examined the contents of the rucksack. It contained basic
provisions: water, bread and cured meats. There was a change of
clothes, dark in colour, a thick wool blanket, several boxes of
matches, medical supplies, a sharp hunting knife and a steel
cup – standard outdoor fare and of little interest. Eli tipped the
rucksack upside down. Nothing else fell out. He felt the lining,
running his finger along the stitches, convinced it held further
evidence. He was right. There was a lump in the material, a
secret pocket. Cutting through the material, ripping off the
patch, he discovered the pocket contained several thin gold
coins, bound in plastic, proof that this was a serious attempt at
defection. Extensive preparations had been made – gold was
nearly impossible to obtain for an ordinary citizen, the inference
was that a foreign country was involved and the man was a professional spy.

The secret compartment contained more than gold. Romm
found two photographs. Expecting them to be classified he was
surprised that they appeared to be worthless from an intelligence
point of view, photographs of two women in their late twenties,
taken on their wedding day. There were also a series of papers. He
opened them, his puzzlement growing as he discovered that they
were a mass of carefully pressed, faded Soviet newspaper clippings
detailing the shooting of a man called Jesse Austin, a once popular Communist singer, murdered in New York by his lover, a
woman called Raisa Demidova. The murder had taken place some
years ago, the articles dated back to 1965. There were extensive
handwritten notes on the articles, in small neat writing,
thoughts on the case, with a list of names, people the man wanted
to speak to. Evidently from these notes the ambition was to reach
New York, the United States – the main adversary. The apparent
motivation was so peculiar that Eli wondered if the papers were in

some sort of code. He would have to report the matter directly to Moscow, to the highest authorities.

The prisoner was in a cell downstairs – shot but not killed by a soldier on guard patrol. After firing from long range with a sniper rifle, the guard had pursued but failed to find the wounded man. Somehow the man had struggled on through the snow. The guard had returned to base, bringing out reinforcements to search the area. Eventually, surrounded by dogs, the man was lucky to be apprehended alive. His injury, a single bullet wound, was not life-threatening and he had received rudimentary treatment at the barracks. The man's tenacity, the fashion in which he'd evaded capture for several hours against overwhelming odds, and the organized, disciplined contents of his bag suggested a military background. He'd refused to speak to the guards or to give his name.

Eli entered the cell, regarding the man seated on the chair. His back was bandaged: the bullet had entered his right shoulder. There was an untouched plate of food in front of him. His face was pale from loss of blood. A blanket had been placed over his shoulders. Eli did not condone torture. His only concern was preserving the integrity of the border and in so doing, his own career. With the newspaper cuttings and the photographs he sat down in front of the man, holding the papers under the man's line of vision. They brought him to life. Eli asked:

— *What is your name?*

The man did not respond. Eli pointed out:

— *You face execution. It is in your interest to talk to us.*

The man didn't seem to be paying any attention, staring at the papers, at the image of the singer Jesse Austin shot on the streets of New York. Eli rustled the papers.

— *What is the importance of this?*

The prisoner reached out and grabbed hold of the papers – his fingers clamped tight around the scraps. Eli sensed that if he didn't let go the man would rip them from his hands. Curious, he released his grip and watched the man gather the papers together in front of him, treating them with as much reverence as a treasure map.

SEVEN YEARS LATER

Greater Province of Kabul
Lake Qargha
9 Kilometres West of Kabul
22 March 1980

With his back to Kabul, Leo stepped into the lake fully clothed, plunging up to his knees and continuing to walk, his khaki trousers bleeding Saturn-rings of red dust onto the water. In front of him the snow-capped teeth of the Koh-e-Qrough mountain range bit into a pale blue sky. The spring sun was bright but not yet strong enough to temper the freezing river waters flush with mountain snowmelt. He knew the lake should feel cold as he raked his fingers through the emerald-green surface yet as the water level rose and flowed over the hip of his trousers he felt wonderfully warm. Were he to trust his body he would've sworn that these were tropical waters as pleasant as the sun on his cracked, tanned skin. He didn't raise his arms, allowing them to sink into the lake, dragging behind him as he walked. Soon the water was up to his shoulders – he was on the cusp of the shallows, his feet arriving at the ledge where the depth increased sharply. Another step and he'd sink beneath the surface, the stones in his pockets weighing him down, easing him to the bottom where he'd come to rest, seated on the silt bed. At the borderline he waited, the water lapping at his top lip, close to his nose, the surface trembling with each slow breath.

The opium was thick in his blood. Until it thinned the drug would cocoon him against the cold, and everything else – the disappointment of the life he was living and the regrets of the life he'd left behind. Right now, in this moment, he was devoid of troubles, connected to the world by nothing more than a thread. He felt no emotion, just contentment, not in the form of happiness but contentment as the absence of pain, the absence of dissatisfaction – an exquisite emptiness of feeling. Opium had made him hollow, scooping out the bitterness and reproach. That he'd vowed revenge, promised justice and achieved nothing did not upset him. His failures had been banished by the drug, a temporary exile, held at bay, ready to return when the opium's effects wore off.

The water lapping at his lips urged him to continue.

One step further.

Why settle for a simulation of emptiness dependent on narcotics when the real thing was so close? Another step and he would be at the bottom of the lake, a trail of bubbles from his lips to the emerald surface the only trace of his existence. The stones in his pockets joined the chorus of whispers, urging him to take the final step.

Leo did not heed their call, remaining motionless. No matter how many times he stood here, no matter how sure he was that today was the day he would cross over, he could not bring himself to cut the thread that joined him to the world. He could not take the final step.

The opium began to thin. His senses reconnected with reality, coming together like planets realigning. The water was cold. He was cold. He shivered, reaching into his pockets and taking out the smooth stones, allowing them to drop beside him, feeling the vibrations as they struck the bed of the lake. He turned away from the mountains, churning the water, and slowly returned to shore, wading back towards the city of Kabul.

Greater Province of Kabul
City of Kabul
Karta-i-Seh District
Darulaman Boulevard
Same Day

By the time Leo arrived at his apartment the sun had set and his clothes had dried, dripping a trail in the dust behind him as he'd cycled back from the lake. With the opium's concentration in decline, running down like the sands of an hourglass, the feelings of failure and melancholy began to circulate in his system, a virus of the mind that had only temporarily been suppressed. He was isolated from his daughters, alone in the city; his only companion was the memories of his wife, thoughts that did not exist without the knowledge that her murderer had gone unpunished. The muscles across his back tightened at the recollection of his humiliating attempt to reach New York, the bullet scar in his shoulder stung as though the wound was raw, his brow furrowed as the details of the case surfaced in his mind. Why had Jesse Austin been shot and how was it connected to his wife? What was the truth behind that night? A dangerous restlessness began to bubble within him – he could not let the matter stand and yet he was further from the truth than ever before. Opium had become not an answer but merely a way of pushing these thoughts back for twelve or so hours.

Not bothering to change his clothes, he collapsed onto his bed, a thin mattress in the middle of the room. This apartment was unwelcoming and functional. He'd refused accommodation in government residences where officials lived safe behind guarded gates and barbed-wire fences, in newly built residential blocks where every apartment was fitted with air conditioning with back-up diesel generators should the electricity fail, which it often did. He never ate with the officers in canteens that served imported, vacuum-packed Russian food, nor did he socialize in the bars established for homesick Soviet soldiers. He existed like a distant moon, in orbit of the occupation but rarely seen, occasionally passing close enough to remind everyone of his existence before spinning into the depths of space on a lonely, elliptical trajectory.

Ignoring protocol, he'd found this apartment himself, agreeing the rent directly with the landlord rather than using the official Soviet channels. He had one criterion – it should be impossible to be mistaken for, or resemble in any way, the home he once shared with his wife and daughters. For this reason he liked the fact that he was near speakers erected outside a tea room that broadcast the muezzin's call to prayer, a sound that filled his apartment, a sound that he'd never shared with his family. His intention was to crowd his life with things that didn't remind him of Raisa – to make his existence so foreign there was nothing that flashbacked to the life he'd lost. The large windows opened to views of the city and the surrounding mountains, a view that could not have been more different from Moscow. Even the layout of the apartment was peculiar: a single room large enough to serve as a bedroom, living area and kitchen. It was imperative there not be separate rooms. Closed doors played havoc with his imagination. His first apartment in Bala Hissar, the centre of old Kabul, had been designed for a traditional Islamic family with a back room intended for a wife and daughters. While living there Leo often heard the muffled sound of Raisa's voice. He'd run to the door and throw it open only to reveal an empty room. Another night he'd heard the sound of Elena's voice, then Zoya, both voices bringing him running. No matter how far-fetched the notion that his family might be together again and living with him, the imagined sound of their voices would bring him checking on empty rooms, sometimes three or four times a night. Insanity was not far away. His temporary solution had been to unscrew the doors, set up mirrors in the hallways so that he could see the empty space at all times. He'd begun looking for a more suitable apartment.

Leo retrieved his pipe: a thin wood tube with a small steel pot roughly two-thirds of the way down from the mouthpiece. There were crude carvings around the rim, a blackened interior where the opium burned. Though it had never been mentioned directly, his addiction was no secret to his superiors. A system of tacit consent allowed soldiers and officials any pleasures accessible to them, a form of compensation to supplement wages that could never be high enough to offset the dangers of Afghanistan. For Leo, opium had nothing to do with pleasure, it was a continuation of the logic he applied to his apartment, making his body foreign and quite unlike the body that had slept beside Raisa nearly every night of his life for fifteen years – an addiction, certainly, but also a strategy to cope with his grief.

He hastened to his stash, breaking off a pea-sized amount, his fingers fumbling, the opium falling to the dusty floor. On his knees, he picked it up, regarding the dust-covered lump. He blew it. The dust remained: the opium was sticky. It didn't matter. He placed it in the cup of the steel holder and lit a candle, impatiently waiting for the flame to take. Opium did not burn easily like tobacco and required a constant source of heat. Lying on the bed, on his stomach, he positioned the steel pot over the candle, eyes on the opium, hungry for it to melt in the flame and the smoke to travel up the pipe. The opium began to burn, the shape of the lump changing. He inhaled deeply, filling his lungs, the smoke slowly dissipating the sense of restlessness, re-dissolving the frustrations and failings.

Sedating his emotions in the way that a surgeon's team anaesthetizes a patient before operating, Leo was able to return to the memories of Raisa, examining them with opium-induced distance as if they belonged to another man from a far-away world. In Moscow he'd been surrounded by the life he'd created with her, from their apartment to the city itself, the parks, the river; even the sound of the tramcars rattling past caused him to stop mid-sentence, his chest gripped by a physical pain. The bitter winters, the hot summers – there was nothing that her memory wasn't stamped upon. In the months immediately after her murder the desire to investigate blazed in his mind as bright as the surface of sun, consuming all other concerns. He had no other thoughts from the moment he woke to collapsing on his bed, catching only a few hours of fretful, disturbed sleep. He petitioned officials, wrote letters, begged for the chance to go to New York only to be told time and time again that what he asked was impossible.

Raisa's body had been returned to Moscow. Leo had demanded a second autopsy. To his surprise this had been agreed to, perhaps in the hope that it would allow him to grieve and drop his incessant requests. The Soviet doctors confirmed the American verdict that she'd been shot from a distance of about ten metres: killed by a single bullet from a powerful handgun, a wound to her torso, entering just underneath her rib. Reading the report, he insisted that he be allowed to see her body. His wife had been laid out on a steel table covered with a thin white sheet. He'd taken hold of the sheet, pulling it back to her waist – a reunion of the most awful kind. Her skin, always pale, was now watery white with trace-lines of blue. He ignored instructions not to touch her, opened her eyes. They'd been so full of intelligence, shrewd and playful at the same time, careful and mischievous, yet there was nothing in these eyes staring at the ceiling. He was so startled by the change that he'd momentarily wondered if this could even be the same woman, as if her life and intelligence were forces too powerful to ever be fully extinguished and some residual vestige would surely remain.

He'd recovered his composure, begun a dispassionate examination as a police officer. He'd taken out a small notebook. He'd picked up a pen. When he looked down at first page of the notebook he saw a scribbled line, involuntarily formed as his hand had trembled across the page. He'd steadied himself, ripping the front page off and noting down several observations, checking them with the doctor beside him. She'd died from loss of blood. A former soldier, he knew vividly from the sight of the wound that such a death would not have been instantaneous but painful and slow. He asked the doctor for an estimate of the time it would have taken from the bullet entering her body to her death. She'd been in Manhattan when the shooting occurred, only minutes from some of the best hospitals in the world. The doctor had been unable to fix a time, saying it varied enormously from person to person and there was no formula. Pressed by Leo, he guessed between twenty and thirty minutes – which surely meant the official version of events was a fiction. Raisa could have been saved. With this fact, his desire hardened – he had to reach New York with or without the State's permission.

Blind as he was to other matters, it was Zoya who forced him to confront the repercussions of his obsessive investigative efforts. In the months after their return Elena's academic work had suffered greatly, she'd lost weight – she'd become reclusive, fearful of making friends and suspicious of friends she'd known for years. She felt it her duty not to leave Leo alone in his tormented state and yet his anguish was painful to witness. Zoya pointed out that this way of living was not living at all. They had to move on as a family. Her determination and intelligence reminded him of Raisa. Though he did not abandon his investigation, he realized that the chances of an imminent breakthrough were slim and he agreed to refocus his energies, pushing the matter of New York into the background, keeping his preoccupation invisible. In this manner of compromise they lived together for seven years. During these years there were many times when Leo was happy, only for that happiness to melt away suddenly when his thoughts returned to Raisa, as they always did. He learned to mask his emotions from his daughters better. He learned to lie, to pretend. Elena recovered. She finished her studies. Zoya became a doctor. They both found love. Elena married first, at twenty-one, throwing herself into a romance, love once again the answer. Zoya waited a little longer before marrying. With both daughters living in their own apartments, Leo considered his promise fulfilled. He was alone and his mind returned to the task he'd never abandoned.

For years he'd considered the case and yet it baffled him. He did not know what lay beneath the plan to murder Jesse Austin. He'd decided that his first objective must be to track down the propaganda officer Mikael Ivanov, the man who'd tricked his daughter. His search stemmed not out of a desire for revenge but because Ivanov would have important information regarding the events of that night. It was logical to find him before attempting to reach New York.

Ivanov was no longer living in Moscow and it took a great deal of effort and bribery to find out that he'd been relocated to the city of Perm, in the central region of Russia. Arriving in Perm, travelling without authorization, Leo discovered that Ivanov had been sent there after returning from New York, working in local government, with a fondness for drink. Several winters ago he'd become drunk and walked out into the centre of a lake, falling through the ice and dying of pneumonia. Some believed it was an accident: others believed it was suicide. Leo had visited the cemetery. The seven-year delay had made it far harder to unearth the truth. Evidence, memories and witnesses faded like the ink in the newspaper articles he'd collected.

No more time could be wasted. He began to devise a way to reach New York, saving up his modest salary to buy gold on the black market, necessary once he crossed the border, carefully plotting a route to the United States. These preparations offered the glimmer of a resolution – no matter how difficult it might be to achieve.

*

Christmas, 1973, he'd eaten dinner with his family, his daughters and their husbands. He'd given them presents. He'd kissed them goodbye. He'd told them nothing of his plans. The next day he began his journey, making his way towards the Finnish border. He'd come close, only metres away before he was shot and caught. The failure of his attempt and his subsequent capture could have resulted in his execution. Once again Frol Panin intervened. Now frail and ill, the old man warned him:

I cannot save you again.

They were words that Leo had once uttered to his own protégé. Interpreting his attempt to cross the border as grief rather than treachery, the State gave Leo an ultimatum – life in prison, or a job so dangerous that no one would ever volunteer for it.

Greater Province of Kabul
City of Kabul
Karta-i-Seh District
Soviet Embassy
Darulaman Boulevard
Next Day

Captain Anton Vashchenko woke at five o'clock, getting out of bed at the first sound of the alarm, not allowing himself a moment's delay, throwing his feet out from under the covers and pressing them against the cold floor. He found satisfaction in such discipline and in the dark found his steel water bottle, containing strong cold coffee brewed last night. He took a long gulp before getting dressed in the dark, putting on running gear, jogging pants, sweatshirt, trainers and a holster, which held his semi-automatic Makarov pistol tight near his shoulder. His route was approximately five kilometres, along Darulaman Boulevard, crossing the Kabul River into the centre of town. It had been suggested that if he wanted exercise he could run at the heavily guarded airport, laps of the runway. He'd dismissed the idea. He would run where he lived, as he had always done. In Stalingrad, where he'd grown up after the Great Patriotic War, he'd run past ruined buildings and unexploded bombs, scampering over rubble – devastation had been the backdrop to his childhood. Here in Kabul, his run took him past slums and bullet-chipped ministries. He refused to live in protected isolation, in the secure military garrisons outside the city. Causing some inconvenience, he'd insisted upon modest temporary accommodation in the embassy despite several protests that it was inappropriate. From his point of view, he'd been tasked with the security of Kabul so living outside the city made little sense. Losing control over these streets would hand their enemy a psychological victory. It was essential that they act and behave like this was their city. Indeed, Kabul was their city now, whether the Afghans liked it or not.

Captain Vashchenko left the gates of the embassy, jogging in the direction of the city centre. Normally, running in Russia, for the first kilometre his muscles would be heavy with sleep, a sensation he'd shake off as he eased into the rhythm of the run and the caffeine took hold. But in Kabul he was alert from the first step, his heart beating fast not because of the exertion or the speed, but because there was a chance someone might try to kill him.

Within a couple of hundred metres gunfire sounded. He suppressed his instinct to stop and duck since the noise had come from far away, a distant neighbourhood. Sporadic bursts of machine-gun fire were a regular feature of city life, along with the pungent smells – cooked food and raw sewage only metres apart. Even as his hand flinched towards his gun, he didn't long to be somewhere else. The captain flourished in extreme conditions. Life in Russia with his wife and children was of little interest to him. After only days at home he became irritable. He was not a good father and he accepted that – it was a skill he would never master. He needed to be tested every day: that was the only way he felt alive. There was no military duty open to a Soviet soldier more dangerous than Afghanistan and for that reason alone there was nowhere else the captain would rather be.

A member of the elite Spetsnaz troops, he'd arrived three months ago, the vanguard of an invasion force sent to save the year-old Communist Revolution from falling apart under inef-fectual rule. There were Soviet advisers already based in the city, but they were no more than diplomatic guests of an independent Afghan state. The captain was part of the Soviet Union's first for-eign invasion in two decades, a complex logistical operation across a vast terrain. Quick success had rested on the gambit that the Afghan Communist regime would not recognize that they were being invaded by their allies, a bold military premise and one that the captain embraced. On Christmas Eve 1979 he'd flown into Kabul airport at the same time as other Spetsnaz troops were flown into Bagram airbase in the north, pretending to be an exten-sion of the substantial military aid already provided to the regime. The first test occurred at Kabul airport when the captain and his men disembarked from the planes that landed without permission in violation of international law, approaching the Afghan gov-ernment troops stationed there, troops with no warning of their arrival. Several Afghans had raised their weapons, cocking their Soviet machine guns at their Soviet allies. In this moment the invasion had rested on a knife-edge and the captain had been the first to react, dropping his gun, running forward, arms high in the air as if greeting a much-loved comrade. He'd expected a chest full of bullets. No shots were fired and the invasion continued under the guise of a military aid programme. New ammunition was promised for the Afghan 7th and 8th Divisions, neutering their guns as shells were neatly lined up in the sand waiting for replace-ments that would never arrive. Afghan tank units were told they'd be receiving new tanks and ordered to drain their fuel to power them. With the fuel in cans, taken away, the heavy armour sat useless as Soviet tanks crossed the border.

The captain had watched the deception play out with mixed feelings. There was only one interpretation of the events – the Afghan soldiers were inexperienced, the disciplines of a modern army were not natural to them. They were gullible because they'd been organized according to Western military concepts, indoctrinated to being told how to behave. They did not recognize when an order seemed out of place. These were the soldiers he and his comrades would be relying upon to defeat the uprisings, inheriting men who had rolled over in muddled disarray as motorized rifle divisions entered Afghanistan from Turkmenistan and Uzbekistan, soldiers who hadn't fired a shot as fifty thousand foreign troops took control of their country. He was not troubled by the Afghan troops' strength, he was troubled by their weakness. The invasion had been intended to capture the Afghan military machine, funded and built up over the years by lavish subsidies. The purpose of the Soviet soldiers arriving in Afghanistan was not to fight the war but to direct it using the Afghan military. But even before the desert dust kicked up by the invasion had settled it was apparent that there was no war machine to capture. As a ring of Soviet troops spread around the country taking the major cities, Herat, Farah, Kandahar and Jalalabad – a near-perfect loop of successful tank and troop manoeuvres – the Afghan forces melted away. On New Year's Day, the Afghan 15th Division revolted in Kandahar. When the Soviet 201st Division entered Jalalabad the 11th Division of the Afghan army simply deserted, a whole division lost in less than a few hours. It was clear to the captain that the real war was only just beginning.

He had never been one of the more bullish officers who considered the resistance to a Communist state primitive, fragmented and disorganized – a tribal opposition equipped with mismatched rifles, some dating back fifty years, and led by squabbling factions. Such an assessment, though accurate in its material analysis, overlooked one key advantage the enemy possessed. This was their home. Superior weapons did not guarantee victory in this mysterious landscape. Smitten with the mystique of this country, the captain had spent many hours reading about the history of resistance in Afghanistan, the defeat of the British and their pitiful retreat from Kabul. One fact above all else had struck him, that since expelling the British:

The Afghans have never lost a war.

What better opponents to carve a brilliant career from? He entered this war from a position of supreme respect for his adversaries but also supreme confidence that he would become the first soldier that these mighty warriors would be defeated by, or, if they preferred, they could die fighting.

Coming to the end of his run, there were the first cracks of sunrise in the sky. Some of the shops were open: new fires in back rooms were burning tinders and twigs. The captain stopped dead in his tracks, drawing his gun and spinning around. The barrel of his gun came level with the forehead of a child directly behind him, a boy running in imitation to impress his small audience of friends. Seeing the gun they stopped laughing. The boy's mouth hung open, terrified. The captain leaned down and gently tapped the barrel of his gun against the boy's front teeth as though knocking on a door.

A scrawny wild dog scampered into the middle of the street, eyes glowing in the last moments of darkness, before running away. Captain Vashchenko's day had begun.

Greater Province of Kabul
City of Kabul
Karta-i-Seh District
Darulaman Boulevard
Next Day

Leo woke, peeling his face from the pillow. He shakily got to his feet, looking down at his outline imprinted in the mattress. His muscles ached. The lining of his stomach was tight and dry like old leather. A hacking cough seemed to take over his entire body. His clothes were the ones he'd been wearing yesterday when he'd walked into the lake. They'd dried stiff. He broke up the folds in his shirt, hobbling to the front door and slipping on a pair of dark green flip-flops. He descended the stairs, plastic soles slapping each step. Throwing open the front door, he revealed the street – from the darkness of his apartment to bright sunshine and city commotion, crossing from one world to another. A *kharkar*, a waste collector, rattled past, whipping a pitiful-looking mule dragging a wagon, wheels squeaking, overloaded with various kinds of city filth. Once the *kharkar* was out the way, Leo breathed deeply, smelling diesel fumes and spice. He wondered how many hours there were before it was night again. The sun broke through the smog, and squinting at the sky he guessed it was the afternoon. As a rule he didn't smoke until it was dark.

Without getting changed, washing, or taking anything to eat, he stepped out, closed the door, leaving it unlocked since there was nothing worth stealing in the apartment. He shuffled down the alley to where his rusty bicycle stood waiting like a devoted mongrel. The bicycle was also unlocked, protected by its worthlessness. He threw a leg over the seat, balancing precariously, and pushed himself off from the wall, wobbling down the alley to the main street, mixing into the traffic of bicycles and mule-drawn wagons. Battered cars honked their horns, exhaust pipes spluttered in reply. And Leo tried not to fall off, rocking from side to side until he managed to find a fragile sense of balance among the chaos.

It was his seventh year as a Soviet adviser providing counsel to the Afghan Communist regime. His area of expertise was the workings of a secret police force, forced into a job no KGB officer wanted. The dangers were numerous. Several advisers had been savagely murdered, regional offices overrun; there had been public decapitations. He was performing the most hated job in a society where he was hated not only as an agent but also as an occupier. His task both now and before the Soviet military occupation was to create an Afghan political police force capable of protecting the fledgling Communist Party. Communism couldn't be exported to Afghanistan without also exporting a political police force: the two went hand in hand, the party and the police, the ideology and the arrests. Having abandoned the profession in his homeland, he'd been forced to return to the job that Raisa had so despised. If he left his post, or failed in his duties, if he tried to run, he would be executed. Military discipline applied. Correctly suspecting the threat to his life might not scare him, it had been made clear that the repercussions to his daughters would be serious, their reputations would be tarnished and their prospects damaged, which tethered him to the job. Locked in servitude to the State, his only choice was to carry out his responsibilities as they'd been outlined – well aware that his superiors did not expect him to survive. Yet he'd clung on, a ragged existence, and he was now the longest-serving Soviet adviser based in Afghanistan.

The Afghan Communist Party was a young creation, formed only a few years before he touched down in a rickety propeller aeroplane at Kabul airport in 1973. Grandly named the People's Democratic Party of Afghanistan, it was led by a man called Nur Mohammad Taraki: an agent of the Soviet Union and codenamed NUR. Since the party wasn't in power there was no way for Leo to establish anything as sophisticated as an official police force and initially his job was merely to keep the party from being destroyed by its enemies both foreign and domestic. It was as if he'd been sent back in time to Lenin's early years: Communism existing as a minority party under mortal threat from all sides. It had been a wretched struggle to deflect numerous CIA plots and resolve internal rivalries. Few were more surprised than Leo when, in the April coup of 1978, the Communist Party seized power. Agent NUR became President of Afghanistan and Chairman of the Revolutionary Council. At that point Leo's duties transformed. He could now advise on how to set up a secret-police force with uniforms and prisons, a force with one purpose – to maintain and preserve the Communists' grip on power.

Trying to eschew the savagery and brutality that had characterized his early years as a secret-police officer, Leo proposed a force that was moderate and restrained. His proposals were dismissed as naive. The police force created by the new Communist regime followed a Stalinist model. It pursued vendettas and arrested indiscriminately. After years of caution and striving to achieve power the President became quickly drunk on terror. Decisions on whether citizens should live or die were presented to him daily, lists of names for him to tick or cross. Ironically, Leo was marginalized by the Party's success. He was no longer needed. He wrote reports to the Kremlin updating them on the nature of the monster that he had helped create.

Unchecked by laws, the President desecrated mosques and arrested religious leaders. The anti-religious campaign was so misguided yet pursued so rigorously, Leo speculated that the concept of God must be irritating to any newly formed dictator, one fashioned with god-like powers. The President's attempts to sculpt Afghanistan into a Communist model overnight were equally misjudged. With Decree Number 8, the President limited the amount of land held to six hectares. The rest was confiscated by the State. The response was uproar among the population. There was a deep cultural attachment between the population and its land. Families lived where they were born: their identity and location were tightly bound together. These sentiments far outweighed any grievances felt by the landless labourers working as tenant farmers. An insurgency took shape while the President tinkered with the things he could control, not his people's thoughts or beliefs, but their flag, redesigned, removing the *minbar*, the pulpit in a mosque, as the emblem and replacing it with a five-point star. On the day the new flag was hoisted, the President ordered the colour red to be celebrated. Pigeons were smeared with red ink, residents of Kabul were ordered to apply red paint to the exterior of their apartments, students painted their chairs and desks red. Leo was sent a note asking him if he'd consider painting his bicycle red. He saved the letter, marking it as evidence and including it with the report he wrote that night to the Kremlin describing the catastrophic failure of their satellite regime and predicting the imminent collapse of the government.

The only choice had been for the Soviet Union to involve itself directly. They invaded at Christmas, 1979, three months ago. With the new influx of soldiers Leo was no longer a solitary Soviet in the city. Russian tanks controlled the streets of Kabul. The former president was assassinated and a new president, Babrak Kamal, was installed, suppliant to Soviet commands. A radio broadcast denounced the excesses of the previous leader and promised to uphold fairness and the rule of law. The new regime was presented as just rather than thuggish, wide-reaching rather than savage and punitive. Yet any goodwill created by the removal of a despised leader was offset by the hatred inspired by the presence of foreign troops, troops the President legitimized by requesting their assistance, as if they had yet to arrive, using the Treaty of Friendship and Good Neighbourliness as the legal framework. It was a political charade, transparently cynical to even the casual observer. In February anti-Soviet demonstrations in Kabul turned into a riot. Three hundred people were killed. Even these deaths were not enough to quell the violence: Kabul's shops were closed for a week. A fly-over of jets and helicopters was ordered, a show of force, an implicit threat that troublesome districts would be destroyed, levelled to the ground if they did not submit.

The need for a powerful and effective secret police force grew more pressing. The force was renamed, now known as KhAD, the State Information Agency – the Afghan equivalent of the KGB. False promises were made. The era of senseless savagery was at an end. No more rivers of blood. No more red pigeons. President Kamal designated 13 January 1980 as a day of national mourning for all those killed by the previous president, and the very next day

Leo began his classes, engaged as a teacher for the newly recruited Afghan agents.

With his coarse grey beard and skin aged and cracked by the hot Afghan summers, his Soviet colleagues joked that Special Adviser Leo Demidov had gone native. They'd concede that he didn't wear a shalwar kameez, traditional local attire, but he didn't wear a uniform either – he was not one of them. His clothes were a blend of styles, locally knitted shirts, Soviet army-issue trousers, American Ray-Ban sunglasses and plastic flip-flops mass-produced in China. He was one of the few Soviet advisers who spoke fluent Dari, a dialect of Persian, the language of the governing classes in Afghanistan less commonly spoken than Pashto. Dari was the first foreign language Leo had learned and he now spoke it more often than Russian. In his idle hours he read about the culture and history of this land and discovered that the only thing to rival the power of opium as a form of escape was academic study. Excluding Communist dogma, for thirty years Leo had hardly read a book; now he did little else.

The authorities tolerated Leo's unorthodox behaviour and eccentricities with a leniency unheard of in the Soviet Union. Rules and regulations that applied back home were quietly ignored here. The concept of discipline was re-defined. Kabul was a frontier town, a revolution perched on a cliff face that every day was in danger of crumbling into anarchy. Many advisers begged to return home, resigning their posts, citing health problems, even cultivating dysentery. They argued that they could never be naturalized in the way that Leo had been. Yet though he was the longest serving Soviet adviser in Kabul, Leo did not consider himself any more Afghani than the day he'd arrived. The claim that he'd gone native was made by scared Soviet soldiers who'd just stepped off the transport plane, many of whom had never been abroad before. None of the Afghans Leo came into contact with thought of him as one of them. He was acquainted with many: he was a friend to none. He was foreign and being foreign was not scored on a graded scale. He was recognized as different from other Soviets. Seemingly without beliefs of any kind, whether nationalistic or spiritual, he did not sing praises for his homeland. While he seemed restless and unsettled, he did not appear to miss the place where he was born. He spoke of no wife. He did not talk about his daughters, nor did he show anyone their photographs. He said nothing about himself. He was not of this land, nor did he belong to the land he'd left behind. In many ways it was easier to understand the more conventional Soviet forces, in uniforms, with ideology and purpose, objectives, strategies and timelines. They represented something, even if it was something to be despised and a force to be defeated. Leo represented nothing. Nihilism was a notion even more alien than Communism itself.

*

Leo squeezed his brakes. Up ahead a truck had caught a tyre in a pothole and spilled thousands of plastic bottles of treated drinking water. There was shouting between those involved. The traffic had backed up. Impatient drivers honked their horns. Leo glanced at the rooftops, at the casual spectators – he'd seen enough road accidents in Kabul to tell when something was staged and the set-up for an ambush. There were no Soviet vehicles in the traffic, and unable to see any reason for the obstacle than the perilous state of the roads, he weaved his way through the scattered bottles, ignored by the angry participants, before continuing past the truck. Glancing over his shoulder he saw children filling their ragged shirts with bottles before scuttling away with their loot. He'd passed through the accident as if he didn't exist.

Picking up speed, he recited a poem by Sabbah, written many centuries ago:

> *Alone in a desert*
> *I have lost my way:*
> *The path is long and I am*
> *Without help or companion,*
> *Not knowing which way to go.*

Unlike the voice in the poem, the destination for Leo had always been clear. The torment was that he could not get there. He knew what he wanted to achieve but could not achieve it. With the road empty, mumbling the words of the poem, Leo closed his eyes, taking his hands off the handlebars and stretching them out to the side, snaking his bicycle from side to side.

Greater Province of Kabul
City of Kabul
Kabul Police Headquarters
Dih Afghanan
Same Day

Trainee agent Nara Mir was content to read her books while waiting for her teacher Comrade Leo Demidov to arrive. He was
several hours late, a not unusual occurrence. Unreliable and
erratic, he was perhaps the most peculiar man she'd ever met, certainly the most foreign, quite alien to her sensibilities. Despite this,
she looked forward to his classes even if it was hard to imagine that
he'd once been a member of the world-renowned KGB. At
twenty-three, her training was nearly complete and soon she
would become an agent supervising ideological education at
schools and monitoring the students, assessing them, deciding
which were likely to be assets to the regime and should be marked
for government jobs and which were likely to prove problematic,
perhaps even a threat. She did not consider such work spying:
every teacher evaluated their students as part of their job, whether
they worked for the State intelligence service or not. Excited by

the prospect, she was at the forefront of the social changes, presented with an opportunity that hadn't existed for women just a few years ago.

Nara's recruitment was recent, part of the reformation of the Afghan secret police instigated less than three months ago. The previous organization, KAM, had been notorious, a cabal of butchers and sadists who pursued no greater purpose and served no ideology. She would never have worked for them. The dark days of their rule were over. A new president promised an era of restraint and probity. The Soviets were intent on developing her country into a great nation, as great as the USSR itself. Nara wanted to play her part in that development. The neighbouring Uzbek Soviet Socialist republic could boast of a population that was one hundred per cent literate. In Afghanistan only ten per cent of men could read and only two per cent of women. Life expectancy was forty years, compared to seventy in Uzbekistan. Almost half of all children died before reaching the age of five. No one could claim the status quo was worth preserving. In order to achieve these breakthroughs radical changes were needed. Opposition was inevitable. For progress to stand any chance people like her were needed to protect the regime. Vigilance was required against those who sought to cling on to the past. There were regions of Afghanistan that were locked in a way of life that hadn't changed for thousands of years and consequently there had been and would continue to be dissent against any reforms. That was inevitable. Unfortunately, there would be loss of life. That was regrettable. In the city of Herat last year there had been an uprising against the compulsory education of women. Soviet advisers working in the city had been dragged into the streets and beheaded, their mutilated bodies paraded in a grotesque display. The only solution was a bombing campaign and the deaths of many civilians before the uprising was tamed. Violence was a necessary tool. She was sure these outbursts of bloody resistance were orchestrated by a few key influential traditionalist elements, men who would gladly see her stoned for taking a job, wearing a uniform. By isolating those dissidents many thousands of lives would ultimately be saved and the lives of many millions would be vastly improved.

She checked her watch. With still no sign of Comrade Demidov, she flicked through the pages in her exercise book, reading over the collection of quotes:

Ideas are more powerful than guns. We would not let our enemies have guns, why should we let them have ideas?

The insurgency was largely illiterate, most fighters could not read or write. Yet they were possessed with a powerful idea – that this was an unjust invasion, that Communism was a foreign abomination and that they would ultimately prevail no matter how many well-equipped soldiers were sent here to die. God was on their side. History was on their side. Destiny was on their side. These ideas were far more dangerous than their outdated weapons. The challenge was how to disavow someone of the belief that victory was inevitable.

Hearing the door open, she looked up. Her teacher had arrived. With silver hair, greying stubble and skin that was much darker than many of his fellow Soviets, he was unique among the foreigners both in appearance and personality. She'd never seen him wear a uniform. She'd never seen him make much of an effort over his appearance. He seemed perpetually distracted, as though in a permanent daydream, with reality only infrequently demanding his attention. He was handsome, she supposed, although she quickly dismissed the observation as irrelevant. Belatedly he noticed that Nara was the only student in the class. He asked, his voice raspy and dry:

— *Where is everyone?*

She said:

— *The others have gone home.*

He looked around at the empty desks neither annoyed nor amused, his expression blank. She added by way of explanation, nervous that it would sound like a criticism:

— *The class was supposed to start at midday.*

Comrade Demidov checked the clock on the wall. He was three hours late. Turning back to Nara, he asked:

— *You've been here for three hours?*

— *Yes.*

— *How long were you planning to wait?*

— *I'm happy to catch up with my work. It's quieter here than at home.*

He walked towards her, picking up her exercise book, reading through her list of quotes. She explained:

— *I wanted to make sure I understood our party's wisdoms.*

Every time she referred to the party, Comrade Demidov would look at her carefully, no doubt evaluating her loyalty. He said, reading from her page:

— *Trust but Check.*

She explained, trying to impress him:

— *No matter how much you trust a person, they should always be kept under watch. The point is that as an agent we do not have the luxury of presuming people to be innocent.*

— *Do you know who said this?*

Nara nodded, and declared proudly:

— Comrade Stalin.

Leo regarded his student speaking Stalin's name as though he were a wise and adored village elder, friend to all and tyrant to none. Nara's facial features were remarkably soft. There was hardly a harsh line in her face, round cheekbones, a small round nose and most notably large pale-green eyes. The weakness of the colour made them more striking, rather than less, as though only a few drops of colour had been mixed with water. They gave an impression of intense curiosity and, combined with her earnestness, it was as if she were trying to absorb and understand every detail of the world around her. Her face and demeanour reminded him of a young deer, an animal striving to appear magnificent, the keeper of the forests, but still young and scared. It was odd to associate her so strongly with a creature she'd never seen, and perhaps never even heard of. From appearances alone he would wager that she did not have the personality of an agent. There was a softness and openness that made it difficult to imagine her taking what were commonly referred to as necessary measures. Could she arrest her fellow countrymen? However, he accepted that appearances could be deceptive and he'd been wrong about people far too many times to put faith in such a superficial observation.

As for her understanding of Stalin's words, they were abstract notions that she'd memorized in order to fulfil her ambitions. She'd never implemented those words, or seen an entire society changed by them, a population unable to trust anyone, even family, friends and lovers. To her *Trust and Check* was a Communist aphorism, something to repeat and to be praised for repeating. She was not merely ambitious but idealistic, a Utopian who genuinely believed in a vision of a perfect society, serious about the promise of progress, without a hint of cynicism, or a doubt in her mind. In this regard, she reminded Leo very much of Elena. Perhaps that was why he tolerated her fanatical loyalty to Communism, understanding it within the context of a character that could not live without a dream of some description. Perhaps also he warmed to her because underneath her certainty there was a touch of melancholy, as if her optimism had been painted over a troubled soul. He did not believe she'd stayed in the classroom merely because she wanted to work. She was hiding from something at home. Related to that, her assertiveness did not come naturally: it was practised. Sometimes she caught herself and retreated from a comment or observation, worried she'd gone too far. And just as Raisa had found beauty to be a dangerous asset, so did this young woman who made a conscious effort to be plain, wearing a uniform that was too large for her, the poor cut hiding her figure. Her hair was always tied back. There was never any suggestion of make-up, never a hint of perfume. Leo had seen her blush at attention, hating to be stared at, perhaps hating her own beauty because of it. Her beauty and her sadness had always struck him at the same time, as if it was impossible to observe one without the other.

Since there were no other students in the class, Leo was about to send her home when Captain Vashchenko entered. It amused Leo that the captain appeared to consider knocking a weakness and barging into a room an act of strength, a triumph over etiquette. They'd spoken on several occasions since the Christmas invasion and Leo found him to be straightforward to deal with. Ruthlessness was often far simpler to understand than moderation. If presented with a choice, the captain always took the most aggressive approach. He didn't stand on ceremony. He wasn't interested in privilege, nor seduced by the comforts available to a military officer. Not particularly tall, he was physically robust, well built; everything about him seemed dense and compact, his body, shoulders, chest and his jaw. To his own surprise, Leo found it hard to dislike him – it would be like disliking a shark, or another lethal predator. There was no outward or obvious psychological darkness, no sadism or perverse relish in violence – he was interested only in expediency. In short, he would do whatever it took and he would never back down.

The captain impatiently addressed Leo, speaking in Russian:

— *A high-ranking officer from the 40th Army disappeared last night. There was no security breach in the headquarters. No sign of a disturbance. We believe it to be a desertion. A car is missing from the grounds. My men are looking for him. We have checkpoints on all the roads. We have found no sign of him. We need your help. No one knows Kabul as well as you.*

— *No one except the Afghans.*

The captain had no time for Leo's flippancy, pressing his demands:

— *If he's in the city, you'll find him, I'm sure of that.*

— *How important is this man?*

— *He's important. More important, we must show desertion cannot be tolerated.*

It was the first desertion that Leo had heard of. He was sure many more would follow. Summers were long and hot, sickness was common, and they were far from home.

The captain seemed to notice Nara Mir for the first time.

— *Is she one of your students?*

— *A trainee.*

— *Bring her with you.*

— *She's not ready.*

The captain shook the concern off with a wave of his hand.

— She'll never be ready if she stays in here. See how she copes with a real investigation. We need agents, not students. Take her with you.

Understanding that she was the subject of the conversation, Nara Mir blushed.

Headquarters of the 40th Army
Tapa-e-Tajbeg Palace
10 Kilometres South of Kabul
Same Day

The palace was perched on a ridge, overlooking a valley that was in turn overlooked by a distant mountain range – a picturesque setting from which to orchestrate the occupation of Afghanistan. By international standards the palace was modest, more like a stately mansion, a colonial outpost, or a presidential dacha, certainly nothing to rival the magnificence of the Tsarist residences. Painted in pale colours and composed of pillars and large arched windows, it was previously a summer pavilion for a king grown weary of his capital's bustle. Such was the abrupt slope of the hill that only the palace occupied the high ground; the gardens were on stepped-terrace fields below. Once irrigated and tended by a retinue of servants, the setting for royal entertainment, they were now neglected, overgrown and weather-beaten, desiccated rose bushes spotted with cigarette butts and bullet casings.

With Nara by his side, Leo stepped out of the car, still wearing green flip-flops and the clothes that he'd walked into and out of the lake. He'd been summoned to the palace before, like a miscreant subject, reprimanded for not wearing appropriate uniform and for not shaving, comments uttered by men who'd only recently arrived and had not yet fathomed the enormity of their task, clinging to petty rules while entire divisions defected and the Afghan military crumbled. Though he had paid no attention to their criticisms and was slovenly dressed, he doubted they would bother reprimanding him again. Several months had passed – enough time for them to be concerned with larger problems.

They were escorted into the building, curt introductions were made, the Soviet command acutely embarrassed by the disappearance of one of their own and resenting their presence, particularly the implication that Nara could help where their own men had failed. The interior had been damaged by battle, regal frivolity dethroned by the business of war. Ornate and decorative antiques were put to functional new purpose, covered with bulky radio transponders. The squatting army's equipment was incongruous and ugly: the original intentions behind the palace, pleasure, decadence and beauty, were not the concerns of the austere new occupants. Maps of the country marked with tank formations and infantry divisions had been hung where works of art and royal portraits once looked down.

They were taken upstairs to the living quarters. The missing officer had been declared a deserter, pre-empting the results of the investigation, although in truth Leo couldn't imagine what other fate might have befallen him. He was called Fyodor Mazurov and he was young for such an important position – in his early thirties. He'd risen through the ranks with admirable speed. Reading his file, Leo noted that the soldier had no experience of living abroad and very little combat experience. He was a career soldier and Leo did not find it difficult to imagine the shock of his arrival in Afghanistan, so far from his familiar world. Nara said:

— *I don't understand why we're coming here. We know he's in Kabul. They've already searched his room here and found nothing. What do you expect to find?*

Leo shrugged an answer.

— *They might have missed something.*

Nara pressed her point.

— *Such as what?*

— *A room tells us a lot about a person.*

Nara scrunched her face up in earnest concentration, trying to figure out how this might be true. Failing, she observed:

— *Searching a suspect's apartment might make sense in the Soviet Union. There are very few possessions in most Afghan homes, some clothes, basic furniture and cooking utensils. A room tells us nothing about the people. Is this not also true for Soviet soldiers too? They are issued with standard kit. What would be different from one room to another?*

— *There are always differences, even if two people own exactly the same objects, how they lay them out would still be of interest. And there are plenty of things that are not standardized. What about money, cigarettes, bottles of alcohol, letters, papers, a diary . . .*

Nara pondered this.

— *A diary? Do many Russians keep a diary?*

— *More women than men, but soldiers often find it helpful to make note of the day's events.*

— *I would be surprised if there were fifty diaries in the whole of Kabul, maybe in the whole of Afghanistan. Do you expect this soldier to keep a diary?*

— *We'll find out.*

Fyodor Mazurov had been appointed a small bedroom on the top floor. It was peculiar accommodation for an officer managing a bloody occupation. Instead of a steel bunk of the kind that the military typically slept in, Fyodor Mazurov had slept in an elaborate four-poster bed, for no other reason than it was there to be used. The room was furnished with a chandelier, entirely smashed, like a collection of splintered teeth, and a walnut writing cabinet, one of the few items of furniture in the palace that remained unscathed. Lenin's portrait stared out from over the bed, nailed up in haste and too small for the space it occupied, the shadow on the wallpaper from the previous portrait dwarfing his image.

Leo walked to the far corner of the room, taking in the sight before him. A man had been given this small space to make his own — his character would surely have made some mark on it. Nara remained by the door, apprehensive of disturbing his process, a sceptical observer. Leo asked her:

— *What can you see?*

She looked about the room without a great degree of confidence, doubting that she would see anything of interest. Leo ushered her over.

— *Stand with me.*

She joined him, regarding the room from the same position. She said:

— *I see a bed.*

Leo moved forward, peering under the bed. There was a pair of boots. He examined the soles: they were heavy duty, standard-issue black leather boots, too hot for Afghanistan, abandoned because they were impractical. He stood up, sliding his hand under the mattress, flipping it over. There was nothing underneath. Moving to the cabinet, he found it had been cleared. There were no papers. He peered into the bin. No rubbish had been thrown away. Leo said to Nara:

— *Finding nothing can be a useful discovery. We know this much. It wasn't a spontaneous or impulsive decision to run. He's thought about it carefully. He tidied the room. He expected us to search it.*

Leo opened the drawer, surprised to see his own reflection staring back up at him. It was an ornate mirror, larger than the portrait of Lenin, a wall mirror. He held it up, examining it. The mirror was heavy, an antique, backed with silver, a pattern engraved around the edge. He looked around the room.

— *Where did this come from?*

Nara pointed to the image of Lenin:

— *Hasn't he swapped the mirror for Lenin?*

— *No, this is much smaller than the picture that previously hung here.*

Leo peered at the surface: the edges were covered with fingerprints.

— *The mirror has been handled a lot.*

Switching into Russian, he addressed the guard standing at the door.

— *Do you know where this mirror came from?*

The guard shook his head. Leo asked:

— *Where's the bathroom?*

Carrying the mirror under his arm, Leo and Nara followed the guard to the bathroom, a gloomy room badly damaged by fighting: the windows were broken, and replaced with temporary boards. The mirrors had been shattered.

— *There's no mirror here.*

Leo addressed the guard again.

— *How do you shave?*

— *I don't live here.*

Leo hurried out of the room, back into the hall, examining the different shadows on the walls. He found a likely one. He hung the mirror: it was the same size, returned to its original place. He glanced at Nara.

— *He took one of the few undamaged mirrors in the building and kept it in his room.*

Nara moved closer, slowly understanding the process she was witnessing, excited by the significance of the discovery.

— *The officer was concerned about his appearance?*

— *And what does that mean?*

— *He was vain?*

— *He met a woman.*

Greater Province of Kabul
Murad Khani District
Same Day

Nara proved invaluable in assessing the lists of women that the deserting officer had come into contact with. She knew most of the names either personally or by reputation and was quick to rule out those who would never have allowed themselves to become embroiled in the scandal of a romance. Leo was not convinced that his young protégée understood that love could make even the most reliable of characters behave unpredictably, doubting that Nara had ever fallen in love. But he decided to go along with her initial observations, having very little knowledge of the women on the list himself.

Despite Fyodor Mazurov having spent three months in the country very few opportunities for romance would have presented themselves. Unlike many war zones and capital cities, there were no brothels in Kabul, though Leo had heard mention from several senior military figures of a desire to create one for the influx of soldiers. The women would be brought in from abroad, from Communist allies in the east perhaps, flown in like crates of bullets or artillery shells with the brothels run not as a commercial venture but as part of the military infrastructure, kept secret to ensure that the pious sensibilities of the local population were not offended. This project, no doubt appointed a lewd code name of some sort, had not yet been implemented and so the young officer must have fallen in love with an Afghan woman. The status of women in the country meant that there were no female shop-keepers, no women at leisure in the teashops, and little likelihood of chance encounters on the street. Nara was adamant that the woman would have come from the upper classes, the only area of society where there was a degree of gender integration. Going through the officer's list of meetings and duties, one woman stood out. He had regular meetings with an Afghan minister, a member of the new government, a man with a daughter in her mid-twen-ties, university educated, fluent in Russian and employed as the minister's translator.

The address led them to a house built in the traditional style, with mud walls and decorative flourishes, hundreds of years old. Many similar houses had been destroyed and this craftsmanship no longer defined entire districts, existing instead as isolated exam-ples, lonely remnants. Positioned on a narrow and ancient street, the colours rich red and brown, Leo thought it appropriate that romance had taken refuge in one of the few beautiful architec-tural areas that remained standing. Once a comparatively wealthy district, catering to the upper classes, it was difficult to view any part of the city as privileged. Nowhere was safe, nowhere was pro-tected from outbreaks of violence.

Leo didn't knock, but picked the heavy iron lock. It was an old design. The decorative engravings were mirrored by the crafts-manship of the mechanics – making it harder to open than many modern locks. Nara became nervous.

— What if I'm wrong? This man is a minister.

Leo nodded.

— We'll be in a lot of trouble. But if we try and obtain permission we'll offend the minister and give the suspect enough time to flee. So, the trick is . . .

Leo raised a finger to his mouth, indicating that Nara remain silent. If they were wrong, they would sneak out without leaving any trace of their search. Eventually hearing the click of the heavy latch, Leo pushed the door.

Were their assumptions to prove correct he thought it unlikely that the minister was personally involved or even aware of his daughter's situation. The risk to the minister was too great and judging from his record he was too canny a politician not to realize the extent of the repercussions, not with his Soviet allies, but with his Afghan colleagues. It was one thing to work with the Soviets, it was quite another to marry a daughter to a Soviet soldier. Leo doubted that the couple had fled the city already, although, privately, he hoped that was exactly what they'd done. His loyalties were not divided: they were firmly on the side of the couple. The daughter, whose name was Ara, was almost certainly sheltering her lover and planning their next move, believing they could wait out the first wave of searches and make their journey when attention was directed elsewhere.

An unusually large house, the ground floor was deserted. Like burglars, Leo and Nara stealthily climbed the stairs. Nara was so young and inexperienced that there was a peculiar sense of play-acting about the moment, as if this were an exercise in agenting rather than the real thing. They arrived at a closed door. Leo pushed it open. Ara was seated at a writing table, papers spread before her, with her back to them. She heard their entrance, stood up and turned around, startled and afraid. There was no longer any option but to commit to the search. Taking a moment to recover her composure, she said, in Russian:

— *Who are you? What are you doing in my house?*

She was remarkably beautiful, with poise and grandeur, typically associated with privilege and education. Her shock was genuine. However, her indignation was forced, her voice trembling not with anger but with nervousness, a quite different tone. The deserter was here, Leo was sure of it.

Leo's eyes darted around the room. There was no obvious hiding place. He spoke to Ara in Dari.

— *My name is Leo Demidov. I'm special adviser to the secret police. Where is he?*

— *Who?*

— *Listen to me carefully, Ara: there is a way for this to end well. Fyodor Mazurov could return to his duties, he could claim he was drunk, or he was homesick, or he thought it was a day off. It doesn't matter what the excuse is. Some lie could be manufactured. He's only been missing for eighteen hours. He has an unblemished military record. This is his first time abroad. Furthermore, your father is a minister. No one wants an embarrassment or a scandal, the Soviets would be as glad to conceal this as they would be to apprehend him. We can fix this if we work together. I need you to help me. Where is he?*

Despite being ready to lie, Ara was tempted by this offer. Leo stepped forward, moving closer, trying to show to her that this was not a trap.

— *We don't have much time. If you lie to me, and the others find him without a deal being brokered, they may not make you the same offer. And they will find you, within a matter of hours. We're not the only people searching for him. We're not the only people who can draw the conclusions that brought us here.*

Ara looked at Leo, then at Nara, evaluating the situation.

— *I don't know what you're talking about.*

Her voice was weak, barely able to finish the denial, the words crumbling away. Leo sighed.

— *Then should I call for the military to search the house? They would be here within minutes. They will rip down walls and smash every piece of furniture.*

Faced with this possibility, Ara abandoned the pretence, lowering her head. She walked to the door, turning back to Leo, imploring him:

— *You promise to help us?*

— *I promise.*

She studied his expression, trying to read into it some sign that he was a good man. It was hard to know what interpretation she drew. More likely, she accepted that she had no choice and led them downstairs, unlocking a door, taking them into a cellar.

The cellar served as a storeroom with low curved ceilings exploiting the naturally cooler air. Ara lit a candle, revealing Fyodor Mazurov in the corner, stunned by the sight of her with two secret police agents. Leo said, in Russian:

— *Stay calm. I can help you. But you must do exactly as I say.*

Mazurov remained silent. Leo noticed that his fists were clenched. He was almost certainly armed. He was ready to die for the woman he loved. With genuine curiosity rather than mocking cynicism, Leo asked:

— *Tell me, what were you planning on doing? Running away together?*

Ara took her lover's hand. It was an audacious display of affection for an Afghan woman and Nara visibly reacted to the gesture. Mazurov replied:

— *We were going to make our way to Pakistan.*

He spoke without conviction. It was a foolhardy mission. They would have to navigate not only Soviet checkpoints but also the insurgents' stronghold on the border. Yet Leo was in no position to criticize outlandish ventures. Feeling a strong sense of empathy towards them, he realized it was more than mere understanding or compassion – it was a desire to go with them. Their plans reminded him of his own attempt to reach New York, brave and stupid in equal measure. He asked:

— *You planned to live there, happily in Pakistan?*

Fyodor was about to contradict this notion when he stopped himself, swallowing the words. Leo guessed what their true aim had been.

— *You were going to seek asylum? From who? The Americans? You wanted them to protect you?*

This fact would guarantee his execution. For Leo to strike a deal and save Fyodor's life, it was essential that they didn't reveal this aspect of the plan. They would have to depict the eighteen-hour absence as a temporary loss of confidence, a night of sexual pleasure. Judging from the preoccupation his military superiors showed towards creating brothels, this excuse might find some sympathy.

Everyone was waiting for Leo to speak, as he assessed what course to take.

— *First, you have to assure me that you'll go along with everything I tell you to do. You must forget this plan to go to Pakistan. It's crazy in any case. If the Soviets didn't kill you, the mujahedin would. Next, you must return to your post and promise your loyalty to the army. Reassure them that this will never happen again.*

Details of his improvised plan were interrupted by a noise above them. There was someone at the door. Leo looked up the stairs, hearing voices, addressing Ara.

— *Your father?*

Ara shook her head. There were many footsteps. Suddenly several Soviet soldiers entered the cellar. Mazurov reached for his weapon. The Soviets raised their weapons targeting Ara as well as him. Trapped, surrounded, the young officer tossed his gun to the floor, raising his hands above his head.

Ara looked at Leo, venomous in her reproach.

— *You promised!*

Leo didn't understand where they'd come from. He hadn't shared his plans: he hadn't told anyone where they were going.

Slowly he turned to Nara. She was standing just behind him, her arms behind her back. Under his stare she said:

— *The captain asked me to keep him informed of our movements.*

Leo had made an amateur's mistake. He'd believed Nara had been partnered with him to learn. She'd been partnered with him as a spy. Considering his own record, it was only logical that the captain should take such a precaution when dealing with a defector.

Fyodor Mazurov was led out under armed guard. Watching him, Ara remained silent, sensing that any display of affection might provoke the Afghan soldiers. She was not arrested: such an event would disgrace the minister. Her punishment would be decided by and carried out by her father. If she were shrewd she would deny that she loved him and put the blame entirely on his shoulders, claiming he was besotted with her. But she was in love and Leo thought it unlikely she'd deny the fact even though it was sure to bring her much hardship and disgrace.

As the last to leave the cellar, Leo said to his trainee, Nara Mir:

— *You have the makings of an excellent agent.*

She took the remark at face value, not understanding its implications. She smiled.

— *Thank you.*

Greater Province of Kabul
City of Kabul
Murrad Khani District
Same Day

The electricity was out across the neighbourhood and Nara was forced to finish her night-time prayers by the flame of a sooty gas lamp. In her thoughts were the lives of the deserter, Officer Fyodor Mazurov, and his lover, Ara, a woman Nara had previously admired as a progressive figure in their neighbourhood. Educated, employed, and intelligent, Ara had been a role model. Though she had behaved according to her duties, she wondered if she'd been right to inform Captain Vashchenko that Ara was their prime suspect. Had she not, Leo might have been able to save both of them. Yet their predicament could hardly be seen as Nara's fault. She'd merely reported on their actions. They must carry responsibility. Not convinced by her own rationale, her prayers were interrupted by doubts. Ara would suffer shame and possibly physical violence. No matter how liberal her father might appear as a Communist minister, sexual politics were separate from mainstream politics and his attitude towards this romance would be conservative. Fyodor would be tried by a military court. Ara would be judged and sentenced by her father.

Breathing deeply, without a sense of composure and balance she normally hoped to achieve through her prayers, she rolled up her mat. It was not expected for a woman to pray in congregation, the emphasis was upon private worship. Though there were no theological reasons why she should be prevented from praying in mosques, the conditions placed upon her attendance were so strict it made public worship onerous. At her last visit she had been accused of wearing perfume, eventually conceding that she'd used soap to wash her hands and that the soap may have been fragranced. After the humiliation of being sniffed by a jury of men, she now prayed in private.

Glancing around her room, at the prayer mat, the clothes, wardrobe, chair, lamp, she thought upon Comrade's Demidov's lesson. If an agent were to search her room the only possessions that revealed something distinct and controversial about her were those given to her by the Soviets – an exercise book and a cheap pen. Normally when she wanted to study she was forced to smuggle her textbooks into her bedroom. The books were stashed outside, sealed in plastic against weather and dirt, in a crevice in the broken mud-brickwork of the narrow side street. It was laborious to remove them without being seen by the neighbours or the boys who played in the alley and she often wondered if she was being excessively cautious, whether her training had altered her judgement. Caution made sense as a tactic: if her parents had reacted coolly to her enrolling in university it was troubling to conceive of their anger at her new occupation, working for the Afghan secret police.

Nara's father, Memar, was one of the country's leading architects. Appointed leader of his guild, he'd been elected as a liaison to the State functionaries, making him one of the most influential voices when it came to any major construction project in Kabul.

A veteran of his craft, known as a master, *ustad*, he ran a programme for apprentices, including Nara's older brother. Her brother had squandered the advantages handed to him. He was lazy, spending most of his time racing through the streets of Kabul on a customized, imported motorbike, impressing his friends. Handsome and popular, he was more interested in socializing than study. Nara had never been asked if she wanted to enrol in the programme, nor had she visited one of her father's construction sites. The possibility of following his career had not only been denied to her, it had never even been imagined. He did not and would not discuss his affairs directly with her. In order to know anything about him she'd been forced to do her own investigations, listening to private conversations, reading his letters – a precursor to the profession she'd chosen.

She'd been able to discover that he had moved to Kabul from the countryside as a young man, funded by his own father, who'd made money smuggling animal skins and karakul fleeces across the Afghanistan–China border. He'd arrived intending to support his family back home, a village suffering from poor harvests in one of the worst droughts the country had ever seen. Keen to fit in with the established middle classes, he was worried that religious conservatism would make him appear provincial. Wealthy and devout, the driving forces of his life were religion and commerce, two energies that did not always harmonize. His business acumen allowed him to compromise. Nara attended school because so did the daughters of his clients. He tolerated her decision not to wear the chador only because his clients did not make their daughters wear it. For a daughter not to wear a veil was a powerful social signal, one dating back to 1959 when women from bourgeoisie families appeared without their veils during the Anniversary of Independence Day in Kabul. But Nara was under no illusion that her father's tolerance was anything more than a commercial strategy. At heart he was strict and pious, and her education vexed him greatly. In business he'd achieved everything he'd set out to accomplish. With regards to his family, he had not. His children consisted of a simpleton son and an unmarried daughter.

Nara spent many hours worrying about the fracture in their family. Not only was she unmarried, no one was courting her, not even the sons of the elite who claimed to be open-minded about her education. In practice even the most liberal men preferred a traditional wife, which was surely why the educated Ara had risked a relationship with a Soviet soldier. No one else would fall in love with her. The same was surely true for Nara. The difference was that she'd resigned herself to this fate.

Nara could have made the decision to split with her family and move out. However, no matter what their difficulties, she loved her parents and understood that moving out might mean losing them altogether. They would not visit her. She couldn't accept there wasn't a compromise. Her father had compromised before: his career was founded upon it. Compromise was the country's future. The new Afghan president understood that. He'd compromised on the issue of faith. Many enemies of the State had claimed it was impossible to work for the People's Democratic Party of Afghanistan while remaining a Muslim. They argued Communism meant bombing mosques and burning the Qur'an. The new president had taken a conciliatory approach towards Islam. Even with regards to the inflammatory issue of female education, the argument made in its defence had been drawn from scripture, quoting the passage in the Qur'an that described the creation of man and woman:

> *A single cell and from it created its mate, and from the two*
> *of them dispersed men and women in multitude.*

There was a religious foundation to ideas of equality. Nara needed to somehow communicate this with her parents. Her faith might take a different form to the worship they recognized but it was just as strong. She considered her family a test model, a microcosm for the country. If she gave up on her family how could she work towards uniting the country?

Nara got into bed, too tired to read or think any more. She wanted to sleep, exhausted by the day's events. She was about to blow out the lamp when she heard a noise. Her parents and brothers weren't at home. They'd gone to visit family in the countryside outside Kabul, a family that Nara had no relationship with. The extended family embodied the worst side of tradition and they would not accept her even as their guest. She crouched on her bed and opened the window. The property had been built on a steep rise of hillside. They lived in the top-floor apartment. She peered into the alley, the hiding place for her textbooks. There was nothing to see. She heard the noise again, a creaking sound. It was coming from inside the apartment.

She got out of bed, leaving her room, bare feet moving silently towards the front door. Their apartment was reached by a narrow brick stairway. Whenever anyone climbed the stairs the timber doorframe creaked. Usually Nara felt no fear even when she alone. There was a security gate at the bottom of the stairway, a grid of thick steel bars. The gate was padlocked. There was no way an intruder could reach the front door. Nara stepped forward, ear pressed against the timber. She waited.

Whether by the force of the door smashing, or out of shock, Nara fell to the floor, looking up to see two men enter the apartment, kicking aside the remains of the timber frame. Nara's body reacted faster than her thoughts: she was up on her feet, scrambling towards the bedroom. One of the men knocked her to the ground. Clawing her way out from under his body, she reached the bedroom. As she got to her knees, the second man kicked her. The pain was unlike any she'd experienced before, a detonation inside her stomach. She collapsed and curled up into a ball, struggling for breath.

The man stared down at her with hate-filled eyes, a stranger who spoke with so much anger in his voice it was as if he'd known her personally.

— *You betrayed your country.*

While he spoke the other man dropped onto Nara, pinning her to the floor. He sat on her chest, his weight forcing the breath out of her lungs. Handed her notebooks, he proceeded to rip them apart, the pages of neat text, the quotes by Stalin, the lessons taught by Leo Demidov, shredded and falling about her face. With a fistful of paper, he tried to force the fragments into her mouth. She pressed her lips shut. The man responded by lifting himself up from her stomach, relieving the pressure, before dropping back down. As she gasped he shoved the paper inside her mouth, his knuckles on her teeth, filling her mouth. The man standing over them commented:

— *You wanted an education . . .*

Nara could not breathe. She scratched at the man's face. He slapped her hands away, pushing more paper into her mouth. There was so much it was pressing down her throat, causing her to gag. She flailed, helpless, hooking onto her bed-sheets, pulling them down.

Unable to focus, her vision blurring, her hand clasped something – the pen used to write her notes. Gripping it tight, she clicked the nib and swung it at her attacker. It entered his neck. She was weak from the attack but it went deep enough to make him cry out. His hands came loose. Free from his grip, she spat out some of the notes, sucking in a partial breath. Able to see again, her thoughts coming together, her strength returning, she forced the pen in deeper, pushing as hard as she could, feeling his blood run down her hand. He toppled, falling on his side.

Nara stood up in disbelief at her sudden freedom, spitting out the rest of notes. She jumped onto the bed, moving as far away as possible within the confines of the small room. The second man was by his partner's side. He removed the pen, causing blood to gush. In the ensuing confusion, the man hopelessly trying to stem the bleeding, Nara assessed the distance to the door. She would pass too close to her attackers. Even if she did sneak past she would be caught in the living room, or the stairway. Feeling the cool night breeze on her bare feet she turned around, facing the window. It was her only chance of escape. She stepped onto the ledge, climbing onto the roof.

With no electricity, there was no residual light from the streets. The city was dark, the blackout stretching across the neighbourhood like an oil slick, spreading across the valley and up distant hills, broken only by the flicker of gas lamps and candles. The more expensive properties and the government buildings had diesel generators and they dazzled: ghettoes of brightness.

She heard the remaining attacker's hand slap down on the roof beside her and set off across the roof, bare feet against the concrete, directing herself towards her neighbours' house, unable to distinguish between the darkness of the roofs and the darkness of the space in between. As her toes crossed the edge of her roof she pushed off, jumping as high as she could manage. Her feet spun in the air before landing on the adjacent roof. She tumbled forward, picking herself up and running again. There were heavy vibrations as her attacker landed behind her. She didn't look back, running as fast as she could, the soles of her feet across the rough concrete, her eyes adjusting. She jumped, landing nimbly onto the next roof. She'd only taken a couple of steps when once again she felt vibrations — he was gaining. Unable to resist the urge to look back she saw his dark form only metres behind her, arms reaching out. Desperate, she turned forward, assessing the gap. It was too far. She'd never jump the distance. But she had nothing to lose.

Her feet left the roof, her body rising into the air. For a moment she was sure she'd land safely, then she began to fall, short of the next roof, hitting the side of the house. She was knocked back, tumbling down. With one hand she grabbed a window ledge. Unable to hold her weight, her fingers slipped and she fell again, landing awkwardly.

She lay still, unsure if she could move. Testing her body, lifting herself up, she felt pain but not enough to stop her. She waited, holding her breath. He hadn't made the jump: she would've heard him. She peered up into the starry night sky, saw his dark form on the edge of the roof. He disappeared. He was searching for another way down.

She picked herself up, hobbling down the alley, stumbling, running, turning blindly. Her only advantage was the blackout, making her harder to follow. Reaching a main street, with no idea where she was or how far she'd run, she saw a woman entering a house. She ran towards her, pleading:

— *Help me.*

Nara was indecent, half naked, covered in dirt and mud. The woman shut the door.

With a stutter the electricity came back on. Streetlights flickered, purring overhead — illuminating her position.

Greater Province of Kabul
City of Kabul
Karta-i-Seh District
Darulaman Boulevard
Same Day

Since returning from the arrest of the deserting officer, Leo had smoked for several hours in an attempt to suppress an almost unbearable sense of restlessness. Listening to the plans hatched by the two lovers hoping to embark on an impossible journey reminded him not only of his own thwarted ambitions to reach New York but also the journeys he'd made with Raisa, across the Soviet Union and into Budapest. Witnessing their determination, misguided though it was, he was forced to ask whether he'd abandoned the dream of solving Raisa's murder. He reminded himself of the conditions he'd been placed under. He could not leave Afghanistan without bringing ruin to his daughters back home in Moscow. Anyway, the advice he'd offered to Fyodor and Ara had been the truth: to reach Pakistan posed insurmountable difficulties. The roads were controlled by Soviet forces: the air was patrolled by fighters and helicopters, while the mountains and footpaths were governed by the Afghan insurgents, who'd kill a

Soviet on sight, deserter or not. In the end, the couple hadn't even made it out of Kabul. Yet there was something noble about their failure. He could not deny the romanticism of such a venture. He thought of Elena: it was the kind of plot she might have become embroiled in had she been born here in Kabul.

Gradually, in the midst of these thoughts, he became aware of a noise, an urgent knocking on the door. He didn't lower his pipe, lying sprawled on his bed — curious as to whether the noise was real or imagined. He had no intention of getting up, content to wait and see. There was a second attempt, even more frantic this time, accompanied by a cry. It was a woman's voice. Leo sucked deeply on his pipe and remained perfectly still, holding the precious smoke in his lungs. He made no move to stand, or open the door, passive and motionless. The voice called out his name:

— *Leo Demidov!*

He exhaled, regarding the opium-smoke shapes, before scratching the side of his unshaven face and deciding the woman was real, rather than imagined. Half-heartedly he called out:

— *The door is unlocked.*

His voice was barely a whisper. And she hadn't heard. She knocked again. It took an enormous effort for him to raise his voice:

— *The door is unlocked.*

The door flung open and a woman caked in mud and dirt ran in. She shut the door, locking it, before falling to the floor in a weeping heap. Hair was strewn across her face, ragged and wild, she looked up at Leo. It was Nara Mir: his most promising student.

Though she was less than a few paces away, her body muddy and bruised, speaking directly to him — a pitiful figure that would surely elicit sympathy from any normal man — Leo felt disconnected from her. The experience was akin to being submerged under bathwater and looking up at this woman. They belonged to different worlds: his was warm and calm while her was troubled and cold. The sensation wasn't indifference, or callous disregard. He wanted to know what she was saying and interested to know what had happened. Feeling the rush from his last inhalation, he sucked in deeply through his nose and imagined if gods existed they would watch mankind as Leo now watched Nara, distant observers of events unravelling before them.

Leo closed his eyes.

*

Nara stopped speaking. Her mentor, the inscrutable Leo Demidov, the man she'd come to in her hour of need, had taken one look at her distressed state and fallen asleep. She hadn't been bundled up in his arms, comforted with a promise that she would be protected. Her teacher allowed her to remain on the floor, bloodied and bruised, without an offer of help or even an expression of concern. Oddly, the lack of attention had a calming effect. By some margin she was the most competent person in the room.

She stood up, moving towards the bed, regarding her mentor with a pipe protruding from his open palm, head and body slumped like a puppet whose strings had been cut. She could smell opium. She hadn't known that he was an addict but it seemed obvious now. He was erratic, absent-minded, unreliable but it was hard when judging a foreigner not to suppose their eccentricities were due to the fact that they were from another land.

Taking control, she assessed her situation. She was inside and behind a locked door. Had the streetlights not come on she might have been able to reach the apartment without being seen. As it was, she'd been chased all the way here, unable to shake her attacker. She hurried to the window, crouching down, looking out. Expecting to see just one person she discovered there was commotion on the street: at least five or six men. She couldn't make out their faces. An angry gathering had formed at the foot of the steps. No doubt the sight of a half-clothed woman running into a Soviet adviser's home at night had caught the attention of the neighbours. Her attacker had been only seconds behind her: he was already with the crowd, stirring their emotions. He would not give up. They were organizing a group, a lynch mob to kill them both, just as had happened in Herat, when Afghan women and Soviet advisers alike had been executed.

Mapping her position in the city in relation to government installations, Nara tried to work out where help might come from. The Soviet Embassy was at the southern end of Darulaman Boulevard. She needed a telephone. She retreated from the window, returning to Demidov on the bed. He was out cold. Abandoning her teacher, she searched the apartment, unable to find a telephone. For a man who believed that searching a person's belongings would reveal details of their character it was odd that he owned so little. There was less furniture in his entire apartment than her room at home. Unless panic had blinded her, there was nothing of any use. She searched the apartment again, thinking that in her haste she must have missed the telephone. On the second search she found the socket and stared at it blankly until she understood he did not own a phone. It was characteristic of him. He would not want to be contacted or bothered. Their best chance of escape had vanished. Panic swelling in her chest, she dropped to her mentor's side, shaking him violently by the scruff of the neck. If he didn't own a phone maybe he owned a gun.

— *Wake up!*

His eyes rolled like two heavy stone slabs, briefly revealing the whites. Nara ran to the kitchen, filled a dirty glass with cold water, returned to the bed and threw it in his face.

*

Leo opened his eyes and touched the spots of water on his face. He'd forgotten the events of the last few minutes and when he looked up to see his most promising student standing at the foot of the bed he wondered what she was doing in his apartment. She was in a state of some disarray. How long had she been standing there and where had she come from? He tried to remember her name but couldn't. Enveloped in a sensation of supreme comfort, all he wanted was to sleep. Feeling his eyes close, he asked, his voice croaky:

— *Why are you here?*

She crouched down, close to him. He noticed that her lip was bleeding and her cheek was bruised. She'd been beaten. Her voice was shrill and loud and it annoyed him to be disturbed in this way. She said:

— *They tried to kill me. They broke into my home.*

Leo felt the opium pipe roll out of his hand. He tried to catch it, closing his palm, but it was too late. His student cried out:

— *Don't you understand? They're outside! They followed me here! We're in danger!*

Leo nodded but he was not sure what he was agreeing with. Breathing deeply, he watched as Nara took the candle and placed it under his outstretched hand. His skin began to burn.

There was a sensation that his brain slowly registered as pain. A patch of skin began to blister. He jerked his hand away, the fastest movement he'd made for hours, studying it as a bubble of red, angry skin took shape. Cracks appeared in his fragile opium shell.

He felt sick, a confusion of pain and opium-contentment, the two sensations clashing. Standing up, unsteady on his feet, he was straddling two worlds: the opiate existence and the real world, where there was pain and grief and loss. Resting against the wall, the sickness grew stronger. He walked to the sink, running his hand under cold water. The pain came and went, then returned even stronger than before.

Leo managed to keep the nausea under control. He turned back to the room, regarding his protégée's injury, slowly deducing the events that must have preceded her arrival. She was only partially dressed and he gestured at the few items of clothing in his possession, spread across the floor and a single chair.

— *Take what you need.*

While she rooted through his slim assortment of clothes, he asked:

— *Who did this to you?*

Before she could answer the apartment went dark. The power had been shut off.

Leo peered out over the city. There were lights on next door. His neighbours had electricity. The wires to the apartment must have been cut. He looked down at the street below. There were at least ten people outside.

— *Who are they?*

— *I don't know. Two men attacked me at home. I injured one. The other chased me.*

— *Did they speak to you?*

— *They'd found out I was working for the secret police.*

He thought for a moment, examining the blister. Nara joined him, wearing his baggy grey trousers.

— *Do you own a gun?*

He shook his head, watching as Nara's strength briefly left her,

her expression seeming to collapse. For the first time she sounded helpless:

— *What are we going to do?*

If the mob broke in Leo knew his time in Afghanistan would count for nothing. The crowd would kill him without a second thought, seeing him as no different to the soldiers who'd recently arrived in Red Army uniforms.

Something struck the timber door. There was another heavy blow and a white zigzag line appeared. They would be inside in seconds.

Leo lifted up his mattress, leaning it against the door. At the base he piled up the bed sheets and his collection of books. He smashed his only chair, kicking the timber fragments onto the heap. Looking around for more things to burn he saw the collection of letters that he'd started composing for his daughters back home. There were at least fifty partially written pages, efforts at correspondence that he'd abandoned, disheartened by his inability to express himself — his writing came across as matter of fact and unemotional, detailing what the city looked like, or how he'd grown to enjoy a new type of food. He was incapable of putting into words the simple fact that he missed his daughters and regretted any anguish he'd caused by his absence.

Nara cried out:

— *Leo!*

The attackers continued to rain blows against the door. They were almost inside. Keeping the letters, Leo picked up the fat-bellied, old-fashioned kerosene lamp. He threw it against the door and it smashed. Kerosene poured down the timber. He picked up the candle, lighting the kerosene. Flames ran across the floor, up the mattress, over the wood. The mattress popped and spat, and in seconds the sheets were ablaze.

Grabbing the spare container of kerosene, he gestured for Nara to join him by the far window.

— *Climb onto the roof.*

The roof was lined with tin, supported by a timber frame. Nara knew it would burn. She said:

— *The roof?*

Leo nodded.

— *We better hope someone saves us before it collapses.*

Their attackers were no longer trying to break the door down, confused by the fire. As Nara pulled herself onto the roof, Leo collected his opium pipe. Perched on the window ledge, he threw the second container into the middle of the fire. The plastic quickly melted. Climbing up onto the roof, feeling a sudden rush of heat, he glanced back to see the mattress consumed with flames, billowing black smoke.

On the roof, he surveyed the substantial smoke trail rising into the night sky. A patrol might come in time. Nara was crouching in the corner of the roof furthest from the fire. Leo sat beside her. He now owned nothing in the world apart from the clothes he was wearing, the bundle of unfinished, inarticulate letters to his daughters and the opium pipe in his pocket. Legs crossed, he watched as the flames broke through a patch of roof. They did not have long. For the first time that night he behaved as any normal man might and put an arm around his injured student.

Kabul Province
Surobi District
Barqi-Sarobi Dam
50 Kilometres East of Kabul
Same Day

Picking from a fistful of sugar-coated almonds, Fahad Mohammad sat near the crest of a hill overlooking the Kabul River. A bright moon hung over the gorge, but even without its light he could navigate down the slopes that dropped sharply to the river. Cradled in between the hills, like a giant concrete mouth, was the Sarobi Dam. It providing a significant portion of the capital's electricity, and its strategic importance to the occupation could not be underestimated. The access road had been fortified with checkpoints and barbed-wire barriers. Two tanks were stationed at the top of the dam, one facing north, one south – guns angled high as if they feared that the mountains would rise up and smash the precious structure. Impressive as these defences might seem to Soviet planners they were of little concern to Fahad. No attack by the mujahedin was ever going to travel up the road. He liked to tell his men:

The Soviets worry about controlling roads. This is not a country of roads. Let them keep our roads. We will keep the rest of Afghanistan.

There were perhaps fifty soldiers in total protecting the facility, a mix of Afghan army recruits commanded by the occupiers. The notion that this was a coalition of equals was insulting – the Afghans were under orders, subservient, slaves in their own country and an abomination in Fahad's eyes. Though the troop numbers were significant, their cautious deployment underscored their belief that mines scattered across the gorge would prevent any attack.

As Fahad chewed on the last of his almonds, he could see one of the mines, a bulbous shape not more than ten metres away. A person might mistake it for a rock, for these mines were not dug in by a specialist team but dropped by enemy planes, scattered from the sky. Specially designed wings spun them through the air to slow their descent, grotesquely copying nature's design of a seedpod, to land softly. They were the most innocuous looking of weapons. Children mistook them as toys since the colour of the plastic case varied according to where they were dropped, whether the reds or yellows of the mountain soil, or the greens of vege-tated areas. Though they could be seen by a vigilant naked eye they were almost invisible to metal detectors, containing only a thin aluminium detonator. Fahad estimated there were several thousand spotted through these hills, none of them intended to kill. An examination revealed that they did not have enough explosives to guarantee death. They were designed to maim. An injured mujahedin was far more valuable to the occupation than a dead man. A wounded soldier could result in an entire operation being called off as the survivors carried him home. The dead pre-sented no such problem: they were left where they lay.

Fahad returned to his team.

— *Allahu Akbar.*

It rippled through the group, and once there was silence Fahad led the descent down the gorge. His team consisted of four other men including his younger brother, Samir — a young man with delicate feminine features. In contrast, Fahad was much taller and leaner. Standing still he appeared awkward. But in motion his body was elegant and nimble, one of the fastest soldiers on foot, able to trek across vast distances without a break, taking only mouthfuls of water from rivers he passed along the way. Fahad loved his three brothers, including Samir, but he held grave reservations about his abilities as a soldier.

Samir was in charge of the explosives, deciding for this mission to use *kama*, a stable mix that wouldn't detonate by accident. It could only be set off by a charge from the inside. It could be dropped, or knocked, the carrier could fall over and stumble without killing the group. Samir spent much of his free time fashioning new kind of bombs, toying with different detonators, experimenting with timers, testing the destructive impact of packing nails around the explosives or ball-bearings, which were much harder to obtain. He had no appetite for hand-to-hand combat and he was no leader. Yet his bomb-making skills were invaluable. Even more advantageous, he had no scars to give away his trade, no fingers missing, no eye full of shrapnel. Perhaps deceived by his soft face, Soviet soldiers never suspected him and he was able to pass through checkpoints with ease whereas Fahad was always stopped and searched, as if it were possible to read in his expression the fury and destructiveness of his intentions. For this mission Fahad had wanted to leave him at home. Samir argued that he was the most experienced with the explosives and he was needed at the dam in order to make the charges, to adapt to the circumstances.

After much disagreement, Fahad had given in. He still felt uneasy about the decision, a niggling feeling in his gut that wouldn't go away.

Once the descent was completed, they would begin their approach a kilometre downstream from the dam, out of sight of the guard patrols. There was no way to defuse the mines but Fahad had cleared a path during the day, marking a safe route for them to follow in the dark. They moved slowly, in single file, unable to use torchlight, guided by the footsteps carefully dug into the ground as markers. As the ground slid under each step they were forced to stop and find their balance, unable to reach out and steady themselves for fear of grabbing a mine. It took almost an hour to reach the bottom of the gorge.

Moonlight caught the Kabul River as it broke over rocks. The enemy had taken many precautions against a possible attack only to ignore the river itself. Their thinking was conventional: their orthodoxy would be their undoing. Fahad stepped into the river, stifling a desire to exclaim out loud at the cold. He could hear the sharp intake of breath as his men entered the water behind him. They had no specialist clothing. They'd abandoned the customary loose-fitting shirts, instead wearing American-style T-shirts that didn't drag in the fast-flowing water. They wouldn't survive long in these temperatures if their heads or necks became wet. They needed to keep their upper torso dry by navigating through the shallows. Stealth was their only chance of survival, rigging the explosives to detonate and then retreating.

The aim of the operation wasn't to bring the dam crashing down. Though it would be a glorious sight, it would be an impossible task, even with Samir's expertise. They were attempting to damage the tunnels underneath it, to cause enough structural instability to shut the facility for repairs. It would cripple operations in Kabul. The Soviet regime would have to concentrate its efforts on energy security, keeping its resources close to the capital, while the resistance could gather strength. It would be a great psychological victory: striking at the heart of the occupation's source of power the same day as Fahad's older brother, Dost Mohammad, murdered an entire class of trainee secret-police officers.

As they navigated the final twist of the river, the dam was directly up ahead. The control room could be seen clearly, the men in charge standing at the windows. The river was at its most powerful here, contained within the narrowest area, the speed of flow controlled by the level of discharge from the dam. At the flick of a button the control room could dump water, enough to flood the riverbed, sweeping the team downstream. Several spotlights zigzagged across the valley and across the river, passing directly in front of Fahad. He sank down, his head just above the water. The spotlight moved on.

Within touching distance of the steep concrete face, Samir began his work. The rest of the team took up positions around him. No longer moving, Fahad shivered. He was unable to stop, his hands shaking. Concerned about his brother's coordination, he moved to help him only to find he wasn't readying the explosives: instead, he was chipping at the concrete.

— *What are you doing?*

The crash of the water released from the dam concealed their conversation. Samir said:

— *If the explosives are planted just a short depth inside the concrete the force of the explosion will travel inwards, through the structure. It might even bring the whole thing down!*

Fahad was furious.

— *This wasn't the plan. We have to damage it, that's all. A hole is too risky. They'll hear us! We don't have time!*

316

— The river is loud enough to conceal the sound of our work.

Fahad implored his brother:

— You don't have to do this to impress me. Set up the explosives and go! Stick to the plan! This isn't about your pride!

Insulted, Samir turned away, striking the concrete again, trying to chisel a hole.

A spotlight snaked along the riverbank towards the face of the dam. This time its movements were deliberate and careful. They'd heard something. Fahad gestured for his men to duck, pulling his brother down with him. The spotlight hit the water, turning it as bright as day. Fahad prayed.

He reacted slowly to the first sound of gunfire, hoping that it wasn't real, amazed by the power of denial, wanting so much to be able to turn back time and order his brother to stay at home. Still underwater, Fahad watched as the water around him turned red. He stood up. There was heavy gunfire, bullets chipping the concrete dam, ripping through the water. One of the men was floating on the surface. His brother was alive, pressed up against the dam, unable to move, paralysed with fear. Fahad reached out for the explosives. They would have to detonate them now, killing themselves but doing as much damage as possible. A bullet hit his brother in the face, his features disappearing. He dropped the bag. The explosives were swept away.

The two remaining men fired back, hopelessly, emptying their magazines at targets they couldn't see. Fahad didn't fire a shot, sinking to his knees, clasping his dead brother. He had failed. His love for his brother had blinded him. The boy was not a soldier. He should never have been allowed to come with them.

There was a rumble and the water level suddenly rose, from his waist up to his shoulders. The entire river swelled. The level of discharged surged. A mass of water was released from the dam. It crashed down around him. Fahad was separated from his brother's body, picked up and lost in the newly created white rapids. Tossed downstream, he was helpless. A poor swimmer, he found himself underwater, his body pounded against the riverbed. He kicked hard, only for another wave to catch him, spinning him round. Smashed against a rock, he lost consciousness for a moment. When his thoughts returned, he was on the surface. The velocity of the river had dropped, the sudden swell had dispersed and he was able to keep himself from going under again.

In a matter of seconds he'd been carried several hundred metres downstream from the dam. The sound of machine-gun fire was distant. Alone, he allowed himself to be carried away by the river. Wretched, he wondered why he'd been saved.

Greater Province of Kabul
City of Kabul
Kabul Police Headquarters
Dih Afghanan
Next Day

Leo and Nara had been rescued from the fire minutes before the roof collapsed. Several members of the mob had tried to climb up, at the points where the building wasn't ablaze. Their determination forced Leo into action, kicking their hands and stamping on their faces. As more of the building was engulfed, including the shop underneath the apartment, the mob waited for the pair to die. Nara buried her head in Leo's shoulder, unable to watch as the flames moved closer. The sheets of tin roofing buckled and bent, becoming too hot for their bare feet, forcing them to hop like schoolchildren playing a game. Just as they were on the brink of deciding whether to jump into the flames or into the mob below, a Soviet military detachment arrived, investigating the disturbance.

Helped down, they were brought to the police station, examined by a doctor, given food, and then told the news. The reason they'd been saved by a military detachment was because martial law had been imposed on the city. The attack on Nara had not been an isolated incident. Every member of Leo's class of trainee students had been targeted in a coordinated series of attacks. Nara was the only survivor. The murders took place within a four-hour period. Marking out the crimes on a map of the city it was evident that one set of attackers couldn't have carried them all out. In total there were fifteen dead: nine students and six family members, either because they'd been obstructive or because they'd been considered complicit in their child's education. The murders themselves were savage. The intent was two-fold: to kill and to provoke. Some victims were found with their throats cut, their tongues sliced off. One man had been decapitated, the Communist sickle cut into his forehead. These were attacks on the institution of the secret police and part of a propaganda war fought not on radio airwaves but in blood, an event with enough scale and horror to be talked about across the entire city. A message was being sent to those considering forming an alliance with the infidel government – death awaited them. Leo took no consolation from the fact that he had always been honest with his students about the dangers of the profession they'd chosen, warning them that they'd experience hatred as they'd never experienced before.

Unlike the other officers, Captain Vashchenko did not appear perturbed or tired, entering the room with his usual abrupt efficiency.

— *Nara Mir, you did well to survive. We're impressed by your strength. You are a powerful symbol that we cannot be beaten so easily. As the only survivor you are also the key to solving these crimes.*

Leo raised his hand, interrupting:

— *Nara has only recently started learning Russian. Perhaps I should translate.*

The captain nodded, showing no embarrassment at his mistaken presumption. Once Leo had finished, the captain continued:

— *These murders are a sensation. They were intended to be. The city's population is talking of nothing else. For this reason, we must solve this crime today. It seems to me no coincidence that at the same time as trainee agents were being murdered an audacious attack was launched on the Sarobi Dam. Had it succeeded there would have been a power shortage across the entire city. The two events together would have dramatically undercut our authority and made it impossible to plausibly assert that we were in control. Fortunately the Sarobi Dam attack failed. We're trying to identify the bodies of the bombers.*

Hearing the translation, Nara asked:

— *What about the man I injured?*

— *His body was removed from your home before we arrived. We found the blood but nothing more. One thing is for certain: this cannot be allowed to stand. In the same way that the deserting officer is to be executed in order to send a clear signal to our soldiers, we must send a clear signal to the Afghans that those who threaten our operation will be killed.*

Leo didn't translate, instead asking:

— *Fyodor Mazurov is to be executed?*

He glanced at Nara to see if she understood. The shock on her face confirmed that she had. It was a lesson that could not be taught – she was forced to experience the sensation for herself, responsibility for another person's death. Blind to the nuances of these emotions, the captain was breezy in his summary.

— *As I said, he must be made an example of. For the same reason, we must make an example of these attackers and return life in the city to normal. I have repealed the order for martial law.*

The impact of these crimes must be reduced, not exaggerated. Life will continue as normal. And we will catch the killers.

There was silence. Nara said, in awkward Russian:

— *And the woman, Ara?*

The captain was becoming impatient with their interest in matters he considered concluded.

— *That is a matter for her father. She has lost her job. He has been humiliated. I would imagine her life is difficult right now. She only has herself to blame.*

Leo was clasping the bundle of incomplete letters in his pocket. He imagined his daughters listening to this conversation, he imagined Raisa standing beside him, and knew exactly how they would react. Outraged, they would plead for clemency; they would petition Vashchenko for Fyodor and Ara to be shown mercy. They would not understand that there was nothing Leo could do. They would not accept that as an excuse to stand idly by. But even imagining their anger, Leo was too beaten down, too tired, to stand up to this judgement, sensing its inevitability regardless of anything he might say or do. He was just an adviser, a man on the margins, paid for opinions whether they were heeded or not. He'd tried to save the couple. The satisfaction he might gain from outrage and indignation were of no use to them now. He mumbled:

— *I tried.*

Vashchenko and Nara looked at him. The captain asked:

— *What did you say?*

Returning the conversation to the investigation, Leo pointed out:

— *How can we solve the murders when we don't even have a suspect? You said yourself the body of the attacker was removed.*

— *We have a lead.*

— *Who?*

Seeming to ignore the fact she didn't speak fluent Russian, the captain addressed Nara directly:

— *Your parents.*

Shocked, she evidently understood what had been said, repeating in broken Russian:

— *My . . . parents?*

The captain registered Nara's distressed response. He turned to Leo.

— *Her parents have been picked up and taken into custody. I want her to question them. I'd like you to help.*

Leo was being asked to act as an interrogator. Nara said again, her Russian improving with the practice:

— *My parents?*

Greater Province of Kabul
8 Kilometres East of the City of Kabul
Same Day

Unaccustomed to using an army vehicle, or any vehicle other than a bicycle, Leo drove slowly. The allocation of a Soviet UAZ-469, a Russian version of the American Jeep with bulletproof windows and reinforced-armour sides, was an attempt to ensure their safety. There were distress flares in the back, spare gasoline, a first-aid kit, water, dry rations, guns and ammunition. Even so, he much preferred his bicycle as a way of getting around. The dust trails launched up from the back tyres of the jeep formed a plume of sand that rose for at least twenty metres, signalling the vehicle's presence to the entire valley. Captain Vashchenko had insisted that they take the UAZ-469, not understanding that driving a conspicuously Soviet vehicle made it far more likely that someone would shoot at you. The belief in technology as a solution to the dangers of the insurgency was flawed. The armour and bulletproof glass might protect Leo and Nara today but in a few months the enemy would improvise new methods of destruction. The Soviet response would be to increase the vehicle's defences, to reinforce the doors and clad the undercarriage. But it was always easier to destroy something than to protect it and that was ultimately why Leo was sure the edifice of this occupation would fail: there was too much to protect, with too many people seeking to destroy it. No matter how many troops were sent, or how much money was spent, the imbalance would remain.

Seated next to him, Nara had hardly spoken since being given the orders to interrogate her parents. Shortly after daybreak, her mother and father had been extracted from their home village, a Spetsnaz team securing the area, pulling them from their house and bundling them onto the helicopter. Hearing this, Nara had asked if they'd been injured, concerned for their welfare, convinced that they were innocent of the allegations. In her mind she was heading to the prison with one agenda: to arrange their release.

Leo preferred to travel in silence; however, in this silence he could hear Nara's thoughts as clear as if she were speaking aloud: her attempts to argue the evidence and to defend her parents' behaviour.

They love me.
They would never hurt me.
They're peaceful people.
They're good people.
I'm their daughter.

Puzzling over how best to prove their innocence, busy constructing explanations as to why her parents happened to be away when the attack took place, Nara finally couldn't resist testing her arguments on him.

— *My father has built more of Kabul than any other man alive. He is a creator, a visionary, not a terrorist. He might be old*

325

fashioned. Most men are. I might have disappointed him in some respects. That does not make him a murderer.

Leo took his eyes off the road, regarding this beautiful young woman with her large pale-green eyes. Quite unlike Raisa, she was naive and earnest – it was impossible to imagine Raisa ever being so gullible. Raisa was a survivor and the shrewdest woman Leo had ever known. He was unsure if Nara Mir wanted him to contradict her. Without answering, Leo turned back to the dirt road. Though the swirls of dust, coming into view directly ahead, was the outline of Pul-i-Charki prison.

Though the plans and design for the prison predated the Communist Revolution, the completion of the facility coincidentally corresponded with the arrival of the Revolution, creating the impression that one could not exist without the other: an infamous political prison required a revolution as much as a revolution required an infamous political prison. Remarkably, this was Leo's first time here. He'd avoided Pul-i-Charki, declining any assignments connected with it. There was no need for him to go inside to know what kind of place it was. Conditions would be inhumane. Degradation and humiliation would be institutionalized. Under the reign of the former president, guards preferred broken soda bottles as a torture instrument of choice, displaying an inexplicable loyalty for an American soda brand that could be bought in Kabul, a type of fizzy, orange-flavoured sugar water called Fanta. There were the more familiar methods, some lifted directly from the Soviet model, including electrodes, bare knuckles and truncheons. Savagery had its clichés too.

The familiarity was not limited to the instruments of terror but extended to the lines spoken by its lead players. Aarif Abdullah, one of the former guards in charge of Pul-i-Charki, had boasted to Leo:

A million Afghans are all that should remain alive – a million Communists, and the rest, we do not need. We'll get rid of all of them.

This indifference to human life, this absurd and chilling pomposity, could have been the anthem of authoritarianism. These grandiose proclamations were made by men drunk on the power of life and death, unaware that they were behaving more or less exactly the same as the Soviet guards and prison governors who'd lived thirty or forty years before them, thousands of miles away, surrounded by snow and ice, rather than dust and desert. Despite their supreme power they expressed no trace of individuality or personality, as if power possessed their minds and made puppets of them, these would-be gods.

As Leo came to a stop, Nara became even more flustered, her hands fidgeting. She opened the glove compartment. There was a pistol and a clip of ammunition. She shut the glove compartment. Briefly, Leo wondered if she was going to be sick. She looked at Leo, utterly lost.

— *But I'm their daughter.*

Leo took out his sunglasses, glancing at the dirt on the lens and not bothering to clean them. They'd arrived.

327

Greater Province of Kabul
10 Kilometres East of the City of Kabul
Pul-i-Charkhi Prison
Same Day

Like a sprawling desert fortress, the prison was surrounded by yellow-brick outer walls, three times the height of a man, running unevenly across the terrain, linking squat guard towers with pyramidal roofs. Rake-thin guards in ill-fitting uniforms slouched in the shadows, antique rifles slung over their shoulders. The scene would not have looked out of place in an American Western, the frontier outpost, housing gunpowder, whiskey and stables. Leo regarded the institution through the smudged lens of his aviator sunglasses, his eyes drawn less to the building itself and more to the vast space around the prison. It was in the middle of nowhere, rising from an arid plain; there was no clue for its existence: a fortress with nothing to protect, no river, or valley, no crops or people, as if it had been built thousands of years ago, surviving while the reason for its construction was eroded by the sand. There was no doubting the symbolism of this far-flung place: geographically and morally beyond the reach of civilization, a world of its own. Leo had heard talk of fifteen thousand people being executed here but he was numb to these statistics, numb to notoriety. Over the course of his life he'd heard so many numbers about so many different prisons, seen so many lists, heard so many whispered atrocities. Whatever the true number might be, it was certain that not one of those men or women had received proper burials, their bodies tossed into shallow graves outside the walls. Perhaps that's why they'd designed the prison to look like a fortress, to guard over the angry souls trapped in the sand. It was a fanciful idea and one Leo might have taken more seriously if he had ever believed in life after death.

He entered the prison-fortress, akin to being allowed into a medieval castle through the great gates. And like a medieval castle, this was a facility concerned solely with the preservation of power. These walls had nothing to do with justice. The Soviet occupation force had immediately recognized the prison's importance and sent a detachment of soldiers, as many as to the power stations and government ministries. This was where the dirty work of protecting a regime took place, processing the risky elements of the population. Soviet objections to the previous President's techniques weren't underpinned by morals, there was nothing wrong with a bloody purge, but murder had to be smart, and for the benefit of the party, rather than a personal grievance. Indiscriminate murder was a tactical mistake, undermining the Communist regime; murder needed to pacify, not aggravate, to make the job of the occupation easier, not more complicated.

Though he did not know them, the Soviet soldiers nodded at Leo as he passed them by, one foreigner saluting another. There was no such camaraderie between soldiers of different nationality: the Afghans and Soviets weren't mixing, separated not merely by language but by profound mistrust. Only three months ago Pul-i-Charki had been under the direct control of a tyrannical president shot dead by the Soviets. Some of his deputies had been also been killed, but many of his prison guards were still here, subsumed beneath a new tier of management. Within a matter of minutes Leo counted three distinct groups: the Soviet troops, the new Afghan guard and the remnants of the old guard. If anyone asked him to write a report he'd argue the chances of an uprising were high. Corruption, betrayals and enemy informers were inevitable. His recommendation would be for Soviet reinforcements to take over the prison entirely. This unreliable patchwork of allegiances was repeated across the army and police. Leo knew of military advisers who believed the only solution was to have the Soviets do everything. Integration and cooperation were a fiction, peddled by politicians reluctant to commit more troops.

Nara had regained some composure, fearful of seeming weak in this fierce and unfriendly environment. As far as Leo could ascertain, she was the only woman officer. Hundreds of eyes trailed her with a muddle of lust and contempt. They were being shown the way by a highly obsequious prison governor, newly appointed by the regime and eager to please. He gave a commentary on his changes to the prison, pointing out various details, including the newly cleaned and improved kitchens that would provide basic but wholesome food. Leo remarked:

— *Not difficult to improve on the food if the previous prisoners weren't being fed.*

The governor seemed stunned that not only could Leo understand and speak Dari, he could also make jokes in the language. He laughed loudly.

— *You are right: any food is better than no food. That is true.*

Unless his good humour concealed a darker soul, the man didn't stand a chance. Leo guessed that he'd last no more than a month.

Nara had fallen back a little, her way of indicating that she wanted to talk out of earshot. Leo waited for the governor to hurry ahead to unlock a door and stopped, turning to Nara. Her voice trembled with emotion.

— *They can't see me like this.*

— *Like what?*

— *In a uniform . . . My parents.*

— *Do they know you're a member of the secret police?*

She shook her head, adding:

— *You haven't taught me how to question suspects. I'm training to be a teacher. I shouldn't be here. It doesn't make sense. There are others more suitable for this job.*

— *You were able to make an arrest. You can do this.*

— *I can't.*

— *The fact that they're your family should make no difference. Your family is the State.*

— *I'm scared.*

If she had not been so merciless towards the deserting soldier Leo might have felt sorry for her.

— *You're not here to ask questions. You're here to provoke them. The captain hasn't sent you because he thinks you're a skilled inter-rogator. There will be people already here who'll handle the interrogation. You're nothing more than a prop.*

— *A prop? I don't understand.*

— *These interrogations are theatrical: people are brought in for effect. You'll be paraded before your parents. That's all. You're not expected to ask any questions.*

— *I can't do this.*

The governor was lingering nearby, trying to ascertain the problem. A trace of impatience crept into Leo's voice.

— *Nara Mir, you're an agent. You work for the State. You*

331

can't find a task unpalatable and refuse to obey. In the end, you do as you're told. You do whatever's necessary. I have failed you as a teacher if I haven't made that clear.

Nara forgot herself, suddenly angry, snapping at him:

— *Would you interrogate your own parents?*

Leo put a hand on her shoulder, a gesture of support that was not backed up by his reply.

— *These dilemmas feel fresh and raw to you. But they're old to me. They're like a song I've heard too many times. Try to realize the awfulness of your position today isn't remarkable, or exceptional, it's ordinary.*

Same Day

An entire wing had been appointed for the more important political prisoners and their interrogations. The stone floors were
cleaner, the guards were more alert, and the overhead fans
worked, a sure sign there was a concentration of Soviet officials
nearby. One man greeted them, another adviser exported to
Afghanistan. His expertise was the handling of prisoners, the
extraction of information — a professional interrogator.

— *My name is Vladimir Borovik.*

Medium build, with greying hair and soft hands, Borovik had
the anonymity of a mid-ranking bureaucrat. He was younger
than Leo, perhaps forty years old, and he displayed unnecessary
deference. It grated on Leo, the implication that he was somehow
the authority in a place like this. More likely, the man was
angling for a friendship, a fellow Soviet to keep him company in
town and show him how to survive the next few months,
where to drink, where to find women. Borovik ignored Nara
completely, despite her being the crucial element in the interrogation. He spoke in Russian, at speed, giving Leo no time to
translate:

— *I only arrived a couple of weeks ago. They have me staying at a military base. I can't say I like this country very much. But the pay is so good I couldn't say no. I'll earn five times the amount that I would back home. I plan to complete six months, maybe a year if I can stomach it, and then go home and retire. That's the dream. I'll probably end up going home, spending all my money in a month or two, and then I'll be back here again.*

Eventually Nara was forced to interrupt, putting to use her limited Russian:

— *Excuse me, I did not understand.*

Leo said in Dari:

— *Nothing worth translating.*

The prison governor had melted away, leaving them alone, not wanting to be involved. As they walked to the cell Borovik whispered to Leo, inexplicably lowering his voice as though they were in danger of being overheard:

— *The woman's parents haven't asked about her well-being or safety, not once.*

He nodded at Nara, continuing:

— *I've told them she was viciously attacked. They don't seem to care. There's no question in my mind that they were involved. The father is a proud man. In my experience a proud prisoner is the easiest to break.*

Nara looked at Leo for a translation. Leo said nothing, allowing Borovik to continue.

— *The father is something of a bore. If he's not silent and solemn, he's ranting and raving about various political issues. The mother is always silent, even when I ask her a direct question. I can't wait to see how they react to their daughter.*

He looked at Nara carefully, adding:

— *She's a tasty one. Any chance she's up for some fun later? She's one of the more laid-back women here, isn't she? I've been*

told only the ones in uniforms are the ones you can mess about with.
A face mask means they don't fuck, right?

Frustrated, Nara implored Leo:

— *What did he say?*

Leo answered:

— *Your parents are not cooperating.*

Reaching the cell Borovik gave precise instructions about the order of their entrance.

— *I will enter first, then you and finally Nara Mir. It is impor-*
tant that there is a gap of at least a minute between your entrance
and hers, so that both parents presume that there are no more new
arrivals. She will then step inside the cell and surprise them.

The cell was unlocked while Leo translated to Nara. She was struggling to pay attention. Finally she gave Leo a small nod, indicating that she understood her part in this performance.

A guard opened the steel door. Borovik entered, Leo followed behind. Her parents were seated on two chairs, side by side. Her mother was not wearing the chador, her face exposed. Ashamed, she remained stooped, hunched over, meeting no one's eye, staring at the patch of stone floor between her feet. In contrast, her father's hands were on his knees, head held high. Leo didn't need to ask any questions. There could be no doubt that this man had either directly sanctioned or been a party to the plans to murder his daughter. Borovik was also right about the man's pride. It bristled around him.

Borovik ushered the Afghan interpreter out of the room. There was no need for him with Leo present. The move surprised Nara's father but he remained silent, waiting for them to speak. At this point Nara entered the cell, pausing by the door, before stepping into the room, hands awkwardly by her sides. Staged like amateur theatre, it was nonetheless an effective device. Her father regarded her uniform: his eyes drilled into the details of her clothes, the colours, the symbols of the new regime. From his reaction he already knew she worked for the government. He regained control of his expression, easing back into his seat.

Borovik leaned close to Leo.

— *Ask him if he's ashamed that he ordered an attack on his daughter.*

Leo translated the question. Before the father could answer, Nara stepped forward.

— *Father, please let me help you. There has been a mistake. I'm here to explain that you had nothing to do with the attacks. If you cooperate we can be out of here within hours.*

A threat of violence could not have been as tormenting to him as this offer of help. Gasping at his daughter's naivety, the father said:

— *You will help me?*

— *Father, the nature of my employment must be a shock for you.*

She continued, deluded, narrating the fantasy of his innocence, a fiction constructed in the drive to the prison.

— *We have our differences. But I know what these men cannot know. There is love between us. I remember holding your hand. You loved me as a child. As an adult, it has not been easy. I wanted to tell you about my recruitment. Consider this, you work for the government. You design buildings. I work for the government too. I will teach in universities, perhaps some of the buildings you helped create.*

Her father shook his head, embarrassed by his daughter's show of emotion and talk of love. He found it humiliating and silenced her:

— *We found your books, your political manifestos and your notes on how to identify recruits for government work and those*

who might be a threat. Were you going to inform on us? One day
you would, if we had said the wrong thing or criticized the
invaders.

— *No, never, I want to help you.*

— *You cannot help me. You have ruined me. Not even a whore*
could have brought as much shame to our family as you have
done.

Nara's mouth fell open. Leo saw her falter, for a moment he
wondered if she would need to steady herself against the wall. She
didn't. Her father continued, sensing weakness, wanting to hurt
her, his desire to inflict pain stronger than self-preservation.

— *I allowed you an education and you taught yourself to be*
blind. You cannot see what is happening to your own country. It
has been invaded. It has been stolen from under your eyes and yet
you celebrate this fact.

Still suffering from shock, Nara clung to one of her previous
arguments, referencing her father's role as a builder, a creator, not
a terrorist.

— *You work with the government. You are an architect.*

— *Shall I tell you what I learned from the history of the*
buildings around us? Hundreds of years ago the British invaders
destroyed the ancient Charchata bazaar in retaliation for the
murder of their envoy. That is how invaders weigh the life of one
of their own against our nation. A whole city is not worth one of
their officers, they would tear it down to rubble. The same will be
true for the Soviets because this is not their home, not their land,
no matter what destruction they bring they can always return to
their cities and their families. I have never worked for the
Soviets. I worked for the people of Afghanistan, the people of
Kabul.

Nara stepped forward, only three paces from her father. Leo

thought there was a chance he'd strike her, even in the cell. His arms and ankles were not restrained. Nara asked:

— *You knew of the attack?*

— *Knew of it? I drew them a map of our apartment and marked with a cross where you would be sleeping.*

Leo had not translated a word. He glanced at Borovik. The interrogator seemed to know exactly what was going on and said:

— *The father has admitted his guilt, yes?*

Leo nodded. Borovik continued:

— *That was the easy part. What we need are the names of those involved.*

Leo whispered:

— *There is no chance he'll give up those names.*

Borovik agreed.

— *The pride that helped us will now work against us. You are right, the father wouldn't tell us the names. His wife is a different matter.*

Borovik gestured at the guard on the door. There was the sound of an adjacent cell being opened. A young man appeared, blindfolded, his hands tied behind his back. Leo didn't recognize him. Nara's mother stood up, raising her face for the first time, hands locked together, pleading:

— *No!*

It was a desperate, animal-like cry. Leo asked Borovik:

— *Who is that man?*

— *It's Nara's brother. The mother seems keen on her son. She agreed to her daughter's death. I wonder if she'll agree to the death of her son.*

Nara had turned almost as pale as her mother. Borovik whispered in Leo's ear:

— I'll wager I can get a name within five minutes.

Like a sultan calling for food, Borovik clapped his hands together.

A guard entered carrying a stainless-steel tray. On it was a single bottle of orange soda, the liquid luminous in the gloomy cell, the colour of the Fanta label a faded blue. The guard set the tray down on a table. He pulled a bottle opener from his pocket with all the formality of a waiter in a luxury hotel. The steel soda top clinked on the floor. Borovik stepped forward and began to drink straight from the bottle in long gulps, a thin orange line leaking from the side of his mouth until the bottle was finished. He placed the empty bottle on the edge of the table and let go. The bottle fell, as was intended, smashing in two. Borovik picked up the largest remaining portion by the neck, creating a jagged glass fist. It was a crude threat, breathtaking in its savagery, exploiting the notoriety of this place. Leo had seen enough. Without saying a word he walked out, brushing past the shocked figure of Nara, leaving the cell. Borovik called out to him from the door but Leo didn't look back. Passing the exiled interpreter, Leo said:

— They need you.

Soliciting the help of a guard, Leo left the wing, keen to get outside, finally managing to gain access to the dusty ground of an empty exercise yard. He walked to the furthest corner and sat against the wall, closing his eyes, his legs stretched out in sun, the rest of his body in shade. Having not slept last night, he was tired and in the pleasant heat he quickly fell asleep.

*

When Leo woke up, the angle of the shade had changed and there was sunlight across half his body. Using the back of his hand, he wiped his mouth. It was only now that he noticed that he was not alone. Nara was seated not far from him, on the dusty ground of the exercise yard, her back against the wall. He had no idea how long she'd been there. Squinting at her, he noted that she had not been crying. Leo asked, his voice croaky:

— *And?*

— *My mother loves my brother. She gave us a name.*

Nara had changed. She was different. She was numb.

Greater Province of Kabul
City of Kabul
Sar-e-Chowk Roundabout
Same Day

Leo surveyed the roundabout, one of the busiest junctions in the city. Sar-e-Chowk was much more than an intersection – it was a marketplace, not just for material goods but for an exchange of information and services. Wagons were set up around the edge of the traffic, displaying produce. Behind them were busy tea rooms populated with men perched on plastic chairs surveying the activity like lookouts on the bows of ships. Clutching glasses of tea, with cigarettes snagged between long thin fingers smouldering dangerously close to their wire-wool beards, no men had ever looked wiser. Deals were done, ideas disputed, people discussed. This was a hub – a commotion of gossip, rumour and trade churned through the population as if by the circular motion of the traffic, a hub entirely outside the Communist regime's control with no phone lines to tap or letters to intercept.

With a calculated air of nonchalance, Leo ambled between market wagons, drifting among the hundreds of people as they headed home at the end of the day. Some were still buying, some were stopping to talk: other vendors were packing up as the day-light began to fade. He did not have long to find his target. Captain Vashchenko was fixed upon taking their prime suspect into custody today. Nara Mir's mother had given them the name of a young man – Dost Mohammad. According to her confession, he was the principal organizing force behind the attacks. He had approached Nara's father with news of the plan, asking them to be away on a specific date.

To the captain, speed was the priority, not prudence. Leo sensed the question of guilt was of secondary interest. There had been no serious investigation into the allegation. The bare minimum of checks had been made. The Afghan police knew very little about the man beyond the basics of his occupation. They couldn't find a photograph among their files. Their bureaucracy was woefully undeveloped. Information was the spine of any credible authoritarian regime – a government needed to know its people. Despite the numerous shortcomings, the captain would not waiver from his determination to make an arrest within twenty-four hours of the attacks.

When Leo had opposed rushing into the market without even knowing what the suspect looked like the captain had chided him, pointing out that in Afghanistan they couldn't behave as the KGB had done in Leo's time, making arrests at four in the morning when everyone was asleep. It would appear to the enemy as a feminine act of deception and subterfuge. If they wanted to subdue Afghanistan they needed to demonstrate bravery, courage and audacity. Guile and slyness were vices here, not virtues. A public display of justice in one of the busiest roundabouts in the city would be a robust and proportionate response to the savagery of last night's murders. As for the danger of resistance within the crowd, the captain did not see this as a problem. He went as far as to hope that the enemy would show themselves. Let them take up arms. They would be killed.

Without a photograph, they knew only that the suspect owned a wagon normally found at this roundabout, selling a variety of typical Afghan sweets, dried fruit and sugared and honey-coated nuts. As a suspect profile, it was one of the worst Leo had encountered. According to some, Dost Mohammad was twenty-five years old, according to others he was thirty. Since many men didn't know how to count, an age was often chosen as a signifier of appearance. Leo would have to strike up a conversation, assess whether the man was Dost Mohammad. He was then to return to the team waiting nearby, allowing them to storm the market and make the arrest. It was presumed that no one would be suspicious of a man in green flip-flops with the telltale signs of opium use in his eyes and face. Leo wasn't so sure.

Searching for the stall, Leo assessed the problems. It would be impossible to secure the area: there were countless exits even with a large team of reinforcements. There were many vantage points for the enemy. There might be lookouts. The suspect had been working here for many years. He knew the market dynamic, the ebb and flow of customers; he would have an instinct for when something was wrong. Leo decided to make a purchase to seem a little less out of place. One old man sold nothing but eggs, cartons stacked high. He showed remarkable composure despite the frantic bustle around him threatening to bring his stock crashing to the ground. At a fruit stall Leo bought pomegranates, and was handed the thinnest of plastic bags that stretched with the weight of fruit – the last batch of the season. He'd almost completed a full circuit of the market. There was only the north end of the roundabout remaining.

He crossed the traffic, arriving at the last few stalls positioned in front of the tea rooms. There were two fold-out tables covered with steel bowls filled with pumpkin seeds, green lentils, pulses and grains. Neither man seemed remotely interested in Leo. He moved on, pausing by a wagon spread with cuts of meat. A butchered cow's head stared into the sky, cheek populated with flies walking a sinew tightrope. Mingled with the smell of offal was something sweet and following the smell he arrived at a narrow wagon covered with wooden boxes. The boxes were like small drawers each filled with an array of sugary snacks, *nuql-e-nakhud*, sugar-coated chickpeas, *nuql-e-badam*, sugar-coated almonds, *nuql-e-pistah*, sugar-coated pistachio nuts. Leo didn't look at vendor, examining the products, choosing one, before making eye contact, saying at the same time:

— Nuql-e-badam, *three hundred grams.*

The man was young, no older than thirty, with smart eyes. Unlike the other two men he was interested in Leo. His expression gave little away and in so doing gave everything away. The control was practised, hatred contained. He filled a paper bag with the sugar-coated almonds. Leo paid for them, reaching for his wallet, putting his pomegranates down on the edge of the wagon. The man took the money and watched as Leo moved off. There had been no opportunity to ask his name without alerting his suspicions, no way of engaging him in conversation. Leo reckoned the odds that he was the suspect were high. However, hatred of the occupation was not confined to the insurgents.

At the end of the road, some five hundred metres from the roundabout, Leo met an impatient captain. Nara was standing beside him. Leo said:

— *There's a man selling sugared almonds at the north end of the market.*

— *Is it him? Is it Dost Mohammad?*

— *I couldn't ask his name.*

— *You have a sense for these things? Was it him?*

Leo had worked many cases, arrested many men.

— *It was probably him. Captain, I should warn you, this is going to end badly.*

The captain nodded.

— *But not for me.*

*

Leo sat on the steps of a house, looking down at the paper bag of sticky sugar-coated almonds. A fly landed, sticking to the nuts, legs flailing, wings congealed with sugar and syrup.

The hidden troops emerged, guns ready. The captain set off, leading his team, intent on making his arrest and sending his powerful statement to the city. Leo closed his eyes, listening to the screech of the tyres, the commotion in the market. There was screaming, shouting, a mixture of Russian and Dari. Shots were fired. Leo stood up. Beside him was the figure of Nara, perhaps the loneliest-looking person he'd ever seen.

Together, they walked towards the roundabout, past the blockade of soldiers, into the crowded market area, arriving at the same time as a helicopter circling low above them. The wind from its blades caught the tarpaulin tops of the market stalls and they filled out like sails. Some turned over, spilling their produce. Leo checked on the eggs. They were smashed, shell and yolk on the ground.

Leo and Nara passed through crowds of Afghans, many on their knees, hands behind their heads, gun barrels pressed against their backs. The man who'd sold him pomegranates looked up at him, full of hatred. With the invasion, Leo could no longer hold a position in the margins, ignored and irrelevant, unseen, living an invisible existence. No longer a ghost, he was the face of the occupation as much as the zealous captain.

The suspect was not dead. The Afghan and Soviet soldiers had cornered him in a space not far from a spice stall. He'd been shot in the arm: his hand was dripping blood. Nara touched Leo, remaining behind him, hidden from the suspect. Leo asked, already knowing the answer:

— *Was this the man that attacked you?*

She nodded.

The suspect lifted up his shirt. Several plastic bags were attached to his torso — the kind used by juice stalls. They were leaking, liquid pouring down his body, soaking his clothes. Then a spark and a flame appeared in his hand, a burning match produced from nowhere. He slapped his trousers and the material caught alight, flames spreading to his shirt, the bags ablaze. In a second he was engulfed. His beard turned to fire. His skin shrank from his bones. The pain became too much and he ran from side to side, arms flailing, flames leaping into the sky. One of the soldiers raised his gun to kill him. The captain pushed the barrel down.

— *Let him burn.*

The suspect burned, eventually collapsing to his knees. The flames died down, the gasoline exhausted. He continued to move, less like a human, more a smouldering corpse animated by dark magic, coming to rest under one of the tables laden with spices. The table began to cook, spice pods popping in the heat. The air reeked, burnt flesh and sumac spice. Leo's eyes followed the unusual coloured smoke into the sky, wisps of blues and greens. At every window, as far he could see, there were faces, young boys, young men, the spectators that the captain had so eagerly wanted for the arrest.

In the tea rooms old men clutched their glasses, cigarettes between their fingers, as calm as if they'd seen this all before and were sure they would one day see it all again.

The Border of Laghman and Nangarhar Provinces
The Village of Sokh Rot
116 Kilometres East of Kabul
9 Kilometres West of Jalalabad
Next Day

Since she was only seven years old, weaving a carpet was considered too difficult for Zabi, so instead she'd spent the morning making two of the colours used in dyeing the fabric. Her nails were stained red from crushed pomegranate rinds. She sucked her fingertip, curious that a colour should have a particular taste: red tasted of sour fruit juice even more bitter and sharp than the foul *chai-e-siay*, the black tea her father drank every morning, stewed so strong it left a smudge around the glass rim. The second urn contained a brown dye, created by grinding walnut husks, more laborious to produce than red. She had to crack the husks, then crunch them to powder with a smooth stone, adding a little warm water, mixing the two together. She dabbed a spot on the end of her tongue. The brown husk paste had its own particular grainy texture but not much of a taste. She decided the colour brown was less of a taste, more of a texture, before deciding that this train of thought was proof that she was bored.

Her mother and her *khaha khanda*, her group of close female friends, were sitting in a tight circle, talking while they crafted their patterned carpets. Some were intended for personal use, most were to be sold. Zabi was supposed to watch and learn. Making dye had been fun for a while, but her arms ached from crushing the husks and her mother was nowhere near finished. They would be working at the carpets for the entire day and perhaps tomorrow too and even the day after that. A square of sunlight appeared on the floor. The clouds had cleared. She wanted to go outside, aware that if she asked she'd be refused permission. Nervous of being told off, she edged along the floor, towards the door, collecting the steel urn that she'd been using to mix the paste.

— *I need some more water.*

Without waiting for a reply she ran out, full of mischievous energy, bare feet fast across the smooth mud path, running past the houses and out of the village.

Her village was set among orchards that fanned out in every direction — the entire valley was green and lush, filled with trees planted so that there was always a new crop coming into season — almonds, walnuts, apricots, apples and black plums. Each orchard was watered by an irrigation system. A deep channel lined with concrete brought water from the mountains, gushing at speed before dividing into a smaller network that spread out across the orchards. According to her father, as a consequence of their ingenuity the village of Sokh Rot was one of the richest in the region, famous for its crops and a grand procession of mulberry trees that welcomed visitors when they travelled up the main road into the village centre.

Despite the beauty of their surroundings, Zabi was the only girl who liked playing outside. Laila and Sahar were sometimes outside but they were only three years old and never ventured much beyond the perimeter of their houses, mostly feeding the goats. The other girls, the older girls, spent their time inside. When they did leave the house they were dressed formally and always on a specific errand, never to play. Zabi could sit with them inside, with her mother, enjoying their stories. And she admitted that sometimes it was fun to be inside, if it was cold or raining, and sometimes it was fun to bake, to cook, stitch and make dyes for carpets, but not all the time, not every day.

She stopped running, far enough away from the village not to be called back. She was still carrying the steel urn and she placed it down, at the foot of the largest apricot tree in the centre of the field third away from her village. She didn't have any shoes on. It didn't matter. She didn't feel cold. Walking through the trees she thought upon something her mother had recently said:

You are almost a woman now.

Being called a woman sounded like a compliment. Even so, the remark had troubled her. The women in the village never played outside, never ran through the orchards and never climbed the trees. If being a woman meant doing none of those things, she'd prefer to remain a girl.

Nearing the outskirts of the orchards, she stood by the main irrigation channel that carried water down from the mountains. The channel was wide and deep: the flow was rapid. She picked up a leaf and dropped it on the surface, watching it speed away. No excuse about fetching water was going to spare her a telling-off. She'd be smacked. That didn't bother her. The punishment she feared more than anything else was to be told that she would never be allowed to go outside. She looked up, mournfully staring at the mountains and wishing that one day she could climb them right to the very top and look down on the valley.

Zabi was startled by a voice.

— *You there!*

She turned around, fearful that she was about to be scolded. An older boy was walking among the apricot trees. In the bright sunshine Zabi couldn't make out his features. He asked:

— *Why do you look so sad?*

Zabi raised a hand, blocking the sun and focusing on the boy's face. It was Sayed Mohammad. Sayed was a teenager, fourteen years old and not at all like his older brothers, who were rarely in the village. Shyly, Zabi stumbled a reply:

— *I'm not sad.*

— *Liar! I can see you are.*

Zabi didn't answer, intimidated by this young man. He was known in their village for his singing and poetry. Despite his youth, he would often sit and talk with adult men, sipping their bitter tea as though he was one of them. She asked, changing the subject:

— *What have you been doing?*

— *I've been composing a poem.*

— *You can do that while walking?*

Sayed smiled.

— *I compose them in my head.*

— *You must have a good memory.*

He seemed to think about this assertion seriously. Sayed thought about most things seriously.

— *I have a technique for remembering poems. I sing them to other people. The ones that aren't very good I quickly forget. Don't you forget the things you don't do very well?*

Trying to imitate his thoughtfulness, Zabi nodded, slowly. Before she could reply, he noticed her fingers.

— *Why are your fingers red?*

— *I've been making dye.*

Zabi wanted to impress Sayed and blurted out:

— *Did you know that the colour red tastes bitter?*

To her surprise, he was interested.

— *Is that so?*

— *I spent all morning making the dye. I tasted it several times.*

— *What is it made from?*

— *Pomegranate rinds.*

Zabi was pleased that she hadn't said something stupid. Sayed scratched his face.

— *Red has a bitter taste . . . I could use that idea in a poem.*

Zabi was amazed.

— *You could?*

— *The Soviet Union's flag is red, so saying red has a bitter taste is a political statement.*

He glanced at Zabi's expression:

— *Do you know what the Soviet Union is?*

— *They're the invaders.*

He nodded, pleased.

— *The invaders! That can be the name of my poem. The first line could say something along the lines of. . .*

He trailed off again, closing his eyes, deep in concentration, trying various ideas.

— *Red flag as bitter as?*

Zabi suggested:

— Pomegranate rinds?

Sayed laughed.

— Doesn't that sound kind to our enemy? To suggest their ideology tastes like our national fruit? We can't compare a fruit that grows here, in the soil of Afghanistan, to the flag of the invaders.

With that proclamation, Sayed walked off, apparently forgetting about Zabi. Wanting to hear more, and not wanting the conversation to end on her stupid suggestion, she caught up with him.

— Can you sing me a poem?

— I don't sing my poems to little girls. I have a reputation to think of. I sing only to warriors.

Hurt, Zabi stopped walking. Sayed noticed her reaction.

— Don't take it so badly.

Zabi wanted to cry. She hated being a girl. He softened his tone, saying:

— Did you know that my father used to despise my poems? He would hit me and tell me to shut up. He said singing and poetry were for women, he told me to be more like my brothers. It is true, some poetry is for women, such as lullabies, or a nakhta, sung by women when they mourn the death of a hero. The nakhta made me think perhaps I should compose lyrics for heroes, not mournful, but triumphant, when they are victorious against the invaders. Poetry must be more than pretty and pleasant on the ear. It must have purpose. It must have anger.

Sayed picked at the leaves of the trees, continuing:

— I sang these new poems to my father. They changed his mind. He no longer hit me. He began to tell me more and more about events in our country so that my poems would be more accurate. Since that change I sing poems about the resistance, poems that are protests against the treatment of our Afghan brothers and sisters.

My father is proud of me. He brings fighters in from the hills. They tell their stories, which I turn into poems. I am compiling a poetic history of our war, thousands of different poems. My father is going to take me travelling, through the hills, performing at different camps. Did you know that my brothers are warriors?

— *I didn't know that.*

— *They're fighting the Soviets. Samir told me he was going to blow up a dam and bring water crashing down, sweeping away the Soviet tanks. They'll come back to the village soon and I'll turn their victories into the best poems I've ever composed. The whole village will gather round and listen.*

Sayed crouched down beside Zabi, whispering as though there were people in the orchard with them who might overhear:

— *Do you want to hear a poem that would have you arrested and shot dead if you sang it in the streets of Kabul? If I sing it for you, you mustn't tell anyone, and no one can ever know. Promise to keep it a secret?*

Zabi was nervous and excited, and not wanting to seem afraid, she nodded.

— *I promise.*

Sayed began to sing:

— *O Kamal!*

He stopped.

— *Do you know who Kamal is?*

Zabi shook her head. She didn't know anyone called Kamal.

— *Kamal is the President. Do you know what a president is?*

— *An elder?*

— *In a way, yes, he's a ruler, a leader, but he was not chosen by us, by the people who live in this country, he was put in power by the invaders to do their bidding. Imagine if our village elder was chosen by another village located thousands of miles away. Would that make any sense? And then imagine if that elder hadn't even been born in our village, but came from outside, came here, to our land and told us what we could and couldn't do.*

Zabi understood: such a system didn't make any sense.

Sayed picked up his song:

— O Kamal! Son of Lenin . . .

He paused again.

— Do you know who Lenin is?

Zabi shook her head. The name was odd to her ear.

— Lenin is the man who created Communism, which is the name of the religion that the invaders believe in. Lenin is a god to the invaders, or a prophet, a divine figure – they hang up photographs of him in their schools and buildings. They read his words and chant them.

Sayed began his song again.

O Kamal! Son of Lenin,
You do not care for the religion and the faith
You may face your doom and
May you receive a calamity, O son of a traitor,
O son of Lenin!

Zabi didn't fully grasp the meaning of the lyrics despite the explanation. However, she loved the sound of Sayed's voice and at the end she clapped.

Smiling, Sayed was about to take a small bow when, like a startled animal, he spun around, staring up into the sky. Zabi couldn't hear anything except the rush of the water in the irrigation channel. Sayed didn't move: eyes fixed on the empty blue sky. Belatedly Zabi heard the noise too, a noise unlike any other she'd heard before.

Sayed grabbed her by the waist, lifting her into the nearest tree. Zabi climbed up.

— *What do you want me to do?*

— *Look into the sky! Tell me what you see!*

Even though she was light, the tree wasn't very old and the branches bent under her weight. The noise was growing louder. She could feel vibrations through the trunk. Unable to climb any further, she poked her head above the top of the tree.

— *What do you see?*

Coming directly towards her, flying low over the trees, were two war machines – giant steel insects with stub wings, each with spinning blades that cut through the air, blurring the blue sky above them. They had windows at the front, a bulb of glass – a terrifying huge monster eye. The flying machines were so low she could see the man seated inside, the pilot's face hidden by a helmet. As they passed overhead, it felt possible to reach out and touch their steel bellies. Sayed was shouting to her but she couldn't hear what he was saying, just the thump-thump of the spinning blades. A gust of air, a man-made storm passed through the trees. She gripped the branch tightly. The entire tree was shaking. Ignoring Sayed's calls for her to come down, Zabi watched as the two giant steel insects circled her village.

The first explosion was so powerful Zabi was punched out of the tree, a force hitting her in the chest, knocking her backwards. She fell, branches breaking beneath her. She would've hit the ground but Sayed caught her. There was intense heat from a fire. A plume of smoke mushroomed above them, rising up into the sky, an angry spirit unleashed. The orchards nearest the village were ablaze, the tops of trees burning. A second explosion, a rush of air, its heat curling her eyelashes. Sayed reacted, he ran, carrying her under his arm like a rolled-up rug. Clods of earth thumped down around them.

Looking back, she saw black smoke ballooning through the trees, rolling towards them like the edge of an evil cloud. Suddenly the cloud broke apart – a flock of mountain ponies burst through the smoke. Their eyes were huge, their manes on fire, skin blackened and burnt. Some were blind, or blind with panic, crashing head-on with the narrow trunks of the apricot trees, the trees splintering, the ponies dropping to the ground. Their hooves ripped up the soil. One pony continued to run even with its stomach gashed open, charging past, while another collapsed to the ground beside them, legs buckling underneath it, tongue hanging out.

The mechanical thumping noise returned. One of the flying machines pushed through the black cloud, hovering directly overhead. Sayed ran faster, his eyes wild with same panic as the ponies crashing about them on either side. There was nowhere to hide.

Zabi saw the irrigation channel ahead. Before they could reach it, a third explosion – the ground collapsing and giving way, every clod of soil, every leaf vibrating. Sayed threw her forward. For a moment she was in the air, then crashing down, landing in the channel, smashing through the surface, submerged beneath the freezing current. She rolled over, looking up through the water. There was no sign of Sayed. A burning pony leaped overhead, hooves clipping the concrete walls. The blue sky disappeared, replaced by fire. The freezing water began to bubble and boil.

Greater Province of Kabul
City of Kabul
Jada-e-Maiwand District
Microrayon Apartment Complex
Three Days Later

The apartment was newly constructed, government-created accommodation. The interior smelled of fresh paint and glue. Leo tried to open the window but it had been bolted shut, perhaps for his security since the Soviet-made glass was shatter-proof, each pane costing more to import than an Afghan glassblower earned in a year. He rested against the window, watching as the sunset refracted through dense city smog, trans-forming a layer of dirt and dust into patterns of red and orange light. He was on the fifth floor, the top floor of what would be, were it situated in the outskirts of Moscow, an anonymous con-crete block of apartments unworthy of a second look. But in Kabul the building's blandness was notable, a foreign anomaly based on Soviet designs entirely unlike the traditional stucco buildings. Built at breakneck speed, using none of the local trades or traditional craftsmanship, these apartment blocks had sprung up across the Jada-e-Maiwand district after the invasion as if from spores. This particular building, finished only last week, had a barbed-wire perimeter fence with security spotlights and was patrolled by Soviet soldiers, not Afghans, a measure of the mistrust between the two forces. Fearing further reprisals after the brutal public spectacle of Dost Mohammad's death, Soviet personnel, including advisers, had been moved into secure compounds. Leo's protests had been overruled. There were to be no exceptions. In a matter of hours they'd created an occupation-force ghetto, exactly the legacy of division and suspicion that Dost Mohammad wanted to leave behind.

Upon moving in Leo had immediately unscrewed the four doors between the rooms, stacking them on the floor. With the doors removed, there was an area in the living room where he could see the entire apartment, could confirm that the rooms were empty, preventing his imagination from tormenting him with the memories of his family. Even so, this layout was far too close to the home he'd shared with Raisa and the girls, a duplication of a typical Soviet apartment, ready furnished with plywood bookcases and wardrobes. Leo had nothing to unpack. All his possessions were on the coffee table, the bundle of unfinished letters to his daughters and his opium pipe. He'd decided not to collect the letters he'd received from Elena and Zoya for the sole reason that he couldn't stop reading them – he'd comb through the contents repeatedly until the words and sentences broke down, no longer making sense. With each reading his uncertainty regarding their true meaning grew, forcing him to read them once more, creating an obsessive cycle. He'd cross-reference letters, wondering why Zoya had only written eight hundred words this time when normally she wrote over a thousand, or wondering if Elena's style had become colder towards him, whether her final remark – *With love* – was written sincerely or out of a sense of reluctant duty. It was impossible to be sure of the tone. On one hot summer's night he'd read a single, one-page letter from Elena, with her neat small handwriting, several hundred times, and would have read it several hundred more times if the opium hadn't sent him to sleep. After that, he'd taken to reading a letter no more than three times before burning it, but he had not received a new letter for several months now. The absence of communication might be down to the unreliable nature of delivery – a stack of three or four could arrive together – but more likely it was because he hadn't responded to the last one. He found it increasingly difficult to compose his thoughts, frustrated with his attempts, starting a hundred times and hating everything he said.

Pacing the coarse synthetic fitted carpet, an aberration in this country since carpets filled with dirt and dust in days, Leo needed to smoke as a matter of urgency. As he prepared his stash, faint music could be heard from the adjacent apartment, coming from his new neighbour: Nara Mir.

After the attempted arrest of Dost Mohammad, Leo had accompanied his only surviving student back to her family home to help collect her belongings, the most important of which – her books on Marxism – had been hidden outside in the failed hope that her parents wouldn't find them. Two Soviet soldiers provided protection. By the time they were ready to leave a crowd had gathered, pushing up to the edge of the vehicle. The soldiers fired shots into the air to disperse the mob while Leo bundled Nara into the car. As they drove through the crowd, a small plastic bag hit the windscreen. Acid leaked out and the glass smoked and melted. Leo ordered the soldiers to continue driving, not to get out of the car, sensing that the provocation was a prelude to an ambush. Nara remained calm, despised by the community she'd once been part of. In response to her exile, she practised her Russian.

— My Russian is not good. I would like to make it better. From now we must speak more Russian.

For the rest of the journey, as the windscreen bubbled and hissed, she read her Russian phrase book as though nothing were wrong.

Curious at the sound of this music, Leo found the discipline to delay smoking, slipping on his flip-flops. He entered the corridor and knocked on her door. Nara opened up, releasing the several heavy locks. She was wearing her uniform despite being off duty. She'd been granted the privilege of Soviet-level accommodation primarily because she was an important symbol of the insurgents' failure to kill all the trainee officers, rather than a gesture of equality between the two forces. She was a talisman of the occupation, and they intended to protect her. Outside the barbed-wire fence and guard patrols she would only last a few hours.

On the living-room table was a bulky cassette player. Nara asked, in Russian:

— Is the music too . . . big?

She couldn't find the word and changed into Dari.

— Is it too loud?

— No.

The music was bootleg Western pop, the kind that could be found in markets, spread out on shawls, with photocopied album covers, shipped in from other countries, sold at an enormous mark-ups, intended for the occupation force. Leo had no idea what the music was, or who the singer might be. The singing was English: the accent was American. The man had an excellent voice. Nara asked, genuinely nervous:

— Is it a mistake for a Communist to purchase the music of an American singer?

Leo shook his head.

— I don't think anyone is going to mind.

— The captain gave me an allowance. I have never had my own money before. I spent it. I spent it all in a single afternoon. I kept buying things I didn't need until the money was gone. Was I wrong to do that?

— No.

— The singer is called Sam Cooke. Have you heard of him?

— I don't follow music.

They listen for a few more moments before Leo said:

— I knew an American singer once. He was a Communist and he visited Moscow many years ago when I was a young man. I provided security for him. He was called Jesse Austin. His voice sounded a little like this man's voice. Except Jesse Austin didn't sing pop songs.

Nara took a pen and pad from the living-room table, writing down the name JESSE AUSTIN, as if he were a suspect she needed to investigate.

— I will try to find him in the bazaar tomorrow.

Leo had never thought of looking for his music.

— If you find it, let me know. We can listen together.

Leo glanced around her apartment, at her Communist books now on display on the shelves, books that she'd once been forced to hide in the brickwork of an alleyway, the books that had infuriated her parents and brought about the attempt on her life. She owned very little else: the apartment was almost as empty as Leo's. The song finished. The tape crackled. A new song began. Nara said:

— Your life in Moscow must be very different from your life here?

Leo nodded, uneasy at the turn the conversation had taken.

— It was.

— Do you miss your family?

361

She'd never asked about his personal life before and he didn't like her asking about it now. He was about to say goodnight and return to his apartment when she added:

— *They're going to execute my father.*

Leo's irritation melted away. He said:

— *Yes. I know.*

— *My mother will be imprisoned. So will my brother. I've never lived without my family before.*

— *It will be hard.*

She looked into Leo's eyes with a pitiful mixture of loneliness and resolve.

— *Does it get easier?*

Leo shook his head.

— *You find ways of coping.*

Leo had not entered the apartment, remaining on the threshold, not wishing to embarrass her sense of propriety. She had not invited him in. It would be culturally inappropriate. However, he sensed that she did not want him to leave and wanted him to ask permission to come inside. She could not bring herself to make the request. Finally, Leo said:

— *Try to get some sleep.*

He turned and left, forcing himself not to look back to see if she was watching him.

Reaching the front door, Leo paused. He pictured her alone in that stark, freshly painted, soulless apartment. It was ridiculous that he should think of going back. She'd lost her family. Of course she wanted company. Was it precisely because she was alone that he wanted to be with her? The two of them were in the same position, alone, outsiders. It didn't need to become awkward. What was wrong with them becoming friends? He slowly turned around.

Nara was at the door. She had not shut it but she was not look-ing at Leo. Captain Vashchenko was at the end of the corridor, a map rolled up under his arm, walking towards them.

— *I need to speak to both of you. Let's talk in Leo's apartment.*

Nara waited until the captain had passed her before leaving her apartment, hiding behind him. Leo did not have a chance to catch her expression.

Inside his apartment, the captain spread out the map on the table, paying no attention as Leo tidied away his opium pipe. The captain took out his gun, using it to weigh the map down. It showed mountains and a valley near the city of Jalalabad, not far from the Pakistan border. The captain explained:

— *I presumed a connection between the murders in Kabul and the failed bombing of the Sarobi Dam. I was correct. Dost Mohammad was behind the murders in Kabul. We found the body of Samir Mohammad at the dam, a known bomb-maker. The two men are brothers. According to our source, there are four brothers in total, a young boy called Sayed and a fighter called Fahad, a man feared as a great warrior. This family is a unit of insurrection. Their target is the stability of Kabul. Three days ago we sent a team to their home village, not far from Jalalabad. Hind helicop-ters were supposed to provide air support for a ground team. We're told that the villagers opened fire. The helicopters retaliated. The conflict escalated.*

He paused, glancing at Leo.

— *Several hundred are dead, including women and children. We now have a problem of a different kind. Stories of the massacre have spread throughout the region. We fear they will inflame the insurgency, not just in the province where it took place but also in Kabul. News of the massacre has reached the capital. People are accusing us of striking the village as an act of revenge. Many of*

our Afghan allies are upset. They see our response as dispropor-
tionate.

Leo guessed where the captain was going.

— *You have military internal affairs. Let them investigate.*
Make a show of justice.

— *This isn't about an investigation of our personnel. They were*
doing their job. This is a public-relations exercise. We need to go
into the region and perform some kind of conciliatory gesture. You
are our most experienced adviser, you understand these people.
These terrorists are causing more problems dead than they did when
they were alive. I want you to broker some kind of peace, some kind
of compensation.

Considering the premise absurd, Leo scratched his stubble.

— *Captain, I'll be frank with you. Going to this village is a*
waste of time. They don't want anything from us, except that we
leave their country. I don't have your authorization to offer that,
do I?

Taking his gun, but leaving the map, the captain didn't register
Leo's objection, saying:

— *We leave first thing tomorrow morning. I need people to nego-*
tiate, people I trust, which is why I want Nara Mir to come with
us. She's proved herself to be a promising agent. It would be good
to have at least one Afghan, for the sake of appearances.

Departing as abruptly as he arrived, he stopped by the door,
looking back at the two of them.

— *You will translate everything I said for her, won't you?*

The captain shut the door, leaving the two of them alone
together.

The Road from Kabul to Jalalabad
100 Kilometres East of Kabul
25 Kilometres West of Jalalabad
Next Day

Leo sat in the back seat of the armoured UAZ beside Nara, the pair of them looking in opposite directions, their bodies angled away from each other. They'd been in this position for most of the long, uncomfortable journey, remaining silent and avoiding eye contact, staring at the view as their convoy had left Kabul, setting out along one of the most dangerous roads in the world, en route to Jalalabad. Forced into taking a diversion around the mountains, humbled before the Afghan landscape, the road passed through the Surobi Gorge where it twisted around sheer drops of several hundred metres, hillsides spotted with burnt-out carcasses of crashed vehicles. This was ambush territory, as lethal as the exit from the Salang Pass where insurgents hid in the mountains, picking off fuel convoys. A military officer was driving with the captain in the front beside him. There was a second vehicle in support with four more Soviet soldiers, a modest military convoy with radios ready to call for air support should it be required. Upon occasion the captain turned around and addressed some comment to Leo, his inscrutable, angular features providing no clue as to whether he guessed what had happened last night. It would be entirely consistent with Soviet protocol if the newly constructed apartment blocks were bugged.

Last night had been a mistake, an impulsive, hot-headed mistake of the most adolescent kind. They shouldn't have kissed. Nara would surely agree. They'd been lonely, two lost souls in their bleak and empty new apartments. He couldn't remember exactly how the kiss had happened – they'd been talking, standing close, examining the map spread on the table. She'd pointed out the village where her family came from, the village where she'd never been welcome. She'd shown Leo the route by which her grandfather used to smuggle fleeces into China, explaining how many of the smugglers died in the mountain passes. As though the thought had only just occurred to her, she realized that her grandfather would have known about the plot to kill her and probably approved of it. She became upset, explaining why. It was possible at this point Leo had touched her, merely to comfort her, or he'd brushed her hand by accident. He couldn't be sure. Though the prelude was muddled in his mind, the kiss was clear, sexual desire for so long repressed by opium, or grief or both. For a moment he'd experienced an uncomplicated pleasure of the kind lost to him, an unstoppable urge, convinced nothing else made sense except following through on this impulse. Yet as he'd gripped her waist he'd felt her body trembling, overwhelmed by emotion, nervous and inexperienced. He'd pulled back. She'd stood before him, her mouth fractionally open as if trying to say something and unable to put together the words. They'd remained opposite each other for what seemed to be several minutes. It might only have been a matter of seconds before finally she'd walked out, quietly closing the door behind her.

After Nara had left Leo had smoked, filling his lungs with opium, his substitute for human contact. Exhausted, he rested his head against the bulletproof glass and closed his eyes.

*

Leo awoke to find the vehicle stationary. Nara wasn't beside him. There was no one driving. He stepped out, opening the heavy armoured door. To his side of the road there were the blue-green waters of a lake. On the other side a steep mountain towered above them. They were at Darwanta Dam, not far from their destination, the village of Sokh Rot located in the valley on the other side of the mountain. The captain was standing with his officers, several of whom were smoking. Nara was by the water, gazing into it, separate from the others. Leo walked to her. Hesitant and conscious that the captain was watching them, he was unsure what to say. He touched the water, rippling her reflection.

— *It doesn't have to be a problem.*

She didn't say anything. Leo added:

— *I take . . . responsibility. You were blameless in this.*

He wanted to stop speaking but couldn't help adding qualifications to each remark.

— *It was a mistake, a mistake that we can put behind us. That's how I feel.*

She said nothing. Leo continued:

— *The best thing would be to carry on as we were before. As though it hadn't happened. We should concentrate on the task at hand. We're close now.*

He quickly qualified:

— *I mean, we're close to the village, rather than you and I, are close, because of last night. I'm not saying we can't be close, in the future, as friends. I'd like to be your friend. If you want . . .*

Leo wished the captain had requested helicopter transport, cutting the journey to minutes rather than hours. But considering the nature of the situation, an alleged massacre by two Hind helicopters, it would have been insensitive to enter the area by air, inflaming the outrage, or sparking panic. Leo did find it odd that the captain had insisted upon handling this problem himself. The intelligence that the massacre was energizing the insurgency in Kabul seemed vague. Equally vague was the notion that forgiveness could be bought with a development project, a medical centre, a school, a well or herds of plump livestock, or why this gesture would take up the captain's time. Leo had packed nothing other than his pipe and a modest stash of opium, predicting that they would be forced to stay in nearby Jalalabad until the matter was concluded.

Nearing their destination, Captain Vashchenko became unusually talkative. He remarked:

— *Do you want to know what my biggest disappointment has been since arriving in this country?*

The question was rhetorical and he pressed ahead without waiting for, or wanting, an answer.

— *During the invasion I was involved in the siege of the President's palace, where the 40th Army is based. Where the defector was living – you went there.*

Nara had understood enough to offer the name.

— *Tapa-e-Tajbeg.*

The captain nodded.

— *The plan was to capture the President. We expected the private guard to surrender. Unlike every other Afghan division they proved resilient. We had to fight our way in. It was the first time I'd ever fought in a royal palace. There was expensive crystal smashed across the floor. Chandeliers were falling from the ceilings. Paintings and works of art were shot to pieces.*

The captain laughed.

— *Imagine fighting in a museum, that's what it was like. You're taking cover behind antiques worth more than I'll earn in a life-time. Considering there was not a hope they were going to win, those guards fought bravely. I guess they knew they were going to die whatever happened. We secured the palace room by room. I wanted to be the one who caught or killed the President. What a prize that would've been! I made a guess he would be hiding in his bedroom. Doesn't everyone retreat to the bedroom in times of danger? People associate it with safety, or the most appropriate room to die in. I was wrong. Another member of my team found the President in the bar. He had his own private bar. He was sitting on a chair, his back to the door, drinking a fifty-year-old Scotch. They shot him in the back, careful not to destroy the decanter. We drank the Scotch to celebrate. But I didn't felt like celebrating. I'm still annoyed I picked the wrong room.*

The captain shook his head in regret.

— *I've never shot a dictator.*

Leo remarked:

— *You've installed another one. Perhaps you'll get another chance.*

To his surprise this amused the captain.

— *If the time comes, I'll be heading straight to his private bar.*

He turned around, an unexpressive man allowing himself a modest smirk.

— *How about you translate that for her?*

It was the last thing the captain had said before leaving Leo and Nara alone last night. He knew that they'd kissed. Leo had been right. The rooms had been bugged.

The Border of Laghman and Nangarhar Provinces
Village of Sokh Rot
116 Kilometres East of Kabul
9 Kilometres West of Jalalabad
Same Day

Approaching the site of the massacre, the landscape began to change. The trees were no longer flecked with blossom; they were charred – branches scorched black, entire trunks burnt, reduced to charcoal silhouettes like a child's pencil drawing. At the epicentre the road disappeared, replaced by a series of ash-black craters, circled by jagged stubs, like trolls' teeth, where the trees had stood.

The captain ordered the car to stop. Leo stepped out, immediately noticing the sharp chemical smell leaching from the ground around him. When the wind blew, fine dust spiralled in the air, coils of black circling around them. Ash crunched underfoot. He caught Nara's eye. She'd never seen the war outside Kabul. She was shocked. He wondered how long it would take her to justify this destruction, to rationalize it and formulate arguments about its necessity. No doubt the process had already begun.

The mud walls of the houses were not in ruins but altogether missing. In a few cases, on the outskirts, there were remnants, mud heaped in a mound, dried out and cracked by the heat. Leo asked:

— *What did this?*

The captain was wearing sunglasses and Leo stared at his own distorted reflection in the lens.

— *These villages seem serene and quaint, your typical primitive backwater with cow-shit houses and kids chasing goats, pots and pans and bags of rice. This was a terrorist haven. The brothers who came from here were armed with enough explosives to create this kind of destruction, or worse. They were going to bring down an entire dam. Do you know how many people would've died, not only soldiers but civilians too? What did this? The villagers who lived here did this. They brought this upon themselves. Our helicopters came under heavy fire.*

Leo didn't know the classified technical specifications of the Hind attack helicopters, but they were heavily armoured: their blades were titanium tipped. Rifle and machine-gun fire wouldn't be enough to bring them down.

— *How heavy was the fire?*

The captain kicked at the ground.

— *The situation we are here to address is not an investigation into whether our pilots made the wrong decision. Fuel-air bombs were an appropriate choice of weapon, in my view. We're here to convince these people that there are better and smarter options than fighting us – that fighting us is going to bring misery to millions.*

Picking up on an earlier term, Leo asked, the jargon meaning nothing to him:

— *Fuel-air bombs?*

He'd never heard of them before. The captain briefly glanced at

Nara. Even though she'd spied on Leo, even though she'd reported on the deserters, she was still foreign and the captain would only trust her so far. He spoke softly, quickly, making sure she couldn't follow his Russian:

— *They produce blasts of a longer duration, a pressure wave that is much harder to survive. They suck up the oxygen from the surrounding air. Normal explosives contain a large percentage of oxidizer. Thermobaric weapons are mostly fuel.*

Listening to the captain, Leo understood why the military planners were so sure they would win this war. They had weapons of such ingenuity that anything other than a victory was illogical. He remarked:

— *To ensure no one survives?*

— *They're designed for cave networks. If the bomb can't destroy the entire cave, it can at least suck out the air, turning a base that is safe structurally into a death trap.*

Leo added:

— *And villages?*

Leo didn't expect an explanation, the captain was already walking away, but he belatedly understood their use. They were weapons that would ensure everyone died, reducing the visible scars of the attack without compromising the lethal intent.

Nara crouched down. There was a steel cooking pot, turned black, but otherwise undamaged. She rubbed a small patch of it clean.

Outside the former centre of the village a shallow lake of ash was forming. The toxic surface lapped at Leo's feet. The network of irrigation channels that watered the orchards had been destroyed in the attack. The water was still being carried down from the mountains but now it had nowhere to go. He scooped up a palm full of water. It trickled through his fingers, leaving a smear across his skin. He rubbed the residue with his thumb. The captain was becoming impatient:

— *We need to move into the hills, talk to the people and discover what they want. Obviously we'll we replant the orchards, clean up the water, and distribute the land to the relatives of those who were killed. You'll handle the negotiations.*

Leo stood beside Nara.

— *Nara and I will go alone. It would be best if you and your men stayed here.*

The captain shook his head without giving the idea a moment's thought.

— *Could be dangerous.*

— *No more dangerous than if you come with us.*

The captain took out a pair of binoculars, regarding the nearest village.

— *They're going to get a medical centre or a school. We don't need to be too precious about it.*

*

The nearest village to the site of the massacre was called Sau. It consisted of a cluster of houses located on the side of the mountain, at an altitude several hundred metres above the valley floor. From their position the villagers would have been able to watch as the helicopters hovered over their neighbours, launching missiles, dropping bombs, fire consuming the trees and houses. Though the village didn't look far away it took almost an hour to cross the scorched land and climb the terraced slopes, following the irrigation channel, walking along the concrete edge. The captain had not only insisted upon coming with them, he'd brought his five soldiers. Leo was confused by his approach. It was true: there was an element of danger. But ambushes were unlikely within the village itself. The mujahedin's tactics were to attack Soviet positions while presenting the enemy with no targets to retaliate against, forces that dissolved into the mountains. Their aim was not to recapture cities since such a victory offered Soviet troops a target to attack. Refusing to engage in conventional warfare, instead, they would slice at the occupation, inflicting upon it a series of cuts, some deep, many shallow. They would bleed the Soviets while the Soviets dropped bombs on dust and rock, or, in this case, apricot trees.

His brow damp with perspiration, Leo wiped his face, studying the approaching village. Sau was small. Whereas the village of Sokh Rot was founded in the lap of once-fertile orchards, this village had no obvious industry other than livestock, herds of goats that scattered as they neared it. For such a small village there was a large crowd in the centre, several hundred men, many times more than would normally be found in a village this size. Leo caught up with Nara and the captain.

— *What do you make of that?*

He pointed at the crowd. More people were arriving, travelling down from the mountain paths and across the valley. The captain surveyed the landscape, observing the crowd. Inscrutable, he remarked solemnly:

— *They want to see the destruction for themselves.*

Leo shook his head, pointing to the opposite side of the valley.

— *Why are they crossing the valley? They can see the devastation from there. Why are they coming here?*

The captain didn't reply.

*

Uneasy, Leo climbed the last few metres, entering the centre of the village and finding himself completely surrounded.

Village of Sau
118 Kilometres East of Kabul
7 Kilometres West of Jalalabad
Same Day

At a casual count there were no more than forty houses and yet in this small village was a crowd of men so dense that many were standing shoulder to shoulder: the centre was as busy as a market in Kabul. There were young boys, grown men, elders. More were entering the village from the mountain trails – so many that some had taken position on the higher ground, squatting on a terrace ledge, lined up like crows on a telephone wire. The village had become a pilgrimage site, drawing people from every direction. Some were carrying gifts: jugs of goat's milk and bowls of dried fruit, nuts and berries, as though there were a religious festival or wedding taking place. The celebratory nature of the gathering should have put Captain Vashchenko at ease. However, he seemed agitated. The Spetsnaz soldiers readied their weapons, taking up defensive positions, none of them going as far as to point their guns directly at the villagers, an act of provocation from which there'd be no turning back.

Appreciating that this situation could rapidly descend into

violence, Leo took the lead, raising his arms, showing that he carried no weapons. He spoke in Dari:

— *I am unarmed. We're here to talk.*

He appreciated that the claim he was unarmed carried little weight considering that he was flanked by heavily armed special forces. A wall of inscrutable expressions made it impossible to judge whether or not they'd even understood. Leo's accent was easy for an urbanite Afghan to follow, perhaps harder in rural areas. He turned to Nara.

— *Speak to them. Reassure them.*

Nara stepped forward, joining Leo.

— *The attack on the village of Sokh Rot was a terrible mistake. It does not represent the regime's intentions. We wish to discuss how to rebuild this area. We want to replant the orchards and clean the soil. We want fruit to grow in those fields once more. We are here to listen to you. We wish to work with you, at your direction.*

She spoke earnestly, with genuine regret at the destruction and sincere desire to rebuild the community that had been lost. Though this attempt at reconciliation was the stated purpose of their visit, the captain's thoughts were clearly elsewhere. He was looking right and left, preoccupied, not asking for a translation and not giving any instructions of his own.

Among the crowd an animated discussion broke out, a pocket of noisy disagreement. Voices were raised, arguments overlapped. The discussion faded as suddenly as it had flared and the crowd returned to its state of silence. Taking a chance Leo moved towards the point where the debate had erupted. Studying the faces of the various villagers, he stopped beside an elderly man with an astounding fire-red beard. Defiance as bright as his beard blazed in his eyes. Fiercely proud, the man was desperate to speak, wanting to make a statement. It took an effort for him to remain silent. Leo suspected the smallest action would be enough to provoke him.

— *The attack on Sokh Rot was an outrage. Help us. Advise us. How can we make it right?*

As expected, the man could not hold his tongue. He pointed to the scarred landscape where the village had once stood.

— *Help you? Here is how we will help you. We will defeat you. We will drive you from this land. And you will thank us for it for you do not belong here. You have powerful weapons. But no weapon built by man compares to the power of Allah. His love will protect us. We have been shown a sign that this is true.*

The crowd reacted strongly. Men cried out for him to be quiet. Leo asked:

— *What sign?*

There were more calls for him to be silent but the old man was keen to speak.

— *A child survives! A miracle boy! Look at all these people that have come to see the miracle! See how it inspires them. Leave our village. We do not want your help. We will rebuild our country without you!*

Several in the crowd echoed his cry.

— *Leave!*

Parts of the crowd came alive, some clapping and cheering, while the more prudent creased their faces in irritation, shouting for the impetuous to be silent. Leo was quick to follow up.

— *A survivor? A boy?*

The old man was being escorted away from Leo. As he tried to follow, other men stepped in his path, blocking his way.

Captain Vashchenko pushed through the crowd, wanting to know more.

— *What's going on?*

Leo explained:

— *Not everyone was killed. A child survived the attack. They're calling it a miracle.*

The captain didn't seem surprised. Leo asked:

— *You knew about this child?*

The captain didn't deny it:

— *We heard talk. First came the stories of the massacre, then stories of a boy. They believe the boy is proof that Communism will be defeated. Our sources in Kabul say that in just a few days the idea of a miracle child has become valuable propaganda for the insurrection. Poems are being sung about the boy being protected by the hand of God. It is ridiculous. But defections from the Afghan army jumped three hundred per cent yesterday alone. We have also lost five police officers: one turned his weapon on his comrades. It would seem that the miracle is more important than the massacre.*

Leo began to understand the captain's interest – a bombed village was hardly worth his attention, a miracle was. Nara joined them. Unaware of the developments, she said:

— *We should leave. There are too many people. We cannot negotiate.*

The crowd had not settled down. The captain shook his head.

— *Tell them I want to see the child.*

Leo was baffled.

— *They're going to refuse. It would be offensive to them. Nara is correct. We need to leave now. We can return when the mood is less volatile.*

As though Leo had not spoken, the captain repeated:

— *Tell them I want to see the child. Translate.*

Leo stood his ground.

— We can come back when there are fewer people.

The captain turned to Nara.

— I want to see the child.

Under orders, Nara addressed the crowd, raising her voice:

— With your permission we wish to see this miracle boy for ourselves.

The request caused fury. Some men raised their arms while others called out, a hundred refusals at the same time. A rock was thrown, hitting Nara on the side of the face. She dropped down, clutching her cheek. Before Leo could reach her there was machine-gun fire. The captain's gun was pointing at the sky. The soldiers were targeting theirs on the crowd. Leo edged to the captain's side.

— If we walk away, no one dies. If we stay, the situation will become violent.

The captain was calm, ignoring Leo, helping Nara to her feet.

— Are you OK?

She nodded.

— Tell them once more to show me the boy.

Nara repeated the command in Dari. As soon as she finished speaking, the captain fired another burst from his gun into the sky. He lowered the gun, aiming it directly at the crowd. One of the soldiers took out a grenade, pulling out the pin and dropping it on the ground. Despite the threats, no man in the crowd made any movement or gave any indication of where the boy might be. Leo said:

— They're not going to show you!

Believing this to be true, the captain moved to the largest house, spying the presents heaped outside. Leo followed. As the captain entered the house, he addressed his soldiers.

— Form a perimeter. No one comes in. Stay alert.

Leo and Nara entered the house. The soldiers remained outside, guns raised.

The interior of the house was dark: a thin layer of smoke had collected under the roof, smoke rippling like a trapped cloud. Candles were arranged in a rough semicircle and incense was burning. The smell was powerful, overwhelming. In the centre of the room, on a platform covered with a beautiful woven mat – arranged like a stage – was the boy. He was dressed in white shawls and was no more than fourteen years old although it was hard to be sure of his age since his appearance was so extraordinary. He was completely bald, with no eyelashes or eyebrows, dressed and positioned like a religious figure. There were no obvious burn marks, his skin was untouched by the fire and shrapnel – he seemed to have no injuries at all. There were two elderly men seated beside him, but not on the stage, framing him, signalling his importance: a fourteen-year-old higher than two elders. Looking carefully at the boy's face, Leo saw that he was terrified.

The captain turned to Nara.

— *Ask them how the boy survived the attack.*

Nara translated his question. One of the elderly men spoke softly using one hand to gesture while the other remained upturned on his lap.

— *You dropped bombs, burning trees and fields and people. Your machines departed, leaving the dead, some bodies as black as ash, others who appeared to be alive, but there was no life in their lungs. Buildings were burning. Trees were burning. Then, as the smoke cleared, we saw this boy. All his hair had been burnt off his body. He was naked. Yet there was not a mark on his body. He had been protected, walking barefoot through the carnage of your warplanes.*

Once the elder had finished, Nara looked at Leo, unable to translate. The captain cried out:

— *Translate!*

Leo obliged, hurriedly summarizing. The elderly man looked at the captain, defiant, saying in Dari:

— *This boy is the reason we will defeat you.*

The captain didn't wait for Leo to translate. He raised his gun and shot the boy in the head.

Same Day

Leo stood, hoping that the miracle might be true and that the boy would rise up uninjured and prove that he could not be killed with bullets or bombs and that he truly was protected by a divine power. The boy lay still, sprawled across the beautiful patterned rug, on the stage, with no trace of blood across his bright white shawls. Captain Vashchenko lowered his gun. Distinguished for bravery and courage, this soldier had shot a teenage boy to prove a point – that there was no God, or if there was, then this God was not in the business of intervening in wars. The Afghans had no supernatural force on their side. And they were fighting a force that would do whatever was necessary. All these ideas expressed in a single gunshot.

Leo stepped forward, reaching the stage, bending down and putting a finger on the boy's neck, feeling the heat of his body. There was no pulse. The captain said:

— *We're done here.*

Leo didn't know this boy. He didn't know his name or his age. Over the course of seven years in Afghanistan, he'd witnessed atrocities committed by Afghan Communists and by insurrection fighters, by religious fanatics and fanatical Communists –

382

beheadings, murders, executions and firing squads. These deaths would continue no matter what he did or said. The captain would argue, correctly, that boy was old enough to fight, old enough to carry an AK-47, to fire at a convoy, to carry an explosive device. If he hadn't died here, he might have died in a bombing raid or stepped on a mine. No one needed Leo's outrage, certainly not the Afghans – they had their own anger. This was a military operation. The captain hadn't lost his temper, hadn't been motivated by hatred or sadistic pleasure, he'd weighed up the situation. The boy was an enemy asset, like a stockpile of rifles. His mission had been simple: disprove the miracle. Leo had been too busy worrying over his kiss with Nara to realize the stated objective of their mission had been a front for an assassination. He'd been blind: dulled by opium and a lack of sleep.

Two of the soldiers peered in, seeing the dead boy, checking that the captain was OK. They'd known the nature of their mission. The captain impatiently ushered Leo and Nara to the door.

— *We leave, now!*

None of the crowd would have been able to see the execution but they would have heard the shot.

Like a statue coming to life one of the elderly men in the hut wailed, a delayed cry of anguish. Startled by the noise, Leo spun round, guessing from the reaction that he was the boy's father. At the same time, outside the house, the soldiers opened fire with bursts from their machine guns. From his position, still kneeling on the floor with his finger on the boy's neck, Leo could see the crowd breaking apart, running, several men falling. The captain moved to the entrance, raising his gun, firing shots from the doorway.

In the confusion, Leo neglected to check the old man. The elder had staggered to his feet and was striding towards him with a curved knife, the blade protruding from his hand like a talon. He raised it above his head, ready to strike. Leo's training and combat instincts deserted him, leaving him helpless before this man's blade.

The elder's arm spun away, as though yanked back by a string. The captain fired again, hitting the old man in the shoulder and stomach. The elder dropped the knife. A fourth shot knocked him to the floor, not far from the body of the boy. Leo remained in the same position, still waiting for the knife to hit his neck. The captain turned the gun on the second Afghan elder: a man who'd remained silent, cross-legged on the ground. The captain fired into his chest, killing him, before returning his attention to the fight outside.

Leo slowly got to his feet, sure that he was going to topple, his legs heavy as lead. He felt delirious. Candles flickered, smoke swirled. An explosion outside brought him to his senses. Despite the fact that upon arrival he'd seen no Afghans carrying weapons, they'd evidently produced some. The captain remained in the hut, now on one knee, reloading then firing carefully from the doorway, entirely untroubled by the dead boy behind him.

A burst of machine-gun fire cut through the roof, the line of bullets running along the mud floor. The trapped smoke escaped through the holes, daylight burst through. The villagers were firing from a position on the ridge. The captain returned fire, at the terraced fields, shouting orders at the other soldiers. He darted out, into the open. Another burst of fire came through the roof, hitting the body of the dead elder. Leo made no effort to find safety. Someone grabbed his wrist. It was Nara, pulling him to the back of the house.

They were in the kitchen. There was a mud stove and beside it four women huddled together, a high stack of flat nan bread beside them, ready for the guests visiting the miracle boy. One nan was on the fire, burnt black. The women were too scared to move, letting the bread smoke. Machine-gun fire surrounded them. Leo crouched by the fire, sliding the burnt nan off the stove, regarding the four Afghan women carefully for the first time. One of them wasn't a woman but a young girl, perhaps only seven or eight years old. The girl's head was almost totally bald except for the odd clumps of hair twisted by heat. Her scalp was red and raw. There were burn marks on her face, burns to her hands. Slowly Leo began to question the things he'd seen. How could the boy's hair have been burnt off by the fire without any damage to his skin? Miracles aside, there was no logic to the boy's appearance. Leo had encountered many men, women and children who'd survived scenes of devastation and none of them looked like the boy – they looked like this girl. He realized the boy's hair had been shaved. His appearance had been altered. He'd been dressed to fit the part. If there had only been one survivor, it hadn't been the boy – it had been this girl. Her place had been substituted for a young man, perhaps someone the villagers hoped would grow into a warrior, or a symbol that could be taken from village to village. They would not have been able to use a girl in that way. The miracle needed to be a boy in order to be a miracle they could exploit. Leo glanced at Nara's expression. She'd come to the same conclusion.

From outside, the captain called their names. Leo raised a single finger to his lips. By the dim light of the stove Nara gave no response, standing still, her face obscured by the smoke rising from the burnt nan bread. Surely she understood the captain would kill this girl as he had killed the boy. The gender of the child was irrelevant.

The captain shouted out:

—*We're leaving!*

Leo moved to the door, gesturing for Nara to follow. She didn't move, speaking in broken Russian, calling:

— *Captain Vashchenko, there is something you need to see.*

Same Day

Not knowing why he'd been called, the captain entered the kitchen cautiously, his gun raised, expecting a trap. Stunned by Nara's decision and convinced she didn't understand the consequences of her actions, Leo tried to hurry them out, offering Nara a second chance to save the girl.

— *Let's go.*

Leo had underestimated the bond between Nara and the party. She'd chosen the State over him, ignoring his advice, ignoring her own moral code – one that he knew she had. He would not allow her to make the same mistakes he had as an agent. She had made one already, showing no mercy to the deserting couple. But from this there would be no going back; she would be changed, like plastic warped in heat, unable ever to return to its previous shape. The conflicting forces were powerful. She was loyal to the party, loyal to the State. The State was her family now and Leo's kiss last night had confirmed what she already knew. No Afghan man would ever marry her. She would be alone, hated by her community, protected only by the captain and men like him. Her life depended upon the occupation. If the Soviets lost the war, then she would die with them. Leo's position, neither a Soviet nor an Afghan, offered her nothing.

Gripping her hand, he said:

— *Nara, let's go.*

She shook his hand free, pointing at the young girl and addressing the captain in awkward Russian.

— *The child.*

The captain's impatience disappeared and his attention focused on the young girl, walking up to her, studying her. It took him no more than a few seconds to realize her significance. Leo cried out:

— *Leave her alone!*

He put a hand on the captain's shoulder. The captain stood up sharply, striking Leo with the butt of his gun.

— *Why do you think I came here personally, Leo Demidov? Why do you think I didn't trust anyone else with this mission? I'm the only one prepared to do what needs to be done. Another man might've taken a look at this girl and not seen how dangerous she is. An enemy drugged on superstition will continue fighting even when they're guaranteed to lose. This girl could cost hundreds of Soviet lives. She could cost thousands of Afghans their lives. Your mercy would result in far more bloodshed.*

He picked up the little girl, carrying her out of the house. Nara followed him. Leo remained in the kitchen with the three women: their faces obscured by the shadows, smoke from the fire swirling around them. Three strangers waiting to see what decision he would make. There was no reason why Leo should care what they thought. He would never encounter them again. It was irrational to be unsettled by their unseen eyes. Except that in the gloom they were no longer strangers for they had become the three women from his own life: his two daughters and his wife, Raisa. And nothing in the world mattered to him more than what they thought. It was irrelevant that he would never hold Raisa's hand again, never touch her or kiss her. In all likelihood, he would never be reunited with his daughters either. Yet they were here with him now, in this room, judging him. The smoke from the fire had become the opium cloud in which he'd hidden. There was to be no hiding now. It was time to decide whether he could fail his family in a way that he had sworn that he would never do again.

Returning to the main chamber, Leo bent down beside the body of the elder and picked up the man's long curved knife.

Same Day

The village was burning. Scores of men lay on the ground. A few
hopelessly clutched their wounds as if trying to put their bodies
back together. Others were pitifully crawling away, leaving bloody
trails in the dust. Leo walked between them, stepping over them,
moving slowly, the knife in his hand, flat against his back.

A house had been destroyed; a grenade tossed inside, a wall had
collapsed, the timber roof was smoking. Three of the Spetsnaz soldiers were dead. A fourth was shot, unable to hold a gun, resting
on the shoulders of the only remaining uninjured soldier. He was
holding two guns, firing at the vantage points above them, bullets
hitting the ridge. His voice was hoarse, shouting out, furious at the
delay:

— *Let's go!*

The captain forced the little girl onto her knees in the centre of
the village, calling out to the mountains, to the hiding places
where the survivors had fled and the fighters had taken up arms.

— *Here is your miracle child! Here is the child that cannot be
killed!*

He put the gun to her head.

Striding up behind the captain, Leo swung the knife, imitating the elder's line of attack and aiming at his neck. He was no longer as fast as he had been, his skills were diluted by age and opium. The captain heard him and turned, raising an arm to block the knife. The blade was sharp and cut into the captain's forearm, slicing deep enough to make him drop his gun. Leo brought the blade up, ready to strike him again. The captain, ignoring his injury, kicked Leo's feet out from under him. Leo fell back, dropping the knife, staring up at the sky.

The Spetsnaz soldier stepped towards Leo, lowering his gun. Leo rolled towards the girl still kneeling on the ground, called out in Dari:

— *Run!*

She didn't move. She didn't even open her eyes. There was a burst of machine-gun fire. But Leo had not been shot. Unable to understand how the man had missed, Leo looked up. He saw the Soviet soldier topple back, taking with him his injured colleague.

Exploiting the distraction, several armed villagers advanced, firing their weapons. Alone, the captain pulled back, unarmed and under fire. Assessing the situation, outgunned, unable to reach the girl, he fled towards the path down the hill, chased by gunfire. Leo checked on the little girl. Her eyes were still closed. He sat up, crawling towards her. He touched her face. She opened her eyes, burnt lashes twisted together. He whispered:

— *You're safe.*

Villagers were returning, armed and closing in. One man was leading them, tall, thin, awkward, armed with a Soviet-made AK-47. He walked up to the fallen soldier, the injured man, and shot him in the head. Turning to Nara, who'd remained motionless, he grabbed her arm, throwing her to the ground beside Leo. The miracle girl was carried away. The leader towered over Leo, regarding him with contempt and confusion.

— *Why did you attack your own troops?*

— *I am not a soldier. I have no allegiance to men who would kill a child.*

— *What is your name?*

— *I am Leo Demidov, special adviser to the Soviet occupation. What is yours?*

— *My name is Fahad Mohammad.*

Leo managed to conceal his recognition of the name. Nara failed. He was the brother of the man they'd arrested and killed in Kabul, brother of the bomb-maker shot at the dam, and brother of the boy killed in the village. Fahad turned to Nara.

— *You know me, traitor?*

Several of the fighters took aim.

Same Day

A safe distance from the village, Captain Vashchenko paused, catching his breath. He was pale, dizzy. The bandage he'd ripped for his wound was soaked through and blood was running into his hand. There seemed to be no one in close pursuit and he was confident he could make it to the jeeps. He turned back, regarding the village of Sau. There was every possibility the fighters would kill Nara Mir and Leo Demidov. But the miracle girl was still alive. The failed attempt on her life supported the notion that she was under divine protection, and proof the Soviets would lose the war. Vashchenko had made matters worse. Five soldiers were dead: their bodies would be picked upon like carrion, their uniforms turned into trophies, their weapons paraded – bullets that failed to kill a young girl.

There was a radio transceiver in the vehicle. He would call for air strikes across the entire mountain face. He would turn these lush green hills smouldering black. He would flatten every house. With this thought, the captain began to feel a little better.

Nangarhar Province
Rodat District
15 Kilometres South of Jalalabad
3100 Metres above Sea Level
Next Day

Though Leo had not been executed, he was far from being safe. Coiled on the cave floor, Leo clasped his stomach. The cramps came in waves. His need for opium felt as desperate as being underwater, unable to breathe – how could he deny his body's impulse to surface? Opium was as natural to him as air to his lungs. His body no longer understood how to function without the drug, physically and psychologically. He'd forgotten how an ordinary person exists hour by hour, how they cope with their frustrations and anxieties. Through narcotics, he'd banished pain and suppressed grief. For seven opium summers he had no needs other than the smoke inhaled into his lungs at the end of every day, achieving a state of numbness, necessary if he was not to attempt something foolhardy. He'd abandoned his grand plans, his journey to America, and put aside the ambition that he might one day find the man who murdered his wife. Though he might not have admitted as much, pretending he was merely delaying the journey, the truth was that he'd dropped the investigation, living solely by the clock of his addiction and the daily routine of oblivion. Without the drug the stark reality of his failure returned. He had not achieved the one thing that mattered most – justice for Raisa – the only thing he could offer her. Instead, he was a grown man who'd made an infant of himself, creating an opium womb.

As Fahad Mohammad had led them out of the valley the withdrawal symptoms had begun, slowly at first, the body's gentle reminder that he was an addict. When the warnings were ignored the symptoms became far worse. Leo shivered as they walked, his whole body trembling with cold even though they were travelling at great speed. Fahad's pace was so remarkable, so quick, his legs so long and nimble that from time to time they needed to jog just to keep up. Leo and Nara took turns in carrying the miracle girl, whose name was Zabi. In shock, bewildered, she made no complaints and asked no questions. When Fahad was out of earshot, Nara wanted to talk to Leo but he was in no state to discuss anything. By dusk his condition had worsened dramatically. His whole body shook with each step and it took concentration just to keep on the path, one foot in front of the other, as his skin turned clammy and his brow dripped with sweat. The first air strikes occurred on the cusp of darkness, a burning bright glow and a chemical-fire sunrise. They paused briefly to look back at the fire sweeping the slopes, the bursts of light, at houses obliterated and fields turned to ash, villages scooped up and tossed into the air. Fahad ordered them to run as the strikes drew closer. Aided by the darkness they'd continued their escape into the night. They could hear, feel and smell the bombing, at one point a bomb detonated so close the entire path was covered with smoke. Fighter jets streaked the night sky, targeting the paths they'd only recently crossed, sending vibrations through the landscape as if this war was against the soil and rock of Afghanistan.

Leo begged for a break, stopping by a river, pretending to sip from the water. He took out his wrap of opium and even though his pipe was smashed, he tried to fashion a way to burn it only to have Fahad grab the drug, crush it in his hand and toss the remains into the river. Crazed with anguish, as though he'd lost the love of his life, Leo plunged into the water, blindly scraping the surface for any trace and pitifully crying out.

Sobbing like a child, waist-deep in the river, he'd turned around to see the three of them staring at him. He was too sick to feel humiliation. Fahad moved off without a word, carrying the girl. Nara waited for a few seconds and then followed, leaving Leo alone. Her departure was fortunate since Leo had lost control of his bodily functions, squatting in the river, throwing up at the same time as being struck by diarrhoea. When he eventually left the river he staggered after the others unable to straighten his back, lurching rather than walking, certain with each step that he'd fall to the ground and never stand again.

By the time they were allowed to rest, he was delirious, barely able to comprehend his surroundings, with no idea where they were or in which direction they were travelling. They'd been given shelter in a village, but he hadn't slept, throwing up at regular intervals until there was nothing in his stomach, coughing up bile and acidic spit, before returning to his foetal position on the jute mattress. At dawn Fahad hurried them on after a breakfast of flat bread and tea. Leo had refused the food, taking only small sips of sweet tea, unable to hold anything else down.

The second day of walking had been worse than the first. Not only did Leo feel sick, he was weak and exhausted. Fahad would not stop and would not slow down, always demanding that they walk faster. The air strikes entered their second campaign but the Soviet bombers were always one mountain range behind. Leo had staggered on without a thought in his mind except for the image of the opium on the surface of the river. Faced with a steep climb up a mountain path he was at the point of collapse. He felt no joy when Fahad had announced that they'd arrived. He merely allowed his legs to give way, falling to the ground at the mouth of the cave.

*

Feverish, huddled on the cold stone floor, Leo slowly realized that there was a hand resting on his shoulder. He rolled over to see that he'd been brought a steel cup of sweet black tea and as he clutched the cup, feeling the heat through the palms of his hands, he saw the woman who'd brought it to him. He sat up, spilling the tea on his fingers, ignoring the pain, astonished as Raisa wiped his brow with a cold rag. He wanted to touch her but feared that she was an apparition and any contact would make her shimmer and vanish. Dumb with joy, he watched her lips as she spoke, each word a miracle. She said:

— *Try to drink your tea while it's hot.*

Leo obeyed, sipping the sweet black tea, while never taking his eyes off her, not even for a second.

— *I was dreaming about the first time we met. Do you remember?*

— *When we met?*

— *I stepped off at the wrong metro stop just to ask your name. You told me it was Lena. For a whole week, I told everyone that I was in love with a beautiful woman called Lena. Then I ran into you again, on the tramcar. I don't know why I was so determined, when it was obvious you wanted to be left alone. I was sure that if*

I could just talk to you then you'd like me and if you liked me a little, perhaps, one day, you'd love me. And if that happened, if a person like you could love me, then how could I be a terrible person? When I found out you'd lied about your name I didn't care. I was so excited to discover your real name. I told everyone that I was in love with a beautiful woman called Raisa. They laughed at me because last week it had been Lena and then this week it was Raisa. But it was always you.

Leo didn't dare to blink, forcing his eyes to remain open, as if a flutter of his eyelids could wipe her from existence. Clutching the tea tight to prevent him from taking her hands, he said:

— *I'm sorry I didn't make it to New York. I tried. If you'd been by my side I know we would have made that journey. The truth is I've never amounted to anything without you. Loving you was the only achievement I've ever been proud of. Since you died, I've been a distracted father and worst of all, I've become an agent once more – doing a job you despise.*

As he began to cry, the image of Raisa became blurred. He cried out:

— *Wait!*

He wiped the tears away only to see that the woman in front of him was no longer his wife but Nara Mir.

Nara sat silent for some time before asking:

— *Raisa was the name of your wife?*

Leo closed his eyes. Immersed in darkness, he breathed deeply.

— *Raisa was the name of my wife.*

In all the years of smoking opium he'd never been gifted with a clear vision of his wife, never experienced a hallucination, never seen her before him or felt her near him even for a fleeting moment. Now, without any drug, she'd been by his side. It was wrong to call these withdrawal symptoms – the opposite was true, opium had been a withdrawal from the world. These were the symptoms of a man returning to the world.

He stood up, slowly. With one hand on the cave wall, he found his way outside. It was night. The moon was bright. Before him, the valley dropped down steeply and in the distance mountains rose like the spine of a dormant prehistoric monster. Village fires flickered like disgraced stars tossed down from the sky while those in the heavens sparkled brilliantly, as numerous as he'd ever seen. No longer numb, Leo felt childlike wonder at this view. He was not yet done with this world. Not only did he feel it, he believed it too.

Next Day

Nara sat at the entrance of the cave watching the sunrise. Light sliced by the jagged mountaintops into uneven beams promised a perfect day. The sight of sun gave her no pleasure and no feelings of hope. On the run, chased by the bombs of the Soviet aircraft, exhausted, she had no time or energy to dwell upon her actions. Reaching safety, taking shelter in the cave, she could think only of her decision to call out for Captain Vashchenko. The sound of her words echoed in her head: her voice was awful, full of self-satisfied pride, deluded belief that she was performing a valuable duty to the State.

There is something you must see.

She'd beckoned him to an injured girl knowing his intentions exactly. He would shoot the girl as he had shot the boy. She could not claim ignorance as an excuse. She had been prepared to watch the execution of a seven-year-old girl.

Her identity had changed and there was no undoing the transformation. Even when her family had plotted her death, observing the hatred in her father's eyes she had never doubted

400

the nature of her character. She was a good person. She had been wronged and misunderstood. Her intentions were noble. She was not like the men who attacked her: she was not like her father planning her death or her mother silently standing by. She would not be defined by rage and anger. She would be motivated by hope, idealism, and she was not afraid to make a stand. Yes, the repercussions were that she was alone and unloved. Better to be isolated than to compromise her beliefs, striving for acceptance from those she did not respect. There was no value in love that was dependent upon pretence. For as long as she could remember she'd been someone who did the right thing, no matter how difficult that made her life. That was no longer true.

The conclusion was inescapable. Having lost one family, she was not prepared to lose another – the State. She was a coward. It begged the question of whether her values had been nothing more than personal ambition reconfigured as ideology. Just as she'd been unable to resist the captain's decision, she'd been unable to support Leo's resistance, standing on the side, incapable of making a stand. She was a traitor in the eyes of the Communist state and a traitor in the eyes of the Afghan people. To Leo, she was morally weak. Had she worked so hard at her education in order that she might manufacture justifications for the murder of a young girl? Was this why she'd read so many books? Her sense of shame was intense. The feeling was akin to grief, as though her identity had died. The prospect of young Zabi waking up and asking for breakfast, unaware of the fact that Nara had called out for her execution, made it difficult to breathe. She sat, snatching gulps of air.

Nara stood up, leaving the cave and moving down the path. They'd not been guarded since any attempt to run was futile, even with several hours' head start there was nowhere to hide. They would be tracked down and killed. Only a few paces away the narrow mountain trail narrowed, with a sheer vertical drop of some thirty or so metres to one side. Arriving at the drop Nara looked down. Without any sense of self-pity she accepted it was the only option remaining. She no longer knew how to live. She no longer knew her place in this world. She could neither go back to the Communist regime, nor could she go back to the little girl. She closed her eyes, ready to step out, falling to her death.

— *What are you doing?*

Startled, Nara turned around. Zabi was standing close by. Responding in an uncertain voice, Nara said:

— *I thought you were asleep?*

Zabi raised her arms, displaying the burns.

— *My skin hurts.*

The pale ointment that had been used to treat the burns had rubbed off. The brittle scabs and damaged skin were exposed. There were raw patches of red. Nara ushered her back, shooing her away.

— *Go to the cave. Please, go back.*

— *But I can't sleep.*

— *Go to the cave!*

At the sound of Nara raising her voice, Zabi slowly turned around.

Alone again, Nara looked down at the drop. Instead of death, her mind was full of thoughts of how to make a new ointment. Without one, Zabi would scratch the scabs and the wounds could become infected. Nara knew a little about the natural properties of mountainside vegetation, taught to her by her grandfather when she was a young girl. She'd cherished those lessons. He knew every plant that grew on the Afghan mountains; during his years as a smuggler he'd been forced to survive off the vegetation on several occasions. Instead of thoughts of suicide, she recalled that juniper berries could be used to create a soothing balm, particularly when mixed with natural oil, such as that pressed from nuts or seeds.

She turned her back on the drop, and ran to catch up with the tiny figure of Zabi. Nara called out to her:

— *Wait!*

Zabi stopped walking. Nara bent down, examining the girl's skin.

— *It's important you don't scratch.*

Zabi whimpered.

— *It itches.*

Hearing the girl's distress, Nara began to cry, unable to stop.

— *I'll make you a new ointment. And then it won't itch any more, I promise.*

Confused by Nara's tears, Zabi stopped crying.

— *Why are you crying?*

Nara couldn't answer. Zabi asked:

— *Does your skin hurt too?*

Nara wiped away her tears.

Same Day

Having slept for the first time in three days, Leo sat up awkwardly, his muscles aching. The cramps were still painful. His hands trembled from dehydration, lack of food, exhaustion. His lips were cracked, his skin broken. His nails were black with dirt. His hair was wild. Without the aid of a mirror, he began to tidy himself up. He used a splintered match to scrape the dirt from his nails, one by one, a thick line of grime accumulating on the match, wiped on the ground. Using a cup of cold water he made an attempt at washing his face, picking the patches of dry skin from his lips and straightening his hair.

The voice inside him demanding opium was a constant nagging rather than a deafening demand, now quieter – more like a distant whisper. He felt strong enough to ignore it. Another voice had returned, his own, and it demanded he concentrate on the matter at hand, escape, not into an opium seclusion, but escape from their predicament. First, he needed to assess his situation: he was not sure how many soldiers there were in this base. He was not even sure where they were located.

As his thoughts turned to the possibility of escape a question arose: to where and to what end? For so many years his life had been directionless, it was hard to remember a time when he was driven by dreams and ambitions of his own. He could no longer drift through days and weeks, in a haze of opium smoke. There were decisions to be made. He had a new family to look after. The plans of the Soviet defector returned to his thoughts, the aspiration of crossing the border into Pakistan and taking asylum with the Americans, seeking their protection in exchange for the information he had about the occupation of Afghanistan. It would serve two ends: survival and an opportunity to reach New York. Yet while that option would protect Nara and Zabi, there would be grave risks to his daughters in Moscow if he defected. His mind had grown slack with opiate-laziness and was unaccustomed to such dilemmas. Sensing the enormity of the journey ahead, Leo felt hungry, a sensation one that yesterday he would've sworn he'd never experience again.

Nara and Zabi were sitting at the mouth of the cave. He joined them, discreetly noting his surroundings and the number of soldiers. The girls were eating *shlombeh*, milk curd with flat bread studded with spices. Though he felt better, he decided against milk curd, instead ripping pieces of the warm flat bread. He ate slowly, chewing carefully. The dough was dense and pungently seasoned with crushed cardamom seeds. He ripped another fragment, the oil turning his fingertips yellow. Watching him eat, the young girl said:

— *Are you better now?*

Leo finished chewing before replying.

— *Much better.*

— *What was wrong with you?*

— *I was sick.*

Nara said to Zabi:

— *Let him eat.*

But Zabi continued her questioning.

405

— *What were you sick with?*

— *Sometimes a person can become sick from giving up. They're not suffering from a disease. They have no sense of purpose, or direction, despair can make a person sick.*

Zabi concentrated on everything he said as carefully as if it was the wisdom of an ancient professor. She noted:

— *You speak my language very well for an invader.*

Zabi was forthright, blunt in her observations and fearless for a girl without a family, so far from home, a home that she'd witnessed being destroyed. Leo answered:

— *When I arrived in this country I was a guest. There was no Soviet army. No military garrisons. And I set about learning your language. But you are right. Now that my country has invaded, I am no longer a guest.*

— *Is Len-In your god?*

Leo smiled at the way in which she pronounced the name. He gently shook his head.

— *No, Lenin is not my god. How did you know that name?*

Zabi took another spoonful of the milk curd.

— *A friend told me. He was going to compose a poem. He's dead now. He died in the attack. My family is dead too.*

— *I know.*

Zabi made no more mention of her family or the attack that had killed them. She ate the milk curd without any showing any outward display of grief. She possessed a degree of introspection unusual in a young child, perhaps a form of retreat from the horror of the events she'd witnessed. She would need help. She was in shock. At the moment, she was behaving as though events unfolding were quite normal. Unsure what to say to her, he noted the burns on Zabi's hands and arms and head – they'd been freshly covered with an ointment. He asked:

— *May I?*

He took her arm and smelled the ointment.

— *What is it?*

Zabi said:

— *It stops the burns from itching. So I don't scratch them and they can heal, that's what Nara says.*

— *Where did you find the ointment? Did the soldiers give it to you?*

Nara answered:

— *We made it, while you were sleeping. From almond oil, boiled juniper berries and some flowers we found outside. The soldiers gave us the oil. We found the rest of the ingredients. Zabi insisted on the flowers.*

Zabi added:

— *We didn't know what kind of flowers they were. I've never seen them before. I've never been this high up before. This is the first mountain I've climbed.*

Nara stroked back Zabi's hair.

— *I tried to explain that just because something is pretty, it doesn't make it harmless.*

Zabi replied:

— *Before I could use it in the medicine, she ate a flower, just to test to see if it was harmful. I watched her put it on her tongue and then swallow it. The petals were blue.*

Zabi paused, looking at her fingers.

— *Did you know that the colour red tastes bitter?*

Without any preamble, apparently for no reason at all, she began to cry, unable to stop. Nara put an arm around her, careful to avoid her burns. Whatever Leo planned to do, he would have to do it with them. They would come with him. He would not leave them behind.

Same Day

After breakfast, Leo waited for a chance to speak to Nara alone. While Zabi reapplied the ointment, he took his opportunity.

— *Walk with me.*

They left the cave, following the path down the mountainside, reaching the steep drop. Despite Leo's urgency, Nara seemed distracted. He touched her arm, trying to get her to focus, unsure how long they had.

— *Nara?*

She looked up, saying:

— *You find it hypocritical of me to look after Zabi as if nothing was wrong. I tried to have her killed and now I tend to her wounds? Tell me, how should I behave?*

— *Nara, you made a terrible mistake. I have been in the same position as you. I have made similar mistakes believing that I was serving a greater good. However, the people who I wronged did not survive. You have an opportunity. Perhaps she is a miracle – she survived.*

— *I will always know what I did, even if she doesn't.*

— *That is true. You must find a way to live with that. It is*

408

possible, difficult, but she will need someone to look after her. She is
alone. You could love her, if she will let you.

No guards had come after them and Leo was pleased that security seemed relaxed. While Nara was still brooding over her
decision, he changed the subject to the prospect of escape.

— *What are the soldiers planning to do with us? Have they said*
anything?

Nara shook her head.

— *They've said very little. They've treated us well enough.*
They've fed us. They gave us the almond oil we used for the oint-
ment.

— *And Fahad Mohammad?*

— *He's here. They haven't allowed us further inside. When we*
arrived they provided us with a blanket and told us not to light a
fire. They were worried it might be seen.

— *And Zabi? How is she?*

— *She's upset . . .*

Leo interrupted:

— *I mean, is she strong enough to run?*

He peered down the path, assessing their position and altitude.
A man leading a mountain pony was climbing the trail towards
them, the pony sighing from the exertion, laden with supplies.
Nara was perplexed by his question.

— *Run where?*

— *We can't stay here.*

— *To escape?*

— *Yes.*

— *How far do you think we'd get? They know these trails. They*
know every village from here to Pakistan. We wouldn't stand a
chance. Why do you think they haven't bothered to guard us? Or tie
us up?

— *I've made difficult journeys before. But I won't do it without you.*

— *I don't know what you've done in the past. This is my country. You must listen to me. I am not afraid of dying. But what you suggest is impossible.*

Before Leo could press his case, a group of mujahedin emerged from the caves. The tall figure of Fahad Mohammad was among them. He did not seem concerned that they were outside the cave.

— *A jirga has convened.*

A *jirga* was a council, a decision-making body composed of elders. Leo asked:

— *You wish me to stand before it?*

— *The three of you will stand before it. Follow me.*

Entering the depths of the cave network for the first time, Leo was impressed by the degree of sophistication in its development. Further inside there were timber steps, a drop of at least ten metres to an uneven passageway – a narrow man-made corridor, blasted with dynamite and supported with scaffolding. There were extensive munitions and food stocks in several uneven-sized stores on either side. At the end of the passageway there were further steps down, leading into a natural chamber, a giant dome, as if a massive air bubble had been trapped in the rock when the mountains were created. There was running water, a mountain stream. The air was cool and damp. There had to be a natural ventilation source for they were too deep into the mountain for air from the entrance to offer enough circulation. The base was an ingenious fusion of the natural environment and the man-made, enabling this central chamber to be inhabited deep inside the mountain with a thousand metres of rock and snow above them as protection.

Leo counted six men. Like elders in a village, they wore no

uniforms, with mismatched weapons by their sides, some with pistols so ancient it was hard to consider them anything other than symbols of war, others with rifles, all crouched in a typical stance, legs tucked under them, bodies hidden beneath thick *pattu*, blankets wrapped around them like seed pods. The lighting in the cave was electric so as not to foul the air with burning torches. A system of wires ran along the floor connecting batteries – it was a dim, bat-like existence, and Leo took a moment to adjust, before being able to observe their faces. He was presented first while Nara and Zabi were held back at the entrance of the domed chamber. The man in the middle of the council, apparently the leader, stood up:

— *The khareji have spent three days bombing the valley and shooting at anyone who walks on the paths. They have sent many hundreds of soldiers to look for you. You are of value to them. Explain this.*

Khareji was a name for a foreigner and was spoken with contempt. Leo couldn't be sure why the Soviets had sent so many troops into the valley but considering the circumstances it made sense to emphasize his importance. He answered:

— *I am not a soldier. I have never fired a weapon in this country. I am an adviser. I have lived in Afghanistan for many years, longer than any other adviser. I know more about Soviet interests in this country than anyone else. I have been writing reports for the Kremlin—*

One man stopped him.

— *What did you say in your reports?*

— *I advised on many different matters, including a recommendation that they should not invade this country.*

— *Your advice was ignored. You cannot be important.*

— *Some of my reports were listened to. Many were ignored.*

411

There was hushed discussion among the council. Finally, the leader spoke again.

— *It is as we thought. You will make a valuable hostage. Fahad Mohammad was correct to keep you alive.*

He waved Leo aside and gestured at Zabi.

— *It has been decided. A boy will pretend to be the only survivor from the village of Sokh Rot. The miracle of your survival is of use to us. We are informed that the story has become a powerful inspiration. You will be sent far away. A new home will be found for you. You will be kept safe from the Soviets.*

He then gestured at Nara.

— *Finally, we come to the woman. She is a traitor. She is worse than a khareji. She is an Afghan, but a slave of the occupation, a murderer. She will be executed. The sentence will be carried out immediately.*

Same Day

There was no discussion. The judgements had been given and before Leo had a chance to protest the council was on its feet. Soldiers dragged Nara away. Leo tried to move after them but a young man, his face almost completely concealed, stepped in front of him, blocking the path. Nara and Zabi were taken out of the cave. Helpless, Leo watched as the members of the council climbed the steps. He called after them:

— *Wait!*

They ignored him, one by one leaving the chamber. Leo cried out again:

— *She could be valuable to you!*

The last member of the council paused.

— *She is of value to us. She is of value dead, as a symbol of what happens to Afghans who betray their country.*

The council member gestured at the guard.

— *Bring him. He can watch.*

The soldier waited until everyone else had left the chamber before allowing Leo to the steps. Trapped at the back of the group, he tried to hurry forward but the men in front of him would not be rushed.

The last to arrive at the mouth of the cave, Leo caught sight of the final preparations. Nara's hands and feet were lashed together. A rope was tied to her wrists, harnessed to the back of the ragged pony he'd seen earlier. The pony hadn't been delivering supplies, as he had presumed, it had been sent as a means of execution. It stood at the mouth of the cave, unsettled by the commotion, kicking at the dusty path and snorting. Nara would be dragged to her death.

Zabi was at the front of the crowd, either by accident or design. She would be made to watch, along with the other soldiers, some fifty or so, gathered for this spectacle. Leo pushed forward. A gun was pointed at him, cautioning him to remain back. He called out in the direction of the council members.

— *I have a proposal!*

The leader shook his head.

— *You think us cruel? How do the Communists deal with their enemies? They torture them. They shoot them. Many thousands of Afghans have died. Many thousands will die. Your soldiers kill innocent families in the hope of killing one fighter. There is nothing you can say in her defence. There is no defence. She is a traitor. There is no deal to be made. You have no proposal that will interest us.*

One of the elders slapped the pony and it began to move. Nara was pulled off her feet, falling to the ground, her face cut open on the cave floor, unable to scream, her mouth gagged. Leo cried out, as loud as he could manage:

— *How many guns would buy her life?*

The pony was walking faster, whipped on by the others. Nara was dragged out of the cave, pulled down the rough grit path, her nose filling with dirt. No one had heard Leo, or paid him any attention. He cried out again:

— *How many guns would buy her life?*

The council leader laughed at Leo.

— *For ten thousand machine guns and one thousand mortars you can have the woman.*

The elders laughed. Leo replied:

— *We have a deal. If you call an end to this!*

The elders stopped laughing, looking at Leo, trying to figure out if he was serious. Leo added:

— *Ten thousand guns, more perhaps.*

The leader raised his arm.

— *I wish to hear what he has to say.*

With the command from the council, the pony was stopped. Nara had been dragged at least twenty metres. She was not moving. Zabi had squeezed both hands into fists, positioned over her eyes. The leader walked up to Leo. He smelt of tobacco. Up close, Leo realized he was much younger than he appeared, his skin cracked, his beard grey, but he was younger than Leo.

— *You are only delaying her death by a matter of seconds if what you say has no interest to us.*

It was Leo's last chance.

— *You have said that the Soviet Union wants me dead. That is true. You admit I'm a valuable hostage. I agree. Ask yourself what would be the worst thing that could happen in their eyes?*

The leader of the council shrugged.

— *The worst has already happened. We have captured you alive. You will tell us the things you know.*

— *I could tell you the specifications of the machine guns on the Hind helicopters. I could mark troop movements on maps. I could give you most of this information in a matter of hours. But that will not give you weapons or mortars, or the ammunition you need. However, consider this. What would happen if the Soviet Union's pre-eminent adviser defected to the United States, if you took me across the border to Pakistan?*

The man shook his head.

— *This is a trick.*

— *No, it is a genuine proposal. Imagine what would happen if I convinced the Americans to support your fight.*

— *How would you do that?*

— *By telling them the truth about the war. By explaining what is at stake for the Soviet Union, their main adversary.*

— *What is at stake?*

— *They have a chance here, in Afghanistan, to deal a blow to the Soviet military machine without provoking a nuclear war. The Soviet military authorities know this to be true. Nothing scares them more. They are counting on American indifference to a country so far away from them. They are hoping that the experience of Vietnam will make them too cautious to realize the potential of this conflict. I will make the Americans understand that this is an opportunity they cannot afford to miss.*

Leo had been a war hero, risking his life countless times to defend the Soviet Union against the advance of Fascist troops. Now he was betraying that homeland, putting Soviet troops in danger, but he had not fought in order that his country might bomb villages and burn farmland.

The council members came together, discussing the idea, murmurs of their conversation echoing around the cave. The other young soldiers remained silent, neutral, as they had been throughout the process, never expressing an opinion. Leo could not look at Nara. She was face down, her clothes ripped. There were cuts on her legs. He was not sure if she was conscious. Finally the council returned their attention to Leo, trying to understand the defection ideologically.

416

— *We find the idea hard to understand. Why would you bring shame upon yourself? You would be a traitor.*

— *My motivation is no concern to you.*

— *We must believe that you are sincere.*

— *Ask Fahad Mohammad. He saw me attack my superior officer with a knife. I wounded him. I am already a traitor.*

— *That could be a trick.*

— *To what end? Ask the man who saw what happened if he thinks my actions were trickery.*

The council turned to Fahad Mohammad.

— *What do you think?*

— *If it is a trick, I do not understand it.*

A careful reply, but not an endorsement, and Leo needed to work harder to convince his audience.

— *I will do what I promise. I will defect. Tell me what you think of my proposal.*

— *It interests us.*

Leo pressed his case.

— *You need American support. You need their weapons, new guns, not the ancient rifles that can't fire straight. Not the rusty pistols you carry on your belts. You need missiles. You need a way of damaging the helicopters and jets.*

The elder nodded, musing on the idea.

— *How would you achieve this? The Americans will not trust you.*

— *Take us across the border, into Pakistan. I know that you are receiving support from the Pakistani secret police. They must have contacts within the CIA.*

— *They might.*

— *Then you have the means to contact the CIA. You can use the Pakistanis to set up a meeting.*

— *And then what? How can we trust the word of a traitor?*

— *You don't have to trust me. The CIA would not protect me unless I was valuable to them. I will tell them everything, or they will turn me loose.*

The elder asked:

— *What is it you want in return?*

— *Nara Mir and the girl would come with me.*

The suggestion caused outrage. Before they could argue, Leo continued:

— *My suggestion offends your sense of what is right and wrong. Yet I know that your decision will be pragmatic. Many of you abhor drugs, yet you trade them for weapons. You abhor the notion of American support to defeat your enemies, yet you know without their support this war will be far harder to win. Not only will my defection to the United States be a psychological blow to the Soviet Union, a propaganda coup for you, I will tell the United States what they need to hear. This is their only opportunity to fight without sending a single soldier. They can cause great problems for the Soviet Union while appearing to be neutral. Would they believe you if you said the same thing? They know you want money and weapons. Would they believe me? I want nothing.*

— *Everyone wants something. And you want her. Foreigners come here and collect our women, that is how it works, is it not? You wish her as your wife?*

— *My wife is dead.*

— *Then you wish to take another? You want her?*

— *She is my friend.*

— *A friend?*

The council laughed at this.

— *We all need friends.*

The leader stopped laughing, sinking into serious consideration.

— *We will vote.*

Hindu Kush Mountain Range
Afghanistan–Pakistan Border
The Khyber Pass
1000 Metres above Sea Level
180 Kilometres South-East of Kabul
30 Kilometres North-West of Peshawar
Next Day

They were to cross the border at night. Fahad Mohammad had volunteered to escort them to Pakistan, adamant that he should be the one to take them. His involvement surprised Leo. The hostility he'd showed towards them was intense – he made no secret of his hatred for them and appeared quite content to watch Nara die. He'd lost three brothers to Soviet operations in three days. Though he was unaware of the precise intimacy with which Leo and Nara were involved in the capture and death of his eldest brother in Kabul, Dost Mohammad, they were agents of a murderous infidel occupation and he hated them as deeply as the helicopter pilots who'd incinerated his village, killing women, children and the elderly. Despite this hatred, he'd put himself forward for the mission after the council of elders ruled in favour of Leo's proposal. The council was divided: a slim majority believed

American support could influence the future of the war, the others considered it an insult to ask for help. However, they abided by the vote and insisted upon sending one of their best soldiers, appropriate for a mission of this importance.

Fahad Mohammad would take them to the Pakistani city of Peshawar, where he'd discuss the intelligence proposal with their most important allies, the ISID, the Pakistani intelligence agency with whom they were working closely, receiving arms and devising strategy. If the Pakistanis agreed with the proposal, and their support was crucial, they would contact CIA operatives, none of whom this fiercely nationalistic faction of the mujahedin had ever met or had any dealings with. Forming a bridge to them through Leo's defection might create a vital connection and the council was keen that their group of fighters be among the first to receive American support, should it ever arrive, appreciating the danger of a rival group being armed while they received nothing. Their eye was not merely on defeating the Soviets, which they believed was inevitable, they were also jockeying for power among themselves, playing a long game that stretched into the aftermath of the occupation's collapse.

Once they reached Peshawar, Leo would make his case for defection. It would not be easy. As he understood the American position, there was strong domestic resistance to involvement in Afghanistan, particularly after Vietnam, a position exploited by the Soviets, aware that the American public would not tolerate another remote and expensive military campaign. President Carter had issued an ultimatum that the United States would boycott the Moscow Olympics if Soviet troops didn't pull out, setting a February deadline. When the deadline passed an official announcement confirmed that no American athletes would take part. Even this symbolic protest had been highly controversial, and if such a passive measure was questioned by the American public, it was hard to imagine them supporting military action. Afghanistan was remote geographically and its strategic importance remote conceptually. It was possible the CIA would show little interest in his defection, or that they'd consider accepting Leo far too politically provocative in the current atmosphere of tension. If the CIA failed to accept the offer, Fahad would surely kill them, a silent threat that hung over the mission. However, that problem was for another day. They were not in Peshawar yet.

To leave Afghanistan they were following the Silk Road, one of the world's oldest trading routes, fought over for thousands of years. With mountains on either side impassable to any except the most experienced climbers, the Khyber Pass was a strategic gateway for armies, rogues, merchants and exiles. With a young girl among their number the pass was their only option, they could not brave the mountains. There were two roads, one for the traditional caravans and wagons, and another for trucks. Both were in the hands of the Soviet forces and the pass was heavily fortified with patrols and checkpoints. Fahad's plan was to shadow the road, guiding them through the slopes on either side. In some places the landscape would pose no problem but in others the cliffs were precipitous. Their journey depended upon striking a balance between distance from the Soviet forces and the perils of the landscape. The further away from the pass the more treacherous the climb. The closer to the pass the more likely they would be discovered.

There was no moonlight, no stars – the night sky was obscured by a violent storm that had swept in unexpectedly, angry clouds twisted and coiled not far above them, moving at speed. Flashes of lightning were the only moments of brightness, like sparks from a flint failing to catch. The wind was cold and strong, opposing their journey, and they walked bent against its force. Progress was slow. Close to the Soviet positions, they had to make the journey by the cover of darkness. Attack helicopters had been circling the mountain paths during the day, firing bursts from their machine-guns at men on the trails. Fahad claimed that not since the early days of the invasion had he seen so many Soviet forces preoccu-pied with the border. Leo wondered if the helicopters were hunting for them. Captain Vashchenko might have guessed their intention. With such intense military pressure it was essential they make the crossing before daylight.

After several hours of walking and climbing, scrambling on their hands and knees, they were crossing a flat hilltop spotted with thin scrub. To the right the landscape dropped sharply, falling down to the Soviet-controlled road, and they could see the lights of troops. Fortunately the wind concealed any noise they made. But for fear of being seen they could not use a torch – even the flame of a match would be visible. Fahad was in front, seeming to sense the path instinctively, and they were entirely dependent on his knowledge of the terrain. Abruptly he stopped walking, looking up at the unsettled sky.

— *The storm is getting worse.*

Leo asked:

— *Do we have enough time to reach shelter?*

— *There is no shelter until we're inside Pakistan.*

— *Should we go back?*

Accustomed to the mujahedin's stoicism, Leo expected the idea to be rebuffed immediately. Yet Fahad gave the idea serious thought:

— *We have travelled too far. It is as difficult to go back as to go forward.*

— *Then we continue.*

About to step forward, Leo felt a tug on his hand. It was Zabi. In the darkness he couldn't see her, able only to hear her say:

— *Listen*.

He could hear the storm. Then, among the noise, was a mechanical sound — jet engines. Though it was pitch-black Leo stared up at the sky in the direction of the plane, hoping the lightning would illuminate the enemy. The edges of the Khyber Pass were an obvious bombing target: the terrain was always a likely concentration of weapons and narcotic smugglers, or in their case, political refugees.

— *We should run!*

Leo's cry disappeared into the storm. There was nowhere for them to run to, no cover on the plateau. The sound of the engines grew louder. Leo crouched down, covering Zabi as the plane passed directly overhead.

The noise of the jet engines peaked and then dissolved, swallowed up by the storm. There were no bombs, no explosions. It must have been a transport plane. Relieved, Leo stood up, looking at the black sky. Lightning flashed through the clouds and he caught a split-second glimpse of hundreds of black specks, a snowstorm — flakes falling towards them. The light disappeared and in the darkness Leo remained staring, waiting for another flash. When it finally came, the snowflakes were only metres above them, revealing themselves not as snow but fist-sized objects twirling through the sky, spinning towards them. Fahad called out:

— *Don't move!*

The first butterfly mine landed nearby, Leo didn't see it but he heard it, a thud on the dust, then another and another, some close, some far away. They weren't exploding, but resting on the surface and surrounding them. Lightning flashed and Leo saw a mine swerving in the sky directly above him, on course for his head. He took a step back, pushing Zabi with him as the mine passed in front of his face, almost brushing his nose, and settled directly on the ground in between his position and Fahad's — at the exact point where he was about to step.

In a matter of seconds the entire plateau had been rendered impassable. They couldn't go forward. They couldn't go back.

Same Day

They were trapped. Even by daylight their progress would be slow, having to tread a careful path around the mines, whose plastic shells would be coloured to match the orange and red hues of the terrain. Nara said:

— *In the morning there'll be enough light to find a way around them.*

The lack of conviction in her voice was damning. Leo muttered:

— *We're only metres from the Soviet border patrols.*

— *We might have enough time.*

— *At sunrise this is the first place they'll search.*

Fahad called out, cutting short the discussion:

— *We must wait till first light. We have no other choice. Be careful not to shuffle your feet, or fall asleep, the only safe ground is the ground you're standing on. We will need to move very fast in the morning, as soon as there's light. Rest now.*

Leo crouched down, rotating, careful not to move his feet. He wrapped his arms around Zabi, keeping her warm. On the other side Nara did the same. Their hands met on Zabi's back, fingers overlapping. The thought occurred to him to move his hand away but he dismissed the idea, instead taking hold of her hand. Huddled together, they waited for the morning.

*

It was difficult to estimate how much time had passed. In the darkness, exhausted, near delirious with cold, time became hard to quantify. The wind picked up, swirling furiously around them, as if trying to force them into the minefield. Even though they were at rest, they were being sapped by the cold. In all likelihood they might be granted a few minutes at dawn before the attack helicopters arrived but it was equally likely that the slim advantage would not be enough. Drained by the savage night, they would struggle to find the energy and pace needed to reach cover.

Something wet hit the back of Leo's neck. He touched his skin, feeling a trace of ice. He tilted his head up towards the sky. Another lump landed on his eyelashes, another spotted his forehead. Out of the darkness the rhythm of the rain increased: they'd be soaked through in seconds. As he thought upon the now impossible challenge of keeping warm until morning the rain morphed into hail, pellets of ice crashing down with such velocity that they stung his skin. Leo felt Nara's hands grip tight around his own, an expression of despair. Their journey was over.

Suddenly, to the side, no more than a few paces away, an explosion – it was small, like a flash grenade. Leo called out:

— *What was that?*

Fahad replied:

— *A mine!*

A second mine detonated, also close by. Leo smelt smoke and felt the blast of air. Another mine, this time the explosion was several hundred metres away. The hail on the pressure sensors was setting them off. Within moments, the plateau was alive with bursts of light and puffs of smoke. As the hailstorm intensified so did the pace of the explosions, now so numerous it was as if they were coming under mortar fire. Zabi cried out, terrified by the noise.

Remembering the mine directly in front of him, Leo let go of Zabi and Nara, turning hastily, once again forced to keep his feet on the same spot. If the mine exploded at this range the blast would injure the three of them. He reached out, trying to guess where it was, shielding it from the hail. His hands were lashed with falling ice. Within seconds he could no longer feel them, numb from the elbow down. The hail continued, the storm interspersed with detonations ringing across the landscape. Leo's arms were shaking. He couldn't remain in this position for long, protecting the very device that had been dropped to kill him.

The hail began to weaken, changing back into icy rain. The rate of explosions slowed down until then finally there no more detonations. Unable to keep his arms out in front of him any longer Leo lowered them. He slapped his hands together, like two slabs of dead meat, trying to restore circulation, his fingers not responding. He was too cold to think about the consequences of the hailstorm, and it was Fahad who called out from the front:

— *The path will be clear.*

Was it possible that all the mines had been destroyed, or had the detonations merely stopped when the hailstorm passed? Beginning to move his fingers again, Leo called out to Fahad:

— *How can we be sure?*

Fahad called back:

— *This mission is blessed.*

Though the notion carried no weight in Leo's mind the indisputable truth was that they would die if they remained here, freezing cold, waiting for dawn. Leo said:

427

— We must take the chance.

Nara was more cautious.

— We don't know that the path is clear. Some mines have been destroyed, surely not all of them, maybe not even the majority of them.

Fahad shouted back angrily:

— You are a non-believer! You wouldn't understand the significance of this event!

Furious, Nara replied:

— My faith doesn't make me stupid. I don't believe I'm invulnerable.

Leo interrupted:

— It is irrelevant what we believe. We cannot stay here! By tomorrow morning we will be too weak to run, too weak to escape. We must press ahead. It is a calculated risk. I will go first.

Fahad replied:

— You are the reason for this mission. You are the person the CIA wants. If you die the mission has failed. The girl should go first.

Nara said:

— I agree. I will go first.

Fahad contradicted her:

— Not you. The girl, the miracle girl, she will find a path. It is no coincidence that she is with us when this happened. We must trust in her.

Aside from the patter of rain, there was silence as Leo tried to unpick Fahad's suggestion. The man was sincere in his belief that Zabi was divinely protected. It was not cowardice that underpinned his suggestion that a young girl should walk first, leading them through the minefield, but piety. Leo was quite sure Fahad's acute sense of pride meant that he would rather lose his own life than appear to be hiding behind a girl. To Fahad it was an insult to God for any other decision to be taken. Nara spoke first, her careful response displaying diplomatic sensitivity:

— I will go first. I will lead. If this displeases Allah I will die, if not, then we need not discuss the matter further. But there is no chance, Fahad, no chance at all, that Zabi will walk first. Not while I am alive.

As expected, Fahad was insulted.

— This has nothing to do with bravery. I would gladly walk first—

Nara didn't let him finish.

— Without you, we're all dead. Without Leo, the mission has failed. I am the only person who we can risk. This isn't theology or bravery. It's common sense. I will walk first. You will follow me.

Leo protested:

— No, Nara, you must carry Zabi. I will walk first.

Nara rejected this idea.

— The CIA is not going to be interested in me. Without Fahad as our guide, we'll be lost. It has to be me. It is absurd to discuss this further. You must carry Zabi.

Without waiting for his reply, Nara manoeuvred around him, hands on his waist, until she was about to step forward. Leo cried out:

— Wait!

He remembered the mine that had landed directly in front. He waited, rain streaming down his face, until lightning flashed in the clouds. The mine was still there, unexploded. Nara had seen it too. She let go of his waist, stepping around the mine and moving to the front, overtaking Fahad.

Leo picked Zabi up:

— Hold on to my neck.

Weakened by the hail, he could feel his muscles struggling even though the girl was light. He stepped around the mine, his legs shaking with fatigue. Nara was out of sight, lost in the darkness, now at the front. He heard her voice.

— *Fahad, follow my footsteps exactly. Put your hands on my waist. That is the only way you can do it! That is the only way we're going to survive.*

Leo wondered if he was going to refuse. Fahad called back to Leo:

— *You must also do the same.*

Leo placed one hand on Fahad's waist, keeping the other supporting Zabi.

Forming an awkward human train they set off, shuffling forward blindly, guided only by the infrequent flashes of lightning. The storm had passed, moving over the mountains of Pakistan. Leo could hear Fahad's heavy breathing. He could hear their shoes on the ground. Each footstep that sank into the damp soil brought a sensation of relief. Leo felt Zabi squeeze his neck in fear. It was the closest he had ever come to praying.

Pakistan
North-West Frontier Province
Peshawar
43 Kilometres South-East
of the Afghan Border
Two Days Later

The truck shuddered over a pothole – one of many in the stricken road – and Leo woke, having dozed on the world's most expensive bed, several million dollars' worth of heroin concealed in flour bags branded with the emblem of a Western aid charity. The voice of his addiction was still demanding that he smoke but it was growing fainter by the day. Though it was a cruel test of his determination, surrounding him with drugs, opium had only ever been a way of suppressing his desire to desert his post, to nullify his restlessness and his impossible hopes of an investigation into the murder of his wife. What had once been unachievable was within his grasp: passage to America and a path to New York.

They'd crossed into Pakistan shortly after clearing the minefield. Since they'd walked in almost complete darkness they were unable to ascertain if all the mines had been detonated. The question of whether they were blessed or whether it was chance remained unanswered. Leo didn't spend too long dwelling on the matter. As a soldier in the Great Patriotic War, he'd seen examples of his friends believing they were saved by a miracle, a bullet lodged in a religious trinket, devoting themselves to understanding the meaning of this only to be killed a few weeks later. Despite his scepticism, he was pleased that their guide's hostility had softened. As the sun rose, brushing away the last of the storm, the four of them had stopped on the crest of a Pakistani hill and looked back to see Soviet attack helicopters in the distance circling the Khyber Pass. Had they waited for daylight they would have been caught. Whatever the truth of the matter, it certainly felt like a miracle.

Cold, filthy and exhausted, they'd reached Dara, a small town in the northern tribal region of Pakistan that existed like the capital city of an unofficial nation. Misunderstood as a lawless buffer state, it was instead governed by the laws of survival and commerce. While Leo had expected the sight of a Soviet civilian, a woman, a badly burnt young girl and a mujahedin fighter to attract attention, this was a town entirely without convention, dominated not by religious stricture or government policy but by brazen material needs – a trading bazaar for three of the world's top commodities: drugs, weapons and information. They were concerned with the questions of what you wanted to buy and what you wanted to sell. There were cottage heroin factories dotted through the town like teashops, bags of unprocessed opium sold for dollars, packed on the backs of mules. Weapons were tested and inspected, taken out of town and fired at tree stumps. Crates of bullets were examined as if they were treasure chests of rubies and emeralds. War funds were raised. War funds were stolen. Allegiances were bought and broken. Intelligence was sold. Victories were invented and defeats denied. From the north there was an influx of Afghan refugees, many with terrible injuries, legs sliced with shrapnel, fleeing the conflict. From the south came a trickle of Western journalists and travellers, some dressed in traditional loose-fitting clothes, others in designer khaki trousers, with sophisticated gadgets. Judging from the small number of journalists, even though this was the closest point of access to Afghanistan, Leo surmised that the war had so far failed to capture the West's imagination. Such an absence of interest did not bode well for his defection.

Though no longer in Afghanistan, they were still in danger. The Soviets were active in the tribal region, crossing the border with a frequency that showed blatant disregard for Pakistani sovereignty. Leo had heard discussion of a series of covert operations intended to destabilize the area and bring pressure on Pakistan to patrol the full length of the border, closing it down. Extreme acts of provocation were being planned as punishment for helping the mujahedin even if Pakistan's stated policy was neutrality. These Communist agents would be Afghan, perhaps disguised as refugees. Some were even corrupt mujahedin. Fahad found it implausible that any mujahedin fighter could be bought by the Soviets. Leo told him that he had seen lists of men who were on the Soviet payroll, identified by code names, arguing that on any side there were always men who could be bought, characters with weaknesses that could be exploited. Fahad had shaken his head in disgust, saying Leo spoke like a Westerner, rotten with compromise and ambiguity.

Fahad had wasted little time in getting them off the streets and into a *chai-khana*, where they were taken to a back room while he arranged transport to Peshawar, the region's capital. Only there could they make contact with Pakistani intelligence, or more specifically the ISI – the Inter-Services Intelligence, known for its close ideological association with Islamic fundamentalism. It was among the mujahedin's most powerful allies.

433

As soon as Fahad left, the three of them fell asleep, a small fire keeping them warm, lying together on a coarse woven mattress with a single thick blanket covering them. They were like characters from a fairytale. When Leo awoke he found Fahad sipping tea by the fire, his long, gangly body tucked under a blanket. He was a truly remarkable soldier, a man who didn't seem to rest, or lower his guard. His strength was not intended to impress, it was not bravado – he had no interest in Leo's opinion of him. Seeing that Leo was awake, he offered him sweet green tea. Leo accepted, joining him by the fire, in silence, improbable allies: but improbable allies would be needed again if the ISID were willing to connect them with the CIA.

*

It was evening by the time they reached their destination. Descending from the truck, Leo was taken aback by the bustle of Peshawar, adjusting to the commotion after their remote, dark days in the mountains and tribal regions. The millions of dollars of heroin they'd been sleeping on would only fetch such a price on the streets of America or Europe, on these noisy streets the sacks were worth no more than a few thousand dollars each. The truck rumbled on, a rickety exhaust pipe spluttering black smoke. Leo wondered whether the drugs had a better chance of arriving in America than they did.

They followed Fahad down narrow side streets, shop fronts and gutters clogged with brightly coloured candy papers, like fallen blossom after a storm. The city was distinct from Kabul with a stronger sense of colonial architecture – ornate, pink-red brick buildings with clock towers framed by tree-lined avenues. Like Kabul, the contrast between ancient and new was sharp. Majestic mosques centuries old stood beside modern buildings that looked as if they would struggle to survive another year. Telephone posts emerged like weeds, at odd angles, jutting up, sprouting hundreds of wires that sagged across streets. Decay and wealth circled each other. The neighbouring war had made this lost outpost important, giving it a new and highly lucrative industry — espionage, professionalized deceit.

Fahad led them to a guest lodge intended for a Western clientele; a painted wooden sign hung from the side of the building, written in English:

GOOD NIGHT

LODGE

A light bulb flickered intermittently in the narrow corridor. An unmanned reception desk was being used to store barrels of cooking oil. Fahad didn't bother ringing the buzzer for attention. He walked straight through, under a broken ceiling fan limp and askew like a desiccated insect sucked dry and left to hang in a spider's web. They entered a small restaurant. Several square tables were lined up against a wall but on one side only, as if waiting to be executed by firing squad. They were covered in red and white plastic tablecloths and set out with bright yellow napkins, unclean cutlery, each with a hundred partial fingerprints. The customers were a mix of strung-out tourists, lost souls running from home, adventurers and mercenaries. They were distinguishable by their physical strength, or lack of, and their kit, wearing leather boots laced up above their ankles or flip-flops with colourfully painted toenails. The Soviet high command had been worried about the mujahedin filling their ranks with Western mercenaries, fighters bought with drug money, believing only Westerners knew how to fight, when in fact the mujahedin, in this terrain, were the best

fighters in the world. Their fight was personal, a matter of principle not profit, and they had no time for mercenaries. They didn't
trust their motives and thought them intrinsically unreliable. The
groups sat at their tables, making plans over plates of oily chips.
There was no alcohol and apparently no staff. Some of the customers turned around, regarding the new arrivals, curious, some
too doped up to care. As Fahad slipped into the kitchen, a cock-
roach boldly passed him by, running out as though he were the
establishment's only waiter. Within seconds Fahad returned with
a key.

On the top floor there were five rooms, three on one side and
two on the other. They took the last room, the corner room, with
windows on both streets. There was a bed, no bathroom – the
facilities were shared one floor down. The floors creaked. The
plaster was stained. The bed sheets had not been washed, only
tucked in after the last occupants. Fahad tossed the key onto the
bed.

— *I will meet the ISI. If they refuse to help us, the mission has
failed. I do not have any contact with the CIA myself. And we
cannot approach them without ISI's permission.*

— *We could go direct to the embassy and make our way to
Islamabad.*

— *Not without Pakistani permission. We're in their country
now. My orders are strict. They will decide what to do. If you try
to reach the American Embassy without me, I'll find you and I'll
kill you.*

With that warning, Fahad left.

Leo picked up Zabi, putting her on the bed. She asked:

— *Are we going to die?*

— *No.*

— *But he said—*

Nara interrupted:

— *Ignore what he said.*

Leo added:

— *We haven't had a chance to discuss what is happening. It must be very confusing. Do you understand why it is dangerous for you to live in Afghanistan?*

She bit her fingernail, saying nothing. Leo carried on:

— *The Soviets fear defeat very much.*

— *Why?*

— *They worry it will make them look weak. They are prepared to go to extraordinary lengths to stop this from happening. They have many weapons. They will use them, on anyone, men, women, children. The country is not safe, not for you, not for me, not for Nara.*

Zabi said:

— *Where are we going to live?*

— *We must find somewhere else.*

— *Can we live here?*

— *I don't think so.*

Nara sat beside her.

— *There are many people from our country here. They have lost their homes, their family, just like you and I. They have nothing. They live in refugee camps, thousands sleeping under sheets of plastic with no clean water. It is a hard life. It would be dangerous, perhaps as dangerous as the war itself.*

With precocious intelligence, Zabi followed the arguments put to her.

— *Where else can we go?*

Leo answered:

— *There is a chance we can travel to America. Have you heard of this country?*

She shook her head.

— *It is far away. It is very different from the world you know. It is a place without war, with clean water, with food, somewhere safe, a place where we have a chance. There is no opportunity for us here. We would spend all our time struggling just to survive.*

Zabi shrewdly asked:

— *What troubles would there be in America?*

— *There will be challenges. It will be unrecognizable to you. And we will be foreign. We will be outsiders. They speak a different language. You would have to learn a new way of life. But if you manage to learn their language and their way of life, you have a chance of being accepted as one of them.*

Zabi asked Nara:

— *Are there mountains like here?*

Nara was embarrassed. She asked Leo:

— *I don't know. Are there mountains in America?*

He nodded.

— *It is a very large country. There are mountains. There are deserts. There are forests. There are beaches. You can swim in lakes or the sea.*

Zabi asked:

— *What is the sea?*

Not only had she never seen the sea, she had no idea what it was. Leo thought for a moment, comprehending the scale of the journey for this young girl. He wondered how best to explain.

— *The sea is an area of water as big as a country. Instead of land there is water, and the water is as deep as the mountains are tall. It is full of animals, like a lake, but some of the animals are very big, as big as this building.*

Zabi was amazed by this idea. She exclaimed:

— *A fish as big as a building!*

— *They're called whales. They're not fish. They breathe air, like us.*

— *If they breathe air why do they live in the water?*

Leo paused, remembering conservations like this with Elena when she was young. She was fascinated by the world, always asking for information. The endless questions, parodied by her sister, were a display of intimacy and trust as much as they were about curiosity. The same was true with Zabi – she was reaching out to him at the same time as she was reaching out to the concept of this new world. Yet this new world would be one without his daughters. If he left Pakistan as a traitor, he would never see Elena and Zoya again. He found the notion impossible to accept, as impossible as the idea that he would never solve the murder of his wife. But the truth was that to return to the Soviet Union, as a known defector, would result in his execution. Even more troubling, there was a possibility both daughters would be punished if it were ever found out that he'd fled the country. Their safety depended upon the presumption that Leo had been killed in the air strikes or executed by the mujahedin. Secrecy was of paramount importance. He wouldn't be able to write to them. He wouldn't be able to call. If he fell sick, he would be alone. If they fell sick, he would not be able to sit by their side.

In a sombre frame of mind he failed to answer Zabi's question, standing up. She squeezed his hand.

— *Tell me more about the sea.*

Leo shook his head.

— *That's enough for now.*

He stroked back her hair. Zabi asked:

— *Have you been to America?*

— *I tried to go there once but I didn't make it.*

— *Will we make it?*

— *We have a good chance.*

Zabi heard his uncertainty. She took Nara's hand.

— *And even if we don't, you'll stay with me?*

Nara nodded.

— *I will never leave you, no matter what happens. I promise.*

There was no uncertainty in her voice. Nara would die for this girl. Leo hoped it wouldn't come to that.

Next Day

Leo waited by the window, watching the street below. Behind him, Zabi and Nara were asleep. Though he wanted to let them rest he was profoundly anxious. Ten hours had passed since Fahad left the guest lodge. In a few hours it would be morning and there had been no word. The option open to them if Fahad should fail was to strike out for the American Embassy on their own, to try and reach Islamabad and make their case for asylum without the Pakistani intelligence service acting as a broker. Aside from the logistical challenges of the journey, Leo wasn't convinced that the deal could be made without Pakistani approval. The only other choice was to run.

He opened the door, checking the corridor. It was empty. He knocked on the door of the room opposite. There was no reply. Examining the lock, he found it so flimsy that a shove with his shoulder snapped the timber frame. A search of the room revealed no bags and no belongings. He checked the window. Unlike the previous room there was a way down to the street – the ledge to the sign to the ground – difficult but not impossible. He hurried back, waking Nara.

— *I want you to stay in the other room. Don't turn the light on.*

Don't make a sound. If anything happens to me, escape. Don't make your way to Islamabad. Don't try to go to the American Embassy. Don't trust anybody. Just run.

Nara didn't argue, picking Zabi up, who was still half-asleep, and carrying her across the hallway. She lingered by the door, slipping back out, kissing Leo on the cheek before retreating to the room and shutting the door.

Leo returned to his room, sitting on the edge of the bed. He looked around for something that might be used as a weapon. Unable to find anything, he caught a glimpse of his reflection in the mirror. His appearance was wild and ragged, not the impression he wanted to present if he was trying to sell himself as an important source of information. He hastily straightened his hair and was about to head downstairs to the bathroom when there was a knock on the door.

Leo stood to the side, calling out:

— *Who is it?*

— *Fahad.*

He opened the door. Fahad entered, with two men dressed in suits. The Pakistani intelligence officer was the older of the two, in his late sixties, with thin hair and lively eyes. The CIA agent was the same age as Leo. His face was gaunt. The whites of his eyes were tinged with yellow. He was a tall man with a slight, skeletal frame. Whereas Fahad's sinewy body suggested strength and dexterity, there was no such implication from the CIA agent, whose physique indicated a life of reading, drink and intrigue. From one addict to another, there was an immediate connection, a silent communication. Unlike Leo, the agents were exceptionally well tailored and tidy, with jackets and crisp shirts, though neither wore a tie. In the case of the CIA agent, there was a sense that his meticulous tailoring served to conceal the subtler indications of his addiction. With the Pakistani agent the tailoring seemed to be an orthodox indication of his power and status. The CIA agent shook Leo's hand.

— *My name is Marcus Greene.*

He spoke perfect Russian, before continuing in fluent Dari:

— *We should speak a language that we all understand.*

The Pakistani agent shook Leo's hand, also speaking in Dari.

— *Abdur Salaam. That is not my real name, but it will do for the purposes of this meeting.*

Greene smiled.

— *Marcus is my real name. I'm not quite as cautious as my friend.*

Abdur Salaam smiled in return.

— *You do not have Soviet agents trying to kill you. Not that I believe our guest desires to kill me. Fahad vouches for your sincerity. He rarely vouches for anyone, let alone a Soviet.*

Greene walked to the window, checking the streets, apparently without any sense of concern, an idle glance, before perching on the window ledge, his legs stretched out in front of him, tidying the line of his trousers while asking:

— *You want to defect, Mr Demidov?*

The tone of the question was flippant. There was scepticism and reluctance. Of more concern, there was very little excitement. Leo answered carefully:

— *In exchange for asylum, not just for myself but—*

— *Yes, for the girl and the woman, where are they, by the way?*

— *They're safe.*

Greene paused, registering the distrust. Leo added:

— *We would want a new life, the three of us.*

Greene replied with a quick nod, as if he'd heard this request a thousand times and was keen to return to the intelligence on offer:

— You're not a soldier, are you? You're a civilian employee of the Afghan government, an adviser. What kind of information do you have?

Leo made his case:

— I have worked for the Afghan government for seven years.

— In what capacity?

— I was training their secret police force. Before the Communist regime took power, I was helping them to survive. After they took power, I continued helping them to survive, the tools and resources changed, the job remained the same.

Greene lit a cigarette.

— What did you do before you came to Afghanistan, Mr Demidov?

— I worked for the KGB.

Greene inhaled deeply, holding the smoke in his mouth. Fahad grew impatient, a soldier, not accustomed to the subtleties of diplomatic negotiations. He snapped at Leo:

— Talk about Soviet operations in Afghanistan, not the KGB. That is the information that we want you to share.

Like a nervous child, Leo hastily listed the points of interest:

— I know specifics, details regarding the equipment being used, tanks, helicopters, anything that is being used or about to be brought in. I know the deployment patterns of the 40th Army. I can tell you the projected mortality rate before the invasion and how that number has been revised since the invasion. I can do the same with the financial costs. I know the names of most of the senior officers and I know their sentiments on the war. I know our limits, how many soldiers we can afford to lose, how much money we're prepared to spend. I can provide information so that you could accurately estimate the point at which the Soviet Union would have no choice but to retreat.

Greene flicked his cigarette on the carpet, watching to see it burn, before stubbing it out under his shoe.

— *Let me explain the situation from our point of view. We're not supposed to be involved in this war.*

Salaam interjected:

— *Pakistan is also not supposed to be involved in this war.*

The remark caused Greene to raise an eyebrow, as if the sentiment could only have been uttered ironically. He continued:

— *In the United States there is no public appetite for becoming embroiled in this conflict. If we grant you asylum we risk opening a major rift with the Soviets, sparking a political fight the outcome of which we might not be able to control. They would demand your return. We would say no. And so on: who knows where it would end up?*

Leo was quick to correct the assumption.

— *I agree. It is essential the Soviets don't find out about my defection. And there is no reason for them to know. They surely believe I was killed in bombing raids. The chances of me making it to Pakistan are slight, and I would never have managed it without Fahad's help. The Soviets would never have imagined that the mujahedin would've aided me. Fahad could even claim that they have me hostage and after a certain period of time announce that they've executed me.*

Leo had not mentioned his daughters in Moscow, not wishing to complicate the issue further. Greene inhaled again, appearing to appreciate the degree of consideration that Leo had given the plan.

— *Your suggestion is smart. Of course we wouldn't announce your defection but there is a chance that they will find out all the same.*

Leo waited, sensing that Greene was about to make his position clear.

— I'm sure you have much information that would interest us. I have a different proposition. We could debrief you here, pay you a sum of money—

— That's no good. We need a new home, a new country. We would be found here, we would be hunted down and we would be killed.

Abdur Salaam glanced at Marcus Greene. The men were working in concert to obtain the information while giving nothing in return. Greene shrugged.

— If the United States were committed to involvement in the conflict, even through covert means, then yes, you would be an asset. The United States is not committed. The United States is undecided. And for that reason I am afraid to say we cannot accept you.

Same Day

Greene and Salaam descended the stairway at a brisk pace, keen to terminate the meeting since no deal could be struck on their terms. Leo followed behind, pleading, the negotiations on the brink of collapse:

— *There must be something I can say to persuade you. Some intelligence I could give you now, to prove my worth.*

Greene answered without turning around:

— *You should tell me as much as possible.*

— *I'm not going to tell you everything only to be left behind.*

— *Then we're at a dead end. I'm going to discuss you with my superiors. It is possible they'll take a different view. You should wait here. It will only take a few days.*

— *You're going to recommend that they refuse my request for asylum? You're going to claim the information I offer is not worth the risk?*

— *In the end, this is not my decision.*

Leo could no longer hide his desperation.

— *They'll listen to you! They'll accept whatever recommendation you make. You're the only person who has met me!*

Greene was about to reply when he stopped so abruptly that

Leo almost bumped into him. Standing at the bottom of the stairs was Captain Vashchenko.

The captain was positioned between two Afghan men, special operatives and his guides to this region since he spoke neither Dari nor Urdu. Vashchenko was dressed as a traveller and wearing Western clothes. His disguise fitted him poorly: he looked awkward in casual clothes. Despite the humid night he was wearing a baggy jacket, no doubt concealing a weapon. Fahad, on the step behind Leo, reached for his gun. Greene indicated that they should remain calm, keen to avoid an exchange of fire in the stairway. An uneasy standoff remained until, speaking in Russian, the captain called up:

— *We can't let you take him.*

Vashchenko presumed that the CIA would accept Leo gladly. Greene could have corrected him, declaring that he had no interest in Leo, which would have ended the standoff immediately. Instead, he gestured towards the restaurant.

— *Why don't we discuss this?*

The Pakistani intelligence officer was less polite. Unable to speak Russian, he addressed Greene in Urdu. Leo couldn't understand what was said, watching their body language. Greene nodded, trying to hold his colleague back, fearing a descent into violence. He replied to Salaam in Urdu, before adding in Russian:

— *Let's talk.*

Leo was impressed rather than surprised that Vashchenko had found him. The military presence over the Khyber Pass suggested that he'd guessed Leo's intentions. After all, he had attempted to reach America before. Even if he didn't know how Leo would try to defect, he'd staked out Peshawar confident that they would travel through the city. The captain's unauthorized presence in Pakistan was audacious. Discovery and capture would create a major diplomatic incident. Leo thought it unlikely the Kremlin would have directly cleared him to cross the border. The Afghan operatives could be disowned but there could be no mistaking a Soviet military officer. It was possible that he was acting alone, out of personal zeal, determined to put right the mistake he'd made in the village of Sokh Rot.

They sat at one of the garish tables, still cluttered with dirty plates that hadn't been cleared. Leo, Greene and Salaam on one side, the captain on the other. Fahad and the two Afghan soldiers remained standing, hands on their weapons, like warrior guards at a meeting of kings. Greene addressed the remaining customers in English. Leo guessed that he was telling them to leave, an order they obeyed without question. Only the mercenaries didn't hurry, wondering if there was a market for their services. As the room emptied, Greene lit a new cigarette, striking the pose of a genial professor ready to listen to a student's presentation. Vashchenko spoke directly to Leo.

— *No one thought you survived. Except for me. I've read your file. You have embarked on some perilous journeys. I knew you'd try to reach Pakistan. I'm here to talk you out of it. Leo, you're a war hero, you have served your country for many years. We cannot allow you to defect. More importantly, I do not believe you want to defect.*

Leo did not reply, waiting for Vashchenko to finish. The gentle persuasion would surely be followed by a threat.

— *Leo, we made a mistake with the young girl. I made a mistake. You were only trying to protect her. I understand why you behaved as you did. I am a father too.*

The sentiment was laughable but Leo was careful not to show any reaction.

— *I honestly believed her death would save thousands of lives otherwise I would never have acted in the way that I did. Maybe I was right, maybe I was wrong. It is irrelevant. The myth of a miracle child has spread and the myth isn't dependent on her. Killing her would have no effect. The story has a life of its own. That is what I failed to understand. Let me bring you back. There will be no charges. The three of you can live in the Soviet Union if you wish. Wouldn't Nara and the girl like that? You have been in Afghanistan long enough. You have accrued a considerable salary. You would live in comfort, in your own land, close to your own daughters. You should think of your daughters. What are their names?*

Vashchenko was perfectly aware of their names.

— *If you follow through with this, they will never see their father again. They might even be subject to an investigation, questions might be asked about their loyalty.*

The threat was shrewdly targeted. The offer was tempting. Leo considered the prospect of returning to Moscow. He would be reunited with his daughters. Nara and Zabi would be safe. Yet could he trust the offer and trust the captain to keep his word? He might be executed as soon as he returned to Kabul. The defector, Fyodor, who'd escaped only for a day, and for no other reason than because he'd fallen in love, had been executed. Leo's betrayal was far more serious.

Allowing Leo to think upon the mixture of incentives and warnings, Vashchenko turned to Greene, angling his attacks at the nation ready to accept him.

— *You should consider carefully whether this man is asset or a liability.*

Before Leo could interject Greene answered in fluent, graceful Russian:

— *We have considered the matter carefully. We've already accepted his petition for asylum. Furthermore, he is not in Soviet-*

controlled Afghanistan, he is in Pakistan, and you have no legal hold over him here. My colleague Salaam is furious at your unauthorized entry into his country. I'm afraid we can't let you have him.

Leo managed enough composure not to exclaim aloud, or gaze at Greene in dumb surprise, trying to react as if this lie were the truth, and an obvious truth at that. Greene toyed with his packet of cigarettes.

— I should point out, were you to be arrested in Pakistan, a Soviet officer – which I presume you to be – the Pakistani government would be upset. You would be classified as a spy. It could cause problems for you, problems far worse than the problems you've come here to solve.

Greene quickly translated his comments into Urdu for the Pakistani intelligence officer, who nodded. Leo knew that there was no chance Captain Vashchenko would ever allow himself to be caught alive. And were he to be found dead in Peshawar, the Soviet government would deny that he was working for them, rolling out any number of excuses.

A timid young waiter arrived at the table carrying four bottles of cola on a steel tray. The captain knotted his fingers together, placing his hands on the table.

— The Pakistanis provide aid and weapons to the Afghans. The pretence of their neutrality is not asset to the Soviet Union. We do not care about upsetting their feelings.

Greene glanced at Salaam, muttering an abbreviated translation, before saying to the captain:

— Where does that leave us? Suffice to say that murdering a CIA operative in Pakistan would change the United States' perspective on the war dramatically.

The captain smiled.

— No one needs be hurt. We just want our man. It is as simple

as that. I believe he is of no use to you. The United States should not be foolish enough to send troops into Afghanistan. Why become embroiled in a conflict so far away? Demidov's information is of no relevance to you.

Though his expression hadn't changed, somehow Greene's face communicated an intense dislike of the captain.

— *I'm sorry, I still don't know your name . . .*

Leo remarked:

— *He is Captain Anton Vashchenko.*

There was silence for a while, calculations being made, options being considered. Greene continued smoking, dumping ash into the untouched cola. The captain was growing impatient. He switched back towards Leo.

— *Demidov, return to Afghanistan with me. You do not belong in America. The two people you are trying to protect are no longer in danger. And your defection would put your daughters at home in a terrible position.*

Leo lowered his head, considering the danger that Elena and Zoya faced if his defection were known.

Judging from the movement of his eyes, Captain Vashchenko had begun to discreetly weigh up the degree of threat. Fahad was his only serious opposition. Greene seemed oblivious or unconcerned, inhaling deeply, blowing smoke through his nose. Leo was convinced that Vashchenko's next remark would be his last before he resorted to violence. The captain said:

— *Do not get involved in Afghanistan. The Afghans hate you as much as they hate us. If you do not interfere in our affairs, if you refuse to supply weapons to the mujahedin, we will bring order and the rule of law within a matter of months. We will open schools, rebuild roads, repair infrastructure. We will educate the population. If the United States joins this war you will condemn the country to years of chaos. You will not find an ally at the end of it. You will create a regime that will despise you as payment for your support.*

Greene dropped his cigarette into the cola bottle, where it fizzed on the surface.

— *I will pass on your message to my superiors.*

Greene translated the conversation. Salaam listened carefully then spoke to Greene for a moment. Greene translated:

— *Salaam will allow you to walk out of here without being arrested. That's the best he can offer. Live to fight another day. He has no interest in escalating hostilities with the Soviets.*

Leo had remained silent through these discussions. They were coming to an end with no resolution between the parties. He had no option but to act.

Using his knee, he shook the table, toppling one of the cola bottles to the stone floor. As it smashed and as the eyes of the men were drawn to the noise, he bolted forward, grabbing a dirty knife from the table and plunging it into the captain's neck. With the aid of the distraction and his senses no longer dulled by opium, his speed was reasonable and Vashchenko failed to block the attack. The knife entered the captain's throat. The two Afghan operatives looked down in horror, having discounted Leo as a threat. Fahad reacted first, drawing his gun and killing the Afghan officers. Fahad did not execute Vashchenko, leaving him seated. Leo grabbed the captain's hands, pinning them down. Even mortally injured, the man was incredibly strong and tried to pull free. Leo didn't let him move, holding his hands tight. The captain's legs kicked, thrashed, he leant forward, almost touching Leo's face. Finally he weakened, his eyes closing, but Leo still did not let go, pinning his hands down long after the captain had stopped moving.

Leo released Vashchenko and allowed him to drop to the floor. He stood up and remarked:

— *He would never have allowed me to live. He would never have allowed himself to be captured. There was no compromise to be made.*

It had been a long time since Leo had killed a man. Still seated, Greene edged his smart shoes away from the blood pooling on the ground, remarking:

— *The Soviets have gone to extreme lengths to silence you. You're worth more to them than I thought.*

Salaam peered at the bodies. He knelt down, searching the captain's pockets. Leo whispered to Greene:

— *Will we be given asylum? Will you support my request?*

Greene considered.

— *Yes.*

*

Leo slowly climbed the stairs, confused whether he should be pleased or apprehensive. He could not be sure his defection would remain a secret. However, at long last, he had a passage to America and no matter what, Zabi and Nara would have a new home. With this thought, he hurried up the stairs, two steps at a time. At the top-floor corridor he ran down to the room, throwing open the door. The curtains were drawn back and a pale orange glow from the street spread across the bed linen. Nara and Zabi were nowhere to be seen. He entered the room, moving around the bed, finding them seated, cross-legged on the floor, hidden in the corner. He sat down beside them, unable to articulate what had taken place downstairs – that there was the chance of a new home. Despite his smile, he saw both Nara and Zabi staring at his hands. In his haste, he'd forgotten to wash them. They were smeared with blood. He considered putting them behind his back. Perhaps it was better that they'd seen. Bloody hands were the price he'd paid for their freedom.

SIX MONTHS LATER

Manhattan
United Nations Headquarters
1st Avenue & East 44th Street
15 November 1981

Leo stood on 1st Avenue, outside the main gates of the United
Nations Headquarters, at the spot where Jesse Austin had been
shot sixteen years ago. Having researched the photographs and
newspaper articles, spending many hours in the New York Public
Library with access to evidence he'd coveted after Raisa's death,
Leo had ascertained the exact location where the crate had been
set up, carried by Austin all the way from Harlem – the stage for
his assassination. There was no plaque to mark the place, no sign
and no statue. It was an unremarkable sidewalk, giving pedestrians
no reason to reflect upon what happened here, the lives lost that
night.

Leo came here often, standing with his hands behind his back,
as if there were a tombstone before him instead of a kerb. He
would ponder the many aspects of the case that he still failed to
comprehend. Fundamentally he could not grasp why Austin had
been killed, nor could he understand why it appeared that the
Soviet and American governments had collaborated in covering

up the murder. Why had the perpetrators planted the gun on his daughter, slipping it into her jacket pocket only to frame Raisa for the murder? The discrepancy suggested a change of plan and subsequent improvisation. Above all, one question remained unanswered:

Who murdered my wife?

The answers in the history books were lies, undetectable to a casual reader caught up in a narrative of adultery and illicit passion, a fanciful story masquerading as a series of bullet-point facts.

When Leo closed his eyes he was transported back to that night, feeling the heat of the crowd and the humid summer air. He could kneel beside Austin's body on the street and stare down at the white shirt turning red with blood. He could see the expression on Anna Austin's face: her mouth open, crying out. He could hear the desperation in her voice, a prescient fear that no help would come. He could picture the crowd panicking, knocking down the barricades – the metal clang ringing out. Leo could see his wife and he'd move closer to her, so close he could hear her heartbeat as she cradled Elena, so close he could hear his daughter's shallow, rapid breathing as her dreams of a better world smashed around her feet.

Like an optical illusion, he could see the episode vividly and yet not understand the things he was able to see. Although a wealth of photographs existed from that night, curiously there was not one photograph with Elena in it. According to her account, she'd been in the midst of the chaos. She'd held up a Soviet flag beside Jesse Austin. Yet there was no evidence supporting that, no mention in any newspaper of her role. A different story had been told, matched with a single iconic photograph, not reproduced in the

Soviet Union, one Leo had never seen before, showing Raisa beside Austin's body. To Leo's eye, she was responding to the cry for help. To the American public, she was a crazed killer, bitter with jealousy. Another photo showed Raisa in Jesse Austin's apartment, the singer's hand on her arm, bed sheets crumpled in the background. Leo knew the photograph was doctored – Elena had told him she'd visited Jesse Austin, not Raisa. Until Leo arrived in the United States, he'd never grasped the public shame that had been heaped on his wife: the degree to which journalists had been captivated by the idea of a tragic Soviet–American love triangle. The shrewdest woman he'd ever known, the only woman he'd ever truly loved, had been logged in the history books as a naive and deluded mistress. The most idealistic man he'd ever known, and one of the few men he'd ever truly admired, had been characterized as lecherous and a liar, a man of such low morals that a bullet through the heart was seen by many as an appropriate end.

On his visits Leo didn't always linger outside. It was possible to go on a tour of the United Nations building and he'd been inside, listening to the guides, understanding only a little of their English. He'd seen the hall where Raisa's concert had taken place, not because it served his investigation but because he enjoyed thinking of her success here – a war refugee who survived Stalin's purges leading a performance in a venue such as this, the diplomatic elite on their feet, applauding her. Zoya told him the concert had gone better than anyone expected, all Raisa's preparations had worked perfectly. While she'd planned for hope and music and song, others had planned for murder.

Twenty minutes had passed and he hadn't moved, standing in the same spot, hands behind his back. The guards at the United Nation were staring at him, suspicious. Taxi cabs slowed to see if there was somewhere he needed to be. But there was nowhere else he needed to be. There were no more journeys to be made. Now his task was purely an investigative one. Peering up at the sky-scrapers he considered them to be holders of the city's secrets, silent giants, answers locked away in steel, concrete and glass. He did not lay a flower. He had no interest in any memorial except to catch his wife's killer.

He'd been instructed not to come here for security reasons. It would be easy for the Soviets to find him if they ever suspected his defection. This would be the first place they'd stake out. As was his way, he ignored the instructions. He walked towards the subway station, conscious that he was being followed. He knew this to be true without stopping and turning around, without seeing the agent on his tail, or glimpsing him out of the corner of his eye. His instincts had been honed over many years. He didn't blame the American secret police for trying to keep tabs on him. Normally he'd allow them to follow him so that they'd feel reassured. But not today – he had work to do, and he did not want the company of the FBI.

Bradhurst
Harlem
West 145th Street

Walking past the apartment building where Jesse Austin once lived, Leo resisted going in. He haunted the location as though he believed that some trace of the past remained, some imprint of the day when young Elena had arrived, with dreams of equality and fairness. His persistence had not yet been rewarded: queries had been rebuffed on every occasion with responses that ranged from hostile to blank incomprehension. There was no one in the building he hadn't approached, acquiring a reputation with the inhabitants as a crank. When he'd knocked on what was once Jesse Austin's door he'd addressed the current occupants, a young couple, in rudimentary awkward English, asking if they knew anything about Jesse Austin. They shook their head, seemingly under the impression that he was looking for someone who lived there now. Unable to articulate his real purpose, he'd taken out the newspaper clippings of the assassination. From their confusion, they had no knowledge of the event, no idea who Jesse Austin was, and certainly no idea why this strange foreign man was asking about him sixteen years after the murder. Though they'd been more polite than most, they'd shut the door and locked it.

Moving away from the apartment building, Leo walked down the street, clutching the articles that he showed to almost anyone, particularly those men and women old enough to have been adults at the time of the murders. While he'd been in the Soviet Union and Afghanistan, he'd always presumed that reaching New York was the main obstacle he faced. He was wrong, underestimating the difficulties an outsider would experience when trying to solve a sixteen-year-old case that no one wanted to remember.

There was a cafe on the other side of the street, always busy and something of a social hub in the neighbourhood, popular with an older clientele. He crossed over and entered. Filled with lunchtime customers, it was noisy and lively, packed with small square tables situated so close together the waitresses needed to side-step between them, which they did with some agility. Wearing blue-and-white-striped aprons they delivered plates loaded with inelegant, delicious-looking food. The kitchen was visible, steam rising. There was an almost constant sound of plates clattering. Many of the men and women eating here were at least fifty years old. Surely someone knew Jesse Austin and the truth about his death, even if it were no more than a rumour. Leo would have gladly listened to even the idlest speculation.

Approaching the woman at the cash register, Leo felt frustrated by his limited English, verbal clumsiness that would not endear him to an already suspicious audience.

— *I want to ask questions. About this man . . . Jesse Austin.*

As Leo unfolded his newspaper articles, the woman cocked her head, a dumbfounded expression he'd seen countless times. She called out towards the kitchen:

— *You better get out here!*

An older woman emerged. As soon as she saw Leo she shook her head. Leo was out of luck, he'd asked for her help before. She'd declined.

— *You got to leave!*

— *Please—*

— *I told you before. I told you no!*

Leo decided to say aloud the man's name, to see if anyone reacted.

— *I want to speak about Jesse Austin.*

— *Get out, right now!*

Her command was loud, silencing the entire cafe, customers staring at him, waitresses staring at him, everyone trying to figure him out. Leo observed one interesting point, no matter how much he annoyed her, no matter how angry she became, she never threatened to call the police. He held up the newspaper clippings, showing them to the customers, and repeating the name.

— *Jesse Austin. Please. Someone. Talk to me.*

He waited outside, loitering on the off-chance someone was going to respond to his request. No one did. He sighed. Hopefully that woman didn't work every day. He would try again, and again. The breakthrough would come.

New York City
Brighton Beach
Same Day

It was mid-afternoon and the subway was nearly empty as it approached Brighton Beach. Leo sat, regarding an advertisement depicting a young, beautiful woman in a bikini, holding a bottle of orange soda labelled:

FANTA

No other passengers appreciated the notoriety of this brand, no other passengers were aware of the ways the bottle had been used in Kabul – the fear that label created in the minds of prisoners awaiting interrogation. Here, in New York, it was a sugar drink, a symbol of frivolity and fun, and no more. Staring at this advertisement, Leo felt like a visitor from another world.

A fellow passenger was reading a newspaper, bags of shopping sagging by his feet. Another man was standing even though there were seats available, hanging from the bar, lost in thought as the train emerged from under the city. A mother sat with her young daughter whose legs dangled over the edge of the seat, not reaching the floor of the carriage. Leo was reminded of the daughters he'd left behind in Russia. There wasn't a day, or even an hour, that passed when he didn't think about them. He hadn't seen them in eight years and he had no idea when he'd see them again. The price for this investigation had been high. The idea that Elena and Zoya did not even know that he was alive made him ache. He couldn't contact them. He couldn't risk the Soviet government finding out that he was alive. If that happened, the girls would surely be targeted. Just as he found it impossible to believe that he would not solve Raisa's murder, he found it impossible to accept that he would not see Elena and Zoya again even if he couldn't rationalize when or how that might happen.

Advertisements aside, Leo found the subway the one place where life in Moscow and life in New York were not so dissimilar. Commuting served as a great leveller of men. He would always watch with interest as the doors opened and a new wave of passengers boarded. The subtle flirtations flickering between passengers were faint echoes of the chance encounter between him and Raisa on the Moscow metro. Far from the memory upsetting him, he'd wonder whether the strangers would part ways, never to see each other again, or try to turn that chance connection into something more.

As he got off at Brighton Beach the sun came out and Leo unbuttoned his coat, feeling warm despite it being late in the autumn. He looked at his surroundings with a sense of wonder, not having adjusted to the fact that this strange new world was home. The notion remained bizarre to him. Perhaps because of his daughters in Russia, he could not imagine ever truly feeling at home. After arriving in the United States, he, Nara and Zabi had spent several weeks moving between temporary accommodation in New Jersey — a disjointed, disruptive experience, but one which Leo found less peculiar than being given a permanent address. He'd insisted upon New York, disguising his true intentions by stressing that this area offered several advantages. There were a large number of Soviet immigrants so his lack of English was not a problem, nor was his foreignness as conspicuous as it would have been in smaller cities. He went largely unnoticed, living under a new name, telling the more curious that he'd fled from persecution.

Zabi and Nara lived in an apartment next to him, also under new names and also with fictional back-stories, pretending to be Pakistani rather than Afghan so that they were harder to trace should anyone come looking for them. They'd wanted Leo to live with them but it would undermine their assumed identities. Arranged in this fashion, they were two different immigrant households who'd befriended each other. Officially, Nara had become Zabi's mother. She had the paperwork to prove it and Leo sometimes caught her studying it as if unable to believe the words. The girl she'd called out to be killed was now legally her child, a contradiction that she would think upon every day. Far from being destructive, though, it made her a devoted mother. Since she was young to have a daughter aged seven, any questions from outsiders regarding the matter were met with stern silence and the suggestion that the explanation was too bleak to detail — a partial truth, at least.

So it was that's Leo's fourth home was on Brighton's 6th Street, in a third-floor apartment. They hadn't been able to secure a sea view, in fact they didn't have much of a view at all, but the apartment was comfortable, with air conditioning, a refrigerator and a television set. Unlike in the apartments in Kabul, he hadn't removed the doors to other rooms. The unbearable restlessness was gone. He no longer needed opium: he was a detective again.

Unlocking the front door and entering the living room, Leo sensed someone else was in the room. Were it a Soviet operative, Leo would surely be killed before he had time to turn on the lights. With this in mind, he reached for the switch.

Same Day

Marcus Greene, impeccably tailored, took out a cigarette and sat down as though this was his home. He said:

— *You seem nervous.*

Leo didn't reply. He disliked the casual disregard with which they broke into his apartment or bugged his phone, and the way in which they searched his belongings when he was out, something that he was aware of since they failed to put items back into the correct position. But he was under no illusion that he belonged to the Americans, a piece of intellectual property, and they would behave exactly as they pleased. It was almost comical that Greene would then ask:

— *May I smoke?*

Leo nodded, taking off his coat, hanging it in the hall. Returning to the living room he stood opposite Greene.

— *Why aren't you in Pakistan?*

— *I'm on leave, visiting my family.*

Greene sucked deeply on his cigarette, with the loving intensity known only to an addict. Leo took a seat opposite, leaning forward, hands on his knees. Greene remarked without self-pity:

— *I have not been a good father. I regret my shortcomings, I suppose. But I haven't done much about them, so I'm not sure what that regret is worth, at least not in the eyes of my wife and my sons. I tell you this because it is part of the reason I'm here. I know how much your family matters to you, not just the family you brought to New York, but also the family you left behind in the Soviet Union.*

Leo asked, his voice strangled with tension:

— What's happened?

— The Soviets suspect that you're alive. We thought that killing the captain might mean your existence would be unconfirmed. Perhaps it is. However, they're testing the water. While I was in Peshawar, they made sure that we became aware of certain pieces of information regarding your daughters. Zoya and Elena . . .

Leo stood up, as if ready to leave immediately. Greene gestured for him to sit down. He ignored the gesture and in the end Greene stood up too.

— We have no means of verifying these rumours. They might be lies intended to flush you out. There was pressure on me not to reveal them to you but I was sure you'd want to know. It's your decision whether you believe the stories or not.

— What stories?

— Because of your defection your daughters have been taken in for questioning. Their husbands have also been interrogated. They have been released, but their futures are uncertain. The next step would be for them to be arrested. That hasn't happened yet, but it could. It is bait, crude, but I can see from your expression, effective.

— If I don't return, they will arrest them? That's the threat?

— Leo, we have no way of knowing if this is just a play. They can't be sure you're alive.

— Do they have an American source?

— I don't believe that's likely. The Soviets have never been very effective at penetrating the CIA. If you do nothing, if you don't

469

react, they will presume you to be dead and nothing will happen to
your daughters. I'm sure of that.

But Leo knew better how the KGB functioned: he knew their
mindset. He remembered how he would have behaved as an ambitious young agent. Shaking his head, feeling sick with fear at the
danger he'd put his daughters in, he said:

— *I don't have much time.*

Same Day

Leo sat in silence over dinner, picking at the food he'd cooked. The threat to his daughters would be carried out even though they were innocent. During Stalin's reign it was established that the son was tainted with the father's guilt. A single crime, a single allegation, could bring about the ruin of an entire family, the toxin of suspicion travelling along bloodlines. Times had changed only so far. This mode of thought remained within the mindset of the KGB, an organization that had always preferred its agents to marry other agents, structuring itself like a dynasty of operatives distinct from the ordinary citizen. This was part of the reason they had always opposed his marriage to Raisa. If Leo did not surrender, his daughters would be arrested, detained in the worst conditions. The KGB's malice would be impersonal, procedural and utterly predictable. Just as it did not matter that his daughters were innocent, it did not matter that they could not be sure if Leo was alive. The Soviet intelligence network in the United States was weak, certainly compared with the European cells of agents. However, they had within their means an easy way of flushing Leo into open. So much had depended upon them presuming he was dead. That plan had failed.

Leo pushed his plate aside. Both Nara and Zabi knew something was wrong, exchanging glances. He could not tell them the news since he'd not decided what to do. The uncertainty would be an unnecessary strain. Zabi had only just returned from a session with a psychiatrist. Though her physical injuries had healed, she was in therapy, two sessions a week, a process delayed for several months while she'd undergone intensive schooling in English, lessons she attended with Nara. Leo skipped most of the lessons, concentrating instead on his investigation. However, he always made time to accompany Zabi to the psychiatrist, surprised that the doctor's office was not in a hospital but a pleasantly decorated room in her house. After the third or fourth session, he'd become more relaxed about treatment. Zabi didn't fear the sessions. Needless to say the American government covered the cost. They covered the costs of all their expenses. In exchange, Leo met intelligence officers, providing information on Afghanistan. His knowledge of the Soviet Union itself was dated, particularly with regard to the KGB and secret police. This information was primarily of interest to historians and academics, a few of whom had been granted security clearance to question him. Only his reports on Afghanistan were classified. It was hard to gauge what impact they were having on American policy – he was never trusted enough to be told anything, only ever questioned. Some of the questions revealed their way of thinking. There were clearly elements in the CIA keen to fund the insurgency, to provide weapons. Whether that was being carried out, Leo could not tell.

At the end of dinner, Leo tidied away the plates, returning to the table with a carton of ice cream that he'd bought from a grocery store run by a woman from Ukraine, one of the few people in the neighbourhood that he spoke to, as unsociable in New York as he had been in Kabul. As he spooned the ice cream into three bowls he said:

— *I'm flying to Washington tomorrow. You remember the work I spoke about? There is an archive of items relating to Soviet espionage in the United States. They want me to take a look, see if I can throw any light on the objects.*

Nara was surprised.

— *I thought you weren't doing that for a couple of months.*

— *They want me to go immediately.*

— *Why?*

The reason was simple: they didn't think Leo would be in America for much longer. Leo kept this secret, merely shrugging.

— *I don't know.*

He added, weakly:

— *I do as I'm told.*

Zabi asked:

— *Are you leaving us?*

Leo couldn't look her in the eye. He toyed with a spoonful of ice cream.

— *I'll only be gone a few days.*

Washington DC
FBI Headquarters
J. Edgar Hoover Building
935 Pennsylvania Avenue
Next Day

Leo was due to stay in Washington DC for a few days, depending on how the work progressed. Resigned to the fact that his time in the United States had been suddenly and dramatically cut short, he was impatient to return to New York – there was now intense pressure on his investigation. In all likelihood he had weeks, not months, before the Soviet Union took further action against his daughters. If they went as far as to arrest Zoya and Elena then he would not be able to hold out – more likely, he would begin to make arrangements to return that same day. A once benign trip to the archive was now a costly distraction.

A friendly man called Simon Clarke had met him at the airport, introducing himself as the archivist, an owlish-looking individual in his fifties with round gold-framed glasses and a gently protruding stomach curving out from his body like a pleasant hillside. He spoke fluent Russian, grammatically perfect, but with an American accent and Leo guessed that he'd probably spoken to very few native Russians. Kind and mild-mannered, Clarke hoped that Leo could illuminate many of the discoveries that had been collecting dust, mysteries that they'd failed to unravel about Soviet espionage protocols launched against the main adversary. Clarke had used Soviet spy slang – *the main adversary* – keen to show that he was acquainted with their secret code.

On a brief tour of the city, before heading to the archive they stopped outside the FBI headquarters. The building was modern, concrete, quite unlike the Russian secret police headquarters, the Lubyanka, with its grand historical facade in the centre of Moscow. The architectural principle of the Hoover Building seemed not that it should appear impressive but that it should appear unbreakable. There was nothing ornate or decorative about the design: it was a hybrid of a parking lot and a power station, as if the FBI were in the same utilitarian category. The archive, not marked on any map or listed in any official registry, was located three blocks back, on 8th Street. There was no sign, no reception, merely an unremarkable door that opened directly onto the street like a fire escape. The entrance was sandwiched between two large offices: a door without a number or mailbox, like a magical portal that everyone on the street walked past oblivious to the secrets it held.

Clarke took out his keys, opening the door, turning on the lights and revealing a narrow staircase. He ushered Leo inside, locking the door behind them before descending the stairs. The air was dry, machine-processed. At the bottom of the stairs was a small drab office where Clarke turned off an alarm system. To the side of the office was a steel door, sealed shut, like a bank vault. After entering a code, there was a faint hiss as the door opened. Lights automatically turned on, fluorescent bulbs slowly flickering one after another in quick succession, revealing the archive's full dimensions.

Far larger than Leo had expected, the archive stretched for

hundreds of metres with row upon row of steel shelves. Unlike a library there were no books. Everything was stored in uniform brown cardboard boxes, side by side – thousands of them, each with the same gap between them. Leo looked at Clarke:

— *All this?*

Clarke nodded:

— *Seventy years' worth of material, most of it understood, some of it not.*

Leo moved forward. Clarke put a hand on his shoulder.

— *Before we start, there are a couple of rules. I've been instructed to search you upon leaving. Please don't be insulted: this is standard policy and applies to all visitors. You must wear these gloves when touching anything. Other than that, you're free to look at whatever you like. Except no fountain pens, or ink of any kind. You don't have any pens on you?*

Leo shook his head, taking off his jacket, hanging it in the office. Clarke noted:

— *You might want to keep that with you. The chamber is cold, air-conditioned for preservation purposes.*

Seventy years' worth of refrigerated spy secrets, thousands of attempts to betray, deceive and murder, preserved as though they were mankind's finest achievements.

The ceiling was not particularly high, but the room was remarkably wide, giving it surreal proportions, the shape of squashed shoebox. The entire archive was concrete, resulting in two colours dominating, the grey concrete and the brown cardboard boxes. There was the hum of air and occasionally slight vibrations from a passing subway train. A passage ran through the middle of the archive from end to end. Each aisle was marked with a number. There were no signs, no written explanations. Clarke must have guessed his thoughts, remarking:

— *Don't worry! We don't want you to look through every-*
thing. I have put aside several boxes that I thought you might be
able to shed some light upon. But you're free to walk around and
see if anything catches your eye. Why don't you familiarize your-
self with the archive before we sit down with the material I've
selected?

Despite the suggestion that he was free to explore, Clarke had
not left his side.

Feeling self-conscious, Leo stopped by one of the aisles, picking
one at random. Each box had a sticker with a number written on
it, a long code that meant nothing to a casual glance. Every box
had a lid, making it impossible to browse. Clarke commented:

— *There is a reference catalogue in the office that matches up*
the codes with a description of the contents. Not everything is
stored in boxes, though: some odd-shaped objects, or oversize items,
stand on their own. They're located further down, near the back.
Let me bring a copy of the catalogue: that might help.

Clarke turned around and hurried towards the office. Leo circled, restless — his thoughts dwelling upon the investigation. Idly
he opened the nearest box. It was filled with money, wads of five-
and ten-dollar bills, low denominations, but pristine, unused, a
small fortune. Leo suspected the money was Soviet-produced for-
geries. One wad of money was inside a plastic bag labelled CAUTION.
The notes probably contained a chemical of some kind, perhaps
even a toxin. Putting the lid back on, he moved down to the next
aisle, selecting another box and lifting the lid. This box was filled
with scientific equipment, a microscope and other apparatus that
Leo didn't recognize. The objects were dated, perhaps fifty or so
years old. Once again there was no explanation: no written documents. After the third and fourth box it dawned on him that the
bulk of this archive would prove to be banal. It appeared as if the

477

Americans had collected everything even vaguely connected to Soviet spy protocols.

About to turn around and wait for Clarke to return, Leo spotted the oversize objects. He walked towards the back of the archive, finding a walking cane made out of gnarled wood. He toyed with it for a while, wondering if there was a secret compartment, some secondary function, a poison spear perhaps. Giving up, he returned it to the shelf. There was an old-fashioned transceiver, perhaps used to make secret communications, as large as a television. Next to that was a suitcase.

Leo crouched down, his hands shaking as he placed them on the case. Though his hands had changed markedly over the years, this case had not. It was old fashioned with a leather-clad handle and rusted steel locks. Despite the fact that he hadn't seen it for sixteen years there was no doubt that it was the same case he'd bought when he was a young secret-police officer.

It was the suitcase Raisa had taken to New York.

Same Day

Leo stood up, peering through the boxes, checking to see if Clarke was close by. There was no sign of him. Returning to the case, his hands still shaking in nervous anticipation, he clicked the locks open and looked inside.

The disappointment was crushing. The case was empty. Recovering his composure, he breathed deeply. He ran his fingers along the lining, searching for a note, a letter hidden in the fabric. There were no knife cuts, no stitched compartments. He examined the outside, turning it upside down, feeling the base and the corners. He could hear Clarke's footsteps on the concrete floor.

— *Mr Demidov?*

The case offered no more clues. He checked the objects nearby: there were at least twenty other suitcases. He recognized none of them. Surely Zoya and Elena's belongings were also here. They'd been confiscated: the girls had returned to Russia with only the clothes they were wearing, everything else had been taken. Leo memorized the item number of Raisa's case. Clarke's footsteps were getting closer: he was only metres away. As he came into view, Leo stood up, moving away from his wife's case.

Clarke smiled at him.

— *Find anything?*

— *No, not really.*

It was a weak denial. Clarke didn't pick up on it. He was carrying a large hardback book protected with plastic.

— *Here's the catalogue.*

Leo took it from him, saying nothing about his discovery, trying to remain calm and unflustered, opening the book and flicking through. Clarke put a friendly hand on his shoulder.

— *I've taken the liberty of putting together a few boxes of items I'd like your opinion on.*

The reading area was near the office, situated inside the archive since no items could be removed. A table had been provided. There was a desk lamp, a chair and several boxes filled with items to look through. Clarke chatted to Leo for a while, explaining his interest in the contents. Leo barely listened to a word, tortured by the delay, desperate to look up the reference number of the suitcase in the catalogue. Finally, Clarke left him alone and he was able to study the entries. The numbering system was complex. From memory he scribbled down the code number of the suitcase. He found the entry log. The description read:

INVESTIGATION RED VOICE

1965 NY

He checked the vocabulary in his dictionary. The use of the word RED was almost certainly a reference to Communism, a prominent Communist voice – surely it referred to Jesse Austin.

Leo stared at the codes trying to figure out how to trace the other documents connected to the same investigation. Unable to crack the system, and reluctant to ask for assistance, he had no choice but to work through every entry, running his finger down the descriptions. He was halfway through the catalogue, constantly checking to see if Clarke was approaching. His finger stopped, pressed against the words:

INVESTIGATION RED VOICE

He wrote down the location for the box – code 35 / 9 / 3.3 – and shut the catalogue, slipping the paper into his pocket.

Standing up, he edged forward, seeing Clarke nearby in the office. He was occupied and Leo took his chance, moving quickly, hurrying towards aisle 35. Reaching the aisle he turned right, his hand moving across the numbers, finding the ninth unit. The box was on the top shelf, third along. He took hold of it, his arms trembling with emotion. The box was heavy and he struggled with it before managing to set it down. As if he was handling a box of precious treasure, he slowly removed the lid.

Inside was a mass of documents, details of the United Nations concert, a programme, official letters written from the Kremlin regarding the trip, discussing the Student Peace Tour, the proposals and protocol. As a former agent, Leo's sense for what was important had been developed over many years of searching through papers and personal belongings. These were formal state documents. They revealed only the surface gloss of the tour. His hand touched the bottom of the box, feeling something hard, the spine of a book – it was a diary.

Leo read the first entry, remembering the words as surely as if he'd written them himself:

For the first time in my life I feel the need to keep a record of my thoughts.

Harlem
Bradhurst
West 145th Street
Three Days Later

In the back of a cab Leo clutched a notebook in which he'd transcribed the most important details from Elena's journal. Unable to steal the diary in its complete form, he'd studied the pages in the archive at every unsupervised opportunity. The timeline ran up until the afternoon before the concert, the last day Raisa was alive. After coming back to the hotel from her meeting with Jesse Austin, Elena had been escorted to her room. Getting ready for the dress rehearsal, she'd snuck into the bathroom and made one final entry. This scribbled, hastily written page was unquestionably the most important. Leo had ripped it from the journal, stuffing it into his sock along with the other notes he'd taken and smuggled them out from the archive.

Most of the diary contained information Elena had already told him when she'd returned to Moscow, including the way in which she'd been approached by the propaganda officer, Mikael Ivanov, and how the relationship had developed between them. It was heartbreaking and infuriating in equal measure to track her emotions, reading descriptions of how she fell for the fiction of her betrayer's love and his noble, lofty intentions. She genuinely believed her mission was to show the abandoned and maligned Jesse Austin that he was still loved by Communist Russia. The depth of her idealism was matched only by her adoration of Ivanov. Everything she'd done – every mistake – had been motivated by love. Leo could only presume that her capacity for love was the reason she'd been targeted and selected for the operation. Reading the honey-dipped words Ivanov had used to seduce his daughter, Leo couldn't help but wonder whether he'd failed as a father, failed to protect his children from the world of deceit that had been his profession. If there was one thing he could have taught them it was how to spot a lie.

Elena had been aware that keeping a diary was risky, particularly considering the secretive nature of her objectives, and she'd resorted to a crude code, numbers for names and a shorthand system of description. If he had not been her father it would have been difficult to make sense of the contents, but he was able to replace numbers with names in the majority of cases. The propaganda officer Ivanov was number 55. Number 71 was Jesse Austin, the number reversed, 17, was his wife, Anna Austin, a choice of code that revealed a great deal about Elena's romanticism. There were a few numbers Leo couldn't identify by name and there was no question in his mind that they were the most important:

AGENT 6.

In her rushed entry she'd described him merely by saying:

He scares me.

The code referred to an FBI detective Elena had seen in Harlem emerging from Jesse Austin's apartment, the man who'd followed her back to the hotel.

This time Leo wasn't going to Harlem alone. Seated beside him was Nara. As a trainee in Kabul she'd only ever been involved in one case – the arrest of a love-struck defector that led to his execution. It felt appropriate that Leo should offer her the chance to close her brief detective career with a case against someone who deserved to be caught. That high-minded notion aside, the truth was he needed her. Nara's command of English was far more advanced than his own. She'd worked tirelessly to improve it, keen to fit in, to make New York City her home and to find a job. In addition to her fluency in English, she was beautiful and charming, whereas he was gruff and scraggy, and she might succeed in persuading people to talk where he had failed. Logically he should have asked for her help from the outset but he'd felt uncertain whether it was wise to involve her. She would feel obliged to support him, regardless of whether or not she agreed with the investigation. As it was a clear violation of the terms of their asylum, seeking sensitive information, he did not want to incriminate her.

Returning from Washington DC, Leo accepted that he didn't have time to waste and couldn't do this without her. Nara listened as he told her everything, the research in the library, his failed interviews in Harlem. She was shocked that his many hours away from home had not been spent exploring the city but delving into the past. As expected, he could tell that she was concerned about upsetting their American hosts. After all, she was a mother now and had Zabi's future to think of. However, she felt a duty to support Leo. She owed him her life. It was with mixed emotions, a sense of foreboding and reluctance, as well as a sense of duty and curiosity that she agreed to participate in the search for Raisa's killer.

The cab stopped. Leo stepped out, holding the door for Nara. He reached into his pocket to pay the driver. Pressed beside his money were the notes he'd copied from the diary and the page he'd ripped loose. In that final, crucial entry, Elena had mentioned that a man had shown her into Jesse Austin's apartment, an angry old man referred to as number 111. Jesse Austin had explained the man's anger to Elena by pointing out that he owned a local hardware store and considered Communism bad for business and bad for the community. It wasn't much of a lead.

Leo decided to go to number 111 on 145th, hoping it would be a hardware store, only to find it wasn't a store, it was an apartment block. After managing to sneak into the communal areas, Leo knocked on door 111. He and Nara spoke to the owner, an elderly man who'd lived in the apartment most of his life, had never owned a hardware store and couldn't understand why he was being asked he if had. Taking a chance, Leo asked whether he knew Jesse Austin anyway. The old man looked at Leo with a peculiar gaze. It was obvious that he knew him, perhaps even knew him well, but he shook his head and shut the door. Glancing at Nara, Leo said, exasperated:

— *This is what I'm up against. No one wants to talk. They haven't forgotten him, but they don't want to talk about him.*

She merely replied:

— *There might be a reason for that.*

Leo was not in the mood for compromise.

— *There's also a good reason for wanting them to talk.*

Walking down the street, Leo raised his hand, gesturing at a run-down hardware store, a ramshackle, old-fashioned affair. The store window was cluttered and dark. Nara looked at him.

485

— How do you know this is the store?

— I don't.

Leo pointed to a hand-painted sign. *A family business for thirty years!*

Opening the door, a small bronze bell rang overhead. There was a musty smell. The shop counter was dusty. The contents were disorganized. On the wall behind the cash register there was a row of plastic drawers, filled with odds and ends, nails and bolts, screws and hinges, drawers stacked as high as the ceiling.

The proprietor was young, a man in his early thirties, emerging from a back room with reading glasses on the end of his nose, regarding his unusual customers. His glance concentrated on Leo and turned unfriendly.

— You've been in here before?

Nara stepped forward, speaking in fluent English, having already gone over the question with Leo at home.

— We're looking for information on a famous singer who used to live near here. His name is Jesse Austin.

Upon hearing the name the man took off his glasses, placing them on the counter.

— That's right, you're the Jesse Austin man. What is it with you, anyway?

— My name is Leo Demidov.

Embarrassed by his English, he turned to Nara. She added:

— My name is Nara Mir. This is my friend. Leo knew Mr Jesse Austin a long time ago. We're trying to find information.

The man studied Leo, saying:

— You knew Jesse Austin? I don't believe it.

— It's true.

— You're not from New York, are you?

— I'm from Russia.

— *Russia? And you knew Jesse?*

— *We met in Moscow.*

— *You met in Moscow?*

The store owner had a habit of turning everything Leo said into a question and Leo was unsure how to respond. The man addressed Nara:

— *You're who? His translator?*

— *I'm his friend.*

— *What do the two of you want?*

Leo said to Nara in Dari:

— *I want to know how Jesse Austin died, the truth, not what was printed in the papers.*

Nara translated. Leo watched the store owner's reaction. He shook his head, waving at the door.

— *I don't know anything. Now get out. I'm serious. Don't bother me again. This is a store. If you want to buy something . . .*

Before the store owner could return to the back room, Leo took a chance, calling out:

— *Your father knew Jesse Austin.*

The store owner turned sharply, staring at Leo accusingly, suddenly angry.

— *How do you know my father? What are you doing dragging him into this? You better have a good answer.*

Leo replied through Nara:

— *Your father met with Jesse Austin the day he was shot. He brought a young Russian girl to his apartment. The two men argued.*

She translated. The store owner was stunned. Recovering some of his composure he said:

— *What do you want?*

Leo sensed he was making inroads and pushed home his advantage.

— *The papers claimed a Russian woman shot Jesse Austin. The papers claim the Russian woman was called Raisa Demidova. The papers are wrong. She did not kill him. That is a lie.*

Leo took a chance.

— *Your father knew it was a lie.*

The store owner listened to the translation before turning to Leo.

— *And how do you figure this?*

Leo had memorized the English.

— *Raisa was my wife.*

Harlem
Bradhurst
8th Avenue & West 139th Street
Nelson's Restaurant
Same Day

The man referred to as number 111 by Elena in her journal was
Tom Fluker, now dead; his son William ran the hardware store, as
Leo had correctly guessed. Once a degree of trust had been established, William was prepared to recollect events from the time of
Jesse Austin's death. He recounted his father talking about Austin,
and how Tom had been furious with him for bringing their community under scrutiny and suspicion.

— *Jesse used to make my father mad. He called him a troublemaker. But the night Jesse was shot, my father didn't say he had it
coming, or anything like that. He did something I never expected
him to. He cried. I remember thinking it was strange that he never
had a nice word to say about Jesse and then he cried when the man
was shot. I was a young boy and it seemed like a contradiction at
the time.*

William had brought them to a restaurant called Nelson's, closing his store and agreeing to show Leo and Nara the way. In his

extensive exploration of the neighbourhood, Leo had passed the restaurant but since it was several blocks from where Austin lived, and looked new, he'd never gone in. There was no mention of it in Elena's diary and he could find no reference to it in any of the articles written about Austin in the press. During the walk William had warmed to them somewhat, almost certainly because of Nara. He'd taken a shine to her and Leo could tell she was flattered. William was a handsome man.

Unlike the hardware store, which appeared not to have been decorated or updated for thirty years, this restaurant had been recently refurbished. Like a tour guide, William gestured at the facade.

— *Don't be fooled. This restaurant has been here for longer than I've been alive. Nelson was the man who opened it and he and my dad were friends. Both of them built up their businesses from nothing. This was the most popular restaurant in the neighbourhood, until . . .*

William trailed off, adding:

— *That's not my story to tell.*

Inside the staff were winding down after the lunch shift, tables being cleared, only a few diners remaining, older men who looked as if they had nowhere to hurry off to, nursing cups of coffee. William caught the arm of a waitress.

— *Can we speak to Yolande?*

The waitress glanced at Leo and Nara, assessing them, before turning around and heading back through the kitchen into an office. Minutes passed before she emerged accompanied by a woman in her thirties dressed in a suit. The woman was tall and striking. She took in every detail of Leo and Nara's appearance before moving forward and shaking their hands. William had phoned ahead. She'd been expecting them.

— Nice to see you, Willie.

She offered her hand to Leo.

— I'm Yolande.

Leo shook it and then Nara. Leo introduced himself.

— My name is Leo Demidov. This is my friend Nara Mir.

She smiled.

— We'd better talk in my office.

Contrasting with her immaculate attire, her office was a jumble. There was a desk piled high with papers and files. Framed photographs and newspaper clippings cluttered the walls. Without waiting for permission, Leo instinctively began studying the photographs. Belatedly he realized that Yolande was beside him. He pulled back, blushing, embarrassed by his lack of courtesy. She gestured for him to continue.

— Go ahead.

One man was central to most of the photographs. Not Jesse Austin – a man that Leo didn't recognize. Yolande said:

— That's my father, Nelson, in his days as a campaigner.

She pointed to one of the photographs, her finger moving away from her father and into the crowd, stopping at the face of a teenage girl.

— That's me.

Leo noted that she did not look as engaged in the march as those around her, a young girl lost in the bustle. Yolande asked, with genuine curiosity:

— Your wife was Raisa Demidova?

Leo nodded.

— She did not kill Jesse Austin.

Yolande smiled kindly, like a benevolent schoolteacher.

— I know that. So does everyone who lives round here. No one in Harlem thinks your wife killed anyone, Mr Demidov. This

*neighbourhood might be the one place in the world where she's inno-
cent. Certainly my father didn't believe it, not for one second. The
press ran the story about how your wife was Jesse's lover. The lie
became truth. There was gossip and slander, written up as journal-
ism, maybe they knew the truth and were too scared to print it.
Can't blame a person for that. Either way, the whole thing was forgotten a few months later and now it's a scandal most people can't
put a name to. The strange thing was that your wife received a
great deal of sympathetic coverage. People said it wasn't her fault.
They said she'd been duped. That all she wanted was to escape
Soviet Russia, she'd been promised a life in America. She was dis-
traught when she realized she'd have to go back. That lie flattered
America. I suppose that's why it was such a smart lie to tell.*

Nara translated. Yolande was content to sit and watch Leo's
reaction. When Nara had finished, Yolande took down a photograph of her father working in the restaurant, handing it to Leo.

— *I was fourteen years old when Jesse was shot. It changed my
life, not because I knew the man but because it changed my father.
Up until then he ran this restaurant and ran it well. He was a busi-
nessman to his bones. After Jesse's murder, he became an activist,
organizing speeches and rallies, printing leaflets. I hardly ever saw
him. The restaurant got into trouble. It became a place to debate.
Lots of customers stopped coming here, scared of being seen in case
they were labelled a radical. Those who weren't afraid, those who
worked with my father, took free meals in payment for their services. Money ran short. Politics got him into trouble with the law:
they almost closed the restaurant down. They sent inspectors who
said the kitchens were dirty, which was a lie because I used to clean
them myself.*

Leo's interpretation of the photograph had been correct: Yolande
had been a girl caught up in the protests rather than being at the

forefront of them. Her heart was here, in the business, not the politics of the time. There was anger too. She saw this restaurant as her inheritance: she'd cleaned it, learned how to manage it, only to have others threaten it. Most of the anger was towards the injustice of the inspectors but some of it was for her father too.

— In the end, my father's health got worse, so I took over the restaurant, changed everything except the name, turned it back into a business. No more politics. No more talk of changing the world. No more free meals.

While Nara translated, William joined the conversation, saying:

— My father used to say the best kind of activism was to run a good business, to pay your taxes, to make yourself the establishment.

Yolande shrugged.

— Jesse paid a lot of tax, more in a year than I've paid in my lifetime. Didn't buy him any favours. They still hated him.

She opened a drawer, taking out cigarettes and a glass ashtray shaped like a leaf. From her reluctance, it seemed to be a habit she was trying to quit. Leo asked:

— Who killed him?

Yolande lit the cigarette.

— Is that what matters to you? The individual responsible? Or the thinking behind it?

Leo checked with Nara to see if he'd understood her question. He didn't need to consider his answer for very long.

— I'm only interested in the individual. I'm not fighting against any system.

Yolande inhaled.

— We don't know for sure who killed Jesse. My father reckoned it was the FBI. I never contradicted him but it didn't ring true. The FBI had already beaten Jesse down. They'd taken everything

he had, his career and his money: they'd smeared his name. It didn't make sense to kill him. Maybe they were just so full of hatred they didn't need a reason but as a businesswoman I find that hard to swallow.

A waitress brought in coffee, pouring it for each of them, allowing Nara to catch up with the translation. Leo took out his notes, transcribed from Elena's diary. He said to Nara:

— *On the day of Jesse Austin's murder, my daughter arrived in Harlem, to speak to him, to persuade him to address the demonstration outside the United Nations. She encountered an FBI agent coming out of Austin's apartment. She refers to him in the document as Agent 6. Ask if they have any idea who this might be?*

Yolande thanked the waitress as she left.

— *An FBI agent at Jesse's apartment. There was a man who'd go round there. I don't remember his name. Anna – Austin's wife – used to tell my father about him. That was a woman full of love, rarely had a bad word to say about anyone, but she hated that agent more than anyone else alive.*

Yolande rubbed her head, unable to recall the name. She took a sip of her coffee, pained by the refusal of the name to come to her. They sat in silence for some time. Leo waited, watching her.

Even though her first cigarette was still lit and resting in the ashtray, Yolande lit a new cigarette and sucked on it, blowing smoke in the air.

— *I'm sorry. I don't remember.*

She was lying. Leo had seen the transition in her expression. She'd tried to conceal the moment by smoking as she was reminded of the price that her father had paid for becoming involved. With the memory of Agent 6's name came the memory of the type of man he was. Elena's description of Agent 6 returned to Leo:

He scares me.

Yolande was scared.

Leo turned to Nara.

— *Explain to Yolande that I understand why she doesn't want to be involved. Promise her that I would never reveal her name. Also say to her that I will find out what happened on that night, with or without her help.*

Listening to the translation, Yolande leant forward, close to Leo.

— *Jesse's murder is a secret that's been buried a long time. Not too many people want you to dig up the truth. Not even people round here. Times have changed. We've moved on.*

She looked into Leo's eyes.

— *I see the same determination I used to see in my father. And my father would never have forgiven me if I didn't help you.*

She sighed.

— *Agent 6 was almost certainly a man called Yates, Agent Jim Yates.*

New Jersey
Next Day

Nara remained silent for most of the bus ride from New York, her attention fixed on the view out of the window. Realizing the depth of the implications, she'd grown ever more certain that the investigation posed a serious threat to their asylum and questioned the wisdom of attempting to expose a controversial case when their lives depended upon the grace of their American hosts. Their actions were wilfully provocative, unwise at a time when their existence was supposed to be secret. What did Leo expect to achieve after sixteen years? There would be no trial, no arrests, his wife's name would not be cleared – the history books would not be rewritten. Though she had not articulated these thoughts, nor had she tried to talk Leo out of his decision, he clearly sensed her doubts. Perhaps, in turn, she did not oppose his plans because she sensed his own thoughts – a confrontation with Agent Yates was inevitable.

After the discussion at Nelson's restaurant, Yolande had taken Leo and Nara to her home, allowing them to search through her father's extensive collection of newspaper articles from the time of the murder, covering the night's events and subsequent commentary on the killings. Yolande kept the book of clippings as if it were a family album. In some ways it was, since it contained the only photographs she possessed of her father through his years as an activist. Most of the articles Leo had read in the public library but there were some, printed in local newspapers and on protest leaflets, that he'd not encountered. Among them there was one reference to FBI Agent Yates. Yolande argued that the largely absent figure of Yates, missing from the mainstream media coverage, was surely proof that he was involved somehow – it was illogical for such a pivotal officer, a man who'd visited Jesse Austin on the day of his murder, not to feature more prominently. The only article that mentioned Yates had been sent to Nelson by a fellow activist in New Jersey two months after the murder, a small article in a local paper, reporting that Teaneck resident Jim Yates had retired from the FBI due to his wife's poor health and was planning to spend more time with her. There was a photograph. The article had spun the news like the man was a hero. Nelson had annotated the article with the question:

What was the real reason for his retirement?

From what Leo could gather from Nelson's comments and scribbled remarks that criss-crossed the clippings, the individual responsible was less important to him than the system they were part of. His energies were directed into trying to achieve wider societal change – a dreamer, just like Elena and Jesse Austin. Leo had given up ideological ambitions a long time ago: they had brought him close to ruin just as they had nearly bankrupted Nelson's business. Dreaming of a better world was not without its dangers.

497

TOM ROB SMITH

As the bus approached Teaneck, Nara turned to Leo purpose-
fully. She took a breath, evidently nervous, before saying in Dari:

— *You're leaving us, aren't you? Don't lie to me. Just tell me the
truth. You're not staying in the United States? Something has
changed.*

Leo regretted not confiding in her earlier. She was no longer a
naive young student. She demanded to be party to his plans and
she had every right to be told the truth.

— *The Soviets know about our defection, or at least, they suspect it. My daughters are being harassed. At the moment the
measures against them are a warning. Should I not turn myself in,
they will be arrested. The only way I can protect them is if I give
myself up.*

— *Who told you that?*

— *Marcus Greene.*

Nara examined the palms of her hands as if the answer were
written on them.

— *So you would return?*

— *What choice do I have?*

— *A return to the Soviet Union might achieve nothing.*

— *My country is not as it once was. They have no interest in
harming my daughters. They are vindictive only if it serves some
purpose. If I return, I believe my daughters will be unharmed. I
can't be sure ...*

— *You will be a traitor.*

— *I am a traitor.*

— *They will execute you?*

— *I'm working for the Americans. I'm giving them information
that will result in the death of Soviet soldiers.*

— *Those soldiers are dying because they were sent to
Afghanistan, not because of you.*

— That is irrelevant. I am a traitor. There is no argument.

— Is your own life so meaningless to you?

Leo thought about the question.

— I see my life only in relation to the people I love.

— You love us?

— Of course.

— But you'll leave us?

— Nara, I have no choice.

Nara was working hard to keep her emotions in check. She was a mother: she had a responsibility to assess the situation with cool logic.

— Bear in mind if you find Agent Yates that you are leaving this country. We are not. We still have to make a life here. Your actions might have consequences for us.

— I would never allow anything to happen to either you or Nara, just as I would never allow anything to happen to Zoya or Elena.

— Going after Yates will not help your daughters.

— That is true.

— Then why?

— I'm not doing it for them.

— You're doing it for your wife?

— Yes.

— I don't believe you. She's dead, Leo.

— I made a promise to her. I can't explain it.

Nara shook her head.

— You're not doing this for her. You're doing it for yourself. Your life is not just about the people you love. It's also about the people you hate.

Leo became angry.

— Yes, you're right. When the person you love more than anyone

else is murdered then it becomes about hate. I hope you never have to experience that.

Nara turned towards the window. She was angry. Leo was angry too. Was his quest for the killer of his wife a selfish act full of hate and bitterness? It didn't feel that way, although he could not explain who else might benefit from his actions. The investigation felt vital, as if he had no choice in the matter. He turned away from Nara and the two remained silent until the bus arrived at its destination: the town of Teaneck.

New Jersey
Bergen County
The Town of Teaneck
Cedar Lane
Same Day

Standing in Teaneck — curled red and yellow autumn leaves around his feet — Leo waited as Nara charmed answers from store owners, working the main street with guile and grace that confirmed she would have made an excellent agent. Leo wondered what career she would eventually take. He imagined she would make an inspirational teacher, much like his wife. Quite unexpectedly, he felt a desire to cry, pained to think of her future knowing that he would have no part in it.

Nara emerged from a grocery store, walking up to Leo. He composed himself, asking:

— *Any luck?*

— *Yates still lives here. His wife died a few years ago.*

— *Did they give you an address?*

She hesitated.

— *Leo, I want to say this one more time, don't be angry with me. There would be no shame in letting this rest.*

— *Nara, a day hasn't passed when I haven't thought about what happened to Raisa. For me, there's been no rest and there can be none, not until I find out the truth. I'm tired, Nara, I've been thinking about this for so long. I want what you suggest: I want to rest. I want to sleep without waking up in a cold sweat, thinking about what happened. I must end this.*

— *What are you going to do when you come face to face with him?*

— *I don't know what he's going to say so I can't predict what I'm going to do.*

Nara's concerns grew. Leo smiled, taking her hand.

— *You're behaving as though I was crossing a moral line from which there's no turning back. You must remember that this used to be routine for me. I've arrested many innocent men and women. I hunted people down for the State, good people, knocking on doors without knowing anything about the suspect except that their name was on a list.*

— *Would you still do that?*

— *No. But I am going to hunt down the person responsible for killing my wife.*

Leo paused, wondering if Nara would want no further part in this.

— *Did they give you an address?*

She looked up at the sky.

— *They gave me an address.*

*

The front yard was overgrown, knee-high weeds and dense bushes — a patch of land entirely out of place in a street where the other yards were immaculately neat and trim. Following the overgrown path, weeds brushing his shins, Leo approached the front door with Nara by his side. There was no car in the driveway. He knocked and then glanced through the window. The lights were off. He tried the door handle. It was locked. Moving quickly, he took out a tension wrench and a paperclip from his pocket. Nara looked at him in quiet disbelief, appearing unable to fathom that he was by profession an agent of the secret police and that he'd broken into the homes of countless suspects. In seconds the door was open. Leo pocketed the tools, entering the house. After a beat, Nara followed, shutting the door behind her.

Yates lived in a large family home laid out over three floors with a basement and a back yard, a model of suburban normality. Yet instead of being familiar and comforting, the atmosphere was unsettling. Everything spoke of decay and neglect, from the wilderness of the front yard to the bland comforts of the interior, decorated in neutral colours, with mock-antiques and a glass cabinet filled with porcelain trinkets. The carpets were plush, as thick as Leo had ever seen, like the fur of an Arctic animal, and were colour-coordinated with the wallpaper – but the colour had been bleached by sunlight over many years. It was a family house without a sign of a family: there were no photographs except for one lonely wedding picture, a handsome man and a beautiful wife, both veiled in dust.

As they explored, each footstep caused a puff of dust, rising up before settling over the toes of their shoes. Only the kitchen showed evidence of recent use. The lines between the tiles were black with dirt. Washing up had been stacked in the sink, coffee cups and encrusted plates. Leo checked the refrigerator. There were cartons of milk. In the freezer was a tower of packaged meals – he counted seven.

Leo could tell that Nara's curiosity had been piqued: a desire to continue was muddled with her anxieties. It was their second search of a suspect's house together as mentor and student. Leo said:

— *I don't think Agent Yates is the kind of person to keep a journal.*

— *What kind of a person is he?*

Once again, Leo recalled Elena's words in her diary:

He scares me.

This house would not have allayed her fears. In deciding whether to explore upstairs or descend to the basement, Leo chose the gloom of the basement, guessing that it might appeal to Yates.

Rectangular patches of carpet had been nailed to the wooden steps down to the basement with no concern for appearances, making it baffling why the alteration had been done at all. The answer was on the ceiling, covered in black soundproof foam. The concrete floor had also been carpeted in a patchwork of material, using the remains of carpets from upstairs. This wasn't about aesthetics or comfort, it was about noise, the creation of a quiet room, a cocoon shut off from the world.

There was a tatty chair positioned opposite a large television set up on a small side table. There was a second refrigerator, this one containing bottles of beer, neatly lined up, labels facing forward. There was a stack of newspapers, recently read, crossword puzzles filled in. Leo looked through the home-crafted bookshelves. They contained various biographies of sporting heroes, reference books, a dictionary for the word games that Yates seemed to occupy himself with. There were magazines about fishing. There was pornography. The room was like a teenager's den buried under a decaying, apparently respectable family house.

The carpeted stairs and soundproofed ceiling meant that neither Leo nor Nara heard Yates arrive. Only when Leo turned to address her did he see the man standing at the top of the padded steps.

Same Day

Yates had been handsome once, Leo thought, remembering the wedding photograph, with his thick dark hair and well-cut suit. But not any more: skin sagged underneath yellow-tinged eyes. Compensating for this slackness in his features, his lips were stretched tight, thin as a washing line. He used gel to smooth down his grey hair, as when he'd been young, though now it looked like a sickly imitation, a pastiche of youth. Likewise, his suit might have fashionable once but now it was dated and worn, the material threadbare and the cut loose around his limbs. He'd lost weight. From the contents of the refrigerator, Leo deduced that his body had been whittled down by drink. But the creeping frailties of old age did nothing to soften his appearance, physical vulnerabilities made no dent on the aggressive force of his presence. Whatever wrong he'd done, whatever part he'd played in the events of that night, this was an unrepentant man, staring at them with brazen confidence and not a hint of remorse. They'd come for him, broken into his house, and it was him who spoke first, assuming a position of power, smug that they had failed to take him by surprise.

— *I've been expecting you.*

506

Recovering his own composure, Leo said to Nara, speaking in Dari:

— *He knows who we are?*

She didn't have time to translate, Yates guessed the question and said:

— *You are Mr Leo Demidov.*

Leo had encountered many brilliant, ruthless agents in the KGB, minds that could calculate a person's weakness in an instant and in another how to exploit it, uncluttered by moral scruples or ethical limitations. It was their absolute certainty that made them so valuable to organizations like the secret police, where doubt had never been considered an asset. Yates was one of those men. Elena had been right to be afraid.

Leo asked Nara:

— *How did he know we were in the United States?*

Yates descended the stairs, at ease, opening the refrigerator, taking out a beer while saying with his back to them:

— *What language is that?*

Nara answered, the tremor in her voice indicating to Leo that, like Elena, she too was afraid:

— *It is Dari.*

— *That what they speak in Afghanistan?*

— *One of several languages.*

— *Maybe that's why your country's in such a mess. A country should have one language. That's a problem we've got here: too many languages creeping in, confusing people. One country, one language – you'd be surprised at how upset people become when you suggest it. Seems pretty logical to me.*

Yates clicked the top off the beer, allowing the cap to fall to the floor, landing silently on the thick patchwork of carpet. He took a sip, licking his beer-wet lips, listening as Nara belatedly translated

Leo's questions: how did he know who they were and how did he know they were in the United States? He gave off the impression that he was enjoying himself, the centre of attention and important in a way he hadn't been for many years.

— *How did I know you'd show up? The FBI informed me you'd been granted asylum, the husband of Raisa Demidova.*

Leo's emotions were stirred by the sound of his wife's name being mispronounced. The clumsy attempt stung as surely as an insult. With remarkable sensitivity Yates picked up on his reaction and repeated the name:

— *Raisa Demidova, she was your wife, am I right?*

Leo replied in English:

— *Raisa Demidova was my wife.*

Leo could not control his tone or expression. He'd laid bare his intentions.

Yates took another long slug of beer, his thin lips sealed around the head of the bottle, his throat gulping as he swallowed – eyes on Leo throughout. Finally, Yates lowered the bottle, then said, his voice heavy with contempt:

— *The FBI didn't think it likely that you'd try to find me. That's what they said. Me? I knew you'd come. I didn't believe it was an accident that you ended up in the United States. They tried to tell me it was a coincidence, that there was no planning, that it had come about by chance, that fate had conspired to bring you to the country where your wife died.*

Yates slowly shook his head.

— *Agents today are so fucking dumb I could cry. They're soft. They have to go to charm school, learn how to eat with four different types of knife and fork. They have first-class degrees and run marathons but they don't know anything about the real world. College kids with guns. They sacked me: did you know that?*

He waited for the translation, wanting to judge Leo's reaction. Leo nodded.

— *You retired only a few months after my wife's murder.*

— *I was one of the best agents who ever worked for the FBI. In my time, there were mavericks in the Bureau, people who got the job done by any means necessary and no questions were asked. We were given space to act, to make decisions. We were judged on results, not on process. We didn't have restrictions, or rules. We did whatever we needed to do. Those times are over. The FBI has changed. They want people who do as they're told, who think in a certain way, company men, no initiative, no guts, every decision needs four per- mission slips to be signed.*

Wistful, he glanced into the near-distance, seeming to forget his guests. Then, abruptly, he turned back to Leo.

— *You're risking a lot coming here. With one phone call, I could have you kicked out the country.*

Nara translated, looking at Leo, her eyes imploring him to leave. Yates immediately spotted the division of opinion between the two of them and added, hastily:

— *Don't get me wrong. I'm not going to do that. I don't get many visitors, certainly not ones I can talk with about interesting subjects.*

He was lonely. He was vain. And he was proud. Like a profes- sional interrogator, Leo weighed these characteristics, evaluating how likely it was that the man would talk and what pressure might be needed. The combination of vices was promising. Yates had remained silent for many years. He was bitter. The fact that the truth had been erased from historical records bothered him as much as it bothered Leo. He wanted to tell his story. He wanted to talk. Leo only needed to flatter him.

Yates sat down, sinking into his comfortable chair, as laid back as if there were a sporting event on television.

— They told me you'd defected? That seems normal for a Communist. In my experience, Communists generally end up betraying their country. You Reds can't stay faithful for long. Loyalty is a virtue I prize. I'm certain the United States has the most loyal citizens in the world, which is one of the reasons why we're going to win the Cold War. Take me, for example: I looked after my wife right up until the day she died, long after she stopped loving me. It didn't matter that she didn't love me. It didn't matter that I didn't love her. I never left her. I knew her every need. I designed this house around her needs. Hard as it might be for some people to accept but I knew my country's needs too — she needed strength against her enemies. I gave her strength. I never compromised. I never pulled my punches. I did whatever it took and I'd do the same again.

Leo listened as Nara translated. Yates interrupted:

— You're here to kill me?

Leo understood the English. Before he could reply, Yates laughed:

— Don't be shy!

Leo used a phrase he'd practised.

— I wish to find out who killed my wife.

— And you wish to kill them? I see it in your eyes. You and me, we're not so different — we do whatever it takes.

Yates slipped a hand into his pocket, taking out a small revolver and putting it on the arm of his chair. He studied Leo's reaction to the gun carefully, then continued speaking as if the gun weren't there.

— You've travelled a long way, so I want to be as helpful as I can. Who killed your wife? Who killed your pretty Russian wife? She was pretty, wasn't she? She was a beauty. No wonder you're sore about losing her. I bet you couldn't believe your luck, marrying

a pretty woman like that. Hard to understand why she was a teacher. Seems a waste to me. She could have had a real career in America – a model, an actress, her face in all the magazines.

Leo said:

— *Who shot her?*

Yates swirled the remains of his beer, as if mixing a potion.

— *It wasn't me.*

Leo had heard thousands of denials in his career. To his disappointment he was certain that Yates was telling the truth.

Same Day

Yates raised three fingers.

— Three people died that night: Jesse Austin, Anna Austin and your wife. A lot of Negroes believed it was me that pulled the trigger on old Jesse. They think I'm the devil and I was the one who shot him even though I was standing on the other side of the street when Austin was killed, with my hands in my pockets surrounded by witnesses, real witnesses too, not the kind in line for a promotion, or trying to duck jail time. Over the years I've received hundreds of death threats.

Yates gestured towards the bookshelves and Leo turned, presuming there to be a bundle of these letters tied together. But there were none and no proof that any death threats had been sent. Yates continued without producing them.

— Negroes complain about lynching but what they're really complaining about is that they don't get to do it to white folks. That's what equality means to most of them: the right to lynch us back. Lynching for all, regardless of colour.

Yates laughed while Nara translated. He was greatly amused by his own joke, which he seemed to consider profound wisdom. He didn't wait for her to finish, keen to carry on with his story.

— The truth is that the idea of killing Austin never crossed my

mind. The idea had never been proposed by the FBI, I swear to God, not once did we discuss it, not even when the old fool was telling the world how he'd rather fight for the Communists than for the United States.

Leo had no interest in this rhetorical performance, nor in hearing the many reasons why Yates hated Austin, and asked:

— *Who shot him?*

— *Your people did. The Communists killed him. Jesse Austin was shot dead by a Soviet agent.*

Leo nodded, he sighed.

— *I believe you.*

Yates lowered his beer, checking with Nara as she translated Leo's statement. He had always believed Jesse Austin's death was a Soviet plot, not an American one.

Leo said in Dari:

— *My daughter Elena was in New York, on that same trip. She was working for a Soviet government agency. She believed that her mission was to rejuvenate the career of Jesse Austin. It is clear to me that this was a lie. She'd been tricked. However, I have never been able to find out why my country wanted Jesse Austin dead. My daughter obviously didn't know.*

Hearing the translation, Yates nodded.

— *Elena? That girl couldn't have explained it to you. She didn't know anything. All she did when we arrested her was cry. She honestly believed she was giving Jesse's career a boost. It was pitiful how stupid she was.*

Leo felt tremendous fury at these words. His daughter had been exploited because she was a dreamer, a young girl who'd fallen in love. Hearing Yates mock her, the desire to kill him was so strong he was forced to shut his eyes briefly, controlling his anger, allowing Yates to speak without interruption.

513

— They needed someone like her to force Austin into the open. He was practically a hermit, never going out. That girl turns up, talks about changing the world, and he can't say no. The only person who could've convinced Jesse Austin was someone like her.

Finally Leo understood that Elena's naivety hadn't merely made it easy for her to be manipulated, it was the key to unlocking Austin's scepticism, the only way to make sure he turned up to the concert.

Yates toyed with the gun throughout the translation. Once Nara was finished, he carried on.

— I'm not surprised you couldn't figure out what the point of the assassination was. It's hard to imagine a scheme more twisted than the one they cooked up. The Kremlin had decided that Austin was no longer an asset. He wasn't on the radio, no one knew who he was and no one was buying his records. He couldn't get a gig in a bar, let alone a concert hall. I'd done my job well. I'd made the old man irrelevant. The Soviets took a long cold look at their biggest supporter and decided that he was more useful dead than alive. Your government was fixated on the idea that the Negro community was the most likely way to start a revolution in America. I suppose since they were downtrodden, the idea was that they'd rise up, rip off their chains and rebuild the State according to a Socialist model. All it needed was a spark and the whole racial tinderbox would go up in flames, bringing down the capitalist regime and turning the United States red. That was the plan.

Yates chuckled at the notion.

— I don't know if they were deluded enough to believe that old man Austin would be the spark but they did believe his assassination would worsen racial tensions. If they shot him, no matter what the truth of the assassination, every black American would think it was the FBI lynching an outspoken Negro. No one would believe it

was a Communist plot, they'd all think it was an FBI hit. The assassination would make the forgotten man famous again; more famous than he'd ever been before, a martyr for the Negro revolution. Malcolm X had been shot only a few months earlier, two Negro assassinations in a year, it looked suspicious, I'll grant them that. They were hoping, after Austin's death, that everyone would buy his music and listen to recordings of his speeches. They thought they could breathe life into his career by taking his life.

Yates smiled through much of Nara's translation, amused by the ironies, fondly recollecting a time when he had power over life and death.

— For the plan to work, they needed him in a public place, with the world's media present. That's why they tagged this plan onto the concert.

Leo asked, in Russian:

— But the FBI would simply tell the public it was a Communist plot.

Nara struggled with the translation but Yates smiled, understanding what had been said.

— The more the FBI told the public it was a Communist plot, the more the public would believe it was an FBI plot. That's how conspiracy theories are born. The official version has to sound like a lie even when it's the truth, and the louder you say the truth, the more people look elsewhere. The Communists couldn't frame the FBI directly: they didn't have the means or the capability. They were going to frame your daughter, Elena, pretend that she'd slept with Jesse Austin. White Americans would believe the girl had shot him out of jealousy. Negroes wouldn't. The plan relied upon innuendo and suggestion: they banked on the fact that the Negro community would automatically believe anything bad about the FBI.

Yates climbed out of his seat, pocketing the gun and walking to the fridge, fetching another beer. He pulled the top off, letting it land on the carpet. He took a gulp, impatiently waiting for Nara to finish. Hearing the translation, Leo asked:

— *How did you find this out? Elena couldn't have told you: she didn't know.*

— *I had it all explained to me by a queer Jew Communist called Osip Feinstein. He'd gotten cold feet about his involvement. Like all Communists, he wanted to switch sides. He wanted me to save him, as if he were a damsel in distress.*

— *He didn't want to be involved in the murder of Jesse Austin?*

— *Maybe he liked the old man's music. I don't know what the reasoning was. But he spilled his guts, ratted out his colleagues.*

— *Did he come to you before or after the assassination?*

Yates considered lying then shrugged and said:

— *What happened was Feinstein ran an agency based in New York that organized trips to Communist Europe for rich dumb Red Americans. He'd managed it for years. Suddenly he wanted to talk. So, I turned up and he asked me to stop the murder. He said I could save Jesse Austin. In exchange, he wanted to go into hiding, protective custody, scared that the Russians would kill him.*

Leo said:

— *You did nothing?*

Yates nodded.

— *I did nothing, well, almost nothing. First of all, I didn't know if anything he said was true. He had switched sides more times than anyone in the history of spying. You couldn't trust him even as your enemy. Second of all, I figured if the Communists wanted to kill one of their own then why should I get in the way? Why should I save old man Jesse, the guy who wanted to fight Americans? I didn't want to hear Jesse Austin bad-mouthing this country any more. Why save a Communist who hated America? Why should the FBI save a traitor? In the end, Jesse picked the wrong side. The decision cost him his life.*

— Why didn't Feinstein tell another officer, if you didn't respond?

Yates nodded, appreciating the point.

— I handcuffed him to a pipe, locked him in his office, to make sure he couldn't interfere, so he couldn't tell anyone else. I let Jesse Austin turn up at the demonstration. That was the extent of my involvement. I didn't orchestrate anything. I didn't kill him. And I didn't kill your wife either. All I'm guilty of is letting the whole thing play out.

Yates leaned against the wall, becoming thoughtful, speaking almost to himself as much as Leo.

— Did I fail in my duty as an FBI officer? I'd argue that I did not. I'll tell you why. I knew Austin's murder wasn't going to cause a revolution. Even if every Negro out there believed that the President Lyndon Johnson himself had personally ordered Austin's assassination, there wasn't going to be any revolution.

The notion of trying to save Austin because he was an American citizen, an innocent man, didn't factor into his equation.

— Most blacks believe in God. They go to church. They pray. They sing. Communists don't. Communists hate God. In the end, there were never enough Godless blacks – there were never enough Jesse Austins for the riots to ever become an uprising.

Yates had said most of what he'd wanted to say. But Leo had not yet received an answer to the question that had brought him here.

— Who murdered my wife?

Yates widened his eyes, as if he'd forgotten about this part of the story.

— You already know the answer to that! After Austin was shot

517

we took your wife and daughter into custody. The precinct was mobbed. There was press in the street. There was a protest. When Anna Austin arrived, they didn't think to search her, the grieving widow. She sat in the office and waited, claiming she had evidence. I'd been interviewing your wife. Soviet diplomats wanted to talk to her. We left the interview room together, walking into the main office. Anna Austin pulled out a gun. She'd always hated me. She must have figured I'd killed her husband. She fired four shots before another officer shot her dead. All four shots missed me. They hit the desk, the walls – one bullet whistled past my ear. It's a miracle I'm alive. One of those bullets hit your wife by mistake – caught her in the stomach. That's all there is to it. It was an accident, no mystery to solve. You've been waiting all these years but you've known the answer all along: the official version is the truth. Anna Austin killed your wife. She didn't mean to, but she did.

Pre-empting his reaction, Yates said:

— There are lots of people that can say it's so. They saw it happen. They saw Anna pull the trigger. They saw your wife go down.

Leo mulled over this explanation, asking:

— Anna Austin never intended to shoot my wife?

Yates moved closer.

— Her intention was to kill me. But she couldn't manage it. She was a lousy shot, probably never fired a gun before. Afterwards we lied about the motives, not about the facts. Jesse Austin was dead. Anna Austin was dead, shot by a police officer. We were in trouble. Two dead Negroes in one night with one shot in the middle of a police precinct? We had to lie. Harlem was going to burn. We were left with no choice. We needed to create a story to confuse the public so that even if they didn't believe us, they wouldn't be able to agree

among themselves what the truth was. We needed to tie the whole thing together. Powers far above me decided that the story about Austin taking a lover would work. We'd tell the world your wife had an affair with Austin and that she shot him dead out of jealousy. Anna came to the precinct and acted out of revenge. It squared with the facts. There were photos of your wife at the murder scene. We doctored some photos so that we had images of your wife meeting Austin in his apartment, cutting out Elena and replacing her with images of Raisa. Those photos were rushed. Take a look at them closely: the proportions are out of line. Osip Feinstein's store was burnt down, with him inside it, the Soviet punishment for betraying them. There were small-scale riots. There were civil-rights marches but nothing of consequence and certainly no revolution. In the end, the majority believed the murders were the result of a tragic romance. Only the Negroes doubted it, and even then, most didn't care. The whole thing worked out so well I couldn't believe the FBI wanted me to quit. They claimed I should have acted to stop the murder of Jesse Austin.

Yates shook his head. It was clear that he was troubled not by the murder, nor by the death of three people, but by the fact that he'd lost his job. He was a villain convinced he was a hero.

As Nara finished the translation, Yates warned them:

— *There's nothing you can do. It's history no one cares about. No one will believe you. No newspaper will publish it. There's no evidence. If you try and cause problems my government will kick you both out the country. I've got nothing else to say. If you expected an apology, you've wasted your time. The affair cost me my job, a job I loved and a job I was good at, so I paid my dues too. Now, we're done talking. If you don't get out of my house right now I'll make the phone call and have you both sent back to that hell-hole Afghanistan.*

Leo gripped hold of one of the biographies on the table. As Yates moved within range he swung it, striking him across the jaw, knocking the former agent to the floor. Moving at speed, he took the gun from his pocket, kneeling on his chest, pinning him down and saying in Russian:

— *I've done worse things than kill a man like you.*

Leo looked up at a terrified Nara, saying in Dari:

— *Translate for me.*

— *Leo!*

— *Translate!*

He turned back to face Yates.

— *My wife didn't die instantly. It took twenty minutes. She died from loss of blood. Maybe Anna Austin did shoot her by mistake but you let her die, didn't you? Maybe you were worried Raisa would tell the world Anna Austin tried to shoot you? My wife was lying on the floor, desperate for help – you saw an opportunity, didn't you?*

Leo struck Yates across the face with the gun, splitting his lip.

— *Answer me!*

Yates spat blood, listening to Nara as she translated. He was calm, saying:

— *No matter what you do to me your wife will always be remembered as a whore.*

Hearing the translation, Leo cocked the gun, saying in English:

— *Tell me how she died.*

Yates didn't answer. Leo moved the gun to the exact position where Raisa had been shot, the barrel pressing against Yates's stomach.

— *Tell me.*

Yates shook his head. Leo pulled the trigger.

Same Day

Nara dropped to floor beside Yates, moving to help. Leo stopped her, saying:

— He's been shot in the same place as my wife was shot. It took her twenty minutes to die. Tell him that he might have that long. But he's older and the bullet was fired at point-blank range. In all likelihood, he has less time.

Nara translated, stumbling over the words. Leo continued, calmly:

— In this soundproofed room no one will have heard the shot. The only way he's going to survive is if I show him the mercy he failed to show my wife. I'll consider doing that if he tells me the truth.

Nara translated, pleading with Yates to speak. Leo directed his Russian at Yates as though he could understand.

— When Anna Austin fired at you, you fired back, not another officer. You shot and killed her, didn't you? And once she was dead you realized the trouble you were suddenly in. You'd visited Jesse Austin that same day. He was dead. And now you'd shot his wife. You saw my injured wife as an opportunity: she was injured, seriously, but she wasn't going to die, not if you'd sought help. The cover-up wasn't your superior's idea. It was your idea. But in

order for your plan to work my wife needed to die. Isn't that right?

Yates squeezed his lips tight, refusing to speak. He tried to stem the bleeding, putting pressure on the wound, ignoring the questions. Leo pulled Yates's hand away: keeping the wound exposed, blood continuing to flow, saying in Russian:

— *Did you do that to my wife? Did you pull her hand away? You let her bleed?*

Yates's brow was covered with sweat, his body shaking. Leo said:

— *You delayed calling the ambulance?*

Nara translated, no longer stumbling over the words, levelling the accusation at him. She wanted an answer too. Yates said nothing.

Leo didn't raise his voice, speaking as though addressing a child:

— *Yates, you're running out of time. If you don't answer I will watch you die as you watched my wife. I will consider the events before me a replay of what happened in New York, and I don't need you to speak in order to understand that night. I'm prepared to watch, like this, as you bleed to death.*

Yates was the master of reading people's weaknesses and could surely see that there was no uncertainty in Leo.

— *You stayed with her, didn't you? For twenty minutes, making sure of her death? You came up with the idea of tying the murders together, claiming that Anna killed Raisa, that it was an act of revenge, but not against you.*

Yates sat up, regarding his bloody shirt, red all the way up to his chest, spreading out across the patchwork carpet. Leo said in English:

— *Speak to me.*

Finally, Yates reacted. He nodded. Leo grabbed his face.

— *Not good enough. I want to hear you speak. Tell me: did you let her die?*

Yates's teeth were bloody. He said:

— *Yes, I let her die.*

Leo's voice was almost a whisper.

— *My wife spent the last moments of her life with you. Describe them for me.*

Yates had turned ghostly pale. He shut his eyes. Leo slapped him across the face, forcing him to respond. Yates opened his mouth but didn't speak. Leo said:

— *Her last minutes. I want to know.*

Yates tried to touch the bullet wound but Leo kept a grip on his hand.

— *You don't have much time.*

Yates spoke. His words sounded like a man struggling to keep afloat, snatched breaths, panicking.

— *I told her there was an ambulance on its way. She didn't believe me. She knew I was lying. She tried to call out for help. Once she realized there was no help she became peaceful. Her breathing was slow. I thought it was going to take a few minutes but almost fifteen minutes passed. There was a lot of blood. I thought she was ready to die.*

He shook his head.

— *She began to speak. Very quietly, like she was praying. I thought it had to be Russian. But she was speaking English. She was speaking to me. So I moved closer. She asked me to tell . . . her daughter . . .*

— *Elena?*

Yates nodded.

— *That she wasn't angry. And that she loved her. She kept mumbling it over and over. Tell her I'm not angry. Tell her that I love her. And then she shut her eyes. This time she didn't open them again.*

Leo was crying. He let his tears run, unable to wipe them away since he was keeping Yates's arms pinned down. He composed himself enough to ask:

— *You didn't tell Elena? You couldn't even do that?*

Yates shook his head.

Leo stood up. Freed, Yates pressed his hand against the bullet wound, stemming the bleeding. His anger and confidence returned.

— *I answered your questions! Call an ambulance!*

Leo took hold of Nara's hand, silently guiding her up the padded stairs. Behind them came the cry:

— *Call me a fucking ambulance!*

In the hallway Leo put the gun down on the side cabinet. The telephone was situated below the wedding photograph, the young, handsome Yates with his beautiful bride, destined for a life together of duty and dislike. Holding the receiver against his ear, ready to dial, staring at this photograph, Leo thought of the details of Yates's confession, picturing Raisa's last minutes – the physical pain, the protracted suffering and the grubby loneliness of her death, bleeding on the floor of a police precinct. There was not a doubt in his mind that Agent Jim Yates deserved to die. It was sentimental dishonesty to believe that a show of mercy would result in a change of heart. Men like Yates regretted nothing. They could not repent and were incapable of uncertainty. Contemplation and introspection served only to underscore what they already believed. They would always be able to justify their actions. A voice seemed to shout at Leo, demanding justice:

Let him die!

That was why he was here, that was why he'd travelled so far and risked so much. How could he come all this way only to save the man who'd murdered his wife? He was not seeking the moral satisfaction of being a better person than his adversary. He would find no sense of pride in saving this man. The anger and anguish he suffered over his wife's death were as raw today as they were on the day he heard the news – those feelings should be acted upon, rather than a preconceived notion of decency. Knowing the truth of what happened was no tonic to his hurt and provided him with no sense of inner peace. His fury was just as strong, his emotions as unsettled as they had ever been. Maybe if he let Yates die, alone in his basement, a sad and pathetic death, one befitting a man ruled by hatred, he would feel differently, he would achieve the peace he'd been seeking.

Let him die!

Let him die.

Nara touched his arm.

— *Leo?*

When he turned to her, he did not see Raisa, but she was by his side as surely as Nara was standing there. The truth is that Raisa would have hated Yates even more intensely than Leo. She would never have forgiven Yates for allowing Jesse Austin to die. She would never have forgiven him for not passing on her last words to Elena. His silence had contributed to Elena blaming herself, carrying a burden of guilt that had altered her character and shaped her life. Even so, even feeling that degree of hatred, Leo was sure that Raisa would call for an ambulance.

He dialled the number, handing the phone to Nara.

— *Tell them the address. Tell them to hurry.*

— *Where are you going?*

— *To help Yates.*

New York City
Brighton Beach
Same Day

Leo sat on the beach watching the ocean break against the shore. The sunset had contracted to a smudge of red, night closing in on what remained of the day. He rolled a smooth stone from hand to hand, back and forth at regular intervals, as if he were an elaborate timepiece counting down to darkness. One fact was clear to him now – the truth had brought him no comfort. His discoveries did not make Raisa's death any easier to bear. With grief, there was no resolution, no closure. There was no end to it. He missed her now, today, on this beach, as much as he had ever missed her. He found a future without her as hard to picture as the moments after he'd first heard she was dead. The thought of waking up tomorrow morning without her by his side, after many years of doing exactly that, still made him sick with loneliness. In truth, his investigation had been an elaborate, fifteen-year-long diversion from the fact that he did not know how to live without her. He would never know.

As contradictory as it might seem, he had been trying to keep Raisa alive by exploring the mysteries surrounding her death, to legitimize obsessing about her by framing that obsession as the work of a detective. In an unsolved mystery there was immortality. Looking back he realized that Zoya had always perceived the true nature of his investigation and had always known it would bring him no comfort. She was right. He had found out who'd murdered his wife, he had found out why and how she'd been killed. He could now picture the events of that night in New York, understanding every detail, fully grasping the motivations. Yet what was important was that he finally grasped the futility of trying to keep Raisa alive, understanding that the unsolved mystery had only ever offered the illusion of her company, a man chasing the reflection of a woman he loved.

He would never see Raisa again. He would never sleep beside her, or kiss her. And with that thought, he let the smooth, heavy stone roll out of his hand. Night had come. The red smudge of sunset was gone. The lights of Coney Island were bright.

Hearing footsteps, he turned around. Nara and Zabi were approaching. They arrived by his side, standing over him, unsure what to say. Leo patted the ground beside him.

— *Sit with me a while.*

Nara sat on one side, Zabi on the other. Leo took Zabi's hand. She sensed something was wrong even if she didn't understand what it was.

— *Are you leaving us?*

Leo nodded.

— *I have to go home.*

— *Isn't this home?*

— *It is for you. I must return to Russia.*

— *Why?*

— *My daughters are there. They're in trouble. They're being punished instead of me. I can't allow that to happen.*

— Can't they come here? They can live with us. I don't mind sharing my room.

— They won't be allowed to come here.

— I don't want you to go.

— I don't want to leave you.

— Can't you stay until Christmas? I've been reading about it at school. I want to celebrate it with you. We can buy a tree and cover it with lights.

— You can still do that with Nara.

— When are you coming back?

Leo didn't reply.

— You are coming back, aren't you?

— I don't think so.

Zabi was crying.

— Have we done something wrong?

Leo took hold of her hand.

— You're the most amazing girl. You're going to have a wonderful life here with Nara. I'm sure of that. You can achieve anything you set your mind to. And I'm going to enjoy hearing about your success. But there is something I must do.

ONE MONTH LATER

Soviet Airspace above Moscow
13 December

Peering out of the window of the passenger plane chartered by the Soviet government to bring him home, Leo was disappointed that Moscow was hidden below angry clouds, as if shunning the gaze of the returning traitor, refusing to show him the city that he'd once sworn to protect against all enemies, domestic and foreign. No matter what rationale he applied, he could not deny that he felt ashamed. He was a man who'd fought proudly as a Soviet soldier and he would gladly have died for his country. Yet he had ended up betraying it. While his sense of personal shame was intense, he felt far greater shame that his nation had squandered its opportunity for social progress, instead industrializing darkness, making its citizens complicit in a murderous command economy, building death-factories in every corner of the country, from Kolyma's gulags to the secret police headquarters, the Lubyanka, a building that lurked somewhere underneath those winter clouds. To the ideals that underpinned the Revolution, they were all traitors to one degree or another.

The journey from New York had been eerie, Leo surrounded by unoccupied seats, the flight empty except for the KGB operatives guarding him and the diplomatic officials sent from Moscow to oversee his return. Upon boarding he'd felt no sense of apprehension, instead pondering the money wasted on his repatriation. As a traitor of international status, he had been granted an entire plane to himself. Recalling the perks he'd once desired as a young agent, he marvelled at the irony that not even the most powerful KGB officer, with the largest dacha and longest limousine, would ever have been granted the use of an entire airliner. It was a simple matter of appearances. Leo's deportation was taking place upon a global stage before a worldwide media circus and no economies would be tolerated. Just as Raisa had been sent to New York in the nation's most modern airliner to impress the main adversary, so the defector Leo would be brought home in the most modern Soviet aircraft available, flying direct to Moscow from New York. The Soviet government was keen to show the world that it was not experiencing financial worries. Carefree spending was an attempt to mask the strain caused by the ever-spiralling cost of the Afghan war, a fact Leo had described in detail to the Americans.

In negotiating his return to the Soviet Union, it was clear that the Americans were pleased to be rid of him. He was a troublemaker, a loose cannon, and they'd extracted the information they needed, understanding from his briefings that Soviet failure in Afghanistan would leave their enemies humiliated. Providing aid to the Afghan insurgency would drain Soviet resources, pulling in more troops and making their ultimate and inevitable defeat even more expensive politically.

As for Leo's incident with former Agent Jim Yates – the attack had been covered up. Yates survived. His revelations would never see the light of day. The history books had been written and they would not be re-written: lies had been chiselled into the encyclopaedias and textbooks. The shooting of Yates in his pleasant suburban house in Teaneck had been blamed on an armed intruder, an opportunistic robbery gone wrong. Leo had assured the American authorities that he would not cause any further problems, or give any statements regarding the death of Jesse Austin, as long as Nara and Zabi were left alone. A pact of silence had been agreed. Leo took some satisfaction from the symmetry of Yates's shooting being concealed as a matter of convenience, just as Austin's murder had been. Though Yates had agreed to go along with the story, he'd pointedly told local reporters that all he remembered about the intruder was that he was black.

With regards to the Soviet government, Leo had been unable to obtain any guarantees except for one – if he returned, the punitive measures against his daughters would stop. He had requested that within twenty-four hours of his plane touching down he would be permitted to see them, but he was in no position to insist upon anything. His guilt was not in question. He'd shared sensitive information with the main adversary and was to be tried for treason, a trial whose verdict had already been decided.

As the plane descended, Leo tried to imagine the events of the past eight years, the things that had happened since he was last in Moscow – eight years in which he'd been missing from the lives of his daughters and their husbands. As he thought upon the letters he'd received, it suddenly struck him that he wasn't anxious about returning to a city filled with memories of Raisa. Something had changed. He was excited. This was the place where he'd fallen in love. He would be closer to his wife here than at any point during his investigation into her death. As the wheels touched down, he closed his eyes. He was home.

Moscow
Butyrka Prison
Pre-Trial Detention Centre
45 Novoslobodskaya Street
One Week Later

Arms and legs cuffed together, secured so tightly that he was forced to stoop even when standing, Leo had been waiting for several hours in an ancient interrogation room within a prison notorious almost from its inception one hundred years ago. He'd supervised this arrangement countless times: the humiliating restraints, the atmosphere of intimidation and psychological pressures of surveillance, watched by guards in all corners of the room. No threats of violence had been made. Instead, a torture far more astute than physical pain had been applied.

This was Leo's seventh day in Moscow and he'd not yet seen his daughters. He hadn't spoken to them by telephone – he'd received no word of their welfare. Every morning upon being woken he'd been informed they would visit him that day. He'd been brought into this interrogation cell and told that they would arrive shortly. He'd waited, eager, feet tapping. Minutes had passed but they'd felt like hours. There was no clock on the wall and no answer ever came from the guards. Part of the torture was the difficulty of judging time. There were no windows, no sense of the outside world. In response, he had devised a way of maintaining his sanity. There was an exposed pipe running across the ceiling. At one of the rusted joints water was leaking, collecting at the line, forming a drop. Once the drop had enough weight it fell and the process began again. Leo counted the seconds of an entire cycle. He then counted them again, and again. There were roughly six hundred and twenty seconds to each drop and he used this number to gauge how long he'd been waiting. So far today he'd been waiting for forty-eight drops, eight hours.

Yesterday he'd sat for twelve hours, counting drops, in a state of great anticipation only to receive word that his daughters were not coming. This excruciating routine was repeated every day, forcing Leo to lurch from hope to despair. He hadn't been given any information on what the problem was, whether his daughters had been spitefully refused permission or whether they did not want to see him. His tormentors were, of course, aware that Leo would obsess upon the possibility that his daughters were choosing not to visit him and they did nothing to alleviate this corrosive thought which, like a pearl of concentrated acid, bored through his thoughts.

There was a chance his daughters wanted nothing to do with him. Leo could not be sure how they had reacted to the news of his defection, or his return. The girls would be angry with him for causing them so many problems – they'd been arrested, questioned, their families collectively punished for his defection. In the six months that he'd spent in America he could not be sure how their careers had suffered, or how their reputations had been damaged. Perhaps they were afraid of visiting him, concerned with how their lives would change. As he ran these thoughts over and over in his mind he could feel every muscle in his back tightening, his hands clenching.

The door opened. Leo stood up as far his restraints allowed, his throat dry, desperate to see his daughters. He squinted at the shadows.

— *Elena? Zoya?*

From the gloom of the corridor a KGB officer entered.

— *Not today.*

Same Day

Leo had been given his own cell – not out of kindness, more likely they feared that as an older man he would be at risk of tuberculosis and might not survive until the trial if thrown into one of the communal cells. At regular intervals the grate in the door slid open and an officer checked that Leo hadn't tried to kill himself. Since his arrival he'd slept for no more than thirty minutes. As the days progressed he'd almost given up on sleep altogether, pacing backwards and forwards – four steps by two steps were the dimensions of his cell – his thoughts revolving around the prospect that he might never see his daughters again.

The cell lights were turned on. Leo was surprised. He received no visitors at night. The door opened. A man in his mid-forties entered accompanied by a guard. Leo didn't recognize him although it was obvious from his smart suit and shoes that he was important, a politician perhaps. He seemed nervous, despite his trappings of power. He would not hold eye contact with Leo for longer than a second. They did not close the door, the guard remaining close by the man's side. It was only at this point that Leo noticed the guard was ready with a truncheon, to protect the visitor.

Plucking up the courage to look Leo directly in the eye, he said:

— *Do you know me?*

Leo shook his head.

— *If I told you my name it would mean nothing to you. However, if I told you the name that I used to go by ...*

Leo waited for the man to continue.

— *I used to be known by the name of Mikael Ivanov.*

Leo's first thought was to step forward and crush Ivanov's throat, assessing the likelihood of success considering his own age and physical condition. Dismissing his instinctive reaction, he managed to control his anger. He had not achieved the one thing he wanted – a visit from his daughters. Whatever blunt satisfaction might come from killing Ivanov, it would guarantee that he would be executed without having seen Zoya and Elena. Apparently relieved that he'd not been attacked, Ivanov pointed out:

— *I was forced to change my name.*

Leo spoke for the first time.

— *A hardship, I'm sure.*

Ivanov was irritated with himself.

— *I'm trying to explain why you couldn't find me. Frol Panin advised me to change my identity. He was sure you'd come looking for me, no matter how many years went by. You did. That was why I had to pretend—*

— *To be dead?*

— *Yes.*

— *Panin was wise. It saved your life.*

— *Leo Demidov, do you believe a person can change?*

Leo considered Ivanov carefully, sensing genuine remorse and wondering if it was a trick – another form of punishment.

Modulating his tone from outright hostility to deep scepticism, he replied:

— *What do you want?*

— *I didn't come to apologize. I know how meaningless that gesture would be. Please do not think me vain or boastful when I say that I have become a man of considerable influence and power.*

— *That does not surprise me.*

Leo regretted the insult, which was childish and petty. But Ivanov accepted it.

— *It had been decided that you would not be given permission to see your daughters. It was seen as the only punishment that would hurt you. You would not hear from them, see them, or talk to them.*

Leo felt weak, unsteady. Ivanov hastily qualified his remark.

— *I cannot intervene in your trial. However, I have been able to petition for Zoya and Elena to be granted permission to visit you. I have succeeded. They will arrive tomorrow.*

The shift from despair to elation was too much. Exhausted from a lack of sleep Leo sat on the edge of his bed, head in his hands, breathing deeply. Ivanov added:

— *In exchange I ask only one thing. Do not tell Elena that I arranged it. Please do not mention me at all. It will ruin it for her.*

It took Leo a moment to recover. His voice was weak, the anger and indignation was gone.

— *You could have arranged this without telling me?*
Ivanov nodded.

— *I could have done.*

Ivanov turned around, about to leave. Leo called out:

— *Why?*

Ivanov hesitated, taking out a photograph and showing it to Leo, his fingers trembling. It was a photograph of Mikael Ivanov seated beside his wife. She was pretty rather than beautiful with generous eyes and open features. Leo asked:

— *You told her what you were doing?*

— *Yes.*

— *Did you tell her why?*

— *She thinks it's a random act of kindness, an expression of my good nature.*

After studying the couple's expressions for a moment, Leo returned his gaze to the floor. Ivanov slipped the photograph back in his pocket, adding:

— *In her eyes I'm a good man. That's as close as I can expect to actually being one.*

Next Day

Once again Leo sat in the interrogation cell with his arms and legs in restraints waiting for his daughters. Once again several hours had passed with no answer from the guards, no clue as to what was happening. He glanced at the pipe in the corner of the ceiling. The thirty-third drop of water was forming at the rusted joint. Almost six hours had passed. Was it possible that Ivanov had lied to him? No, the remorse he'd seen in his face had been real and impossible to feign. But he might have been manipulated by more important men, lied to and falsely assured that he could deliver the good news only so that the traitor would suffer even more today when they did not arrive. Hope and despair were the torture instruments in play: the authorities switching between the two with such expert cruelty that Leo struggled to breathe as he imagined the future. He would remain here in ignorance, tormented by broken promises. He would never know if his daughters wanted to visit. He would never know if it was their decision to stay away. Not knowing would break him and it would break him long before the trial reached its inevitable conclusion. As the thirty-third drop of water fell Leo could no longer fight back his frustrations and he leaned forward, bowing down before his torturers, sinking his head to the table.

Some time later, the cell door opened. Leo didn't sit up. He didn't look. If he allowed himself to picture his daughters at the door when they were not there, he might not be able to survive the disappointment. He could feel his heart weakening with the pressure of the past week. However, he could not suppress a faint hope and he listened carefully. He could only hear one set of footsteps – heavy boots – it was the KGB officer. Leo closed his eyes, grinding his teeth in expectation of those awful words:

Not today.

But the guard said nothing. After a moment Leo opened his eyes, scared by the flutter in his chest. He listened again, hearing the unmistakable sound of someone crying.

Leo sat up sharply. His daughters were at the door. Elena was crying, Zoya was holding her sister's hand. Both of them were beautiful in their different ways, both of them were scared. Leo froze, unable to speak or smile. He would not allow himself to feel happiness until he was sure this was not a dream, or a deception conjured by his sleep-deprived mind. Perhaps he was delirious, imagining his daughters when in fact he was still lying on the table. His mind had played games with him before. He had seen a vision of Raisa in the Afghan cave. She'd been a comforting illusion, one that had dissolved and disappeared when tears formed in his eyes.

Leo stood up, his steel restraints rattling. His daughters stepped into the cell, walking slowly towards him. Watching them in motion, observing the details of their posture, he was amazed by the lifelike details of this apparition. But he would not feel joy. He would not laugh or delight in this moment. He could not commit to it. He had no doubt, no doubt at all, that they would vanish as soon as he touched them, or if he closed his eyes their surface would shimmer, the light would break apart and they would be gone and he would be alone. They were a projection from his mind, a mirage, constructed to protect himself from the bleak reality that he would never see them again.

Exhausted, trembling and on the brink of insanity, Leo said to them:

— *Make me know that you are real.*

He noticed that Elena was pregnant, a fact he had not known, or been told. As he began to cry, his daughters hurried forward, wrapping their arms around him. And finally Leo allowed himself some happiness.

ACKNOWLEDGEMENTS

A special mention must go to my good friend Zoe Trodd who shared her research, her time, insights and support as I wrote *Agent 6*, particularly with relation to the subject of American Communism, and including guided tours of the relevant locations in New York. Zoe has been an invaluable source of information – she's a wonderful friend, and a brilliant mind.

I have been lucky to have the support of two great editors, Mitch Hoffman at Grand Central Publishing, and Suzanne Baboneau at Simon & Schuster UK. I'd also like to thank Felicity Blunt at Curtis Brown for all her help with this novel and Robert Bookman at CAA – I owe a great deal to both of them. And finally I'd like to thank Ben Stephenson for his support over the past two years.

CHILD 44

TOM ROB SMITH

NOMINATED FOR 17 INTERNATIONAL AWARDS

Moscow, 1953. Under Stalin's terrifying regime families live in fear. When the all-powerful State claims there is no such thing as crime, who dares disagree?

WINNER OF 7, INCLUDING THE GALAXY BOOK AWARD FOR BEST NEW WRITER

An ambitious secret police officer, Leo Demidov has spent his career arresting anyone who steps out of line. Suddenly his world is turned upside down when he uncovers evidence of a killer at large. Now, with only his wife at his side, Leo must risk both their lives to save the lives of others.

AN INTERNATIONAL BESTSELLER IN OVER 30 LANGUAGES

Inspired by a real-life investigation, CHILD 44 is a relentless story of love, hope and bravery in a totalitarian world, and is a thriller unlike any you have ever read.

OVER 1.5 MILLION COPIES SOLD

ISBN 978-0-85720-408-0

TOM ROB SMITH

FROM THE AUTHOR OF INTERNATIONAL BESTSELLER
CHILD 44

Moscow, 1965: a society trying to recover from a time when
the police were corrupt and the innocent arrested as criminals.

Detective Leo Demidov, former Secret Police Officer, is forced
to ask whether the wrongs of the past can ever be forgiven.
Trying to solve a series of brutal murders that grip the capital,
he must decide if this is savagery or justice.

NOMINATED FOR 17 INTERNATIONAL AWARDS,
WINNER OF SEVEN

Quickly it becomes apparent that Leo himself – and his
family – are in danger from someone intent on revenge.
Desperate to save those he loves, he is offered salvation from
an unexpected source – and at a terrible price.

THE MULTI-MILLION SELLING TRILOGY
CONTINUES…

From the streets of Moscow in the throes of political upheaval,
to the Siberian gulags, and the Hungarian uprising in Budapest,
The Secret Speech is a breathtaking novel that confirms Tom
Rob Smith as one of the most exciting authors writing today.

ISBN 978-0-85720-409-7